Abou

Lara Temple writes stron~~~~ about complex individual~~~~ with plenty of passion. Sh~~~~ ~~~~ ~~~~ her husband, two children and one very fluffy dog, and they're all very understanding about her taking over the kitchen table so she can look out over the garden as she writes and dreams up her *happy ever afters.*

Regency Rebels

Regency Rebels:

Opposites Attract

LARA TEMPLE

MILLS & BOON

First Published in Great Britain 2024
By Mills & Boon, an imprint of HarperCollins*Publishers* Ltd,
1 London Bridge Street, London, SE1 9GF

www.harpercollins.co.uk

HarperCollins*Publishers*
Macken House, 39/40 Mayor Street Upper,
Dublin 1, D01 C9W8, Ireland

ISBN: 978-0-263-32311-5

MIX
Paper | Supporting
responsible forestry
FSC **FSC™ C007454**
www.fsc.org

This book contains FSC™ certified paper and other controlled sources to ensure responsible forest management.

For more information visit: www.harpercollins.co.uk/green

Printed and Bound in the UK using 100% Renewable Electricity at CPI Group (UK) Ltd, Croydon, CR0 4YY

LORD HUNTER'S CINDERELLA HEIRESS

To Myrna, Mark and Arik, who miss David
as much as I do.

He couldn't hold on but gave so much love
while he did.

Prologue

Leicestershire—1816

'You're wanted, Miss Nell. The master has some viscount or other wanting to take Petra through her paces. Lord Hunter, I think his name was. Knowing fellow.'

'Another one? I hope she takes him head first through a hedge, Elkins,' Nell replied, her voice muffled as she bent to examine Pluck's fetlock.

'She'll have to go to someone and he seems a fair choice—no bluster about him.' The elderly groom smiled.

'I don't know why Father insists I escort his guests anyway. As head groom you are far more qualified than I.'

'It's simple, miss. You've got the best seat in the county and that gives them fellows the idea their wives or daughters might look the same if they took home one of these prime bits of blood. They won't, no how, but there's no harm in it. Your father's a hard man, I know, but he's right proud of the way you are with horses. You're like him there, see you.'

Nell wrinkled her nose—she didn't want to be like

the brutish sot in any way whatsoever. She secured the stall door, but Pluck shoved her arched neck over the side and shook her mane. Nell relented and came back for one more stroke.

'No, you can't go to your mama yet. And, yes, I will go and see if he is worthy of her and if he isn't I'll have her toss him into a pond. You like that idea, don't you, you little rogue? Father and Aunt Hester will skin me, but for Petra I just might find the nerve. Now I *must* go or I will be late and Father will be furious and then Aunt Hester will be furious, too.'

There was no way the filly could understand how serious that was, but Pluck's head ducked back into the stall.

Her father was already in the stable yard. He was hard to miss—even braced on his cane and his face lined with pain and puffy from years of hard drinking, his height and booming voice intimidated everyone around him. However, this time he was diminished by the man who stood by his side. Not in inches—they were probably of a height and the stranger certainly hadn't her father's massive and blustering look. In fact, the first thing that struck her was that he was very quiet.

They hadn't seen her yet and she watched as the stranger approached Petra. His movements were economical and smooth, and his hands, though they looked large and strong, were calm and travelled slowly over the mare as he examined her. It was just the right way to approach a high-spirited horse.

It was only when her father called her over that she looked at the man's face. He was probably close in age to Charles Welbeck, who had just turned twenty-five the week before she and her father had gone to Wilton, but he *seemed* older. There were creases of weariness about his eyes and a bruised look beneath them as if he had not slept well for a long time.

She couldn't imagine such an expression in Charles's cheerful blue eyes. But other than that she had to admit he was almost as handsome as Charles, though in a completely different manner. She wondered if he was perhaps part-foreigner and that might account for the dark chestnut hair and the warm earth tones of his skin and the sunken golden brown of his eyes. It wasn't a comforting face—its sharp sculpted lines didn't make her think of princes and dancing through the night at the village fête in Wilton; it was an arrogant face more suited to the weighty matters of a beleaguered king and she doubted a glance from his tired eyes would make her think of dancing.

Not that Charles had ever asked her to dance. He hardly even looked at her for more than a kind greeting. Except for just once, when she had been fourteen. Her father had been furious at her for cramming one of his horses at the Welbeck jumping course and she had stood, humiliated and wilting under his wrath until Charles put his arm around her and said something which made the men around them laugh, but the smile in his eyes as he glanced down at her told her it wasn't unkind. It had calmed her father and filled her with a peaceful warmth she had begun to forget existed. At that moment she had known there would never be anyone else for her but Charles.

She had no illusions her love would ever be reciprocated. Charles was perfect and she…she was a beanpole, almost as tall as he but painfully scrawny. The village boys would snigger and call her Master Neil behind her back and she was accustomed to the dismay in young men's eyes when she was partnered with them at the informal dances held at her best friend Anna's home in Keswick. It was only when she was on a horse that her height didn't bother her. In fact, very little bothered her when she was on a horse.

So as she watched Lord Hunter mount Petra she hadn't in the least thought about him as a man, or herself as an unattractive and overly tall seventeen-year-old. She was Miss Nell and she could ride a horse better than anyone—man, woman, boy or girl—in the county.

She tensed as Petra sidled at the man's unfamiliar hand and weight and was immediately checked, but so gently that the motion was almost invisible. She couldn't decide if his calm was innate or assumed, but she met Elkins's gaze and shrugged. He would do.

'Fells Pasture or Bridely field, then, Miss Nell?' Elkins asked.

'Fell's Pasture, I think,' she replied and turned to the man. He was watching them with a slight smile, clearly aware he was being weighed and judged. His eyes gleamed gold at the centre, or perhaps that was a trick of the sun, which was just catching at the edges of the trees behind her. She herself preferred light-haired men, like Charles, but Anna would probably think him very handsome.

'Is that good or bad?' he asked.

'It means we presume you can stop Petra from throwing you, Lord Hunter,' she replied, surprising herself. She was not usually so direct. 'But if you aren't comfortable with her yet, we can start with some easy riding. It's just that Fell's Pasture has a few miles of open runs and safe jumps. Alternately once you ride her I can show you her paces myself. She is probably our fastest mare and it would be a pity if you didn't see just how beautifully she gallops.'

He cocked his head to one side with a glimmering smile that turned the lines of tension she had noticed into laugh lines. She had probably been wrong about the signs of strain; his smile didn't allow for the presence of the darkness she had sensed.

'I don't think you meant any of that as an insult, did you?'

Nell stared at him, running through her words in her mind.

'Not at all, my lord. You appear to handle her well enough, but I just want to do justice to Petra. Father must have told you she can be a little resistant at first, but she knows me and will open up more easily with me in the saddle. I merely thought you would want to see her at her best.'

'We won't have time to switch to side saddle anyway, so let's just see how I manage, shall we?'

She shrugged and turned to Hilda, her mare, allowing Elkins to help her mount.

'We don't put a side saddle on Petra; she's trained for a man's saddle and weight. But as you said, we'll see how you do.'

This time she heard the condescension in her voice and almost smiled at it.

'I'm almost tempted to do an abysmal job of it just to see what you mean, Miss Tilney.'

He didn't, of course, and as she watched him gallop across the field she didn't know whether to be relieved that Petra was being delivered into the capable hands of a man who would treat her right, or disappointed that she hadn't been given the opportunity to show him her mettle. In this one corner of the universe where she was completely capable, she rarely wished to show off, but today she felt that urge. She watched as the man stopped just short of where she and Elkins waited. There *was* gold in his eyes, she realised, and the colour was heightened by the clear enjoyment on his face, making him look younger.

'Can you match that?' he demanded, bending forward to stroke Petra's damp neck.

Elkins chuckled and Nell didn't need further prodding. She tossed her reins to Elkins and slipped off Hilda.

Clearly Lord Hunter hadn't expected her to actually accept his dare because he looked disconcerted, but she just laid her hand on Petra's muzzle and raised her brows, waiting.

'Are you serious?' he asked. 'Now? But she's probably winded and you can't ride her in skirts…'

Nell unhooked the fastening that held the wide train of her skirt and hooked it over her arm.

'These skirts work as well on a regular saddle. I made them myself. And far from being winded, Petra is just warming up, so instead of sitting there while she cools down, you can dismount and I'll show you what she can do and then you will probably ask Father to buy Pluck, her filly, as well. Now, down you go.'

He dismounted meekly, still watching her with curious fascination as she placed her leg in the stirrup, swinging her other leg over, and with a practised flick cast her skirts over as well, the long folds of fabric covering her legs to her boots and obscuring the riding breeches she wore underneath. She plucked out the pin which held her riding hat and handed them to Elkins, and then she was off.

Petra didn't disappoint her. If ever a mare flew, the grey blood mare rose off the ground, as smooth and slick as water, her small head down and extended like an arrow. Nell didn't bother with proper lady's riding posture, but leaned low into the shape of the horse, laughing as Petra's mane stung at her face like a brace of tiny whips. Nell wanted that man to appreciate what he was getting, and if she managed to convince him to buy Pluck as well, it would be worth it. She hated when mare and filly or foal were separated too young.

She took Petra over the hedge at the far end of the pasture as if it wasn't even in the way and then led her back for the long jump over the stream. When she drew up she was bursting with the excitement of the run. She could even cope with the knowledge that she probably looked a fright. Her hair was too straight to stay confined by pins and she could feel it hanging down about her face.

'Well? Isn't she amazing?'

He took the reins she held out to him as she swung out of the saddle and she realised he really was very tall because she actually had to look up, an unusual feeling and one she didn't quite like since it reminded her too much of Father stalking at her. She hurried to mount Hilda, her exhilaration fading.

'Indeed she is,' Lord Hunter said as he stroked Petra's sweating neck. It was easier now that she was mounted and he had to look up at her. 'What is the name of her filly?'

'Pluck. Well, that's just my name for her, though Father prefers to call fillies and foals after their sires, so she's known as Argonaut's Filly, but that's a mouthful, so I just call her Pluck, because she is. Plucky, that is.'

'Like you.'

Her eyes widened.

'Hardly. I'm the least plucky thing that ever was.'

'Now that's not quite fair, Miss Nell,' Elkins interjected as they turned back towards Tilney Hall. 'There's none like you for throwing your heart over a fence.'

She shrugged, annoyed at herself and at them, though she didn't know why.

'That's different. I know what I'm doing when I'm on a horse. You can see Lord Hunter to the house, Elkins. Goodbye, Lord Hunter.' She rode off, feeling very young and foolish she had succumbed to showing off. He had been kind about it, but she still felt ridiculous.

She hoped her aunt didn't have one of her whims and insist she dine downstairs because then he would see how wrong he was about her pluck. She wasn't yet formally 'out' in society and she rarely dined with guests, which suited her just fine because those occasions when her aunt did demand her presence were sheer purgatory. Her father's temper was nothing next to Hester's vindictiveness.

Just when Nell thought the hour of danger had passed, Sue, the chambermaid, rushed into her room.

'Her majesty says you're to join the guests for supper, Miss Nell.'

Nell shook her head, desperately trying to think of some way to avoid this disaster, and Sue clucked her tongue.

'There ain't nothing for it but to go forward, chick. Hurry, now. Luckily I added a flounce to your sprigged muslin and it isn't quite so short now, but you'll have to keep the shawl over your shoulders because there's nothing we can do now about the fact it won't close right.'

'I can't... I won't!'

'You can and will. There isn't aught else to wear, chick. Really, your father should know better but men are fools. That's right—best heed me. Men are fools and you're better a mile away in any direction!'

Nell stood like a seamstress's dummy, rigid and useless as Sue busied about dressing her in her one decent muslin dress with its childish bodice and equally childish length. Though Mrs Barnes was an excellent cook, neither she nor Sue were capable seamstresses and the new flounce was clearly crooked and this would surely be the night the straining fabric would finally give way to her late-budding bustline. She would sit down and there would be a horrible rending sound and everyone would look at her and her aunt would sneer and oh so kindly suggest Nell go change and perhaps ask her why she had insisted on wearing that dreadful old dress and really she despaired of the girl because no matter how hard she tried to make her presentable there was only so much one could do with such a hopeless long meg... Nell would leave the room and of course not return because she had no other dress that was suitable for evening wear and because she couldn't face their contemptuous and condescending stares and sniggers, and tomorrow her father would rant at her for having humiliated him in front of his guests and for being as dull as dishwater and less useful.

'I can't do it. I can't. She is just doing it so she can make a fool of me again. I won't.'

Sue squeezed Nell's hand.

'I wouldn't put it past her but it will be worse if you don't go. Here, don't cry now, chick. Think—in two days you'll be on your way back to school.'

Nell pressed the heels of her hands to her eyes.

'I wish I could go tonight. I hate coming here. I wish I could stay with Mrs Petheridge always.'

'Well, Ma and I are glad you are here summers at least.'

Nell scrubbed her eyes and blew her nose.

'Oh, Sue, I didn't mean I don't love you and Mrs Barnes. You know I do.'

'Aye, you don't have to say a thing, chick—we know. I wish for you that you *could* stay there year-round. Lucky your aunt doesn't know how much you like that school or she'd have you out of there in a flash. Proper poison, she is, and no mistake. Now go stare down at your nose at the lot of them. Lord knows you're tall enough to do just that. Bend your knees so I can get this over your head, now. Goodness, what do they give you to eat in them Lakes? I swear you've grown a size since you had to wear this just a month back.'

Nell chuckled and slipped her arms into the sleeves, struggling against the constricting fabric. Thank goodness for Sue. She was right—Nell could survive two more days.

This optimistic conviction faded with each downward step on the stairs. Her aunt was already in the drawing room and the familiar cold scrape of nerves skittered under Nell's skin, almost painful in her palms and up her fingers, like sand being shoved into a glove. She kept her eyes on her pale slippers peeping out and hiding back under her flounce as she made her way to the sofa where she sat as meek and as stupid as a hen, praying that was the worst people thought of her.

The door opened again and out of the corner of her eye Nell saw two pink confections enter the room, followed by an older couple. She had learned to look without looking and she inspected the two pretty, giggling girls and their mother, who wore a purple turban so magnificently beaded with sparkling stones Nell couldn't help staring.

'Stop gawping, girl!' a voice hissed behind her. 'Keep your eyes down and your mouth shut or I'll send that slut of a maid of yours packing, cook's daughter or not! And pull that shawl closed. You look like the village tart with your bosom spilling out like that. Ah, Mr Poundridge, and Mrs Poundridge! So wonderful you could come for supper. So these are your lovely daughters! Do come and meet Sir Henry's daughter, Miss Helen. She is not yet out, but in such informal occasions she joins us downstairs so she can acquire a little town bronze. Sometimes I wonder what we pay such an exorbitant amount to that school for, but what can one do but keep trying? Perhaps your daughters could give her some hints on the correct mode of behaviour in company. Oh, what lovely dresses! Do come and meet our other guest tonight, Viscount Hunter...'

Nell kept her eyes on her clasped hands as her aunt sailed off, dragging the Poundridges in her wake, only daring to raise her head when she heard her aunt's voice mix with her father's. None of them was looking at her except Lord Hunter. He stood by her father, flanked by the old suits of armour Aunt Hester had salvaged from the cellars, and together they looked like Viking and Celtic warlords under armed escort. She hadn't seen him when she entered because she hadn't looked and her mortification deepened as she realised he must have seen everything.

Nell's eyes sank back to her hands. The gritty, tingling pain and the clammy feeling was still climbing, and though it hadn't happened quite so badly for a while, she knew there was nothing to be done but wait it out. If she was lucky it would peak before her legs began to shake. She tried to think of Mrs Petheridge and her friends at school, but it was hard. Her left leg was already quivering. She wanted to cry at how pathetic she was to let this woman win each time, but self-contempt didn't stop her right leg from beginning to quiver as well. Think of brushing down Petra. No, Father was there, glaring. Think of Mrs Barnes and her cinnamon bread... No, her mother had died with an uneaten loaf by her bed, so she could smell it. Of Charles's sweet smile as he helped her mount the first time they had come to the Wilton breeders' fair; of how he had put his arm around her when Father had raged. If he were here, she might be able to bear this...

Two days. Just today and tomorrow. Her right leg calmed and she pressed her palm to her still-shaking left leg. In two days she would see Anna and sit in Mrs Petheridge's cosy study with the chipped tea set and ginger biscuits, helping the girls who cried for home or who threw things, because she was good with them. She breathed in, her lungs finally big enough to let the air in, and the clamminess was only down her spine now and between her breasts under the scratchy shawl.

'Your father has agreed to sell me Pluck as well. Will you miss her?'

The sofa shifted and creaked as Lord Hunter sat and she looked at him in shock.

'What?' Her voice was gritty and cramped and his golden-brown eyes narrowed, but he just crossed his arms and leaned back comfortably.

'I went to look at her as you suggested and I have to admit she is a beauty. By the length of those legs she might even turn out to be half a hand taller than her mother, but time will tell. I'm hoping she will win me points with Petra. What do you think?'

Think. What did she think? That any minute now her aunt would come and sink her fangs into her for daring to talk with someone. What was he talking about? Petra and Pluck. He was taking Pluck, too. It had been her idea. Yes, yes, she would miss her, but she would be gone by then, just two days. Oh, thank goodness, just two days. Just two. Say something...

'I think...' Nothing came and her legs were starting to shake again.

'Do you know I live right next to Bascombe Hall? Were you ever there?'

Why was he insisting? She wished he would go away! Bascombe Hall...

'No. Mama and Grandmama didn't get along.' There, a whole sentence.

'No one got along with your grandmama. She was an ill-tempered shrew.'

She stared in surprise. How did he dare be so irreverent? If she had said something like that...

'That's better,' he said with approval, surprising her further. 'I understand you inherited the property from your grandfather, but that your father is trustee until you come of age. Since she never made any bones about telling everyone she had disapproved of her daughter's marriage to Sir Henry, I'm surprised she didn't find a way to keep you from inheriting.'

'She did try, but the best she could do was enter a stipulation that if I died before my majority at twenty-one, my cousin inherits. Once I'm twenty-one there is nothing she can do.'

'Well, with any luck she'll kick the bucket before that and save you the trouble of booting her out of the Hall.'

She pressed her hand to her mouth, choking back a laugh. Surely he hadn't said that! And she hadn't laughed... She rubbed her palms together as the tingling turned ticklish. That was a good sign; it was going away. Had he done that on purpose? He couldn't have known.

'I keep hoping she might actually want to meet me. Is she really so bad?'

His mouth quirked on one side.

'Worse. I know the term curmudgeon is most commonly applied to men, but your grandmama is just that. You're better off being ignored.'

Oh, she knew that.

'Had you ever met my grandfather?'

He nodded.

'He was a good man, very proper, but he was the second son and he only inherited it when your great-uncle died childless. Those were good years for us.'

'Why?' she asked, curious at this glimpse of the relations she had never met.

'Well, the Bascombes control the water rights in our area, which means all our crops are dependent on them for irrigation and canal transport, and for those few blissful years we had a very reasonable agreement. When he died your grandmother made everyone in the area suffer again. Thankfully your father is trustee now, which means he has the final say in any agreement.'

'But if I'm the heir, I can decide now, can't I?'

'Not until you're twenty-one and by then you will probably be married, so do try to choose someone reasonable, will you?'

A flush rose over her face and she clasped her hands again. Charles's smile shimmered in front of her, warm and teasing.

'I don't think I shall be married.'

'Well, you're still young, but eventually—'

'No,' she interrupted and he remained silent for a moment. He shifted as if about to speak, but she made the mistake of looking up and met her aunt's gaze. Pure poison, Sue had said. She pressed back against the sofa and drank in some air. The man next to her shifted again, half-rising, but then the door opened and the butler announced supper.

Hunter smiled at the pretty little brunette who was chirping something at him. She didn't require any real answers and he could cope with her flirtatious nonsense to her utter satisfaction with less than a tenth of his attention.

Tomorrow he would have to return to Hunter Hall. It had been cowardly to escape the day after Tim's funeral, but as he had watched his brother's grave being filled with earth, the thought that it was over, all of it, pain and love, hopelessness and hope, had choked him as surely as if it was he being smothered under the fertile soil. He had needed some distance and the negotiations with Sir Henry over the fees for access to the waterways controlled by the Bascombe estate had provided an excuse to disappear. At least in this Sir Henry appeared to be reasonable, unlike his dealings with his daughter, and it appeared they would not be required to pay exorbitant waterway fees to the Bascombe estate, at least until the girl inherited.

No wonder Sir Henry had let drop that he was concerned his daughter, who would come into the immense Bascombe estate in four years, would be easy prey for fortune hunters. After her performance that afternoon Hunter had assumed that was because Sir Henry wasn't confident he could keep such a mature little firebrand under control. But it was clear this girl would probably throw herself into the arms of the first plausible fortune-hunting scoundrel simply to escape this poisonous household.

He glanced down the table to Sir Henry's daughter. She was barely eating, which was a pity because she was as thin as a sapling. She definitely didn't look strong enough to have ridden Petra so magnificently that afternoon. In fact, if it hadn't been for the fact that he knew she was an only child, he could easily believe this girl was a pale twin. No wonder she had recoiled at being called plucky. When she had entered the dining hall that evening he had stared with disorientation at a completely different person from the pert and intrepid horsewoman. A prisoner on the way to the guillotine had more jump in their step than the pale effigy that had somehow made her way to the sofa in the corner. Her skin had been ashen under its sun-kissed warmth, almost green, and he wondered if she was going to be ill. Perhaps someone petite might have looked fragile, but she just looked awkward.

He had almost started moving towards her when her

aunt had reached her, and though he had only been able to make out part of her words, the vitriolic viciousness had been distressingly apparent and the coy comments to the Poundridges had almost been worse. She had humiliated the girl in public without compunction and Sir Henry had stood unmoved as a post.

It wasn't until he sat down by her that he had noticed she was shaking and immediately he was back with his brother. Tim's legs would leap like that at the onset of the attacks of terror; that was how he could tell it was starting. He hadn't even been able to hold his one remaining hand or touch him because of the constant pain. All he could do was sit there with him until it stopped. Not that it had helped in the end. To see that stare in the girl's face and the telltale quiver of her legs had been shocking. She had finally calmed, but he hadn't. He was still tight with the need to do damage to that vindictive witch. That poor girl needed to get away from this poisonous house.

He glanced at the girl again. She still wasn't eating, just sitting ramrod straight, staring down at her plate. But there was a stain of colour on her cheeks as the aunt leaned towards her. She was at her again, the hag, he thought angrily. Why doesn't her father do anything about this? If she had been his daughter he would have ripped this woman's head from her shoulders long ago.

Something the pink-festooned brunette said to him required his attention and he turned to her resolutely. This wasn't his affair and it wasn't as if he had been so successful helping the people who mattered to him. It had been his father's death that had partially released his mother from her humiliation, not any of his puny efforts to protect her. And Tim... He might have saved his brother's broken body from a French prison, but he had failed on every other level. This girl was just another of a multitude of cowed women, just like his mother, beaten down until they could no longer imagine standing up for themselves. There was nothing he could do to change the trajectory of her fate.

'Are you really fool enough to try and flirt with Lord Hunter? Do you really think someone like him will be interested in you?' Aunt Hester hissed under cover of the conversation. Her witch's smile was in full bloom, the one she used while spewing hate in company.

In a year this would be her life, Nell thought. She would be eighteen and for three long years until her majority she would have to suffer the whip of her aunt's tongue and her father's anger and indifference. No, she couldn't do that. She wouldn't.

'He doesn't need your money, so don't think you can snare someone like him just because you're an heiress. Like mother, like daughter. That's how your slut of a mother caught Henry, you know…'

Nell stood before her mind registered the movement.

'You will not speak about Mama. Not a word. Not ever.'

She hardly recognised her own voice. It was low, but the room fell into shocked silence. Her aunt's face was turning the colour of fury, but Nell was far away. Soon the walls would collapse on her, but for a moment time had stopped and she could walk through this frozen little world out into the night and keep walking until she reached Keswick.

Then she saw Lord Hunter's face. There was a smile in his honey-brown eyes and he raised his glass towards her and time moved again and she realised what she had done. Her aunt surged to her feet, which was a mistake, because she was much shorter than Nell.

'If you cannot behave in a ladylike fashion, you will beg everyone's pardon and retire, Helen.' The words were temperate but the message in her aunt's eyes wasn't. I'll deal with you later, they said.

Nell almost hung her head and complied, but looking down at the purply-red patches on her aunt's cheeks, the thick lips tinted with the pink colour she favoured, she felt a wave of disgust, not fear. She took a step back and turned and curtsied to the others.

'I apologise for not behaving in a ladylike fashion. I hope you enjoy the rest of your evening. Goodnight.' She turned back to her aunt. 'I will never listen to you again. Not ever. You have no voice.'

She heard her father bellow her name, but didn't stop. She would leave for Keswick in the morning and she would never return.

Chapter One

London—1820

'There's no one there, miss,' the driver of the post-chaise said impatiently as Nell stared at the empty house and the knocker-less door. How could this be? Her father's last letter had been sent just two days ago and from London. As far back as she remembered he always spent the week before the Wilton horse-breeders' fair in London, assessing the latest news and horses at Tattersall's.

'We can't leave the horses standing in this rain, miss; they've come a long way.'

Nell turned back to the post-chaise. The driver was right. The poor horses had made excellent time over the last stage and they must be exhausted. But where could she go?

'Do you happen to know where Lord Hunter resides?'

The words were out before she could consider and the driver cocked a knowing brow.

'Lord Hunter, miss? Aye, I do. Curzon Street. You quite certain that's where you'll be wanting to go? Not quite the place for a respectable young lady.'

Nell breathed in, trying to calm her annoyance and fear. Nell knew memories were often deceptive, but she had found it hard to reconcile her memory of the troubled and irreverent young man with Mrs Sturges's report of a noted Corinthian addicted to horse racing, pugilism and light women. Nevertheless, it was clear the driver shared Mrs Sturges's opinion of her alleged fiancé's reputation. Mrs Sturges might teach French and deportment, but she was also the school's resident expert on London gossip, and when Nell had received the shocking newspaper clipping sent by her father, she had immediately sought her advice. Mrs Sturges had been delighted to be consulted on such a promisingly scandalous topic as Lord Hunter.

'He is a relation of mine, so, yes, that is precisely where I'll be wanting to go,' Nell lied and leaned back into the chaise as it pulled forward. She, like the horses, was tired and hungry and just wanted to sleep for a week, but she was not going to back down now. She was twenty-one and financially and legally independent, and no one…no one!…was going to decide her fate any longer. She didn't know whether it was her father or Lord Hunter who was responsible for the gossip in the *Morning Post*, but she wasn't going to wait another moment to put a stop to it.

'This here's Hunter House, miss.'

Nell inspected the house as the postilion opened the chaise door. It looked like the other houses on the road— pale, patrician and dark except for faint lines of light sifting through the closed curtains in the room on the right. The hood of Nell's cloak started sliding back and little needles of rain settled on her hair. She tugged her hood into place, wondering how on earth she was going to do this. She turned to the driver.

'Will you wait a moment?'

The driver glanced at the sluggish drizzle and a little rivulet of water ran off the brim of his hat onto his caped greatcoat.

'We'll see if there's someone in, but then we'll have to get the horses to the Peacock Inn, miss. You can send for your trunk there.'

She almost told him to take her to the Peacock as well, but the thought of asking for a room in a London posting house without maid or companion was as daunting as bearding the lion in his den.

Not a lion, she mused, trying to recall what Lord Hunter had looked like. Too dark for a lion. Too tall and lean for one, too.

Whatever the case, he was unlikely to be happy about her appearing on his doorstep at nine in the evening. However, if he had a hand in this outrageous stratagem, he didn't deserve to be happy. She still found it hard to believe the handsome and wealthy rake described by Mrs Sturges really wanted to wed her at all, especially after her shocking behaviour four years ago, but it was equally hard to believe a columnist would dare fabricate such a libellous faradiddle.

She climbed the last step, gathering her resolution, when the door opened and golden light spilled out and was immediately obstructed by a large shadow. She stepped back involuntarily and her shoe slipped on the damp steps. She grabbed at the railing, missed and with a sense of fatality felt herself fall backwards. She instinctively relaxed as she would for a fall from a horse, adjusting her stance, and she managed to land in a crouch on the bottom step. She pushed to her feet and brushed her gloved hands, glad the dark hid her flush of embarrassment. The figure at the top of the steps had hurried towards her, but stopped as she stood up.

'That was impressive.' His deep voice was languid and faintly amused and she glanced up abruptly. Apparently she did remember some things about her betrothed.

'Lord Hunter…'

'Impressive, but not compelling. Whatever is on offer, sweetheart, I'm not interested. Run along, now.'

Nell almost did precisely that as she realised the driver had been true to his word and was disappearing down the street at a fast clip. She drew herself up, clinging to her dignity, and turned back to the man who was thoroughly confirming Mrs Sturges's indictment.

'That's precisely the issue, Lord Hunter. I am not interested either, and the fact that you don't even recognise the woman that according to the *Morning Post* you are engaged to only confirms it. Now, may we continue this inside? It's cold and I'm tired; it was a long drive from Keswick.'

At least that drew a response from him, if only to wipe the indolent amusement from his face. The light streaming past him from the house still cast him into a shadow, but she could make out some of the lines of his face. The dark uncompromising brows that drew together at her greeting, the deep-set eyes that she couldn't remember if they were brown or black, and the mouth that had flattened into a hard line—he looked older and much harsher than she had remembered.

'Miss Tilney,' he said at last, drawing out her name. 'This is a surprise, to say the least. Where is Sir Henry?'

'I don't know. May we talk inside? It is not quite…'

She paused, realising the irony of suggesting they enter his house to avoid being seen on his doorstep. His lips compressed further, but he stood back and she hurried into the hall, her heart thumping. Everything had been much clearer in her mind when she had been driven by frustration and anger and before she had made a fool of herself tumbling down the steps.

'This way.'

He opened a door and she glanced at him as she entered. She went towards the still-glowing fireplace, extending her hands to its heat and trying hard not to let her surprise show. How had she managed to forget such a definite face? Had she remembered him more clearly, she might have reconsidered confronting him alone. She had vaguely remembered his height and the bruised weariness about his eyes; even his irreverence and his tolerance of her skittishness. But she hadn't remembered that his brows were like sooty accusations above intense golden-brown eyes or the deep-cut lines that bracketed a tense mouth. If she had grown up he had grown hard. It was difficult to imagine this man being kind to a scared child.

'Lord Hunter,' she began. 'I—'

'How did you get here from Keswick?'

She blinked at the brusque interruption.

'I came post. What I wanted to say was—'

'In a post-chaise? With whom?'

'With a maid from the school. Lord Hunter, I—'

'Is she outside?'

'No, I left her with her family in Ealing on the way. Lord Hunter, I—'

He raised a hand, cutting her off again.

'Your father allowed you to travel from the Lake District to London and come to my house in the middle of the night, unattended?'

He spoke softly but the rising menace in his voice was unmistakable.

'My father knows nothing about it. Would you please stop interrupting me?'

'Not yet. What the…? What do you mean your father knows nothing about it?'

'My father sent me a letter on my birthday informing me I have apparently been betrothed for four years. I wrote back and told him I most certainly wasn't. His response was to send me this clipping from the *Morning Post*.' She fumbled inside her reticule for the much-abused slip of paper and shoved it at Lord Hunter. He took it, but didn't bother reading it.

'And rather than communicating your…distaste in a more traditional manner, you chose a melodramatic gesture like appearing on my doorstep in the middle of the night?'

Although his flat, cold voice shared nothing with her aunt's deceptively soft but vicious attacks, Nell felt the familiar stinging ache of dread and mortification rising like a wave of nausea. She gritted her teeth, repeating for the umpteenth time that Aunt Hester had no power over her and that she was no longer a child. She was twenty-one and very wealthy and she was done being treated like chattel.

'Do you find it more melodramatic than concocting this engagement behind my back and keeping it from me for four years? You have no one to blame but yourself!'

That might have been going too far, Nell told herself as his stern face lost some of its coldness, but she couldn't tell what the increasingly intent look on his face portended.

'Clearly,' he said, still maddeningly cool. 'Where are you staying in town?'

Some of her bravado faded at the thought of the disappearing post-chaise.

'Nowhere yet. I thought Father was in town, but the house is empty and the post-chaise is taking my trunk to the Peacock in Islington.'

The gloves jerked in his hands again.

'I see. And now that you have delivered your message in person, what do you propose to do?'

Nell had no idea. She was miserable and confused and hungry and she wanted nothing more than to sit down and cry.

He moved away from her and for a moment she thought he might just leave her there and her shoulders sagged, almost relieved. But he merely strode over to the bell-pull and gave it a tug. At least in this her memory had been accurate—he walked lightly, unusually so for someone of his size, but it just added to that sense of danger she had not associated with him at all from their meeting all those years ago.

'Sit down.'

He tossed his gloves on a table and took her arm, not quite forcing her, but it was hard not to step back and sink into the armchair. It was as comfortable as it looked and for a moment she contemplated unlacing her shoes and tucking her cold feet beneath her, leaning her head against the wings, closing her eyes… Perhaps this would all just go away.

He stood above her, even more imposing now that she was seated. Neither of them spoke until the door opened.

'Biggs, bring some…tea and something to eat, please.'

'Tea?'

Nell almost smiled at the shock in the butler's voice. Lord Hunter glanced at him with a glint of rueful amusement just as the butler caught sight of Nell. All expression was wiped from the butler's face, but something in his stoic expression reflected the brief flash of amusement in his master's eyes and Nell didn't know whether to be relieved by this first sign of some softer human emotion from the man she was engaged to.

'Tea. Oh, and send Hidgins to the Peacock and ask him to retrieve—' He broke off and turned to Nell. 'Let me guess—you gave them your real name, didn't you? I thought so. To retrieve Miss Tilney's baggage. Discreetly, Biggs. But first have him drive by Miss Amelia to tell her to wait up for me; I will be by within an hour with a guest for the night.'

Nell started protesting, but the butler merely nodded and withdrew.

'I can't stay with you!'

'Don't worry; I never invite women here and certainly not my betrothed. I will take you somewhere a damn sight more respectable than the Peacock is for a country miss with no more sense than to try to stay at one of the busiest posting houses in London without a maid or chaperon. You may not want to marry me, but I'm damned if I am going to have the woman whose name has just been publicly linked with mine create a lurid scandal through sheer stupidity. I admit your father and I agreed on the engagement four years ago, but I understood he would discuss it with you and inform me if there was any impediment to proceeding and that in any case it wouldn't be relevant until you came of age.'

'Because I wouldn't inherit Bascombe until then, correct?' she asked, not concealing her contempt.

He breathed in, clearly clinging to his calm.

'Correct. I don't see anything outrageous in wanting to ally the Bascombe and Hunter estates. I admit I should have probably discussed the matter with you myself, but since you disappeared from Tilney and since I was in mourning at the time, it seemed sensible to let your father discuss the issue with you. I had no idea he hadn't done so and I had nothing to do with that gossip in the *Morning Post*. Believe me, I am suffering as much as you from that nonsense.'

Nell shrugged, her anger dimming, but not her depression.

'That was probably my father's heavy-handed way of trying to force my submission, but it won't work. If I have to personally demand the *Morning Post* issue a retraction, I shall do so.'

'No, you won't, not unless you wish to escalate this into a full-scale scandal, which I, for one, prefer to avoid. We will deal with this discreetly and that means if you want my co-operation you will go to my aunts and once you are rested we will discuss our options. Until then I suggest we put a moratorium on this discussion. I never decide on important matters when I am tired, hungry and upset. I suggest you adopt this policy, at least for tonight.'

Nell didn't answer and the tense silence held until the butler entered with a tray bearing a pot of tea and a plate of sandwiches.

'We don't have any sweetmeats, I'm afraid, sir,' he

said as he placed the tray in front of Nell and she smiled gratefully.

'Never mind. I don't like sweetmeats. This is perfect.'

The butler's brows rose, creating a row of arched wrinkles on his high forehead. Again she saw the glimmer of amusement in the glance he directed at his master.

'You don't like confectionery, miss?' he asked as he poured the tea, and both the action and the question surprised her. 'Such a distaste is uncommon in young women, if you pardon the impertinence, miss.'

The scent of steaming tea was heavenly and her mouth watered. It occurred to her this particular servant was allowed a great deal of latitude, which surprised her given Lord Hunter's controlled demeanour.

'If my aunt is to be believed, my not liking sweetmeats is the least of my peculiarities. Thank you.' She took the cup and saucer he held out to her.

'You're welcome, miss. But eat those sandwiches, do. Anything else, sir?'

'No, thank you, Biggs. That is more than enough.'

Nell once again heard the mocking note in Lord Hunter's voice.

'Very good, sir. Shall I also send a message that you are...otherwise engaged?'

A flash of annoyance crossed Hunter's face.

'Yes, do that.'

Biggs bowed and withdrew.

'I'm sorry I ruined your plans, but really there's no need...'

'It doesn't matter. Eat something and I'll take you to Amelia.'

'I really don't think...'

'We've established that already. Eat up. And next time

you plan to stay alone at major posting houses, use an alias. I suggest "Mrs Jones, widow". Widows are granted more leeway.'

Nell was tired in body and soul, and disheartened, and miserable, and his brusque, matter-of-fact approach pushed her over the edge. Even the sight of the food wasn't enough to counter the fury that caught her. She put down her cup and saucer with more force than grace and stood up.

'What useful advice. I will apply it at the next hostelry. In fact, I will try it right away. Goodnight, my lord. Have a lovely life and when you speak with my father tell him to have a lovely life as well.'

He blocked her path, his hand closing on her arms firmly but without force.

'Don't be a fool. Come, I will take you to my aunts and tomorrow we will figure out what to do with you.'

'You will *not* figure out what to do with me. I am not a...a witless dummy to be manipulated. I promised myself years ago I will *never* again be bullied and I don't care how tired and hungry and upset I am, because if you say just one more nasty thing to me I will walk out of here and if you try and stop me I will scream at the very top of my lungs and enjoy every second of it!'

Once again his fleeting smile flashed.

'I'm certain you will, for a moment. But it's not very practical, is it? You would probably call the Watch in on us and you look done in and I don't think you want to spend the next hour explaining the whole story to magistrates and strangers, do you? Can we compromise?'

'Compromise how?'

'You eat up and I take you to my aunts and then tomorrow we discuss this. Calmly.'

'That isn't a compromise since I still do what you want,' she said, well aware she sounded like a resentful child.

'Yes, but tomorrow you can send me to the devil and I will not lift a finger to stop you.'

'That's still not a compromise.'

'Well, it feels like one to me. What on earth are you thinking of doing? You can't go to the Peacock, especially now I've sent Hidgins for your baggage, and if you are contemplating doing something so rash, I just might choose to communicate some interesting information to the landlord that will make your stay more uncomfortable than it already appears to be.'

'You wouldn't!'

'Try me. I'm damned if I'm going to have someone whose name has been tied with mine in an unfortunately public manner make a fool of herself in one of the busiest hostelries in the city.'

'So you are threatening to compound my folly with yours? That doesn't make much sense.'

'Don't start preaching sense to me, young woman. Well?'

She raised her chin, trying to find a better solution and failing.

'Fine. For one night. Your aunts will probably think you drunk or mad and I won't blame them.'

He smiled.

'Not them. They're used to my eccentricities.'

Nell felt a snide comment wavering at the edge of her tongue, but held back and sat down again. It felt so very good to lose her temper, a luxury she rarely indulged, but the truth was that he was right—she was hungry and tired and upset and more than willing to postpone coping with the consequences of her actions until tomorrow.

'Fine. And please stop swearing at me. It is very improper.'

'Fine. Eat up.'

Hunter watched as she finally did as she was told and took one of Biggs's bread and cheese creations. He walked to pour himself a glass of port so she wouldn't see his smile. Admittedly when he and Sir Henry had agreed on the betrothal four years ago he hadn't been at his best, but he wondered how his memory could be so seriously flawed. He knew people changed a great deal in four years, he certainly had, and not for the better, but the contrast between this young woman and that girl was extreme. Despite her height she had struck him as rather mousy, all long limbs and very little else, her pale hair showing a distinct tendency to fall out of its pins and obscure her face. She hadn't been ugly, just... awkward. He remembered her expressions more than her face, from the joyful light after that incredible gallop on Petra to the sheer terror when she had come under her aunt's attack. Then, in that last minute when she had marched out of the drawing room, there had been something else—for a moment she had taken full advantage of her height and looked almost regal.

She wasn't a beauty, but mousy or gawky were definitely not the right words to describe her. He wasn't quite certain what words were applicable, but those blue-grey eyes, sparked with the fire of temper and determination and with a faint catlike slant, were anything but plain, and though she was still lean and athletic, as her limber recovery from the fall on his steps indicated, even under her countrified cloak he could see that her girlish slimness had filled out quite nicely.

In fact, as far as looks went, she was much more appealing than he remembered. But what she had gained in looks, she had lost in temperament. He certainly hadn't remembered she was such a prickly thing, though now he could recall some of her critical comments during that ride four years ago which should have forewarned him. It appeared he had as thoroughly misread her character as he had been mistaken about her appearance.

It hadn't taken him long to regret his agreement with Tilney, but he had comforted himself that at least he would be gaining not only Bascombe but a docile, compliant wife grateful to be saved from her less-than-satisfactory life, content to stay in Hampshire and leave him to pursue his work and other interests in London. Well, that conviction was clearly nothing more than a fantasy. There was still something skittish about her and her words about bullying were telling, but she was about as docile as she was mousy.

He savoured his port as he watched her. She might not like sweets, but she was certainly doing justice to Biggs's sandwiches. She put down her empty plate with a slight sigh and he smiled involuntarily. She was a strange little thing. No, not little.

'Better?'

Her mouth wavered, as if she was contemplating holding on to her anger, and then settled into a rueful smile.

'That was the best sandwich I have ever eaten, I think.'

'I will inform Biggs of your appreciation. He takes bread and cheese very seriously.'

'A sensible man.' Her smile widened and he could see

that girl again who had slid off Petra after her gallop, confident and confiding, but then she was gone again.

'He is. Now that you are fed, I have a suggestion to make. When I go to Wilton I will confer with your father and when I return we will all sit down—'

'Wilton? You're going to the breeders' fair?' Nell asked, leaning forward.

Hunter raised his brow at the interruption. Her face had transformed again and was now alight and eager.

'Yes. I've gone for the past couple of years. I'm looking for a stallion to breed with Petra. Why?'

Her gaze remained fixed on him, but he could have sworn that for a moment she wasn't there, had left her body and travelled to some place lovely and warm because her cheeks and lips lost their pallor, warming to a shade of a very edible peach, and her pupils shrank, turning her eyes more silver than grey. For a split second he thought this is what she might look like after she climaxed, full of warmth and light, afloat. Then it was gone; she looked down at her hands and pressed them together as if about to pray.

'I will agree to your compromise. On condition.'

Oh, hell. Somehow he thought he wouldn't like this.

'What condition?'

'I will come with you to Wilton.'

It was not a request. This girl was definitely not turning into the biddable bride he had thought she would be.

'I am not saying that I agree, but may I ask why?'

She shrugged and tugged at her gloves.

'Well, clearly we need to speak with Father about repudiating this rumour and if he isn't in London he has most likely gone to Wilton early. Surely there is no harm in merely driving with you since we are, for the moment at least, engaged. Well?'

Well, indeed? Why should every one of his instincts be on alert? Ever since Kate had shoved the newspaper with that blasted gossip at him he had known his life was going to take a distinct turn for the worse, but somehow he had hoped he could put off dealing with this particular commitment for a little while longer. He was used to the occasional sniping column about his affairs and activities and accepted them as part of his choice of lifestyle, but the deluge that had appeared in today's papers following the appearance of those two sentences about his purported betrothal was trying his patience. It didn't help that Biggs had indulged his sense of humour by acquiring several newspapers and spreading them around the house carefully folded open to the most damning, including one entitled 'Wild Hunter Bagged at Last!', which had been borderline libellous and peppered with the initials of the women reputed to be mourning his removal from the field.

All told he had been looking forward to confronting Tilney at Wilton and telling him what he thought of his management of this affair. What he had not counted on was that Tilney had clearly never told his daughter about the arrangement or that she would descend on him from the wilds of the Lake District demanding a disavowal. He walked over to the fireplace and shoved in another log. She wanted conditions, fine.

He stood and brushed the slivers of wood from his hands.

'Very well. As long as you meet my conditions as well. Unfortunately, as far as the world is concerned we are betrothed and to deny that now will cause precisely the scandal we're trying to avoid. So while at Wilton we present ourselves as such until we can consider how to end this engagement without turning us into a laughing stock. In addition, my co-operation is conditional upon reaching some reasonable long-term agreement about the water rights. I'll be da—dashed if I have to negotiate yearly fee agreements with my once betrothed or your bridegroom of choice when eventually you decide to marry.'

Hunter trailed off as she blushed so hotly she might as well have been wearing her heart fully emblazoned on her sleeve. No wonder she wanted out of this betrothal. His forced fiancée clearly already had a bridegroom in mind.

As the blush faded she canted her head to one side.

'Somehow that amounts to quite a few more conditions than mine.'

'I'm not negotiating. Well?'

She gave a brisk nod and he relaxed.

'Good. Off we go, then. Just keep your hood pulled low. I prefer not to be seen abroad with such a reckless character as yourself at this late hour.'

She laughed and stood, pulling on her hood, and he felt a twinge of regret. He reached out and arranged her hood so that it better covered the silver-gold glints of her hair. Her eyes rose to his in surprise and he didn't immediately release the soft fabric. Her irises were an interesting combination of shades of grey and blue—from slate to ice to a rim of darker blue. This close he caught her scent, something warm, like a field of wildflowers in summer. His eyes glided down towards her mouth, slightly parted in surprise. A very generous mouth. For a moment he was tempted to taste that lush curve. The memory returned of her coming towards him on Petra, her hair tumbled and her face alight, except that now his imagination embellished, it was no longer a girl but this young woman coming towards him, and now he was drawing her down onto the grass, spreading that fairy hair out on the wildflowers her scent evoked...

He didn't move, noting with cynical amusement the enthusiastic response of his body. Trust it to show interest now that he was within arm's reach of escaping this engagement. Whatever the case, he had no intention of acting on the urge. He stepped back and held out his arm.

'Shall we?'

Chapter Two

Nell obediently kept her head down as they descended from the hackney cab. At least that had been her intention, but a quick glance at the building they approached made her look up in swift surprise and her hood slipped back. She grabbed at it, but stood staring upwards. She had expected a house similar to Lord Hunter's or like her father's more modest town house. This looked more like a rambling school and took up half the road on this side.

Lord Hunter noticed her shocked expression.

'I know, not ideal, but it's the best I can do at such short notice. Aunt Sephy and Aunt Amelia live in a separate apartment. Their entrance is down this alleyway.'

He took her hand and placed it on his arm, leading her towards a narrow gap between the building and a row of modest-looking houses scantily lit by a single oil lamp at the corner. His arm was very warm under her gloved hand and it spread a pleasant heat through her, like the comforting animal warmth of leaning against a horse in a cold stable.

She smiled at the thought. Lord Hunter would probably not appreciate being compared with a horse. In fact, she had no idea what he might appreciate. He was not at all what she had expected. Neither the perplexing young man she remembered nor Mrs Sturges's debauched rake. There was still that rather irreverent amusement hovering in the background, and sometimes not so far in the background, but she certainly didn't feel threatened by him. Perhaps just a little when he had helped her with her hood; something unsettling in his eyes had set off alarms, but it had come and gone too quickly for her to act on her need to draw back.

Still, it wasn't wise to trust this man and she shouldn't presume that she understood him simply because he was so unfashionably blunt. As someone who kept most of herself firmly out of public view, she had a good eye for identifying people whose surface differed from their interior. She could see beyond painfully shy or boisterously loud exteriors and she had used this skill time and again helping Mrs Petheridge with the schoolgirls and even with recalcitrant or challenging horses. Not that he appeared to be masking vulnerability or fear, but there was definitely something behind the urbane façade that outweighed it, and until she understood what it was she would do well not to take him at face value, no matter how charming the face.

As they weaved their way into the gloom she realised she was being all too complaisant about being led into a dark alley by a man she hardly knew. Admittedly the mention of an Aunt Sephy and Aunt Amelia didn't exactly invoke images of rape and pillage, but still…

'What is this place?' she asked in a whisper, slowing her steps, but just then the alley curved into a small courtyard set around a single tree. The cobblestones glistened with the remains of the drizzle and light shone through curtains which were definitely pink and embroidered with flowers. Even in that weak light Nell could see the façade here was well tended and the tree surrounded with chrysanthemums. It was so far removed from the dour impression of the front of the building that she couldn't help staring.

Hunter stopped as well and his hand covered hers where it lay on his arm. He stood with his back to the faint light from the window, once again a dark-on-dark shape like that first moment he had opened the door, but this time it was a different kind of shock that spurted through her. There was enough light to infuse his eyes with a startling burn of gold and his smile was so enticing that her hand began to turn under his. She froze before she could complete the gesture, but she was incapable of doing anything else but waiting for his move, as surely as if this was a game of chess and these the iron rules of a game they had engaged in.

He wasn't doing anything, just looking down at her, but in her weary and overwhelmed state he seemed to grow, take on the dark of the night, expand and envelop her. She had never been fanciful but she imagined Lucifer might look like this the moment before he claimed a failing soul for his own. It would feel like this, too: hot, terrifying, all encompassing, seductive. If she leaned forward she might fall into that heat and be consumed by it, claimed and changed for ever. It would be inescapable.

Then he spoke and the moment broke.

'A bit of a surprise, isn't it?' he said and there was nothing in his voice to reflect the swirling heat of the moment. She stepped back, pulling her hand away. It must be the weariness and the confusion, that was all.

More proof that she should not trust him, even if that moment had been merely her imagination.

'I can't go in there!' She heard the panic in her voice, but couldn't help it.

He took her hand again, layering it between his own. This was no longer Lucifer, and though the warmth flowed through her, now it was soothing.

'It's all right. You will like them and they will like you, I promise. There is nothing to be afraid of.'

She tried to resent being spoken to like a child except that it wasn't the patronising tone of some of the school-mistresses. It was an offer, but the decision would have to be hers. She glanced at the pink curtains and nodded. She had little choice, after all.

He tapped lightly on a lion's-paw knocker and the door was opened immediately by a round little man who bowed and stood back.

'Good evening, my lord. Miss Amelia is waiting for you in the parlour. Miss Sephy has of course retired.'

Lord Hunter urged Nell up the stairs into the well-lit hall.

'Thank goodness for that, Bassett.'

The butler's mouth relaxed as he opened the door into a room at the back of the house and stood back to let them enter.

'Indeed, my lord. May I bring refreshments?'

'You may. Tea for Miss Tilney and something stronger for me.'

Nell cringed at the trouble she was causing and almost began apologising, but Lord Hunter ushered her into the parlour where a woman moved towards them with a smile in honey-brown eyes that clearly were a shared family trait. She also had her nephew's strong brows and slightly aquiline nose. It was a formidable face, but contrarily Nell didn't feel at all intimidated. In fact, and very uncharacteristically, Nell liked her on sight and met the woman's smile with one of her own.

'Amelia, this is Miss Helen Tilney. Miss Tilney, this is my aunt, Miss Amelia Calthorpe. She lives here with my other aunt, Miss Seraphina Calthorpe, who is thankfully asleep because her rampant curiosity would keep you awake until dawn if let loose. Amelia, we have an emergency. Miss Tilney needs a place to stay for a few days until she decides on her future path. May she stay here? I've sent Hidgins to collect her luggage from the posting house, but if he's delayed she might need to borrow some gear from you.'

Nell was grateful for the soft light, though she was sure her flush of shame was still as apparent as in broad daylight, but Amelia's face betrayed none of the shock and scorn Nell had expected.

'Of course you may,' Amelia said without hesitation, holding out her hand to Nell. 'And you needn't worry about your baggage. It reminds me I once lost my trunk and I was miserable because I had just bought the loveliest bonnet. Do come with me and we will have something warm to drink while Bassett is preparing the guest room. Did you travel far today?'

Nell followed her in something of a daze.

'I…from Keswick…'

'Oh, of course. I just realised who you are! I am not very good with the papers, but Sephy did show me the column in the *Post* today, or was it yesterday? I have been meaning to write you a note, Gabriel. Why didn't you tell me this is the woman you are engaged to?'

'Not any more. Miss Tilney plans to jilt me as soon as we can do so with minimal fuss.'

'Dear me, what a pity. Was it something you said?'

'I think it might be something I didn't say.'

'Of course. I quite understand, Miss Tilney, and I must say that though I personally adore Gabriel, I can see your point. From the age of four he was always one to go his own way and let the world follow if it can. Oh, thank you, Bassett. Just put it on the table. I will pour.'

Nell accepted the cup of tea Miss Calthorpe handed her, trying very hard not to give in to the urge to giggle at this increasingly improbable scene. She looked away and met Gabriel's eyes and the lazy invitation to share in his amusement evoked an involuntary response in her. If ever a look said 'I told you so' without exciting the least resentment, this was it. She drank her tea, answering Miss Amelia's questions as faithfully as possible, but without much awareness of what she said. She laid down her cup on the small round table by her chair, but it tilted alarmingly and the cup and saucer slid away as she watched, too tired and sluggish to even realise what was about to happen. But Lord Hunter leaned forward with a swiftness that made her jerk awake and caught the cup and saucer with a smooth motion.

'Thank you,' she murmured, flushing, and his eyes moved over her, intense and questioning.

'You're tired. I'll go see if Bassett is done.'

'Please, don't bother…' she began, but luckily Bassett entered.

'Miss Tilney's room is ready, Miss Amelia.'

'Thank you, Bassett. Come along, Miss Tilney. May I call you Helen, or is it Nell? Leave your cloak. Bassett

will give it a good brushing. Goodnight, Gabriel. You
may come by tomorrow.'

Nell allowed herself to be propelled out of the drawing room and up the stairs, resisting the childish urge
to remain with Lord Hunter. It was a sign of how shaky
she was that she was beginning to consider an irreverent rake a safe haven.

Chapter Three

'He wandered, lost and dreaming of his love...'

Hunter turned with a resigned sigh as a tall dark figure crossed the street towards him.

'And so it begins. Want to lampoon me out here, Raven? Or shall we wait until you can entertain Stanton as well?'

'Both, thank you. This merits quite a bit more ribbing than can be accomplished on a doorstep. Besides, I need a drink. I just walked over from Jenny's and I'm frozen through.'

'Didn't she warm you sufficiently? Either you or she is slipping, Raven. Good evening, Dunberry,' Hunter greeted Stanton's butler.

'Speaking of slipping, I frankly never thought you'd take the plunge; it was a bit of a shock to have that gossip in the *Morning Post* pointed out to me.'

'For me, too.'

'You don't remember proposing? And here I thought you had a hard head.'

'I remember proposing. Her father and I settled it four years ago but I thought common courtesy would require he speak with me before discussing it with gossip columnists. I didn't appreciate Kate bringing it to my attention.'

Ravenscar winced.

'I suppose she was peeved?'

'I was too distracted by being "peeved" myself to notice and it rather ruined the mood, so I didn't linger to chat...'

They entered the library and Stanton glanced up from the book he had been holding, but didn't bother rising from the sagging armchair by the fire.

'You're late.'

'May I have something to drink before you begin the catechism?' Hunter asked politely.

'Help yourself.' Stanton waved towards a decanter on the sideboard. 'What happened? You two having a hard time finding your timepieces amidst the tangle of sheets?'

'Good God, Stanton, tell me you've read the papers these past two days,' Ravenscar said with disgust.

'Of course I read the papers. A great deal more closely than you do, Raven. What does that have to do with your mistresses?'

'Other than the political pages,' Ravenscar corrected, taking his glass and settling in his usual armchair, his long legs stretched out to the fire that shot his black hair with a jet sheen that made his name singularly apt.

'In that case, no. Why, has something happened?' Stanton's blue eyes narrowed in concern.

'Hopeless,' Ravenscar murmured. 'Shall I tell him, or shall you, Hunter?'

Hunter took his usual seat as well.

'I wouldn't deprive you of the pleasure for the world, Raven.'

'Thank you. It appears we are to wish Hunter happy. He is betrothed.'

'What? When? To whom?'

'I think "Why?" might be more to the point,' Ravenscar replied and Hunter sighed.

'She's Sir Henry Tilney's daughter and heir to the Bascombe estate. Her father and I agreed on the engagement when I went to negotiate the water rights after old Bascombe died.'

'Wait, I remember now. You bought Petra and Pluck from Tilney. Right after Tim's funeral.'

Eventually this reflexive stiffening of his muscles at the mention of Tim would fade, Hunter told himself for the umpteenth time.

Stanton continued, his controlled voice far worse than Ravenscar's jibes.

'You've been engaged for four years and never once mentioned it.'

'I didn't mention it because the engagement was… conditional. The girl was just seventeen and Bascombe's will stipulated she inherit only when she turned twenty-one. If she died before that, married or not, the property went to some cousin. Her father agreed that it would be unreasonable to expect me to commit to a public engagement until the inheritance was legally hers.'

'And she accepted this cold-blooded arrangement? Well, you definitely have reached the mecca of complaisant and biddable brides, Hunter. I salute you.'

'Not quite. I presumed her father would discuss it with her, but it appears she didn't know about it until recently, and when she balked her father decided the best way to force her hand was to make it public.'

'Just so I understand,' Stanton said carefully. 'You entered into this engagement without ever asking the girl to marry you?'

Hunter rubbed his forehead.

'I couldn't very well make any announcement at the time anyway because of Tim. So it made sense to wait until the main reason for marrying her became valid. She was only a child, for heaven's sake, and the last thing she was ready to cope with at that point was someone else imposing their will on her. Her father and I agreed she would be better off remaining in the care of her schoolmistress as a boarder until she inherited. The corollary was that for the past four years we've enjoyed the best terms on the Tilney waterways in generations. I thought it was a damn good arrangement at the time.'

Stanton stood up himself and moved with uncharacteristic restlessness around the room.

'Are you saying you asked her to marry you because you felt sorry for her?'

'I told you, there were also the water rights. Put like that I know it sounds foolish...'

'Foolish doesn't begin to cover... Hunter, didn't it occur to you that making such a decision just days after Tim's death wasn't very wise?'

'You do have a talent for understatement, Stanton,' Ravenscar mocked.

Hunter rose as well and went to stand by the fire, watching the flames dance cherry and gold in his brandy.

'Very well,' Stanton said carefully. 'Now that her enterprising father has forced your hand, what do you intend to do?'

'Since I am honour-bound to stand by my offer, my intentions are irrelevant. She, on the other hand, intends to jilt me.'

Ravenscar grinned.

'This keeps getting better.'

'I still don't see anything wrong in principle with marrying in order to ally my land with Bascombe,' Hunter replied defensively. 'It's been done since time immemorial. Now you can take ten minutes to rake me down and then I suggest we get down to the business of finding a property for Hope House in the west country.'

'More important than my friend making a monumental mistake?' Both Hunter and Ravenscar straightened at the uncharacteristic bite in Stanton's voice. He rarely used his *last-chance-to-negotiate-surrender* voice with them. 'The only sensible thing about this whole fiasco so far appears to be Miss Tilney's reaction! I make every allowance for your original decision having been made in rather trying circumstances, but do you really mean to tell me that for four years it didn't occur to you once to seek out this girl and find out whether your decision was a wise one? I don't give a damn about what people have done over time immemorial! I know you've lived your whole life thinking you can rescue people and depend on no one, but you are not as clever as you want to believe and this, let me tell you, is sheer, abject stupidity. Ravenscar I could understand cold-bloodedly deciding to marry an heiress, but you don't even need the funds; the Hunter estate is one of the wealthiest in Hampshire...'

'Yes, but we depend on Bascombe for the water...' Hunter raised his hands placatingly, trying to stem Stanton's rising outrage. It was clearly a mistake. Stanton, renowned for the lightest of diplomatic touches on the most sensitive affairs of state, rarely allowed himself to descend into blasphemy but he did so now, with all the thoroughness he applied to his diplomatic concerns. When he was done the silence was of the calibre often experienced in the studies of the better tutors. The moral point having been made, behaviours examined and condemned, silence remained to let remorse and counsel rise to the surface and prevail. Hunter had had to share quite a few of those moments at Eton with both Stanton and Ravenscar by his side. Predictably Ravenscar broke first.

'What is she like? Ugly as nails? Heiresses usually are. When can we meet her?'

Hunter hesitated. Before this evening he would have known what to answer. After seeing her again he wasn't so sure. She was certainly no beauty like Kate, but she was…different. Unpredictable. Intriguing. He decided to keep it simple until he knew what he himself thought. Not that it would make any difference. If he could convince her to hold her course and withstand her father's ire, she would be someone else's problem.

'Not that it matters since I am about to be jilted, but she is neither ugly nor a beauty. More…unusual. I've never seen a woman with a better seat on a horse. On the other hand, she had a brutal harpy of an aunt living with them who reduced her to the state of a quivering blancmange, which when you're as tall as a Viking looks just a bit bizarre. Then halfway through one of the most tedious dinners I have yet had to plough my way through she suddenly transformed into an avenging fury, told the aunt to go to the devil with biblical panache and the next day she ran back to her school without a word to anyone but the cook and groom. Then tonight she appeared on my doorstep unchaperoned and determined to consign *me* to the devil. I'm glad you find this so amusing,' he concluded a bit sourly as his friends sat with various degrees of grins on their faces.

'You would too, man, if it wasn't happening to you,' Ravenscar replied. 'And I think you could call it a very auspicious beginning. Since marriage is a fate worse than death, it sounds as though you are getting a very fair preview of your future if you can't convince her to sheer off.'

'Thank you, Ravenscar. I can always count on you for perspective. I admit she wasn't quite what I had bargained for when I was resigning myself to the benefits of a modest, country-bred wife who would be happy to live at the Hall tending to children and horses and leaving me to my concerns in London.'

'Ah, the sentimental musings of today's youth...'

'You can be as caustic as you like, Raven. You're one of the least sentimental people I have ever met.'

'I have my moments. Luckily none of them involved an offer of matrimony.'

'So what are you planning to do?' Stanton interceded practically. 'You need to find the girl's father first thing.'

'He's likely at the Wilton breeders' fair and the girl is raring to go there, which is lucky because the sooner I hand her to her parent, the less likely we are to turn this fiasco into an outright scandal. If she is serious about jilting me, I will need to manage this carefully.'

'Do you really want to nip this affair in the bud?'

Hunter shrugged. It was probably the wisest course of action. He had worn out his chivalric fantasies trying, and failing, to save Tim and his mother. Even before Tim's death he, Ravenscar and Stanton had acquired a reputation for wild living and for accepting any and all sporting dares. After a particularly difficult midnight race down to Brighton, society had delighted in dubbing them the Wild Hunt Club. Since Tim's death he had more than earned his membership rights in that club. He often spent his nights wearing himself down to the point where sleep captured him like the prey of the mythical wild hunts he and his friends were styled after. Whatever still remained of his chivalric impulses he channelled into his work at Hope House and he didn't need anyone outside his friends, his work and the uncommitted physical companionship of women like Kate. The thought of being saddled with a frightened, easily bullied near-schoolgirl was so distasteful he wondered why he hadn't just gone down on his knees and thanked his lucky stars the moment she had sent him to the devil. He had certainly been dreading the moment Tilney would come demanding his due.

It was just that he had been surprised. He had done a very effective job of putting her out of mind since that day at Tilney and coming face-to-face with her had disoriented him. She certainly didn't act like a frightened girl, despite a few moments when he had seen alarm in her silvery eyes. As for near-schoolgirl...those lips and that body were anything but schoolgirlish.

He sighed. None of this mattered. The key was to grasp this reprieve with both hands. He would take her to her father and see if he could extract himself from this fiasco without too much damage.

'Well, whatever you decide, I have faith in your ability to talk her into your way of thinking,' Ravenscar said. 'I've yet to see anyone get by you when you bend your mind to it.'

'Tim did.'

The words were out before Hunter could stop them. They would have been completely out of place, except that these two men had also risked their lives to rescue Tim from France during the war and they knew what caring for Tim until his death had done to Hunter. Ravenscar's cynical smile disappeared.

'Tim was lost the moment that French devil of an inquisitor got his brutal hands on him. We might have managed to salvage his body, or what was left of it, but five months in that prison was five months too long. It was damn bad luck the French were convinced he knew something of value simply because he was on Wellington's staff. They should have realised a boy of nineteen was unlikely to be privy to staff secrets.'

Hunter's stomach clenched as his younger brother's tortured, scarred hands appeared before him as they did in his nightmares, and his face—staring, shaking, wet with tears, begging for the release from mental and bodily pain that the opiates gave him and which Hunter had been forced to ration as Tim's dependency grew.

'That bastard would have continued torturing him anyway. But it was my fault allowing him to join up in the first place.'

'That's nonsense,' Stanton said curtly. 'You took better care of Tim than your parents ever did since the day he was born and he wouldn't have lasted a day after we rescued him if you hadn't nursed him. If there is anyone in this world who should feel no guilt over Tim, it's you. I'm damned if I know why you do.'

Hunter's shoulders tensed as the memories flooded back. For two years he had tried everything he could to help his brother heal, but nothing but laudanum had succeeded in dimming the daily agony of his pain and his attacks of terror. Hunter would never be certain if that final dose was intentional, but he was as certain as he could bear to be. He remembered Tim's words that night before climbing the stairs to his childhood room for the last time.

'You've always been so good to me, Gabe. If there is any way to stop anyone else from going through this, you'll do it, won't you? You promise?'

He would have promised Tim anything at that point, if only he had made an effort to… It was pointless. After the initial shock of finding Tim dead the next morning he had spent a year full of guilt and self-contempt that he had failed his younger brother, or worse, that he had somehow willed Tim to finish it because his agony was too much to bear, and yet worse—because he could only look ahead to years of servitude to a broken boy. Eventually he had dragged himself out of that pit with the help of Ravenscar and Stanton and their work at Hope House. But his grief and guilt and sense of failure clung. He had enough distance now to know that his pact with Tilney had been formed from the ashes of his failure with Tim. Bascombe, water rights and a young woman who was clearly in need of salvation and therefore likely to be grateful for what she could receive had been presented to him on a silver platter and he had taken them, platter and all, more fool he.

'Are you still having nightmares?' Stanton asked, dragging Hunter's thoughts back with unwelcome sharpness. He could feel the sweat break out on the back of his neck and he rubbed at it, but nothing could erase the sick feeling of helplessness. He knew Stanton meant well, but he wished he hadn't asked.

'Sometimes.'

'Since this piece of gossip showed up?'

'Yes.'

Both nights. The dreams were one reason he never stayed the night with his mistresses and another reason, if he needed any, why the thought of marriage was so distasteful. It was one thing keeping this secret from the women he chose to visit on his terms. He couldn't imagine the strain of keeping his fatal flaw a secret from a woman living in his own home. The realisation that he would have to go through with this marriage was probably bringing the worst of it to the surface. It was bad enough having his friends know about them, but he could trust Stanton and Ravenscar with his weaknesses. The thought of that girl…of anyone seeing him while he was in the throes of those moments that left him soaked in sweat… It was unthinkable.

'All the more reason to extract myself from this mess. I don't think my bride would appreciate finding out about my less-than-peaceful nights. She'd probably run for the hills.'

'If you found someone you cared about, you wouldn't have to hide this from them,' Stanton replied.

'That will never happen.'

'What? Loving someone or sharing your weakness?'

'Either. What the devil are you talking about anyway? Love is just another name for dependency or lust and I've had enough of the former in my life and I'm quite content with what I have of the latter. I have no intention of aping my mother or brother by letting myself depend on anyone as they did on me. It didn't do them any good, did it? Or me either.'

'It doesn't have to be such an unequal equation. I

liked Tim and your mother, too, but they drained you dry, man. I don't call that love.'

'You go too far, Stanton!' Hunter said and Stanton raised his hands in surrender.

'Fine. I've no right to preach anyway. Aside from my parents I've never seen evidence of the fabled beast myself.'

'You're too cold-blooded to fancy yourself in love, anyway, Stanton,' Ravenscar stated, swirling his brandy as he watched them. 'And I'm too hot-blooded. So let's put that topic to rest and leave Hunter's Viking bride for the morrow and focus on our business. You'll be pleased to hear I have found a reasonable location for a new house near Bristol. It belongs to a relation of mine who has seen the light and wants to go succour the poor in warmer climes than Gloucestershire. The only problem is that it is distressingly close to Old Dame Jezebel's lair.'

Hunter gratefully accepted the reprieve.

'Your grandmother? Good Lord, she would never countenance a charitable institution within a hundred miles of her domain. She'll never include you in her will if you do this.'

'Since I am already permanently excluded from that honour, her outrage will be well worth it.' Ravenscar winked.

Chapter Four

'You are early, Lord Hunter,' Bassett said as he took Hunter's hat and cane.

'Is that an observation or a hint, Bassett?'

'An observation, my lord. Miss Seraphina is having her cocoa in bed, and Miss Amelia is not yet awake, having read late as usual. Miss Tilney, however, is awake and Sue has gone to tell her breakfast is served. Is there anything I can bring you?'

'Just coffee, thank you, Bassett.'

'Right away. Oh, the newspapers are on the table, my lord.' He nodded at the pile on the breakfast table.

Hunter glanced up in suspicion at something in Bassett's tone, but the butler was already on his way out, so he turned to the dreaded society pages in the rag Aunt Sephy adored. He found his name quite readily and sighed again as he read through the latest creation of the columnists who were clearly having a great deal of fun at his expense.

'Bad news?' a voice said next to him and he whirled around. Nell was standing just beside him, frowning at the paper. She had entered so quietly he had not even realised she was there. He held back on a childish urge to tuck the paper behind his back. Very casually he turned the page.

'Good morning, Miss Tilney.'

'Good morning, Lord Hunter. May I see that?'

Hell.

'It's just the usual nonsense. I ignore it. So should you.'

Nell didn't look up from the paper, even though it now merely showed an advertisement for a cream to counter the ravages of the outdoors.

'Lady F. That's Lady Katherine Felton, isn't it?'

Double hell. How would she know that?

'You shouldn't believe everything you read in the newspapers. Not that this is a newspaper, just a glorified gossip column. Aunt Seraphina lives on a diet of gossip and cocoa.'

The silvery eyes rose and he felt an uncharacteristic heat prickle in his cheeks, throwing him back to the experience of standing before Nurse and a broken window, desperately trying to hide a cricket bat behind his back. He drew himself up. This was ridiculous.

'Shall we…?'

'You needn't be embarrassed you have a mistress. Mrs Sturges assures me most dandies in London have mistresses.'

'I'm not a dandy!'

'Aren't you? Oh, right, she said you were a Corinthian, not a dandy. Though there doesn't appear to be a great difference between them and I suppose they have mistresses, too.'

'There is quite a gulf between a dandy and a Corinthian,' he replied, annoyed at her dismissive tones and momentarily distracted from the fact that the last thing he should be discussing with his betrothed was mistresses.

'I suppose so, but they both are rather profligate and slavishly obsessed with things that matter to no one but themselves. There isn't anything in that column I didn't already know. Mrs Sturges told me all about you and your exploits.'

'My exploits!'

'That's what Mrs Sturges called them. She is very Gothic and talks in capital letters. I rather thought she had exaggerated, but the columnist obviously shares her opinion. She told me all about midnight races and something called the Wild Hunt Club, if I remember correctly. Strange—you don't seem like a dissolute rake. You certainly didn't take advantage of me yesterday, though I suppose that is not quite a criterion since I can't imagine anyone, even if he was a rake, making advances to every woman he comes across, especially if she isn't in the least pretty. It would be quite wearying, wouldn't it? Particularly if he already has a mistress and Mrs Sturges said that Lady Felton is an accredited beauty. In fact, by that logic rakes would be less likely to make advances to all and sundry, wouldn't they?'

Hunter struggled to find a reasonable response to this barrage, or even to manage his own response to her. Out of all the improper and thoroughly damning statements she had let loose with such insouciance, the one that caught his attention was her condemnation of her own looks. It was said with such matter-of-factness and with just a touch of wistfulness that he almost protested. But the need to contradict her statement was submerged by the same confusion he had experienced when facing her last night. In the light of day the difference between this woman and the girl he had thought he was engaged to was even more pronounced. The sun-kissed face looking at him in uncritical interest, though not beautiful, was remarkable in its way. Her wide grey eyes were slightly slanted and framed by the most amazing eyelashes he had ever seen, long and silky and definite and, like her brows, several shades darker than her hair. Her mouth, too, was remarkable—generous and lush and there was a faint white scar just below its right corner. Without thinking, he reached out and touched his finger to the line.

'I don't remember this when I saw you in Leicestershire. What happened?'

Her lips closed tightly and she stepped away from him and he could have kicked himself not only for his insensitivity but for his irrational reaction to that imperfection, a surge of concern and protectiveness that only arose with regard to the very few people he considered under his care. But if his intention had been to deflect her from her inquisition, it worked.

'I was thrown from a horse. It was my fault. But Juniper—the horse—is fine. I know it's ugly.'

'What? No, it's just—' He broke off. There was nothing he could say to explain, to her or to himself, why he had reacted that way. Why he had wanted to touch it and the line of her lip as it curved in. He looked down at the newspaper, trying to find his footing. Then he turned back to her resolutely.

'Why don't we sit down, have something to eat and then talk this over sensibly?'

Her eyes glinted at him.

'There is a pattern forming here. You appear to think I will be more amenable once fed.'

'I certainly will be. I'm useless without my morning coffee.'

Her smile widened, but she nodded and went to the sideboard. He kept the conversation light as they ate, telling her about Petra's and Pluck's successes at the racing meets, a topic which she clearly was happy to explore until she had finished her last finger of toast.

'I'm so happy they are content with you. I still miss Pluck, but I knew Father would never let me keep her, so I'm glad she is with Petra. Well, now that we've eaten I admit to being impatient to hear what you are planning.'

'What makes you think I am *planning* anything?'

'I don't know, but I'm quite certain you are. You have a look.'

Hunter, who had a reputation for being unreadable at the piquet table, barely refrained from asking what this 'look' was, drummed his fingers on the table and wondered how to play his cards. This was not precisely how he had imagined his dealings with a near-schoolgirl would progress. For better or worse she was a bright young woman and he had better start treating her as such.

'May I ask what you plan to do once you are freed of this engagement?'

She considered him, clearly debating whether or not to confide in him.

'I will probably go to Bascombe, but first I will find someone respectable to act as companion or Father or... or my aunt will think they have a duty to come...'

Her voice faded and the haunted look he had seen at Tilney returned. The last time he had seen that expression before her had been on Tim's face. Every day since he rescued him from that French hell and until the day he killed himself. Hunter uncurled his hand from the cup before it shattered. He was right to run. He didn't need this.

'Bar the gates, then,' he said, a bit more roughly than he had intended. 'Bascombe's gates are flanked by two portly gargoyles which make the point quite vividly.'

Her eyes focused back on him and he relaxed as the edge of a smile returned as well.

'Gargoyles?'

'Your grandmother's idea. At least if they were decent sculptures it might be forgivable, but they look like drunken gnomes about to fall off toadstools.'

The smile widened.

'Then my first order of business shall be to remove them. I don't think they would intimidate Aunt Hester anyway. She might even like them. She has the most awful taste.'

'I remember she told me the horrific banquet room at Tilney Hall was her design. Send her the gargoyles as a gift, then.'

She half-laughed and covered her mouth to stop the sound.

'I'd just as happily drop them on her,' she said daringly and he smiled. 'Meanwhile I shall write to a schoolmistress I know to come stay with me.'

'And then?'

She smoothed the tablecloth with her finger.

'I haven't decided yet. But I do know I don't want a marriage of convenience without affection or love.'

He managed to stop his expression from exhibiting what he thought about that last statement. Of course the girl would be dreaming of love. She came from a girls' school, for heaven's sake. The place must be a hotbed of silly novels and soulful sighs.

'Those are two very different qualities. What people call romantic love is not much more than a glorified term for mundane physical passion and tends not to outlive it.'

She flushed, but met his gaze squarely. 'I concede that passion is important, but love is an entity in itself. You are completely wrong to dismiss it so cavalierly.'

He raised a brow at her dismissive tones.

'Of course I am, being so very green,' he said quietly. There was a limit to the abuse he would take from this young woman.

'No, you're not green, just wrong. I may have had very little experience of the world, but I have also been very lucky. When I lost my mother I thought I would never find anyone else who would care for me as much, but now I have other people I love, really deeply love, like Mrs Petheridge and my best friend Anna, and it would be devastating to lose them. I may not expect to find that depth of feeling with a husband, but there must be elements of that for it to be worthwhile marrying. That is what I mean by love. Working in a girls' school where children can't help but mirror the joy or pain of their families is a fairly good arena to explore that particular topic. I have had excellent opportunities to observe the products of the kind of union this betrothal might lead to and I have excellent reasons for refusing. I grew up knowing what it is like to be insignificant and powerless and I will never put myself in that position again.' She leaned back, her Nordic sea eyes narrowed and challenging. 'But this discussion is pointless. Why don't we discuss what you are really interested in—the

Bascombe water rights. Well, I promise I won't be in the least unreasonable. I don't want to be at war with my neighbours. There is no reason why we cannot come to an agreement that is fair for all parties.'

Hunter shifted in his chair, battling the urge to give her as thorough a lecture in return. It would be cruel to take from her anything that had been so painfully won by pointing out that relations between men and women were substantially different than the kind of familial friendships she had thankfully developed away from Tilney. He knew the value of friendships all too well and he knew the pain of loss that came with loving someone who was brutally snatched out of reach, and those, thankfully, had nothing to do with the institution of marriage. To point this out would not only be churlish but counterproductive. He focused instead on her statement about the water rights.

'Though I appreciate your good intentions, if you are indeed set on finding your perfect prince, once you wed it will be your husband who decides on such matters. I suggest you keep that in mind because once it becomes known you have inherited Bascombe Hall some very skilled fortune hunters will be lining up and professing precisely the kind of emotions you appear to value so highly.'

He winced at the harshness of his words, but she just stared coldly back at him.

'I dare say I should be grateful you didn't bother to do the same in your quest to secure Bascombe for yourself. I rather thought you had enough wealth already, or is it never enough?'

He supposed he deserved that.

'I admit my concerns were practical. I never made

any pretence that this alliance wasn't primarily one of good sense. You might think me a profligate fellow, but I take my role as custodian of the Hunter estate seriously and of course I thought it made sense to ally our estates. But I have no intention of forcing you or your father to stand by your engagement, and though if I chose to be unpleasant I could have both of you before a court of law for breach of promise, I prefer to settle this peaceably. So I suggest we try to resolve this like adults. Is that reasonable?'

'Quite. I'm not very happy about the implied threat, though. Are you one of those litigious individuals like Father, who are always suing people over imagined grievances? I find that very self-absorbed people are very quick to find offence at the most absurd things.'

'It was not a threat, but an observation,' Hunter replied, his composure beginning to wear thin. 'And though I have never sued anyone in my life, I would be tempted to begin with you if you insist on continuing with your insults.'

She surprised him, the anger melting away from her eyes as she smothered a ripple of laughter.

'But I didn't insult you. Those were all general statements. You are far too sensitive.'

'Unbelievable. I think I will retire from the lists before I suffer further damage. But before that I just want to make my position quite clear—I went to Tilney Hall to negotiate terms with your father and having met you I thought an alliance between Hunter and Bascombe Halls was a perfect solution. I wouldn't have contemplated it if I hadn't liked you.'

'Don't bother lying! There was nothing to like! I was

pathetic!' Her words were so fierce he physically drew breath. The ice kept getting thinner and thinner.

'Your *aunt* was pathetic,' he replied quietly. 'Your father was almost as bad, and the worst is that they had no redeeming qualities. I don't remember you being pathetic. I remember a girl who was pushed to the edge of her endurance, but who still managed to be the most fearless rider I have seen and who showed more courage that night standing up to her oppressor than many men who went into battle. Don't let that harpy win by perpetuating her poison in your own mind.'

She brushed her fingertips over her eyelids and then rubbed her eyes like a tired child.

'Thank you. I was right that you are kind. You're clever, too. I won't marry you, but I will talk to the lawyers and see if there is a way to sell you some of the riverfront, which is what you obviously are truly interested in, so you needn't worry that my naïveté will land me with a fortune-hunting husband who will make you suffer like Grandmama did.'

He let this manna from heaven settle in the silence between them.

'You would sell me part of the water rights?' he asked cautiously.

She dropped her hands. Her eyes were red and her lashes stuck together like the spikes on the Bascombe gates, and she looked both very young and very adult.

'None of the land is entailed or obviously I wouldn't be able to inherit. I asked for the estate maps when Grandmama passed and I remember the river has a curve near your land before it branches off into the canal that feeds your fields, so if we split ownership of that portion of the river then you could build a canal from there instead. It would just be another, what, fifty yards? And then neither the Bascombes nor the Hunters would be able to control the flow and river traffic. So if I do marry a nasty fortune hunter, or if I don't marry anyone and eventually my cousin or his children inherit, they wouldn't be able to change anything. Correct?'

It was a perfect solution. Talk about keeping his cake and eating it, too. He would happily pay for such a concession. It wouldn't even be taking advantage of her youth—it was actually a sensible solution. The ongoing squabbling over those rights cost both sides funds and unnecessary anxiety and acrimony.

'That's a very sensible solution,' he said slowly and was rewarded by the same smile she had tossed at him last night after Biggs's sandwich. A mix between satisfaction and the dispensing of well-being. 'I will even happily concede Pluck to you to sweeten the deal. Meanwhile we go down to Wilton, sit down with your father and discuss how we are going to proceed. Agreed?'

'Agreed. I'm very glad you are being so reasonable about this. If I had to become engaged to and unengaged from anyone, I'm glad it was you.'

Hunter burst out laughing and stood up.

'That might be the nicest thing anyone has said to me in a long time, sweetheart, and I happily return the compliment. I will send word to your father and the Welbecks that we will drive down tomorrow.'

'But I can't stay here. Your aunts…'

'Will be delighted. They aren't very fond of society, but they love company. Do we have an accord?' He held his hand out and after a moment's hesitation she stood and held hers out as well.

'Yes.'

Hunter took her hand. It was a little cold and he could feel the calluses at the base of her fingers. Clearly she still rode, even up in her rainy mountains. Her hand warmed in his, the stiffness seeping out of it, but the pliancy that did nothing to mask the strength in her long fingers brought a responsive surge of hunger and a curiosity to see if he could make the rest of her warm and pliant. There was fire here; he was certain of it. She might not be aware of it, but it was there, just waiting for someone to show her precisely what she was capable of.

Not that it was his concern any more, he told himself, holding still as his body rode out a wave of physical awareness. Then he let go of her hand before he spit in the eye of providence and succumbed to the need to do something foolish.

'Come, Miss Tilney. There is something else we would like to show you,' Amelia said with the tone of someone who had come to a decision.

It was already well into the afternoon and Nell was tired but glad the sisters had allowed her to join them on their rounds at Hope House. She had had no idea that so much suffering continued to linger so long after the wars. If it wasn't the ravages of physical and mental damage it was the destitution and lack of employment that faced the men who had returned from the wars, having given their souls for King and Country, only to find that King and Country had made no provisions for their return. At least not alive.

Now Nell followed the sisters into one of the most peculiar rooms Nell had ever seen. It might once have been a library, because two walls were lined with shelves and the other two with framed paintings and drawings and there were chairs and two tables. But unlike the libraries at Mrs Petheridge's schools, there were very few books and the objects on the shelves reminded Nell of the pawnshop in Keswick. There were figurines, mugs, pipes, rolled-up belts, small metal boxes that might have been for snuff, some tinderboxes and a multitude of other objects. She turned, puzzled, to the hanging pictures and there the confusion deepened. These weren't family portraits or the tame landscapes and botanists' prints she was used to either. They were sketches of men, some serious and some caricatures. The landscapes were raw with minimal colour, of mountains, of a village market with a man leaning over a stall piled with fruit, of soldiers by a campfire… She stopped in shock by a small portrait of a handsome young man in an ensign's uniform looking directly at the painter with a smile that was surprisingly sweet. He might have been fifteen or sixteen and she recognised him. She shook her head. No. It looked incredibly like Lord Hunter, but not quite.

'Who is this?' she asked Amelia, who had come to stand behind her. For a moment the sisters were silent. Then it was Seraphina who spoke.

'That is Timothy, Gabriel's younger brother. He was never strong, but he was the sweetest boy you could imagine, full of light. He adored Gabriel most of all, perhaps because Anne, their mother, never fully recovered her health after the birth and because their father was so rarely there.'

'Thankfully!' Amelia added with a dismissive snort.

'He was not a good man,' Seraphina conceded. 'It was always a worry Gabriel might take after him, but though he was so very self-sufficient and has a tendency to be…well… It was quite clear he did not take after his father in any way that mattered.'

'Most certainly not,' Amelia interceded. 'Gabriel had that household in order before he was off leading strings. When we came to stay after Timothy's birth he made it very clear we were welcome but not needed.'

'He was always a trifle high handed,' Sephy conceded. 'But he took such good care of poor Anne and Tim. We would, of course, have preferred that his protective nature towards Tim not manifest itself in terms of violence towards offenders, but he was, after all, a very physical little boy. In others that might have lent itself to disdain of a brother who clearly did not share any of his outdoor interests, but it was quite the opposite. He had more patience for Tim than anyone. Especially those last two years.'

Her voice thickened and she raised a handkerchief to her eyes in a gesture that might have looked theatrical, but just squeezed at Nell's heart.

'Timothy died almost exactly four years ago,' Amelia added and Nell's mind shot back to a memory she hadn't even realised had lingered, of Lord Hunter, his face worn and serious beyond his age as he inspected Petra.

'I'm so sorry,' she said uselessly, but her mind struggled to understand. Four years ago the war had already been over.

'Timothy was taken prisoner and badly wounded in the war,' Amelia replied to the unspoken question. Then she nodded at the wall. 'This is the memory room. Those that come here or work here can bring mementoes of those they lost to war, or even just for themselves. You might think it ghoulish, but I find it is a beautiful room.

It is better to share pain than hug it to yourself. It binds us as surely as love.'

They stood for a moment in silence, absorbing the weight of those present in the room. The immensity of it sank in very slowly and Nell looked around the room again, her own words to Hunter the previous day coming back to her. There was so much about love she had yet to learn. At least she was open to it. She must not give up on that.

'You are right. It *is* beautiful.'

Amelia smiled and took her arm and as they left Nell glanced back at the small portrait in the corner.

Chapter Five

'My dear, you look lovely, quite like one of *La Belle Assemblée*'s prints,' Sephy chirped as Nell entered the parlour the following morning. 'That shade of fawn is particularly becoming with that ivory trim and those blue ribbons.'

Amelia inspected Nell from head to toe and gave a brisk nod.

'Most becoming. I have a weakness for bonnets myself, and the trimming, I see, is particularly fine.'

'It was shockingly expensive,' Nell admitted.

'Quality usually is,' Amelia concurred approvingly and Nell smiled, wondering how she already felt so comfortable with the two vastly different ladies after such a brief stay. Sometimes bonds like that were immediate and inexplicable and it was best not to dissect the whys and wherefores.

'Thank you so much for allowing me to stay with you, especially under such irregular circumstances.'

'My dear, it truly was our pleasure, but please remember not to tell Gabriel about joining us on our rounds. He might be upset that we exposed you to such sights...'

Nell straightened.

'Lord Hunter does not decide what I can or cannot do.' As she saw the worry on Miss Sephy's face she relented. 'I shan't tell him if you don't wish it. But I do hope you will allow me to visit again.'

'Ah, that is no doubt Gabriel now,' Amelia said at the sound of the knocker. 'Do come in, Gabriel. You have arrived just in time to stop our goodbyes from turning maudlin.'

'I am very glad to hear that. The thought of conveying a watering pot to Wilton does not appeal.'

He spoke lightly, the faint smile curving his lips taking the bite out of his words, and she smiled back before she even realised she was doing so. She looked down to the gloves she was pulling on, suddenly shy. She had managed to convince herself over the past day that the unsettling sensations she had experienced in his presence were the result of nerves and weariness rather than anything intrinsic to Lord Hunter. This conviction received a much-needed boost by the excitement that rose in her at the thought that she would soon finally, *finally* see Charles again, a thought which bubbled as happily as water on the boil throughout the day. Therefore it made little sense that her anticipation should stutter and turn as flat as a tarn in midsummer when Lord Hunter entered the parlour.

It wasn't that he was too large and out of place in the frilly room with its embroidered cushions and baskets of darning and wool, but that he actually wasn't. He was completely at his ease as he went to kiss each aunt on the cheek, stepping back to inspect Miss Calthorpe, his hands on her shoulders.

'Aunt Sephy, surely that fetching cap is new? Is that

for my benefit or is some gentleman about to be very lucky?'

Nell watched with amusement as Miss Calthorpe giggled and tapped Lord Hunter playfully on the arm with her knitting needles.

'It is indeed new and you are shameless, Gabriel. What your sainted grandpapa the vicar would say about you I do not know. Off with you now. I know you don't want to keep your precious horses standing.'

'My precious groom is walking them, love. But we should be off so Miss Tilney can arrive there in time to rest before supper. Shall we go, Nell?'

Her friends called her Nell, but somehow in Hunter's deep voice it sound different, gliding down at the end and giving it a foreign ring, something more connected to myth and dusk than to her. She turned to the mirror to make certain her bonnet was straight and for a moment she had a peculiar sensation of seeing a stranger and expected her to move out of the way to reveal the real Nell. She raised her chin and the feeling dissipated.

As they exited the alleyway her attention was caught not by the elegant carriage, but by a perfectly matched team of chestnuts harnessed to a sleek curricle. She moved towards them instinctively, running her hand down the leader's neck.

'Oh, they're beautiful! Where did you acquire them?' she asked in awe, completely forgetting her constraint.

Lord Hunter came to stand behind her. 'They're Irish bred. I bought them from a friend of mine who went to India. Do you like them?'

'They're absolutely perfect. Can I drive them?'

The groom standing at the horse's heads choked and tried to mask it with a cough. He didn't look much like a groom. He was too large, for one thing, and he looked as though he had been in one too many stable brawls, with his broken nose and rough-knuckled bare hands.

'What is your name?' she asked him and the groom's eyes flew to hers with alarm and then darted past her shoulder to Lord Hunter.

'Tell Miss Tilney your name,' Hunter said, his voice low and amused.

'Hidgins, miss.'

'You don't think I can drive this team, Mr Hidgins?'

'It's just Hidgins, miss. And I wouldn't be so bold as to think anything, miss. Would I, sir?'

'I'm not sure you should apply to me to back your word, Hidgins. Miss Tilney is convinced I'm a sadly frippery fellow. Sorry, I believe the term profligate was employed.'

'And overly sensitive,' Nell added. Somehow everything was always easier around horses. 'Obviously I was right if you remember my comments so faithfully. So how would you like a wager, Hidgins?'

The look he sent Lord Hunter went beyond alarm to entreaty. But she had clearly hit a sensitive nerve and she could see the groom's interest awaken.

'A wager, miss?'

'Yes. I will engage to drive this team on the first stage towards Wilton without any aid either from you or Lord Hunter. If I fail I engage to pay you ten guineas…within one month,' she added, conscious of her need to spread out her funds until she met with the Bascombe banker in Basingstoke.

'Ten guineas, miss? A bit steep, don't you think?'

'Not at all, because I shan't lose. Done?'

Lord Hunter cleared his throat.

'I hate to point out the obvious, but these are my horses and neither of you has the right to make any wagers regarding them. So if you don't mind, we should be going.'

'But ten guineas, my lord!' Hidgins practically wailed.

'Surely you're not frightened of being driven by a woman, are you, Lord Hunter?' Nell asked, trying not to show how very, very much she wanted to drive these beautiful animals. 'I presume you could always come to my aid if you see I can't hold them. Or are you worried you might not be able to bring them under control if they bolt with me?'

'Now that was shamelessly transparent, young woman. You must think I am very easy to manipulate. Into the carriage with you.'

Nell sighed and let him lead her towards the carriage. It had been worth a try, but she wasn't surprised. Most men did not like anyone else driving their cattle and certainly not women. It was the one area where she had always appreciated her father's open-mindedness. As long as he judged she was physically strong enough to control a particular horse or team, he had never stopped her from riding or driving anything, and though these chestnuts looked very powerful indeed, she could tell by their stance they were so well trained their power could be directed and checked with skill, not brute strength. Mostly. All she needed was to feel them.

Halfway to the carriage Lord Hunter stopped.

'You can come with me in the curricle as far as Potters Bar.'

She glanced at him in gratitude as he led her back to the curricle. 'And drive your team?'

'Don't push your luck. Up you go.'

She settled in and sighed again as Lord Hunter took the reins and Hidgins jumped onto the perch behind with something very close to a huff.

'Are you both going to sulk all the way to Wilton?' Lord Hunter asked politely as he set the curricle in motion. 'If so, I won't bother trying to make conversation.'

'I am not sulking. I am disappointed,' Nell said with dignity.

'And you don't pay me to sulk, sir,' Hidgins added with equal dignity.

'Very true, Hidgins. Are you comfortable, Miss Tilney? Would you care for a rug?'

'Yes. No. Is this a custom-built curricle? It feels very light on the road even with the two of you in it.'

'Do you hear that, Hidgins? Miss Tilney thinks we are fat.'

Nell glanced over her shoulder at Hidgins with a complicit smile.

'No, no. Large boned. There are benefits to that, like the difference between an Arabian and a cob. Keeps you more firmly on the ground. But I'm not sure I'd like to race with you in the curricle.'

'As the saying goes, no one asked you; and annoying me is not likely to convince me to let you drive my horses.'

'Are you saying there is something I could do that might?' she said hopefully and he glanced at her. There was always a mix of rather cynical amusement and calculation in his honey-brown eyes. As if he knew something that explained the game they were engaged in and was toying with the possibility of letting her in on the secret. It should have intimidated her, but it had precisely the opposite effect. He was like one of Mrs Petheridge's little puzzle boxes. Nell had always been quickest at solving them and now she felt the same as when facing one of those wooden conundrums—confused but tantalised and very much on her mettle. Right now trying to make sense of all the disparate pieces of what she knew of Lord Hunter was stretching her intellect, which only made the pursuit all the more fascinating.

'Perhaps,' he replied lightly, giving nothing away. 'I might ask you to forgo these charming insults for half an hour, but I doubt you could comply.'

'I'll try—really I will.'

He laughed and the heat touched her cheeks again. She was acting like an over-eager child. She should really try to be a little more refined.

'All right,' he conceded. 'Once we clear the worst of town traffic I will let you try. Hidgins, be prepared to abandon ship.'

'Not without my ten guineas, sir.'

'Who's being insulting now? How far is Piccadilly?' she asked.

'Just coming up. I hope you will be more patient with my horses than you are with me, Miss Tilney.'

'I'm always patient with horses. Is this Piccadilly? What chaos.'

'It is and I hope it makes you appreciate my decision to wait until we are out of this chaos to let you drive.'

She nearly responded to this provocation when she remembered her pledge.

'It is very gallant of you, my lord.'

He guided his horses around a top-heavy wagon.

'I think I prefer your insults. They are more sincere.'

She glanced at him, unsure of his tone, but at Hidgins's snicker behind them she relaxed. She was always so much more comfortable with people when around horses. Perhaps because they didn't judge or condemn. They just were and so she could also just be.

'Very well. Hidgins, remind me that I knowingly took my life in my hands if we end up overturned in a ditch. *Mademoiselle*, your reins and whip.'

She didn't bother answering. Horses with mouths this fine would sense the change in driver immediately and their reaction could be unpredictable. She had been watching Lord Hunter's driving carefully and appreciatively and she could tell she would have her work cut out for her. It wasn't just her anticipation of driving a wonderful team of horses, but the need to prove herself to these two men.

The horses were well behaved in the city, but were clearly used to fast driving, and the moment they had cleared the worst of the traffic they lengthened their stride, eager to pick up pace. It would take both skill and strength to convince them to respect their new driver. She could tell the wheeler would be difficult and almost immediately he proved her right, his stride becoming uneven. She gave him a very light flick of the whip and caught it again about the base and with a shake of his mane he fell back into pace. Out of the corner of her eye she had seen Lord Hunter reach forward, but he sat back and she kept her attention on the horses. After a few miles she had their measure and they had hers and she started enjoying herself. The roads were good and not too crowded and she even had the opportunity to execute a very nice pass by a lumbering coach that tested her passengers' nerves, looping a rein and letting it slide free. Once past she grinned at Lord Hunter and he shook his head ruefully.

'Keep your eyes on the road. You can gloat later. Thankfully we've almost reached Potters Bar.'

'Sorry. I didn't mean to scare you.'

'I thought you promised no more insults.'

'That was an apology, Lord Hunter.'

'We clearly have different understandings of the term. Here, take the right side of that fork.'

As they approached Potters Bar she reluctantly handed the reins over, still full of the pleasure of driving such beautiful cattle. Then she sat back with a sigh and turned to Hidgins.

'I won't say I'm sorry about winning, Hidgins.'

'I won't say so neither, miss. It was a right pleasure to be driven by someone with such light hands.'

'*Et tu*, Hidgins?' Lord Hunter demanded. 'Is there prize money out there for taking me down a peg?'

'Eh, sir? I weren't talking about you.'

'That's even worse, man!'

Nell laughed, amused by the unusual camaraderie between the two men, but then there was something about Lord Hunter that invited informality. He didn't appear to take himself—or anyone else, for that matter—too seriously. Perhaps that was why she had been comfortable with him all those years ago. And now. Up to a point. Because there was also that watchfulness that stood back from the world and the distant memory of his eyes sunken with strain until he had smiled. She shouldn't presume to know this man because he was choosing to be kind for the moment. She knew better than to relax her guard, especially not when so much was at stake.

He turned into the cobbled courtyard of the White

Hart posting inn and two ostlers in smocks immediately ran forward.

'Here we are, and thank goodness. I don't think my vanity could take much more abuse. That is not an invitation, Miss Tilney,' he added quickly as she opened her mouth. She laughed again.

'I was merely going to thank you for allowing me to drive your beautiful horses, Lord Hunter.'

'I should have known you would find a way to put me in the wrong again.' He sighed and jumped down from the curricle.

Nell scooted over to where he was waiting to help her descend, holding down firmly on a smile. She jumped lightly to the gravel drive, inspecting the bustling courtyard. It took her a moment to realise Lord Hunter was still holding her hand and a flush of warmth, like embarrassment, spread up her arm, tingling in her chest and cheeks. The urge to pull back to safety was so strong and so distinct from the heady feeling of freedom she had experienced during the drive that she forcibly resisted it and looked up to meet his eyes.

It wasn't just the impression that he was enjoying some private joke that struck her, but a considering look that found an immediate answering chord in her, a warmth that was deepening into heat as he assessed her. She wasn't used to men looking at her like that and she had no idea what to do with the tingling that was spreading through her like a rash, making her very aware of her skin, of the tightness of her pelisse, even of the uneven cobblestones under her feet. Then he turned away and she was released.

She had been right. He was not to be trusted.

Once inside he led her into a private parlour at the

back and through the mullioned windows Nell caught the view of a garden rich with flowering bushes and beyond it a glimpse of a stream lined with weeping willows.

'What a lovely garden,' she said and immediately regretted it. The look of slight surprise on Lord Hunter's face indicated one did not normally gush about the ambience at posting houses.

'Why, thank you, miss,' said a deep voice behind them. 'The garden's my wife's pride and she's always pleased to have her labour appreciated. Good morning, Lord Hunter. Some of the house best for you and some lemonade for the lady.'

The burly innkeeper placed a tray on the table and rubbed his hands on his apron.

'That's perfect. Thank you, Caffrey.'

'Do you know him?' Nell asked curiously once he left.

'I know most innkeepers on the posting roads,' Lord Hunter answered casually. 'It's useful.'

'For what?'

He pushed her glass of lemonade towards her.

'Are you always this inquisitive?' he asked and the sting of the implied criticism sent an inevitable flush of heat up her throat and cheeks.

'For racing,' he said and she looked up. He was regarding her thoughtfully. 'In answer to your question, and at risk of providing more grist for your critical mill, during my *profligate* youth I accepted any and all wagers for curricle races and Caffrey here was well recompensed by us flighty youths to turn our teams around with all speed and efficiency. Not to mention that he won quite a bit on the back of my successes and he never begrudged me my losses. Gambling builds bonds between men…and women, for that matter.'

Nell cradled her lemonade. She didn't know whether to be grateful for his attempt to smooth over the uncomfortable moment or annoyed that he saw through her so easily.

'Do women also gamble on curricle races, then?'

'Not in public, or at least not respectable women.'

'Sometimes I truly wish I wasn't.'

'That's because you haven't seen the other side of the equation. Believe me, not being respectable is no guarantee of a happy life.'

He would know, too, she thought with sudden rancour.

'Nothing is a guarantee of a happy life. I would settle for an interesting one.'

'I seem to recall you said you enjoyed the school you attended. Weren't you happy there?'

Had she said anything about the school? Perhaps she had, but she was surprised he would remember any details of that meeting years ago. That was rather bad luck because it probably meant he remembered her horrific behaviour during that dinner. People tend to remember the bad more than the good.

She sighed.

'I am very, very happy there and truly I have nothing to complain about. I know how lucky I am. Which is precisely why I want to go back there once everything is arranged at Bascombe.'

'You want to go back? To school? Aren't you a little old for that?'

'Not to study. Though I suppose one is never too old to study. It is like trying to empty an ocean with a teaspoon; there is always so much more to know. But, no, I teach.'

'You teach. I understood you were just boarding with your schoolmistress and that she has been paid handsomely for keeping you. Do you mean to say she has made you work?'

There was a sharp bite in his voice and it raised her own inner temperature. It felt very much like her father had been reporting on her to this man, as though she was an investment.

'She did not *make* me work. What on earth would I do there year-round? Stare at the walls? Or course I worked. If you must know, I am not only a teacher, but I have invested my pay and part of my allowance in the school and I am now a partner...'

The gold in his eyes darkened into amber.

'I see. She took your fees, your allowance, your salary and your labour and gave you an alleged share in a girls' school in the wilds of the Lake District. A very enterprising schoolmistress. There surely is a great deal to learn from her.'

Nell stared at the transformation from the easy-going rake to this man who looked as though he was about to pounce across the table and rip someone's head from their shoulders. As always, just watching anger gather was emptying her from the inside, draining her enjoyment of the ride, the horses, the freeing informality of his company. The only difference was that she was watching it happen, watching herself like a timid wren perched on the windowsill. She could almost see the colour fade from her face and lips; could see inside herself to the sand grating under her skin.

He must have also marked the change and he reached towards her across the table.

'Never mind. It's none of my business, Nell.'

But it was too late. The wren had breathed in, filled, and was fast transforming into whatever avian species strongly disliked having their nest threatened. It was one thing to poke fun at her, but the way he had spoken of Mrs Petheridge...as if he knew her, which he didn't. He had no right! She could feel the heat in her cheeks; it still grated, but this grating felt good. It felt like talons ready to rip into something soft and yielding. It felt *powerful*.

'You just know *everything*, don't you!' she interrupted, surging to her feet, bumping the table and sending lemonade sloshing onto the tablecloth. 'Let's just assume Nell is a naïve little girl who people can order about as they see fit. Well, I will not sit here while you make facile assumptions about me and the people I love. If this outrage is because you are worried I have frittered away what you very prematurely presume to be your property, let me tell you that I meant what I said— I have no intention of marrying you and I have, in fact, already made a substantial profit when we sold one of our properties to the Blaketon School for Boys. If you ever insult Mrs Petheridge again, who was the first person since my mother who actually *loved* me, I will...'

She groped futilely for a retribution sufficient to the offence.

'I'm going to see if the horses are rested. And I don't want any more lemonade!'

She stopped before she further ruined the grand effect of her tantrum. She wished he had yelled back because the way she felt now she just might have yelled some more herself, but he just sat there, looking at her with a strange look of concentration on his face, as if trying to understand a voluble foreigner. It wasn't quite as rewarding as she had hoped a tantrum would be. She turned towards the door but he reached it before her and started opening it. He didn't speak and his eyes were downcast, but in the firmly held line of his mouth she caught the faintest quiver and a different kind of outrage slammed through her.

'Are you *laughing* at me?' she demanded, her voice rising further.

He surprised her by closing the door again and leaning back against it. There was definitely laughter in his eyes and she began to flounder, desperately trying to cling to the firm boulder of her outrage as something stronger was doing its best to knock her off it and into a fast-moving current.

'Only at myself. Just telling myself to remember this when I am next struck by one of my now-rare chivalric impulses. My only defence is that I did mean it for the best. Forgive me?'

Her boulder turned out to be a soap bubble and it burst and she sank into the current. She tried not to, because although she wasn't used to cajolery as a means of getting her to yield, she still knew it for what it was. This was what this man did. He could charm an innkeeper and a groom just as he had once charmed a frightened and lonely girl, and now an angry and nervous young woman. She took a step back, finding the safety of the shallows, but still very aware of the current tugging at her.

'Of course. We should be on our way.'

She shouldn't have sounded so grudging because clearly he wanted more from her. He reached out and raised her chin, and she forced herself to meet his gaze, hoping she looked both forgiving and unaffected, whatever that looked like. There was a challenge in his eyes and even in the shift of his thumb on the slight cleft in her chin. Then it rose to briefly skim the scar below her lip and once again the rush of inner heat pulled at her, towards him, and she almost turned her head to catch the slide of his finger with her mouth when he dropped his hand and turned to open the door.

Hunter had had every intention of putting her in the carriage for the second part of the journey. But though the carriage had arrived he led her past it to the curricle where Hidgins waited, ignoring her surprised look and his own mixed feelings about subjecting himself voluntarily to another stretch of her less-than-complimentary comments and this increasingly uncomfortable physical urge to cross the line into her private domain. He was used to flirting, but only with women who knew the rules of the game where it was an equal exchange. Here he was crossing a strict line in the sand as if it was merely a polite suggestion. If he wasn't careful the next thing he would be doing was giving in to this foolish urge to kiss her and he would likely end up with a boxed ear or, worse, more firmly engaged than ever.

For the first few minutes of the drive the discussion was distinctly stilted until Hidgins broke the awkwardness by telling Lord Hunter he had met Lord Meecham's groom in the stables and had a good chat about that time they raced to Brighton overnight.

'Ah, those were the days.' The groom sighed gustily.

'You moaned the whole way,' Hunter reminded him curtly. He wasn't in the mood for Hidgins's attack of nostalgia. He didn't know what he was in the mood for at the moment. Or if he did, it wasn't likely to be realised. It was his fault for trying to soothe the chit when she had turned into a spitting kitten and her fault for shifting from one mood to another with a mercurial agility that would have done the most temperamental of his mistresses proud. She had surprised him in there, flying to her schoolmistress's defence as if he was bent on rape and pillage when all he had been thinking of was her own good. She clearly didn't want or need his protection, which was fine with him.

For once Hidgins didn't take the hint.

'It was December! It *rained* the whole way!'

'Oh, the poor horses! They must have been quite frozen through!' Nell said and Hunter tried to resist the way his muscles relaxed at this sign that she had obviously calmed down. It was one of his iron rules not to let women's moods rule his, but he was letting this woman...this almost-schoolgirl, he corrected...do just that.

'You needn't worry. The punch thawed them out quite nicely once we made it to Brighton.'

'You give your horses *punch*?'

'Don't you?'

Her outrage transformed into a delighted smile in another shift that caught him off guard.

'Oh, I actually believed you for a moment. Though I suppose if someone had placed a wager on it you might have done so.'

'You wrong me. There are some things I don't wager on, the welfare of my horses being one of them.'

'And what else?'

He glanced at her for a moment. All the haughty fury had flown and she now merely looked as curious as a schoolteacher's dream pupil and he had no idea why that should be just as unsettling as her surprising show of temper and why he actually felt he should be careful what he told her. This was no schoolgirl, however inexperienced. She was actually trying to catalogue and analyse him and he was damned if he was going to be the object of whatever academic exercise she was engaged in.

'What else what?' he temporised.

'What else won't you wager on?'

'What I consider to be certainties, like the probability that you will find some new and creative way of insulting me again before we reach Welbeck.'

'But I have never insulted you.'

'Quite right. It is just that I am sensitive—I forgot. Hidgins remarks on it all the time, don't you, Hidgins?'

'That I do, sir. It's a fair shame the way I have to tippy-toe around him, miss.'

Nell laughed.

'I promise I shall do the same for the rest of the drive. Especially if you let me drive again,' she added, her voice rising hopefully.

'After the next toll you can take the ribbons. For a stretch.'

As before she glanced quickly back at Hidgins with a complicit smile and Hunter didn't have to see his groom's face to know he was grinning. He relaxed, but kept his own smile at bay. She was actually right; he was being far too sensitive. There was no call for this instinctive need to repel her curiosity. Her inquisitiveness and over-sharp wit were just the signs of a young woman let out for the first time from a confining environment and eager to explore the world. There was no reason to let it unbalance him. He should remain focused on his objective of easing out of this engagement as smoothly and painlessly as possible, and for that he needed her co-operation and her trust.

Chapter Six

W̲elbeck Manor was a sprawling Tudor structure which each generation but the last two had added to with a great deal of vigour and very little architectural grace. It had been four years since Nell's last trip to Wilton, but the tingle of happiness as they crested the rise was wonderfully familiar. She sighed as the curricle rolled up the wide drive and the view of the house disappeared behind a clump of old oak. Before the fiasco of the betrothal she had fantasised about meeting Charles dressed in her new finery and, if not dazzling him, at least showing him that she, too, had attractions worthy of being considered, even if they were primarily pecuniary. But now she was arriving at Welbeck an engaged woman in the eyes of the world. Engaged to a handsome, charming man who by all accounts made Charles's mild flirtations look monklike by comparison.

She glanced at the striking profile of the man beside her. She had no doubt if she were to tell him what was going through her head those brown-gold eyes would fill with contempt. He might be easy-going on the surface, but with every light-hearted comment she heard the echo of another thought, something firmly with-held. She didn't know whether there was ruthlessness or pain there, but whatever the case, that side of him would probably have no sympathy for her childish dreams. He would certainly be contemptuous of her plan to pay for a bridegroom. If only Charles could come to see her as a woman. Maybe even as a desirable one...

Impulsively she placed her hand on Hunter's arm.

'Could you stop, just for a moment? There is some-thing I would like to ask you before we arrive.'

Hunter checked his horses and with a quick nod Hidgins went to stand at the horses' heads.

'Well? Cold feet?' Hunter asked with a quirk of his mouth, but his eyes held the same considering look she had seen before.

'Not precisely. I have a favour to ask. I was wonder-ing if you would... If when we arrive at Welbeck... Oh, this is difficult!'

'Come, it can't be that bad. Out with it. What would you like me to do?'

'Flirt with me.' As his brows drew together she hur-ried on. 'Just a little. I mean I know we aren't really en-gaged, but everyone will think we are and I don't want them to think...'

She rubbed her hand to her forehead, trying to chase away her discomfort.

'Look at me.'

His voice was calm, but there was an edge to it and there was no amusement in his eyes now.

'I would have thought that such a request goes against your plan of calling a halt to the engagement. Unless you have another reason...'

He trailed off as the blush that had started in her chest

flowed upwards like lava escaping Vesuvius. Still, she tried to sustain his gaze. She had foreseen contempt and it came.

'I see. The real reason why you wanted to come to Wilton,' he drawled. 'So, I am to earn my keep this week.'

She looked down, feeling childish and strangely hollow.

'You don't have to. I just thought…'

'It is quite clear what you thought, sweetheart. Very well. It's no hardship on my part. As long as we keep to our agreement, never let it be said I don't provide value for money. Now we should move on. Hidgins!'

Hidgins hurried back to his perch and they drew forward. Nell felt her anticipation dim. She hadn't meant to insult him and she wasn't precisely certain how she had done so.

They drew up in front of the house and she kept her eyes down as he dismounted and came to help her down. She started towards the steps, but he moved to block her path, raising her chin so that she was forced to look up. The contempt wasn't there any more, just that serious look.

'I'm sorry. You trod on my vanity and I reacted badly. You surprised me again, that's all. Forgive me?'

A weight slipped from her shoulders.

'It *was* foolish of me,' she answered quickly. 'Of course you needn't…'

'I shall flirt with you with great pleasure.' He surprised her by smiling and the relief was so strong she couldn't help laughing.

'If it isn't young Nell! And, Hunter, good to see you again, man. Welcome, welcome.'

They both turned towards the stairs as two men approached and Nell stiffened. She would have much preferred her first meeting with Charles to be in one of her new dresses rather than in an outfit dusty from the long drive. She turned instead towards the portly man who approached them, his hand extended in greeting.

'Good afternoon, Lord Welbeck, Mr Welbeck.' Her voice wavered on the last and she raised her chin.

Lord Welbeck grasped her hand between his own, shaking it vigorously as he addressed Hunter.

'M'wife received your note about Nell here. Glad to have her. Congratulations all around, eh? Tilney already told us the news when we met him at Tattersall's last week before he hared off north.'

'Tilney isn't here?' Hunter asked.

'Heard a tip that Buxted is rolled up and selling off his stables, so off he goes to steal a march on the market. Wouldn't have minded doing so myself, but the dibs aren't in tune just at the moment, eh, Charles?'

'You couldn't very well disappear now just as the fair is set to start, Father.' Charles smiled at Nell and held out his hand invitingly. After a second's hesitation Nell held out her hand as well and he grasped it.

'Hello, Miss Tilney. Your father did say he means to join us here when he closes with Buxted, so of course you must stay until he does. Mother is delighted to have another female guest to commiserate with. Congratulations, by the way,' he added, his eyes sliding momentarily towards Hunter.

'That's right,' Lord Welbeck continued. 'Fine work, eh? We didn't even know the Bascombe land was to come to you, lass, or I'd have made a push to snabble you for my boy. Your father kept that card mightily close to his chest, didn't he, eh? Well, I'm particularly glad you've come, gel. There's this new filly I could use some help with and you might be just the one to do the trick. Lovely legs, but won't let anyone near her. She's in the far paddock. Have a look at her first thing and let me know if there's a point in keeping her, will you? Well, I'm off to the stables to see all's ready for the week. Say your hellos, Charles, and join me when you're done.'

He strode away with a buoyancy that was in stark contrast to his weight, leaving them to sort themselves out. Nell detached her hand from Charles's a little reluctantly. There was a moment of awkward silence and then Charles turned towards the curricle.

'Are these your famous matched chestnuts, Lord Hunter? Beautiful beasts.'

Nell stood back as the two men turned, glad for a moment to recover. Charles was bending down to inspect one of the horses, his golden hair catching the afternoon sun already scraping the treetops to the west. In a second she was cast back years ago to a moment in the Welbeck stables when she had seen him very much like this, his attention on one of the mares, painfully handsome and wholly oblivious of her.

She looked away and met Hunter's eyes. She had no idea what he had seen on her face and how he connected that with her wholly regretted request, but she rather feared he saw right through her. For a moment there was a hard, contemptuous light in his eyes that sobered her, like the burst of cold air after stepping out of a warm house. Then the butler appeared in the doorway and everything moved again. Nell followed the butler up the wide stairway with a strange sense of fatality, like a prisoner being led before a judge and jury. It was fanciful, but she felt the course of her life would be decided between these walls, in this week, and she hoped she had the strength of character to be an author of that future, not just its subject.

Chapter Seven

'Miss Tilney, wait...'

Nell's heart hitched and she stopped halfway down the stairs. There was never much light in the low-roofed corridors of Welbeck Manor and as Charles descended the stairs towards her his face was cast in shadows, only his smile glinting brightly.

'Has it really been four whole years since we saw each other last? I am sorry about your grandparents' passing, by the way.'

He stopped on the step above her, giving him some extra inches and making her feel, for a change, almost normal. Except for her thudding pulse and the heat in her cheeks which she hoped the gloomy light masked.

'Thank you, Mr Welbeck. But since I never met them I hardly mourn them.'

She moaned inwardly. She hadn't meant to be so blunt. He blinked and his smile wavered, but returned.

'Well, whatever the case, I am glad you came this year. That is quite a piece of news, your engagement. Congratulations.'

'Thank you. We are very happy.'

Oh, help, what an inane thing to say. She didn't know whether to revel in the fact that Charles was actually talking to her like an adult or to wish someone would come and relieve her of her embarrassment. No, it was now or never if she meant to impress upon him that she was indeed an adult. And a woman.

'Lord Hunter can be very…persuasive.' She smiled, trying to invest the word with all manner of meaning, and Charles's affable smile stiffened.

'Yes, I've heard that about him.'

There was no mistaking the undercurrent in those words. What would an experienced woman do? Nell thought. Anna would probably turn up her nose and march off, but that didn't suit Nell. Besides, any reaction other than amused condescension was good, wasn't it? She wasn't fool enough to believe Charles might be jealous, but perhaps he wasn't indifferent to her engagement. Or perhaps he just didn't like Hunter. That, too, was highly possible. She imagined Hunter rubbed many people the wrong way. Before she could think of an answer he smiled.

'Now, that was uncalled for, wasn't it? If you like him I'm sure he's a capital fellow. Forgive me?'

'Of course, Charles… I mean, Mr Welbeck.'

'If memory serves me right, we called each other Charles and Nell since before you put up your hair. I think we can dispense with such foolish proprieties, don't you?'

She smiled, warming from the inside out.

'Of course. Charles.'

'Oh. Good evening, Mr Welbeck.'

They both turned as a husky voice slid down the stairs. Nell wouldn't have been surprised if the woman's appearance was accompanied by trumpets and the strewing of petals—even in the gloom her beauty glowed. In colouring she was Charles's twin, with golden hair and sky-blue eyes, as if she had been created to stand by his side in the illustration for a fairy tale. She descended with leisurely grace, her eyes smiling into Charles's. She came to stop just a step above them and her tongue briefly caressed her lower lip in a gesture Nell had never seen before, but which must be universal because if ever there was an invitation, this woman was extending one to Charles.

The woman finally descended the last step, increasing Nell's agony. She was beautiful and perfectly rounded, her bodice cut as low as decency allowed, and worst of all, she was tiny, accentuating how awkward Nell's inches made her. Charles's mild gallantry towards her just a moment ago, which had filled her with such hope, just deepened her despair. As long as a woman like this wanted Charles, what chance had she?

'Won't you introduce me to your friend, Mr Welbeck?' the vision said and the prompt just made it worse. Charles introduced her as Lady Melkinson and somehow Nell answered, aware she was being as gauche as a child, and they moved towards the drawing room. Inside she scanned the room for Hunter, but he was nowhere to be seen and so she mutely moved towards the corner where Lord and Lady Welbeck stood speaking with Lord Meecham, feeling lost and hopeless.

Hunter entered the drawing room, stifling a resigned sigh. In past years he had avoided most evening events at Welbeck, preferring the conviviality of the horse breeders at the local inns to the stuffiness of the Welbeck drawing rooms. His reputation as one of the Wild Hunt Club always made respectable hostesses somewhat wary of his presence in their drawing rooms anyway. But with Tilney absent he couldn't disappear and leave Nell to cope alone, though judging by her strange request and by her blush when they had arrived, she might be glad to have the opportunity to spend this time with young Welbeck.

It was hardly surprising such a sheltered girl would fancy herself in love with a young man who looked like a storybook hero, and though he doubted Welbeck would fulfil any of the criteria she had championed so hotly, that wasn't his concern. What was his concern was that from his experience of the extravagancies of the Welbeck stables they would be only too happy to grab Nell's inheritance and were unlikely to honour her generous offer regarding the water rights. In fact, he didn't particularly want the Welbecks laying waste to Bascombe simply to feed the bottomless pit of their stables. She wanted to flirt? He had no problem with that. He might even enjoy it and Nell might come to realise she had better things to do with her life than moon over a fundamentally weak vessel like Charles Welbeck.

He scanned the room in search of her and his gaze paused on the woman standing in the centre of the room. It had been quite a few years since Lady Melkinson had tried to add him to her impressive list of wealthy lovers, but she hadn't changed much and was still doing her best to command male attention. Almost every man in the room was at least partly focused on her décolletage as she leaned to inspect a flower arrangement, holding the pose just long enough for conversation around her to sink and fade.

'Oh, aren't they lovely?' she asked no one in particular. There was a rumble of shared assent among the men, though no one was looking at the flowers, and Hunter had a hard time holding back a laugh. Then she held out her hand to her husband, but her eyes briefly caught and held Charles Welbeck's and Hunter's mood brightened. Well, well, apparently Nell's shining prince was otherwise engaged. What a pity Nell hadn't seen that telling meeting of eyes.

Hunter scanned the room again, wondering why Nell hadn't appeared yet, when he noticed her, half-obscured by Lord and Lady Welbeck and watching Lady Melkinson with an expression as telling as the act put on by the lady herself, though less intentional. She was pressed against the wall, using her hosts' impressive bulk as a shield. Someone smaller might get away with the wallflower manoeuvre, but in her case it was a futile effort. Against the dark old wood and in her long silvery dress she looked as dramatic as Lady Melkinson, but from a very different kind of play. Not a rococo farce with frills and tossed-up skirts in the rose garden, but a Saxon princess about to be bartered to an enemy tribe. Someone predatory like Lady Melkinson could have made mincemeat of a rival's petite plumpness if she had possessed Nell's attributes, but it was becoming clear Nell was completely unaware of her charms. He was tempted to show her she had no reason whatsoever to be envious of someone like Phyllida Melkinson, but that lesson wasn't his to give.

Hunter moved towards her and when she saw him her face relaxed into a smile. Clearly she already regarded him as a safe haven, which was a good sign. He never flirted with marriageable misses, but in this case there was no harm in fulfilling his part of the bargain—since her affections were firmly focused on Welbeck she wasn't at risk of taking his attentions seriously and she could probably use a boost of confidence. When he reached her he took her hand as he let his gaze move over her, taking his time.

'It's quite lucky you taught in a girls' school. I can't imagine any boys being able to concentrate on their declensions with you by the blackboard.'

She flushed a little at his examination, but her eyes lit with amusement, dispelling the tragic Saxon. She twitched her skirt, setting off a silvery wave on the gauzy overskirt.

'It's not me—it's the dress. It was shockingly expensive, but Mrs Sturges insisted. She has very strong ideas about fashion.'

'And about gossip, if I remember correctly. But it is unfair to blame the dress; the culprit is most definitely you, sweetheart. Do you mean to tell me there are no mirrors in a girls' school?'

'Not many, but Mrs Sturges has two full-length mirrors in her room set so you can see yourself fore and aft, as she says. She made me exhibit all the dresses as soon as they were delivered. It was excruciatingly embarrassing, but she was so excited I couldn't say no.'

'And to think I missed it. I might have to request a private viewing.' He dropped his voice, watching her closely. She hadn't even appeared to notice he still held her gloved hand and was gently caressing her palm with his thumb. Standing this close to her also made it clear there were distinct advantages to tall women. She would fit against him so easily and all it would take was a gentle lift of her very determined chin... He gave in to the urge to just touch it lightly and finally an edge of awareness entered her silvery eyes.

'There is a perfectly serviceable full-length mirror in my room,' he observed softly.

Her breath caught and a gentle flush warmed her full lips to a soft peach colour. He watched it, fascinated by this quite unique and very appealing transformation; then he looked up and met her eyes and was surprised to see that they were brimming with laughter.

'I think I might actually enjoy this,' she half-whispered.

'What?' he asked, confused.

'Flirting. I think I'm starting to understand how it works.'

A slap might have been more painful, but no more sobering. For a moment he had actually forgotten what he was doing this for.

'That's good. Feel free to experiment. Despite my name, I don't mind being hunted.'

'I'm not sure how. I don't think I could ever do what Lady Melkinson does.'

He caught the hopelessness in her voice.

'You won't know until you try,' he said lightly and this time her eyes were assessing. Then she half-lowered her long lashes so that the silver irises glimmered through them.

'Like this?' she asked huskily, leaning towards him, the tips of her fingers just making contact with the sleeve of his coat. Then her lips parted and the tip of her tongue touched her lower lip, drawing it in gently and letting it go. As far as seductions went it was very mild, as hesitant as a girl dressing in her mother's finery. There was no reason it should have felt like the blood was reversing course in his veins.

'A very good start,' he managed and was rewarded with another smile.

'I'm not the only one working on my flirting. Betsy, the maid, is already quite sweet on Hidgins. You should warn him he is a marked man.'

'She told you that?' he asked, surprised.

'Well, they used to assign her to me when I came as a child, so she and I know each other quite well and she tells me things. I was even thinking of asking Lord Welbeck if I might take her to Bascombe when I leave. I will need a personal maid.'

'You're still determined to live there on your own?'

'Of course. I've already written to ask Mrs Calvert to come to Bascombe. She is lovely, rather like your aunts.'

'There is no one quite like my aunts. I don't know how comfortable someone like Sephy would be for a young woman living on her own. Every time I come to dine she remembers she is a parson's daughter. Serving up the late Reverend Calthorpe's views on my unlikely prospects for redemption with the syllabub tends to wreak havoc with the digestion. I suggest that if you must employ a companion, find someone who teaches progressive topics such as geology or biology, perhaps with a particular interest in crustaceans.'

'I hate syllabub anyway, but sermons will definitely be banned from the supper table. As would be any discourse on crustaceans. Mrs Calvert taught music.'

'Will I still be welcome to visit you once you are settled at Bascombe? Or are we to play this along tragic lines of jilted lovers, smiting brows and scowling darkly when chance meetings occur.'

Her laugh, tumbling but quickly checked, made him want to shake it free, just as he wouldn't mind seeing her silky hair shake free again as it had four years ago.

'Of course you will be welcome! You must come and give me advice on my stables and of course you will come when you bring me Pluck.'

'Ah, I see you won't forget that offer.'

'Are you reneging?' she challenged, raising one brow at him in an impressive golden-brown arc.

'I never break my word. If I can help it. Giving you Pluck will give me even more reason to visit because Petra is certain to miss her.'

Her expression shifted so rapidly it was almost comical.

'I hadn't thought… Perhaps it isn't a good idea after all.'

He took her hand and gave it a little squeeze, touched by her concern. Mother–daughter relations were obviously a sensitive point for her.

'Nonsense. They will both be fine. We can do it gradually if you like.'

She nodded in relief.

'Yes, that will be best.'

'You know, it just might be that Pluck will miss me more than she will Petra. I have a way with mares,' he mused and she laughed. He caught her hand as it rose to block the laugh.

'Why do you do that? You have a beautiful laugh.'

She shook her head, her eyes catching on his with a flash of fear. Then she shook her head again and her eyes cleared.

'It is silly, isn't it? Anna makes fun of me for doing that. Not in a bad way, I mean. My aunt always said laughing aloud was ill bred, and so if I ever found myself laughing when she was about, which wasn't often, I would hide it. I still do it when I'm nervous.'

'I see. So I make you nervous?'

She tilted her head to one side, considering him.

'Actually, no. Which is strange. I should be more nervous around you than around anyone else here practically. Perhaps it is because you don't take yourself seriously.'

'I beg your pardon. I take myself very seriously.'

Her smile returned, sunny and intimate, and he realised it *was* strange that she was treating him with such friendly ease on such a short acquaintance. Especially someone as sensitive as she.

'No, you don't,' she said easily. 'I think the list of things you take seriously is very short, but perhaps you regard those things as very particularly serious so that might atone for the rest. Oh, dear, that sounds very patronising, doesn't it? I didn't mean it like that. It's just to say that I'm glad you decided to let me come to Wilton with you. I'm usually quite nervous the first day here until I settle in. It's different having you here.'

Hunter took a moment to work through his reaction to her casual but rather brutal dissection of his character. In anyone else he would swiftly discourage the freedoms she was taking, but beyond a reflexive rejection of anyone's attempts to come too close, he really didn't mind her less-than-complimentary observations.

'You know the Welbecks and you must know some of the other regular guests as well. It's rather strange that you would need someone who is essentially a stranger in order to feel comfortable.'

If he had been fishing for compliments at the expense of the Welbecks, he came up empty.

'Well, ordinarily after the first day I do begin enjoying myself, but I promise I won't drop your acquaintance when that happens.'

For a moment he nearly took her seriously, she looked so sincere.

'Do you know,' he said slowly, assessing her, 'you may not have much experience flirting, but you certainly know how to tease.'

This time she laughed openly and Hunter noted, and not completely with satisfaction, that as many eyes strayed to her as had followed Lady Melkinson's manoeuvre. The main difference was that his betrothed clearly neither expected nor noticed the attention. One of those observers headed towards them and Nell's smile wavered.

'Hello, Charles.'

'Hullo, Nell. You look like a princess in that dress.'

Hunter watched in disgust as Nell blushed.

'Meecham has agreed to let me take his bays for a turn tomorrow,' Charles continued. 'Will you come with me? That is, if Lord Hunter doesn't mind?'

'I'd love to.' Nell nodded. 'And of course he won't mind, would you?'

'Not at all,' Hunter lied.

'Perhaps we might even organise a friendly race with your team.' Charles smiled, clearly extending an olive branch.

'I think that would be up to Meecham,' Hunter replied and Charles's cheeks reddened at the rebuke, but the boyish smile held.

'Obviously. Just getting ahead of myself. Well, there's

Mama come to herd us into dinner. You're sitting next to me, Nell, so you can tell me everything you have been doing these past four years.'

Hunter hoped that the Welbecks' ploy in seating her next to Charles was as obvious to her as it was to him, but by the glow in her eyes he doubted it.

After dinner the men remained to savour their port and cheroots, but as soon as they joined the women in the drawing room Hunter watched as both Charles and the young man who had been seated on her other side during dinner headed towards the sofa where Nell was seated next to Lady Welbeck by the windows opening to the veranda. The evening was unseasonably warm and a set of long doors at the end of the drawing room had been opened and the lawn and gardens lit with hanging lanterns so the guests could stretch their legs and digest their meal.

Hunter was tired and he was tempted to leave her to her little victory, but when the two men fell into a laughing rivalry over who would take Nell for a turn around the gardens, Hunter's patience faded and he moved towards them. There was a limit to the leeway he was willing to grant her—having his betrothed, real or not, make a laughing stock of him by wandering a darkened garden with another man was just such a limit.

'I believe in such cases the third option is often considered the least controversial.'

'Are you willing to come in third? That isn't what one hears of the members of the Wild Hunt Club,' Nell said daringly, her shining look still very much in evidence, and his resentment faded. She looked very different from the timid girl he had seen when he first entered the drawing room that evening.

'In this case the prize for third is well worth throwing the race.'

She laughed and shook her head, but gave him her hand with an apologetic smile to the other men.

'Don't forget we are to go driving tomorrow morning, Nell,' Charles tossed in with a smile that had lost some of its exuberance.

'Now that your morning is so pleasantly accounted for, you are free to dedicate the rest of your evening to me,' Hunter said, holding her gaze, and she pressed her full lips together like a child trying not to laugh. Behind her he spotted Charles Welbeck already moving towards Lady Melkinson, her coral-pink dress and gold curls glinting in the crowd like a tropical fish strayed into a village pond. He didn't want Nell to have any illusions about Welbeck, but neither was he anxious to see her smile extinguished, so he guided her towards the terrace. Outside a large group of the younger guests were already gathering, the men laughing and the women flirting with their fans, and he led Nell down the lantern-lit path to a spot where they were caught in the shaded darkness of a yew hedge. He knew he shouldn't risk their absence being noted, but he could use a moment of quiet.

She didn't speak, just waited with a look he was becoming very familiar with. Direct, curious and making it very clear that though she might be cowed in certain circumstances, there was an inner core of steel he wondered if she was even aware of herself. He sighed and shrugged out of his coat, draping it over her shoulders.

'I know it's not really proper to be out here like this,

but I can't stomach any more drawing-room conversation,' he said truthfully.

She tucked her arms into his sleeves and smiled as the ends flopped over her hands.

'I'm not surprised. You must be exhausted after that long drive and I admit I have had enough for tonight as well. We should probably go to bed.'

Watching her efforts to roll up his sleeves, Hunter wanted to agree wholeheartedly.

'Wouldn't that be a little improper?' he asked politely.

She glanced up, her dark gold brows gathering in confusion. Then realisation dawned and she burst out laughing.

'Are you never serious?'

'I am very serious. Very often. It just doesn't always show.'

Her face was still alight with amusement, but even in the gloom he could make out the return of her assessing look.

'I think that was one of your honest moments, whether you meant it or not. Aren't you cold? I feel guilty about taking your coat.'

She moved to slide it off, but he caught it, holding the lapels and gently easing it back onto her shoulders.

'I'm not in the least cold.' That, too, was very honest. He wasn't certain what was wreaking more havoc on his self-control, her comments or the sight of her wrapped in his coat, the dark cloth bracketing the pearly rises of her breasts above the silver and ivory bodice, their juncture marked by a single-tear pearl pendant hanging from a long chain.

She might not be abundant like Lady Melkinson, but her breasts were perfectly shaped and they would fit marvellously in his palms... He must indeed have been more tired than he thought because it didn't make any sense that he couldn't just slide his hands under his coat to her waist and pull her towards him and do something about this rising ache, like stripping away that silvery sheen of a dress, leaving her in nothing but his coat, her hair against the dark fabric, her skin like moonlight and shadow underneath...

Without giving himself time to consider, he gently plucked the pearl necklace from its resting place, the backs of his fingers skimming the silky skin that curved enticingly into the lace-lined bodice. The pearl was warm and he balanced it in his palm, feeling the heat rise from her skin not an inch from his, wondering what he was doing. She seemed to be wondering the same thing.

'Is this significant? This necklace?' he managed, just to say something, waiting for her to pull back, but she nodded.

'Yes. It was my mother's. Her father gave it to her when she married and it is the only thing I have from her that meant something to her. She never cared for jewels or fashion. She liked animals.'

'Like her daughter.'

Her alarm faded, replaced by her sudden smile. It was a wholehearted smile, full of love and the warmth of memory, and it pressed further at the edges of his control.

'Not really. Or rather, much more than I ever did. She was only ever comfortable around horses. I like animals, but I like people more. Some people, at least.'

'Some more than others. As with animals I would

just advise you are certain they genuinely like you back before approaching them with overtures.'

He should have kept quiet. Even in the dark he saw the flush of colour spread upwards from her bodice and she stepped back and he let the pearl slip out of his fingers and it snaked its way back down between her breasts. He stopped himself from following her, trying to ignore the thud of desire that was spreading through him.

'I know I must appear very foolish to you,' she said. 'But I'm not as naïve as you think me. I saw him go to Lady Melkinson just now. I'm not surprised he is attracted to her; they're both so very perfect, after all.'

She was trying to speak lightly but he could hear the anguish in her voice. The need to reassure her battled with the need to maintain his distance. Whatever pretensions to save people from themselves that remained in him after his disastrous failures should be firmly confined to people he could ultimately walk away from like the veterans at Hope House. If this conceit that he could protect her was what had drawn him to this girl four years ago he should be thanking the stars she wanted none of him. He was no one's champion. In fact, if he ever did decide to marry, he should probably choose one of those spoilt, shallow society misses London excelled in producing who needed nothing more from him than his title, an open purse and the chance to lord it over society. They would leave him alone much more effectively than his fictitious biddable country-bred wife.

'Perfect? Are they? You have a rather shallow understanding of that term.'

Her mouth parted in surprise at the mockery in his

words and even in the dim light he could see colour rise on her cheeks. He waited for the hurt to push her away. Let's just finish this.

'I suppose I do.' She frowned. 'Beauty has a mesmeric effect, doesn't it? The lakes are beautiful and when I look at them everything I see is tinged with a sense of well-being, but when you break down the landscape it's just rock and ferns and water and people's houses with regular lives. I suppose it's a matter of perspective. But I don't think my feelings for Charles are based on his looks. I've known him for years, you see, and he is a kind man, even if he is beautiful.'

Her calm acceptance of his condemnation just raised his tension.

'If we are talking about perspective, do you really think you have any on Welbeck? Not that it is really any concern of mine if you want to tie yourself to him, but you were a child when you knew him. Are you really willing to stake your entire future on a childish infatuation?'

She raised her chin.

'Perhaps I am. Children are not necessarily fools and their intuitions about people can be very sound. I was a child when I met you and I think my intuitions about you, despite our short acquaintance, were just as sound.'

He wasn't going to rise to that bait. This was just what was wrong with this girl. She didn't stay where she was put; she had to go turning tables all the time. He barely resisted the childish urge to demand she hand back his coat.

'We should go inside now.'

She nodded, her mouth curving in a rueful smile. 'You see? You really are better off taking my offer of the riverfront and being grateful you aren't saddled with me after all.'

She began slipping off his coat and he grasped the lapels, stopping her again. He shouldn't ask. He knew he was going to regret it.

'All right, what were your intuitions about me?'

Her laugh was just a quick intake of breath.

'Nothing bad. That you were a good person. That you were too aware of people...not just of people; that's why you were so good with Petra... You thought of her before you thought of your own needs. You can tell a great deal about people from the way they are with animals. But I also remember not knowing if that calm you had with her wasn't covering something else.' She hesitated. 'I didn't know about your brother then. I do remember thinking you looked tired and very sad. I'm so sorry.'

Nothing bad. All in all it was a rather kind, if damning, assessment. He should be flattered, not flicked on the raw. It was also confirmation that he was right—she was precisely the wrong combination of clever and needy. She was already tempting him to step back into his old and futile role of protector, except that in time she would probably see his pretensions for what they were. He didn't need this schoolmistress dissecting him like a specimen at the Royal Academy. He didn't want to live his life with someone like her constantly reflecting back his failures. She wasn't one to let things be, and much more than he wanted to bed her, he wanted quiet. He wanted to be left alone.

'We should go back inside,' she said and handed him his coat and he put it on, aware of how her warmth lingered in the pliant fabric in a way that he knew was ridiculous.

'You're right. Let's go in.'

Hunter woke with his fingers still digging into the mattress. He loosened them slowly, but otherwise didn't move, letting the sweat cool on his skin which always felt pinched and raw after the nightmares. Eventually he turned and groped on the floor for the blanket he had thrown off.

It had been worse this time. No, not really worse, just different. For the first time since the nightmares had started four years ago the images had changed. Not just Tim writhing in pain as their mother serenely plummeted off a cliff into a river of blood fed by Tim's wounds. This time a new figure had been standing there, watching his futile efforts to stop the tragedy, her long hair streaming out and colouring the grey cliffs a silvery gold.

Actually, it *was* worse. The curious, watchful pressure of her eyes had added shame to his agony and his sense of failure, but at least this time he had woken before he himself had been dragged down into that chasm as he tried to cling to Tim's disintegrating body. That anomaly was also her fault—she had started walking towards them and he had tried to stop her and both Tim and his mother had slipped away before he could grab them and then he had woken, their names choking in his throat. It was a small mercy that he didn't make too much noise during these nightmares, that the primary damage was to the bedclothes he scattered around the room and sometimes to his own skin.

The house was very quiet, enough to hear the creaking of the wood and the distant cry of a night bird. He closed his eyes. His pulse was slowing, but the familiar sluggish mix of despair and disgust was taking the place of the frantic fear of the dream. He was so tired of this. There was nothing he could do about the guilt of failing his family, but he kept hoping he could at least, finally, be rid of these nightly accusations. Perhaps one night he might manage to stop them from destroying themselves. And him. Not likely, though.

He wished he could just rest.

He was so tired…

Chapter Eight

Nell raised her face to the sun. It was still cool as Charles guided the curricle out the gates, but the bite of autumn was more than recompensed by a perfectly blue sky. She smiled in wonder that she was here, being driven by Charles, looking as good as Betsy could make her in a lovely pale peach jonquil pelisse over a sprigged muslin dress. All she needed to complete her happiness was the nerve to ask Charles to let her drive Meecham's lovely team. After all, she had had no such qualms about demanding to drive Hunter's horses and he was practically a stranger. It was peculiar to feel so much less comfortable with Charles, whom she knew so much better.

'So, Nell, tell me what you have been doing these past four years. Breaking hearts in the Lake District?'

Nell's attention was on the way his whip snapped at the leaders as they came over a gentle rise, resisting the urge to tell him not to hold the reins quite so tightly.

'Hardly. I have been too busy teaching.'

'Teaching? As in schoolmistress?'

Nell tried very hard not to stiffen at the shock in his

voice as she had yesterday with Hunter. Apparently this concept was hard for some people to grasp.

'Yes. I happen to enjoy it. Very much.'

Charles looked at her briefly and then smiled.

'That's nice. Will you miss it when you're married?'

'I won't stop teaching just because I marry. I am even planning to open a school. Not right away, I will need to find the right people and, well, there are a lot of considerations, but eventually.'

His eyebrows disappeared beneath the tumbled locks of golden hair on his brow and she forced herself to change the subject before she completely scared him off.

'How are your stables faring?'

He sighed and guided the horses around the village green where workmen were already busy preparing for the upcoming fête, which was the highlight of the breeders' fair.

'Hopefully the fair will go well. I don't know how your father does it, honestly. I would swear our stock is as good as his, but… Anyway, let's talk about happier things. Your engagement, for example. When is the wedding?'

Nell's heart gave a great big thump and then settled into a rapid tattoo in rhythm with the horses' hooves.

'We haven't settled on a date yet. After all, we have just become engaged.'

'But we understood from your father this was a long-standing arrangement?'

Trying to convey availability while not revealing that Hunter had no interest in anything other than her inheritance was a stretch of Nell's flirtation skills. What would Lady Melkinson do?

'It is, but I was very young at the time. I'm afraid I still don't know my own mind.'

Oh, dear, that sounded dreadfully missish. Anna would probably start giggling at this point. Hunter would probably say something unrepeatable.

'I see. You deserve better, Nell.' Charles's hand squeezed hers briefly and she flushed in a mixture of excitement at the gesture and shame at her perfidy. It wasn't that far from the truth.

She looked at his perfect profile, at the soft line of his cheek and the way his wheat-gold hair curled over his forehead. The memory of that day he had defended her came back sharply and she spoke before she could think.

'I always wanted to thank you, Charles, for that day you defended me against Papa. I know it was years ago, but it meant a great deal to me.'

'I did?' He looked surprised.

'Oh, it was years ago, at the jumping course. I think I must have been fourteen at most.'

His frown cleared after a moment.

'Goodness, I remember that. He was ranting about you cramming your horse. No offence, but he was always foul-tempered. I remembered we had Lord Davenport there to look at some stallions and your father was embarrassing everyone. Luckily Davenport didn't shy off; bought Jade Dragon that year, which was a good sale. Your father should have known better than to put you on the course at that age in the first place. Why, you were nothing but a child.'

Nell watched him flick his whip at the horses as he urged them up the incline turning into the drive and felt as if the leather had stung her as well. It made no difference, she told herself. Of course that moment had meant more to her than it had to him; there was no reason for her to feel so let down. It was a miracle he remembered it at all. It was her own stupidity for even mentioning it. This was Charles, here and now, with her, listening to her with that gentle smile. She should be grateful, not disappointed. Still, she was relieved as they approached the house. Make one last effort, Nell, she admonished herself. She tried out the smile she had practised on Hunter last night, up and half through her lashes.

'Nevertheless, it was very kind of you, Charles.'

The only problem was that he was watching the horses. She held the smile resolutely as he pulled the horses to a halt and finally he turned to her. Apparently it was not a bad effort because his cheeks tinged with colour and his sky-blue eyes settled on her mouth. The sheer absurdity of what she was doing made her smile falter and she looked down at her gloves.

'Thank you for inviting me.'

'I'm glad you came, Nell. Good morning, Lord Hunter.'

Nell swivelled in her seat to meet Hunter's gaze where he stood by the curricle, waiting to hand her down. She had been so focused on Charles she hadn't even noticed the curricle standing by the stairs. He had probably seen her laughable attempt at being seductive.

'Good morning, Welbeck. You have timed your arrival well; I was just looking for Miss Tilney. Shall we go look at the filly Lord Welbeck mentioned, Nell?'

Nell nodded as he helped her alight, trying to read his expression, but he was giving nothing away. There wasn't even the cynical but tolerant amusement she was becoming used to—still, her shoulders tightened with unease and her face heated under the force of his golden-brown eyes. This was ridiculous—she was mounting a defence and she didn't even know if she was under attack.

Hunter watched Welbeck reluctantly climb the stairs as the groom drove the curricle to the stables. He knew drivers like Welbeck—he had raced their type often enough—they were skilled but commonly lost in the end because they wore their horses out too soon. It gave him a little satisfaction, but not enough to counter the effect of the sunny smile on Nell's face as she had sat staring at her prince or the intent look in Welbeck's eyes, as he finally began seeing her clearly. He was tempted to tell her what he thought of such a blatant display of juvenile adoration, but he was aware it would not only put up her back, but smack of jealousy, which was ludicrous. He wasn't going to marry the girl, so there was no need to play dog-in-the-manger.

'Do those bays drive as well as they look?' he asked, searching for a neutral opening. She looked at him and he grimaced in annoyance as her smile sparked the increasingly familiar kick of lust.

'They really are beautiful steppers, though the wheeler is just a little short in the shoulders, so it's not a perfect match. Did you see?'

Hunter felt his antagonism melt at her obvious excitement about the horses.

'Don't tell Meech that. He doesn't have your discerning eye and he'll be devastated.'

'Still and all, the lady's right,' Hidgins assented behind them. 'Just a little short. Fine forward action, though. I'd like to see their paces up a hill.'

'Charles took them over the rise once you pass the

village and they took it, crest and all, as if it was a walk.'
She glanced over at Hunter. 'Your team is just as evenly
paced and perhaps have a little more staying power,
though.'

Hunter resisted the urge to smile, barely, and some
more of his tension faded. 'Are you placating me, by any
chance? Precisely how old do you think I am?'

'Ancient,' she replied promptly and with all seriousness and Hidgins gave a snort of laughter, hastily subdued. 'I wasn't trying to placate you. It was just that you
looked a little annoyed just now. I know it's never easy
to see a team you know is just as good as your own.'

'I would debate that they are quite their equal, but
in the end it is also the driver that wins the race, not
merely the team.'

She clasped her hands in front of her and nodded,
eyes wide.

'What the devil does that expression signify?' he
asked, trying to hold on to his annoyance.

'That's how I look when Elkins, our head groom, tries
to teach me something about horses that is painfully obvious, but I don't want to offend him. It is supposed to
convey interested attention.'

'Well, you just look like a dyspeptic owl.'

She laughed and walked over to Hidgins and stroked
the lead horse's sleek neck.

'I was going to tell you Charles mentioned that Meecham is bringing a stallion here for sale, too. A grey. I
saw him when he was just a foal and he's probably a
beauty now.'

'Meecham?' Hunter enquired politely and her smile
glinted at him over the horse's neck.

'Meecham is a darling, but I don't think anyone

would call him a beauty. My point is that I remembered you mentioned you were looking for a horse up to your weight and he stands over sixteen hands.'

Hunter came to stand on the other side of the leader. She had taken off her gloves when she approached the horse and he watched as her hand moved with calm rhythm down the horse's neck.

Hers weren't the plump pampered hands of a society miss, nor the carefully soignée, white hands of someone like Lady Felton. They were warmed to a pale honey and looked strong, and when she brushed her fingers along the horse's mane he saw the pucker of calluses on her palm.

He pulled off his own gloves and placed his palm on the firm muscled neck between them. The short hair was warm and vibrated with the blood and life beneath. It was ridiculous to be envious of a horse simply because a young woman was petting it. To be reduced to stroking the same horse simply to approach her was a tactic he would have thought had gone the way of his schoolboy days.

'Are you making fun of my size again, by any chance?'

That won him another teasing smile which gave him far too much satisfaction.

'I'm not one to say anything about being too big, unfortunately. But it is worth looking at him. Apparently his name is Courage, which is a bit pompous, but he's too old to change it, I would think. Or perhaps you could call him Coleridge, which is close enough, no?'

'There is no possible way I would name a horse after a poet.'

'What's wrong with Courage?' Hidgins asked. 'Fine

name for a stallion. We have a good strapping gelding named Valiant, don't we, sir?'

'Don't give her grist for her mill, Hidgins. There is only so much abuse I can take before noon.'

'Valiant is a very charming name,' Nell said, her tone blatantly propitiating. 'I'm sure many medieval knights named their steeds Valiant and Intrepid and…and Fearless.'

'How about Impudent? Or Shameless?' Hunter replied, edging Hidgins out of the way. She was getting all too comfortable poking fun at him and that came at a price. Hidgins, good man that he was, took the hint and moved towards the curricle. Hunter completed the manoeuvre, boxing Nell in between the horses. She glanced up in surprise and tried to pass him, but he didn't move.

'Don't run away just yet. You did ask me to flirt with you, didn't you? And I presume Welbeck won't be able to resist taking a peek on our progress from the windows. Besides, all this talk about medieval knights and steeds makes one want to do a little marauding. You might think,' he continued, stroking the horse's neck and stopping just short of where her hand rested, 'that it isn't easy to maraud in broad daylight in full view of the front door of a country home, wouldn't you?'

She did the same thing with her lips, that faint lick and tug, but though this time it was completely unconscious, the gesture and the coral-coloured flush, that winter sun-coloured hair between him and those lovely, firm little breasts…

'I would have thought it is close to impossible,' she murmured as the silence stretched.

He slid his other hand down this time so that his thumb just came to rest against her wrist, then very slowly slid under it until he could feel her pulse, warm and fast, against the pad of his thumb.

'Be you ever so close to impossible, you remain in the realm of possibility.'

'Who said that?' she asked, her voice husky. She raised her wrist almost imperceptibly, so that his fingers could slide under into the warm cavern between her wrist and the horse. He found it hard to believe she had no idea what she was doing. In anyone else he would have considered this behaviour to be a blatant invitation to take this flirtation to its natural conclusion. If she were anyone else he would do just that.

'I did.'

'It sounds impressive. Rather like a heraldic motto. Ours is *Qui edere vult nucleum, frangat nucem.*'

He frowned, momentarily distracted.

'"If you want to eat his centre, break his nuts"?'

'Dear me, you would have failed my Latin class. It means "he who wants the kernel must crack the nut".'

'I would have failed your Latin class because I would have found it very hard to concentrate. On the other hand, if you taught anatomy...'

He slid his hand between hers and the horse, his fingers tracing the dip at the heart of her palm up to the rasp of the calluses at the base of her fingers and then on until his hand laced with hers. She still didn't pull back. He almost wanted her to because he was beginning to feel very much like that schoolboy he had described. He knew she was enjoying this exploration of what he suspected was a very passionate nature, but it was also obvious she trusted him to set the boundaries and keep her safe. She was here to learn theory, not practise. And he...

A distinct throat-clearing from Hidgins made them both turn their heads. Just as a day earlier, a group of men were coming around the house and Hunter moved back. Impossibility had won this time. She looked suddenly much younger and quite shy, reminding him precisely what she was. He placed her hand on his arm and he led her away from the horses.

'Porridge,' he said decisively and she looked up in surprise. 'Sounds just as much like Courage as Coleridge does, no?'

'Porridge?' Her voice shook with laughter and the shyness faded. 'You would never call a horse Porridge.'

'I'd sooner call him suet pudding than Coleridge, darling. Now we'll let Hidgins take the horses to the stables and we can go see this filly Lord Welbeck mentioned yesterday. Unless you would like to ask young Welbeck to take you?'

She actually had the audacity to consider his question for a moment.

'No... I don't think I should seek him out again so soon. I prefer that he sue a little for my attention. Is that awful of me?'

'It is in the finest of feminine traditions, at least.' He tried to keep the edge out of his voice.

'I don't think you are in a position to accuse anyone else of being flirtatious. Certainly not me. This is my first real taste of it.'

'Then you are an extremely precocious pupil.'

'Some credit must go to my teacher, then,' she conceded gallantly. 'Is it terrible to admit I enjoy it?'

'Appalling. Up there with necromancy and slave trading.'

'I just knew I was a hopeless case,' Nell said with

relish and he couldn't help laughing. It might not be very comfortable, but he could surely survive a little misplaced attraction, and it appeared to be doing her a great deal of good, so it was churlish to resent her artless enjoyment.

The path separated a collection of buildings that surrounded the stables from the paddocks and they had just come to the last of the buildings when a snort and the sharp strike of hoof against wood made Hunter turn abruptly.

'That's probably Griffin,' Nell said. 'They keep him in the small stable away from the other stallions. He's a beauty, but he's the most ill-tempered horse I've ever seen. He's just not meant to be domesticated.' She paused. 'You're curious, now, aren't you?'

Hunter laughed, not surprised she had seen through him so clearly.

'A little. Let's go take a look.'

The stable was a small one, with just four large loose stalls, all of which were empty but the last. The moment they stepped in, a large bay head surged over the stall door which squeaked in protest as the stallion's body hit it with a thump. Hunter took a step forward, but stopped as Nell grabbed his arm. He closed his hand on hers reassuringly, rather pleased she was concerned for his safety.

'Don't worry; I won't go too close.'

The stall door creaked again as Griffin pushed against it, tossing his head up, ears flat and eyes wide. Then his meaty lips pulled back, displaying very large teeth, and he surged forward again, his teeth closing with a sharp snap on the air.

'Well, that answers that question. We're definitely not welcome here.'

'I'm afraid it might be too late to help him. Some people are like that, too. There was a girl at school who enjoyed hurting other girls. Nothing we tried made the slightest difference. I was very glad when she left.'

'Did she hurt you?'

She looked up at the tension he hadn't even realised had entered his voice and her brows drew together.

'No, not me. She was quite little and she went after smaller girls. She did try to bully my best friend Anna once, but that earned her a nosebleed. Anna has six sisters, you see.'

'That would teach anyone survival skills. Anna is your best friend?'

'Since we were ten. She lives near Windermere and I spent all my holidays with her family. Her parents even have me call them Uncle Arthur and Aunt Ginnie. They are more family to me than my own.'

'They sound nice.'

Again the careful glance at him.

'You would probably like Anna. She's small and quite as lovely as Lady Melkinson, but she has black hair and eyes. All the boys always fall in love with her.'

'Are you jealous of her?'

He expected a denial, but she just sighed.

'That's awful of me, isn't it? I love her dearly, but I can't help wishing I was also tiny and dark and her hair has a lovely natural curl. It really bounces. Not very nice of me, is it?'

He took her hand, turning her towards him. They had reached the folly, a small brick tower around which a copse of old oaks created an intimate and private cavern.

'It's honest, but misplaced. I wouldn't be surprised if she was envious of you.'

Nell shook her head.

'She did say she wished she was tall and pale, but she was just being nice. She is like that.'

Her full lower lip was curved in a soft smile and it occurred to him that this strange girl had made a completely new life for herself away from her cold and damaging home. She spoke of her schoolteacher and friends with more warmth and protectiveness, and even with the expectation of being loved in return, than most people he knew spoke of their own families.

Her insecurity always centred on her height and looks, which was nothing short of baffling. It was true that at seventeen, aside from her performance on the horses, she had shown all the gawkiness of a girl grown too much too fast. But the woman who stood before him, because she was definitely a woman, might not be conventionally pretty like the petite china-doll girls she admired, but she was far more attractive and exciting than someone as transparent as a Lady Melkinson. It was clear she had no idea of the damage she could do with her elegant body and quicksilver eyes. Part of him wanted to teach her, but another part didn't want to give her any more help in her aggravating plan to capture Welbeck.

As he remained silent, her smile dimmed.

'You would probably like her, too.'

'I'm not sure; my taste runs along different lines.'

She half-snorted.

'I know. Lady Felton and opera singers.'

His mouth quirked and he stepped forward, moving his hand lightly up her arm.

'Longer lines. Much longer. There are distinct advantages to a woman who fits against you…perfectly.'

He took another step, moving his hands to her waist.

'See?' he asked, trying to keep his body in pace with his mind. 'And I happen to appreciate Saxon princesses with North Sea eyes. They tend to bring out the medieval warrior in me.'

Her lips parted and their colour warmed to the lovely pink peach that kept tantalising him.

'Do you know many Saxon princesses?'

He liked the way her voice, already deep, sank and thickened, increasing the feeling of being lost and isolated in a fog-bound moor.

'Just one,' he answered, letting sensible considerations slip away. She was clearly ready to carry her experimentation a little further—she wouldn't stop him. No, she *wanted* this, and he…needed this. For a moment the truth of that alarmed him but he shoved it down hard, touching the tips of his fingers to her jawline, to her cheek, raising her chin with his thumb, very slowly. 'But she's not a princess—she's a queen. Princesses are soft and middling; queens are strong and weak in equal measure. And fascinating. And worth fighting for…'

He was using his voice like his hands and body, but the words rang true even in his own ears. Her mouth bowed a little and her eyes fell away.

'That's beautiful,' she breathed. 'Thank you.'

It took him a moment to realise she thought this was part of their charade of flirtation and another moment to remind himself that it was. But it didn't stop him. His hand tightened on her waist, closing the distance between them. Her hair, sliding between his fingers, was hot and silky, soft as liquid, and he twisted his hand in it, raising her face the last inch towards him.

'Nell,' he murmured, feeling the flush of his breath

against her cheek and then against her mouth. Finally.
His mind was still struggling to describe just what it
felt like when with a small sigh that sucked the breath
out of him she opened her mouth under his, just canting
her head a hair's breadth so that the fit was…perfect. He
stopped thinking, at least with his mind, and let every
instinct take over, talking with her and listening to her
by all other means.

And she was a symphony of contradictory and conflicting answers. Her hands moved first in feather-light,
tentative brushes against his coat that reflected the light
teasing slides of his mouth over hers as he waited for a
sign she was ready for more.

He shouldn't have been surprised that the surrender,
when it came, would be so thorough. The moment his
tongue lightly caressed the silk of her inner lip, where
the skin was warm and full and smooth as mother-of-
pearl, her arms rose to wrap around his neck with a sigh
and her body sagged against him with the abandon of a
collapsing marionette.

For a moment he froze, holding her to him, his hand
deep in her hair as she clung to him like to a mast in a
storm, waiting. Then forces of nature won out over the
strange surge of fear and his hand moved down to the
rounded rise of her backside, pulling her against him as
he indulged the urge to lick and tug at the soft and lush
lower lip that had done so much damage to his control.

This time her sigh was more a moan and her muscles
gathered with purpose as she dug her fingers into the
hair at his nape, pulling herself against him, opening
her mouth for him, her lips catching against his, and it
was his turn to groan. It was obvious she wasn't used
to being kissed and it was even more obvious that she

liked it. She didn't even pull away when he deepened the caress, his tongue finding hers, stroking it slow and long. She just moved against him, tasting and seeking and rewarding him with little whimpers of pleasure that were as devastating to his control as the urgent movements of her body.

He had been so right about how perfectly she fit against him. It would take so little to push her against the wall, pull up those skirts, warm and heat and dampen her until she was ready for him and then...

'Hunter...' It came out a whisper and a plea and his whole body contracted as if he was about to climax just at the sound of her and the slide of her breath into him. He leaned one hand against the wall of the folly, holding her tightly to him with the other, aware at some level that he was in the act of committing a folly of his own. That, madness aside, there was no possible way he could follow through on what body and mind were begging for. That he had to stop. Now.

He pulled back, registering with some surprise that his arm was shaking as it leaned against the stone surface.

'Nell, I don't want to stop, but we have to... Anyone might come by here.'

Her eyes opened slowly and he forced his gaze from the plump, reddened dampness of her lips to her eyes. Unfortunately, they met his with a dreamy, dilated shimmer that was almost as bad for his control. What did he care if someone saw them? The worst that could happen was that they would have to carry through on this engagement. But as he was about to lean back into her, her hands fell from about his neck and the dreamy look was replaced by one of mingled surprise and awareness.

'Is this how you kiss all women?' she asked huskily.

The introduction of other women into the moment was so out of place he struggled to even understand what she was asking. His brain, already in a losing position, told him to keep his mouth shut while his gut was demanding he answer a resounding 'no'. His other instincts, scrambling to recover lost positions, told him to tread very carefully.

'Of course not!'

Her mouth drooped.

'Did I do it wrong?'

A laugh escaped him at the absurdity of it all.

'If doing it wrong means taking me within an inch of losing all control, then yes.'

He was sober enough now for the admission to cost him, but he was rewarded by one of her sudden joyous smiles.

'I would have thought that meant I did it correctly. Must we stop?'

He leaned forward, pressing his lips against the soft hairs at her temple, breathing her in. Oh, he loved her scent. He had no idea what it was, just that it was the most beautiful...

'Yes, we must. For now.' He spoke against the tickle of her hair. He was so damn tempted to take her into the gloomy entrance of the folly, braving cobwebs and mice and headless spectres if need be just so he wouldn't have to take his hands off her. He let them curve one last time over her hips and behind, trying not to pin her to him again so she could feel precisely why they had to stop now.

'It doesn't feel done yet,' she whispered, turning so that he felt the last words flutter against his neck.

'Why not?' he asked. He was falling again. It was as though in a dream, watching himself do something he knew he shouldn't, but being incapable of moving to stop it.

'I don't know. I feel…awake and asleep. Buzzing. It doesn't feel right to stop now.'

'Oh, Nell. Please stop talking. I can't think.'

'I don't want to think…'

'If we don't stop now, we'll be exchanging vows by the end of the week,' he said desperately, as much to himself as to her, but apparently it was enough for Nell. He hadn't realised how pliant her body was against him until she froze; then her elbows shoved between them, pushing him away.

Without another word they turned and continued, their feet scrunching on the gravel path. It wasn't far from the folly to the paddock and the filly had obviously sensed them coming and retreated to the far end, her ears flat and her eyes wide. Nell stopped and leaned on the paddock fence, watching the filly, and Hunter did the same a yard away, his hands pressing against the sun-warmed wood as he tried to understand just how on earth he had lost all judgement.

For a while neither spoke as they watched the filly. The buzz and chirp of insects and birds and the gleam of the sun on the late summer wildflowers created an idyllic setting, but he just stared at it grimly.

She bent and tugged at a dandelion that was tapping against the fence.

'Well, at least I can see why you men do this all the time.'

He closed his eyes briefly, wishing her a thousand miles away until he was himself again and his body stopped dancing to the tune of her voice and her art-less remarks.

'We don't precisely do this *all* the time.'

'No, it would be quite tiring, I suppose. Still...'

The sound of hooves made both of them turn. Hunter realised that his half-prayer that something save him from his baser instincts had taken a distinctly unwanted form—the last person he wanted to see right now was Charles Welbeck.

Charles nodded to Hunter, but addressed Nell as he dismounted.

'Well, what do you think of her?'

Nell's smile shifted into the serious look she reserved for equine matters and Hunter was at least glad to see that in her master-of-the-horse mode she showed no in-clination to blush in the presence of her prince. What amazed him even more was that she showed no sign of what had just taken place between them. She might not have much experience, but she was taking to this new sphere like a duck to water.

'She is beautiful, her head and shoulders are perfect, but it's not a good sign that she has kept her ears back ever since she sensed us, even though we are nowhere near her. Did something happen to her?'

'She had a hard birth and her dam rejected her early on. I told Father to sell her, but he said someone might pay a good price for her if we could calm her. I think it's a waste of time. She just doesn't have the makings of a good breeder.'

'I don't agree, but we shall see. Has she been named?'

'We just call her Buckminster's Filly after her sire. You name her, then, Nell.'

Nell's gaze followed the filly, her mouth softening.

'Daisy.'

Hunter watched with mute frustration as Charles's eyes skimmed from Nell's profile to her other attributes and his mouth bowed into a sweet smile as Nell turned back to them.

'Daisy, then,' Charles assented.

Chapter Nine

Nell slunk past the door of the drawing room as the women bent over the latest fashion plates. The weather was still lovely and the last thing she wanted to be doing was exchanging gossip with the matrons. She would take this opportunity to go see Daisy on her own. Perhaps without two very tall, very male individuals by her side, the filly might be more amenable.

She also could make use of some time alone after her inexplicable behaviour with Hunter. She was clearly taking this whole flirtation idea too far. It wasn't surprising that Hunter was very, very good at it or even that she enjoyed it so much. After all, she had always wished she could flirt like Anna, and to do so with someone so handsome and adept was an opportunity not to be missed.

Already it was making her much less affected by Charles's presence. She had actually felt quite his equal during that exchange down by the paddock and during the walk back to the house. It was very kind of Hunter to be so obliging, though kind was probably not the right word. He probably hadn't abandoned his plans for Bascombe, but she sensed that he was someone who would take his failures with good grace and probably be quite content with just the water rights in the end.

A sudden roaring cheer from the direction of the stables made Nell pause and then change course. On a grass clearing a large group of men, gentry, servants, grooms and stable boys stood shoulder to shoulder, clearly enjoying some spectacle at their centre. Standing back from the crowd, but with an excellent vantage point on stacked bales of hay, was Hunter's man, Biggs.

She stopped next to him. 'What on earth is happening, Biggs?'

Biggs, caught in mid cheer, gaped down at her.

'Miss Tilney! You oughtn't to be here.'

'Why not? Is there a fight? Help me up.'

Seeing he was too shocked to comply, she clambered up herself. Sometimes there were advantages to being tall. From the hay she could see over the crowd to the two men who were... Her hand flew to her mouth as Hidgins's fist drove itself into Hunter's middle.

'Oh, no! Why are they fighting? I thought they were friends.'

It was a strange thing to say of a master and a servant, but the words were out before she could consider their wisdom.

Biggs looked startled, but recovered himself.

'They are, miss. This has become a yearly tradition at the stables, so to speak. His lordship and Hidgins being proficient in the Fancy, they draw a fine crowd and excite not a little bit of wagering.'

'The Fancy?'

Biggs tore his eyes away from the fight and smiled reassuringly.

'It's just sparring, miss. Fisticuffs for pleasure.'

For pleasure! Hidgins stumbled back under a blow and the crowd shifted to give him room to rally, re-forming again as he propelled himself headlong into Hunter.

'You needn't worry, miss. They've been sparring since they were boys, Hidgins being the eldest of the old groom at Hunter Hall.'

'You knew Lord Hunter when he was a boy?'

'You might say we grew up together at the Hall, miss.'

'But you and Hidgins are older, I think, no?'

'We are, miss, but his lordship was always old for his age.'

Biggs glanced at her momentarily and then continued, his eyes fixed firmly on the fight.

'If you'll pardon the impertinence, miss, but don't let his lordship's manner fool you into thinking there's no substance there. I don't know how it was, but there wasn't one that didn't know who ran the Hall and saw to Lady Hunter and Master Tim long before the old lord passed. He never asked for help, always stood firm on his own two feet. There's no better man or master I know.'

Nell smiled at Biggs's obvious pride, but couldn't help a prick of annoyance at the way he regarded Hunter's self-sufficiency as evidence he didn't need anyone. Hunter's aunts had said something very similar. It was impressive that Hunter had taken such responsibilities on to his overly young shoulders, but someone should have interceded on his behalf. She had seen enough during her years at the school to know children should always have someone to lean on if they are to feel safe in the world; their strength shouldn't come from being strong for someone else, but from believing themselves valued and protected. Her mother had been her protector and, when she had died, Nell had luckily settled on Mrs Petheridge as another source of strength. Perhaps she had been luckier than Hunter after all. She tried to shrug off her sense of unease. She was clearly exaggerating. Hunter was a grown man and had obviously come through these imagined emotional privations with minimal scars, except those incurred by being bludgeoned by fists. He wasn't a pupil of hers to be worried over.

'His lordship wouldn't like you to be here,' Biggs said with great resolution, distracting her from her thoughts, but his eyes remained firmly on the fight.

'But I'm not here, Biggs,' she murmured, her own attention returning to the rhythm and force of the exchange. She could see now that Hunter's catlike grace and reflexes had distinct advantages when it came to beating opponents into a pulp. Hidgins's lunges and jabs were quick and brutal, but though Nell cringed each time they shot out, not many managed to make contact. But Hidgins was as broad and thick as a brick wall and just as hard to fell, and when his fists did finally make contact with Hunter her own body contracted with sympathetic pain.

'Do they beat each other until one of them breaks the other's nose?'

His thin lips quirked and settled back.

'No, miss. After the first year it was decided to establish some rules to ensure presentability after the encounter.'

Nell was used to schoolmistressy euphemisms.

'No blows to the head, then?'

Again the prim quirking of lips.

'Precisely, miss, and none below the…if you will excuse the word…waist, miss.'

She almost said that it was silly to be prudish about the mention of a perfectly everyday part of human anatomy, but her eyes dropped to Hunter's waist just before it was blocked from her view as Hidgins came forward with an impressive jab and blow. She winced at the rush of concern that coursed through her and a parallel rush of heat at that very brief and utterly inconsequential consideration of Hunter's waist. She had seen his waist and other men's waists before and it certainly had never been an issue. Perhaps the difference was that she had actually felt that waist against her, hard and urgent and making her disastrously aware of her own waist, her legs, the way her skin felt, the way her hands had wanted to touch...

She tightened her cloak about her and tried to focus on feeling disapproving at this very childish exhibit. Fisticuffs and betting in a stable yard! It was so typical of Hunter—he probably went to drink ale in the village inn afterwards and then to share his waist and everything else with whatever maid he could charm. Charles would probably never engage in such activities. She couldn't imagine him with his hair all tousled by rough handling and his shirt being mangled by Hidgins as the groom tried and failed to deflect a blow to his stomach. As the crowd sang out their approval and agony she turned resolutely to Biggs.

'Have you placed a bet yourself, Biggs?'

He shook his head mournfully.

'No, miss. It wouldn't be quite proper.'

'To bet against Lord Hunter?'

'Against Hidgins, miss. His lordship's pride is rather more...flexible.'

Once again the two men went down onto the grass.

'Those stains will never come out.' Biggs sighed.

The crowd had closed again and for a moment it looked as though they might all join in the fray and she lost sight of the two men on the ground. Then both a great concerted groan and a rival cheer stretched out.

'He has him pinned,' Biggs informed her and the groan and cheer scattered into laughter and the settling of debts. The knot unravelled, revealing the two dishevelled men who might just have well been rolled down a hill into a bog, Nell thought as her breath finally began to settle.

Then Hunter turned and saw her and her breath lost its rhythm again. He came towards her, his strides long and less graceful than usual. There was almost a bounce in them, as though he might suddenly leap from the ground. She tensed because his stride spoke of anger, but his face was still alight with laughter even though she could see he was trying to school it into disapproval. The combination was doing something to her and it wasn't just the saggy platform of hay under her feet that made her feel off balance.

He wore no coat or cravat and his shirt was untucked and marred by various stains which were likely, as Biggs had said, to resist extraction. It was also rent at the shoulder, revealing a triangular patch of skin which was almost the same warm tan as the skin at his neck. He must go shirtless quite often for his shoulders to be sun-touched like that, she thought. Where on earth could a gentleman do that? At Hunter Hall? If she had agreed to marry him, would she see him striding towards her just like that, but bare chested, with those powerful shoulders she had clung to and those arms that could control a four-horse team with less effort than it took most men to drive a gig?

'Biggs, why didn't you see Miss Tilney back to the house? It's not proper for her to be here.'

The words were perfectly sensible and in complete discord with the movement of his body and the brandy and honey eyes which were as hot and enticing now as the spirits they resembled.

'Who, my lord?' Biggs asked and received a quick sardonic glance.

'Subverting my servants, Nell?'

'I think that is a lesser sin than beating them up,' Nell replied. 'Are you all right, Hidgins?'

Hidgins grinned at her and pressed his hand to his ribs with a pitiful moan.

'I think you broke a rib, sir. I'll be laid up for a week, I will.'

'Oh, poor Betsy,' Nell said before she could stop herself and Hidgins dropped his hand and burst into laughter. Then, with a glance at Hunter, he and Biggs headed off towards the central stable. Nell realised she and Hunter were the only ones remaining on the patch of grass and she was still standing atop her perch as Hunter looked up at her with a very unsettling expression and resembling a pirate after a pitched battle. An incredibly handsome pirate. Most pirates would probably be grimy, with missing teeth and perhaps stunted from scurvy and not at all an object for admiration, she told herself, but the image clung. At least to her less-than-sensible imagination he did look like a pirate with the wind tangling in his warm chestnut hair with its shades of bay and cinnamon and flapping the edges of his shirt, threatening to lift it up so she might be able to see if his abdomen was also that colour as it dipped downwards into his buckskins, whether he was heat and warmth everywhere.

She tried to be sensible.

'It really is quite silly to be brawling like that. You two could have hurt each other!'

He grinned, tucking in his shirt and looking very much like a boy just returned from a successful raid on a neighbour's trout stream.

'Not really. This is what is called mere flourishing. After the first time, Hidgins and I agreed we would avoid blows to the head and below the waist. This way the only marks are easier to hide than a black eye.'

Another allusion to waists! She was not going to look or think about tucking in the ruined shirt herself and wondering if he would feel soft or hard there.

'So Biggs explained. Have you ever had a black eye?'

'Several.'

'Several. That is impressive; most people can only have two.'

His grin widened.

'Very amusing, Saxon. Now come down before I decide to put all this hay to good use.'

She really should come down, but she didn't want to, not yet. As she remained unmoving the raffish quality of his grin shifted, mellowed, his lashes dipping.

'You do look like a Saxon queen up there, about to bestow her favour on her knight,' he observed and Nell planted her feet more firmly as the bale quivered beneath them, or maybe that was just her legs that had wobbled. She was used to looking down at men, but very contrarily looking down at him made her feel dainty. Dainty?

'She would probably be a Norman queen if there were knights,' the schoolmistress corrected, and then, more to the point and in a less resolute voice. 'I don't have anything to bestow.'

'Yes, you do.'

How could three words turn a quiver into a blaze? He might as well have touched a match to the hay the heat was so intense. Also the sense of danger. He was making love to her in the middle of a stable yard without raising a finger and she didn't want it to stop. *This is not making love, just flirting*, the schoolmistress pointed out and was kicked off the bale of hay.

'I do?'

She would have preferred his hands, but his eyes were just as thorough and they left a scalding trail as they moved over her, a light shining and picking out the elements of her body, one by one, and she felt them as clearly as if he pressed his mouth to each point—to the skin just where her cheek sloped towards her ear, to the hollow below her chin, to the rise of her breast under the soft scrape of her fichu. All the way down her arm and so warm into the palms of her hands, telling her they could touch him, slide under that torn linen shirt...

'Your ribbon,' he said. He must have moved closer without her noticing. Now she could see the thick strands of his hair rising and falling against his forehead in the mounting wind, just touching the beautifully sculpted cheekbones. Was it ridiculous to feel envious of the wind that was doing what she so desperately wanted to do? It had to be.

'I will settle, for now, for your ribbon.' He spoke slowly, as if aware she wasn't quite listening.

'My ribbon.'

He nodded and took her by the waist and lowered her to the ground so gently and slowly she realised there must be even more strength in those arms than she had imagined. Now she was so close she could see the shading of his eyes. How could there be so very many shades of brown and how could they be so very warm? His scent, too, was composed of the same elements of sultry warmth, reaching her below the familiar scents of the stable yard and fields beyond. She had been cold a moment before, wrapping her cloak around her. Now it choked her, she wanted it off...

'This ribbon.' His voice was even slower now, treacle slow and warm, and when his fingers caught the fluttering end of the ribbon of her bonnet it became a thread of tingling, an extension of her dancing nerves.

'Why?'

'Your hair. I need to see it.'

Her hair, her hopeless, shapeless pale-as-dust hair, and he wanted to see it. Either she had no better charms or he actually, really did like her hair. He *needed* to see it. She could feel the truth of that word and it was very strange.

He didn't wait for her permission. The ribbon tautened, pressed over her bodice and down, and the slide of the satin fabric over the layers that kept her at bay was torture. She wished he could keep pulling and everything between them would unravel and peel away.

Her bonnet landed on the bale of hay and inevitably her hair, released so incautiously from its cage, slipped from its knot and settled on her right shoulder. The wind, scenting new prey, set about making as much of a tangle of it as possible. While he just stood there and watched it dance and flick about, his hands fisted on her cloak.

She shivered and it wasn't from the cold, but the sense of being bare though she was fully clothed. But it did make her think of him in his linen shirt. He must be freezing. She wrapped her cloak about his hands, drawing them into hers. They weren't in the least cold, but she chafed them anyway.

'You must be cold.'

'I am many, many things at this moment. Cold is not one of them.' But he didn't draw away his hands.

'Sorry, my hands are rough,' she said as she slid her palm over his, feeling his calluses and hers, regretting all those years of reins and harnesses and brushing down horses because at this moment she wished her hands were as silken and soft as his lovers' probably were. She wanted to be a woman in every sense of the word.

'The hands of a queen are never soft. They aren't passive. They take what they want. They are beautiful and elegant and strong. You can take what you want.'

She didn't know what she wanted beyond this pure present instant. She wanted time never to exist again so she could remain just there in the universe created around his voice throbbing inside her and her palm against his. But the moment the thought of time intruded, it began to rush again. She could hear horses coming along from the gravel drive. A curricle and riders. For a moment his hands moved deep under her cloak, catching her and pressing her the length of him convulsively, his face sinking towards her. It was seconds, but she felt the hard ridge press against the pliant skin of her stomach and her whole body clenched against a rush of heat that centred between her legs, making her squirm against him, seeking.

'Nell.' His voice was a warning as he whispered her

name against the corner of her mouth. Then his lips brushed up and against her and he was already a few steps away, taking his coat from where it hung on a railing. By the time the riders appeared he had knotted his cravat and was now marginally presentable but still looked like a pirate, just in rumpled riding clothes.

'What? Did we miss the match?' Meecham called out, his pug-like eyes crestfallen. He bowed and smiled shyly at Nell. 'Hello, Miss Tilney.'

'Did Hidgins win this time?' another man asked hopefully as he inspected Hunter's dishevelled state.

'Sorry, Walters. Maybe next time. Now, if you will excuse me, I need to see Miss Tilney back to the house.'

Nell followed meekly, still shocked at her own behaviour. With that light, humorous and wicked charm he kept slipping through her defences and she didn't even realise it until he was ready to make it clear, as he just had. This man was a walking, talking Trojan Horse.

They came around the paddock by the small stable and she caught sight of Charles holding Griffin's reins well near the bit. The great dark stallion was clearly being his endearing self, shaking his head, his hooves tattooing on the ground, his rear dancing even as Charles tried to control his front. In the neighbouring paddock a large bay stallion was tethered to the fence and he also didn't look overly happy at being so close to a rival stallion.

'Oh, no. Stop,' Nell cried out, but it was too late. Griffin ripped the reins from Charles's grasp with a great backward heave and shied away, bouncing off the ground.

'Charles, get out of the paddock. Leave him be.'

She kept her voice low, but either Charles didn't hear

her or he chose to ignore her because he kept moving towards Griffin. The stallion's movement was so quick it was over in seconds. He had stood with his rear to Charles, but in a flash he turned, lowered his head and charged like a bull, slamming Charles into the fence and dragging him along it before pulling away. Charles dropped and half-rolled, half-crawled under the fence and straight into Nell's arms as she knelt on the grass to pull him through.

'Don't move, don't move.' Her voice was tight with shock, but her hands moved swiftly and surely over his ribs and arms.

'I'm all right,' Charles croaked. 'I'm all right.'

'Well, you don't deserve to be,' Nell said, her voice still shaky. 'What on earth were you thinking, trying to discipline him when he is in full territorial mode with another stallion right there in the next paddock? You are lucky he didn't break your back and bite your hand off into the bargain!'

Charles's cheeks went from chalk to cherry as he shoved to his feet, brushing the dirt from his clothes, but before he could react she reached out.

'I'm sorry, Charles. I didn't mean to scold. I was just frightened.'

He laughed shakily and took her offered hand.

'Don't apologise—I deserved that. I let my temper get the better of me. I should be the one apologising, Helen. I've quite ruined your dress.'

Nell glanced down at the grass stains on her muslin dress.

'That doesn't matter. I'm just glad you're not hurt.'

'Yes, well, we had all best change. It wouldn't do for us to be seen like this.'

Nell flushed at the suspicious look he cast at Hunter's ragged state and the tousled hair escaping her bonnet. She should be happy at this sign of jealousy, but her shakiness just increased as Hunter took hold of her arm again, more stiffly than before, and they moved towards the house.

She cast a glance back at Griffin, who was still cantering around the small enclosure like a tiger pacing its cage. It might be foolish to be worrying about that devil of a horse, but despite what she had told Hunter, she did not really believe anyone was irredeemable. It was a matter of time and patience, and once she established her own stable, and her own school, she would do her best to reach precisely those who erected the most effective barriers against warm human contact.

As they approached the house she realised she had been distracted from her plan to go see Daisy. She would return once she was alone; she could use some time to sort through her own thoughts and she was always clearest when facing a serious equine challenge.

The small stable was empty, which meant Daisy was already out in the paddock, but with the clouds sinking lower and lower the afternoon fog had also rolled in over the low-lying field, obscuring most of it. She ducked under the paddock fence and leaned against it, rubbing her cold hands under her cloak. Then the fog shifted, swirled, and a dark figure came towards her with the speed of a hurtling stone. She held still as Daisy pranced close to the fence, her tail up, her thin forelegs high off the ground. Nell stood with her back half-turned, one hand on the top rung of the fence, her eyes on the ground, and waited. Again and again Daisy made the circuit, but even when her lovely tail flowed out, like hair in water, and grazed Nell's shoulder, Nell kept her gaze on the shift and eddy of the mist around her legs, waiting. Finally a whicker just behind her told her Daisy had stopped and when the filly's breath settled warm and moist against Nell's cold fingers where they lay on the fence she moved very slowly away and into the paddock, her head down. She could feel Daisy just a yard or two behind her at all times, her curiosity and need for contact battling with nervousness. Nell knew what that was like.

Once she completed the circuit she allowed herself a slow glance up. The filly stood quite close, her eyes a wide liquid brown. Very slowly Nell reached out and stroked her neck, just once. Daisy held still and then lowered her head, edging closer. Nell allowed herself another couple of gentle caresses and then placed her hand back on the fence. After a moment the filly nuzzled her hand and then turned away, rising on her hind legs and doing a strange little dance before bucking playfully and cantering off again. Nell burst into delighted laughter at the beautiful animal's surprising show of character and at her own success.

'I'm glad at least you find this amusing.' Hunter's harsh tones snapped her out of her reverie and she whirled around, raising her hands.

'Hush!'

'Lady Welbeck sent your maid for you and the poor girl enlisted Hidgins's help when she couldn't find you. We've been looking everywhere for you!'

She hugged her cloak to her, not sure whether the shivering was from the cold or his anger.

'I'm sorry I caused a bother. I should have asked

Betsy to tell Lady Welbeck I had a headache or something. I wanted to see Daisy.'

'Alone? And in this weather?'

'Yes, alone. I wanted to see Daisy without anyone distracting her. Stop treating me like a child!'

'You are quite right—you aren't a child. You're a damn walking provocation. You can't just go tramping around the stables and fields on your own with impunity. Anyone could have…'

He half-turned away, his jaw tight, and contrarily her resentment faded as she registered his tension. Just as Biggs had said earlier, he took his responsibilities far too seriously.

The wind shoved at them and when they still didn't move it flicked some needles of rain at them. Hunter took her hand and turned her towards the house.

'Your hand is frozen. These gloves are hardly any more than a scrap of cotton. Don't you know to put on real gloves before you go out in this weather?'

She laughed at the scold.

'I forgot.'

'Very childish. Come, we need to warm you up.'

She didn't answer. It wasn't so terrible after all to be treated like a child sometimes, being led by a very large and warm hand. She hadn't quite realised how cold and stiff she had become until his fingers forced hers apart and laced between them with his palm pressed against hers.

When they reached the door to her room she turned to thank him, but there was a burst of laughter from the stairs and she suddenly found herself inside her room with Hunter.

'You can't be here,' she whispered. 'What if Betsy comes?'

He turned the key in the lock.

'Problem solved. Besides, you need someone to light your fire.'

She frowned at his back as he took the tinderbox from the mantel and bent down to the grate. She nearly answered that she was quite capable of lighting her own fire, but that seemed the wrong response to his words. Instead, she unfastened her damp cloak and hung it from a peg by the wardrobe. When he rose from the burgeoning fire she stepped back.

'Thank you. Now…'

He took her hand and sat her down on a chair by the fire.

'Now we thaw you out. You're turned to ice. Little fool.'

He sank down on one knee and cupped her clenched right hand. Reality swirled and for a moment she thought of a knight presenting a precious offering to his sovereign. He took off her glove and gently rubbed and chafed her hand until it tingled and pulsed.

'Here, I think we've thawed this one out. Let me see.' He touched his mouth to the back of her hand, turned it over and gently smoothed out her clenched fingers before pressing the same light kiss to her palm.

'Now let's have the other hand,' he said, placing her warmed hand in her lap and holding out his own hand, his eyes on hers.

She gave it to him and just sat as he continued his ministering. Except that it wasn't the same. When he had propelled her into the room she had felt embarrassed and foolish and he had been in full imperious mode and she had hardly noticed when he had taken off her glove.

Now something had shifted. The fabric of her glove caught and pulled and slithered over her cold skin, and when he cupped her fist and very gently blew upon it, like a mother warming her child's hands, the heat was too intense, like hot water poured on a limb recovering from frostbite. She tried to draw it away, but he held it without force and it stayed there. After a moment he began the same calming ritual as before. His thumb moved gently over the bones of her wrist, the back of her hand and the sweep between her finger and thumb.

She watched his long elegant fingers move between hers, darker and more powerful and so gentle. She watched him, the dark chestnut gleams in his hair, the black lashes shielding the gold in his eyes. She wanted so much to touch that hair, the sharp ridge of his cheekbone. There was a little white scar there, a slightly tipsy letter L, hardly visible, and she remembered the way he had touched the scar by her mouth and she wondered she hadn't seen it before. He was slowly coming into focus for her. Element by element.

'What is this from?' She touched her finger to the scar and his hands stilled, his eyes glinting like a cat ready to spring.

'What?'

'The scar, the little L. Here.' She touched it again. She wanted to do more than that, place her now-warm palm to it, bend down to brush it with her mouth.

'I don't remember.' His voice was already closing down and she felt it in his hands, too, as they gently placed her left hand in her lap, but she turned it and caught his wrist and he didn't immediately draw it away.

She was walking the edge of his pain and any moment now he would repel her, either with mockery or teasing or anger.

'I was trying to rescue my brother's cat. It wasn't grateful,' he said after a moment and she thought of that sweet boy's face in his ensign's uniform and of Hunter as the fierce little warrior protecting his domain and subjects.

'Your brother probably was.'

His eyes flicked to hers again, the danger more evident now. Even his breathing had changed. Her insides started to grate with the inevitable reaction to anger, but she wouldn't stand down. Hunter wouldn't hurt her. Not like this, anyway.

'It's unusual for a boy to have a cat,' she said into the silence. 'Did he like animals?'

He pushed up from his knees and turned towards the door, but then walked towards the dresser.

'He was often ill and bedridden as a boy, so I brought him the kitten to keep him company when I went away to school. Why he ever went into the army I'll never know. I told him he was a fool. I should have stopped him.'

'Maybe he had something to prove.' It must have been hard having an older brother who was so very good at everything male.

'He had nothing to prove. Everyone that mattered loved him. It was my fault for thinking it was a good idea he be sent to school. It took me months to realise he was miserable there and I only found out by chance because one of the boys there was the younger brother of a friend of mine. He never complained. The fool even apologised for making me come all the way there to bring him home. He was just like that. He gave back a hell of a lot more than I could manage to give him. He was the last person on earth who should have had to prove anything to anyone.'

Nell watched him pace the room.

'He sounds as stubborn as you in his own way. You probably couldn't have stopped him.'

'I should have found a way. I knew it was wrong for him, but I never thought... I should have stopped him.'

'He was a grown man by then. Even if you considered yourself responsible for him, you couldn't live his life for him.'

'I didn't want to live his life, just try to prevent his death! I failed him when I let him join and I failed him when I couldn't stop him from taking his own life. Don't you understand? When he came to me saying he wanted to join up, I actually encouraged him. I thought it would finally force him into the world. I never thought they would send someone like him to the Peninsula, let alone put him on Wellington's staff. I knew it was wrong, but he was so damn proud of himself I allowed myself to believe he was finally ready to stand on his own two feet. That's the worst. I was so damn relieved he was finally growing up, that... What a selfish fool I was...'

The room itself was thudding with the restless energy of his pacing and she held herself very still, wondering how to keep him talking.

'How long was he in the war?'

She wasn't certain he would answer, but she waited.

'Just under a year. Six months before he was captured and then five months in that hell. He was so broken they had to move him to a monastery because the gaolers couldn't stand his screaming every night. The abbot was so horrified he actually helped us... He woke up screaming to the end.'

Her mind worked away at the pieces even though her heart was wholly caught in Hunter's agony and guilt and loss. She could feel them as palpably as if each was a living, beating organ on its own. But it was her mind that spoke, too shocked to hold back the words, because the threat to Hunter felt real and present.

'Helped you? You went to rescue him yourself? During the war?'

It was a mistake. He turned back to her and she could see him gathering in and carefully shutting down. Pain and guilt were returned to their drawers and the door firmly closed on her.

'It's already past six. You should dress. I will see you downstairs.'

She stood, trying to think of something to bring him back.

'Gabriel, you aren't to blame for what happened to him...'

'I will see you downstairs.'

He reached the door and turned to her and she had never heard him speak with such a bite of ice in his voice.

'I am not one of your homesick little schoolgirls to be soothed and mollified. You don't know me and you certainly didn't know Tim, so I would appreciate if you would refrain altogether from discussing the subject. I don't like meddlers.'

Chapter Ten

Hunter watched Charles bend over Nell's shoulder as he leaned to turn the page of the *Illustrated Collection of Thoroughbreds* balanced on Nell's lap, his hand so close to a flaxen curve of hair resting on her nape that if she breathed in deeply the man's fingers would tangle in it. From the easy intimacy of Charles's posture it was obvious Nell's scold after Griffin's attack had shifted the balance between them and for once Welbeck's eagerness in her presence didn't appear at all forced.

His own absence today had probably helped as well. He hadn't joined her or the Welbecks the previous evening and had spent the morning down in Wilton, but he had known he had to show his face eventually, if only to tell her he had decided to return to London. She was safe enough with the Welbecks until her father came for her. Safer than she was with him. It hadn't taken the recurrence of his nightmare that night to remind him that he was still paying the price of allowing himself to care for people who were too weak to care for themselves. It was only getting worse. This time she had also been at the centre of his dream, walking blithely towards a rearing, raging black beast while he tried to stop her, weighed down by Tim's pain-racked body. He had saved neither of them and had awoken shivering, his nightshirt soaked in sweat.

He should have left right away, but he had gone to Wilton instead and now it was too late to drive to London today. Besides, he had to face her and tell her he was leaving. The problem was he had no idea what to say to her after his outburst the previous evening. He had never lost his calm like that, not even when the pain and guilt at failing the one person in the world he needed to protect above all had still been so raw he had thought it would submerge him. He still didn't understand why he had lashed out. So what if she had seen through him and shown him a little compassion? That was her nature, the same impulse that drove her need to worry about Daisy or her schoolgirls. Nothing more. There was no reason for it to have felt like danger. Not from her, but from something inside himself. Something dark and sluggish had stirred in response to her warmth and the invitation to share, something he knew very well was not to be set loose.

He shouldn't have gone into her room in the first place. He was already raw when he reached the paddock, worrying that she might have gone to see that devil Griffin, or perhaps been accosted by someone. She was far too trusting when around horses and someone might misread her warmth as an invitation. The relief of finding her safe by the paddock had been overtaken by something else as he stopped to watch the peculiar courtship between her and the filly. He had been mesmerised by her stillness, the calm and calming presence that drew the nervous filly towards her, closer with each circuit, the young horse's whole body easing until it had finally come to a stop. When the filly had nuzzled Nell's hand on the fence, a thunderclap of lust so powerful had struck him and he had almost moved after her as well when she began walking. But he kept still, waiting for it to pass like the first shock of a bee sting before it settled into a persistent ache and itch. By the time she and the filly completed the calm, companionable circuit and climbed out of the paddock, he thought he had regained some control. But he had been wrong. The sting had subsided, but the ache had only deepened.

He watched her and Welbeck's golden heads bent close together. He might not think much of Welbeck, but there was no denying the man was a damn sight more respectable than him and it was beginning to look like her dream of having her prince fall in love with her might not be so far-fetched. All the more reason to step back. The only problem with this resolution was the heat that was even now simmering in him as he watched her; his attention kept snagging on elements of her—on the shadows and lines marking the winged perfection of her collarbone, on her elegant fingers as they turned the pages, on the slope of her shoulder that Welbeck kept hovering over, adding the burn of anger to the mix of snapping desire. It must be because he was unused to dealing with innocents, but just sliding his fingers over the ridge of her wrist bone, into the soft valleys between her fingers, had packed a greater erotic punch than a full naked display. By the time he had moved to her second hand he had been harder than he had ever been with Kate and that was without Nell even touching him. Then she had touched his cheek, her finger as soft as a raindrop on his skin, falling on painfully fertile ground—it had taken all his will not to accept that invitation and make use of the bed behind him.

It was just Nell being Nell, he told himself. There was nothing to read into it, certainly less than the shocked panic she had exhibited running towards Charles in the paddock. He could forgive her for her unintended seductiveness, but it was harder to forgive her for the way she had made him reveal things about Tim—treacherous things, showing Tim in his weakness and his dependency and raising the edge of the cover on Hunter's lifelong frustration with his younger brother. He could never have explained to anyone why he had always been envious of Tim. He had told her that Tim had never asked for anything and it was true, but from the day his brother was born he had received a full measure of love and a cocooning care that no one had ever thought to offer Hunter.

His mother had told him that he had come out ready to fight and had taken whatever he wanted without waiting to be offered. She had actually been proud that he had never needed shielding, not even from his drunken libertine of a father. Far from it, he had become her champion at the tender age of six and it had been as natural as breathing to extend that shield to Tim, who had always been dreamy and fragile and who had looked up to Hunter as a demigod at least. He hadn't even known there was something wrong with his mother's and Tim's dependency on him until he had brought Tim back all broken and had to come to terms with their weakness. In the end he had shattered along with Tim and he hated being reminded of it. Nell had blindsided him in there, taking advantage of that moment of weakness to make him betray Tim and his own perfidy. He was losing control of the situation to an inexperienced virgin.

It was a stark reminder it was time he returned to London. She was safe enough here with the Welbecks. Depending on one's definition of 'safe', he thought, as he watched Welbeck laugh at something she said and lightly brush the curve of her shoulder as he turned the page. Hunter saw her shoulder hitch just a little and his fists closed reflexively. He might not want to marry her, but he was damned if he was going to let them paint him a cuckold while he stood just two yards away.

'Do let the girl have some fun, Hunter.' Lady Melkinson glided into his path as he began to move towards Nell, her childish blue eyes raised to his in the sweetest of smiles. 'She's been aching for it for *soooo* long, apparently.'

'Phyllida. Engaged in procuring now? Aren't you concerned your swain might stray?'

'Darling Hunter, always so distressingly direct. You cannot seriously think I find that long meg a rival? I am fond of Charles and he has his heart set on expanding his stables. If it's the land you want, I am certain some agreement can be reached without you having to abandon your hedonistic lifestyle. He has no interest in Hampshire and you can more than afford it.'

'I'm curious—has he sent you to negotiate or is this your own initiative? In any case, it is rather late in the day for that. She is, after all, engaged to me.'

'Well, precisely, my dear. To you. Had it been a love match naturally Charles would concede defeat. But apparently Tilney in his cups was quite revealing. Charles knows this engagement is mercenary on your part and everyone at Welbeck knows the chit has held a candle for him half her life, and though you are admittedly a very handsome and charming rake likely to appeal to women of more…mature tastes, Charles is the epitome of any girl's dreams, isn't he?'

'Apparently not just girls.'

Lady Melkinson laughed and tapped his arm with her fan.

'I do admit there is something scintillating about waking next to a man quite as beautiful as I. I simply knew I must have him when I saw him.'

'All those mirrors in your rooms no longer satisfying, Phyl?'

'The pleasure is thus doubled,' she replied with a mock-innocent fluttering of her lashes.

'I'm not sure I can stomach the image. Now, if you will excuse me, I will go and relieve your pretty prince of his chivalric duties. I wouldn't be quite as certain as you that he is not enjoying himself far more than you would care to admit, Phyl. There is a saying—be careful what you wish for.'

He walked around her, barely refraining from walking through her. Not even her quick frown of doubt gave him satisfaction. Nell and Charles looked up as his shadow fell across the illustrated plate of the stallion they were examining, and though Charles straightened, he didn't relinquish his position by her side. Nell's gaze flicked past him towards Lady Melkinson.

'Lord Hunter.'

He had been wrong that she was angry at him, he realised. Just wary. He had begun to forget how sensitive she was to anger. Another mark against him and another reminder of why he should stay away from her.

'Shopping for new inmates for Bascombe's stables?'

he enquired. 'I don't think Tiresias is for sale. Portland is quite attached to him. But he might be willing to part with Bull Dog.'

'I was just looking,' she said wistfully, her shoulders releasing some tension. 'He is quite beautiful. And look at this lovely brood mare, Lady Grey. Her stallion Gustavus won the July Stakes. I heard he's a perfect grey. Did you see him?'

'It was a wonderful run,' Charles interposed. 'I wish you would come to the races, Nell. Newmarket and Epsom are quite respectable and it is a great pity your father never brought you. Perhaps once you are married you will attend.'

His tones were both teasing and caressing and Hunter's jaw tightened.

'That's an excellent idea. If we forgo the banns and can track down a handy bishop we can make it to the Newmarket Meeting, Nell,' he offered.

'Attending the races is not a sufficient reason to rush into wedlock, Lord Hunter,' Nell replied primly, but the laughter had returned to her eyes.

'Certainly not. There are many better reasons, both sufficient and necessary. Excuse me, Welbeck. My betrothed apparently needs my help listing them.'

Hunter sat down by Nell and Welbeck was forced to retreat. Once he was gone Hunter turned to Nell.

'I'm sorry about yesterday.'

Her mouth parted in surprise and she shook her head.

'No, it was my fault. I shouldn't have pried. You had every right to warn me off. I just… You have nothing to apologise for.'

'Yes, I do. I am not accustomed to speaking about Tim and I reacted badly. Not even my aunts know everything, just the two men who were with me in France. I wasn't angry at you and I don't really think you were meddling. Forgive me.'

She shook her head again.

'I knew it wasn't really at me and it was foolish to expect you to talk to me about something so precious to you. As you said, we hardly know each other. I don't particularly like talking with people about what hurts me, either. Perhaps because I already told you things I only told my closest friends and I wanted to help and I didn't know how and I made a mull of it; I know it was presumptuous of me. Do you forgive me?'

Hunter reminded himself he was in a civilised drawing room under the very watchful and hostile eyes of his hosts. He had no idea what to do with the fist clenching around his lungs, but doing any of the things the rest of his body was clamouring for was strictly impossible. He took the book and closed it, allowing himself a light brush of his hand along her fingers, trying to ignore the dangerous heating in his groin. He was allowing this aggravating lust to dictate his actions again, but at the moment he was too unsettled to care. Besides, he had to tell her he would be returning to London and he preferred to do that without an audience.

'I hear the Welbecks have a very fine Stubbs of Diomed. Have you ever seen it?'

'Yes, it's in the green room,' she replied as he drew her to her feet, the telltale tinge of colour filling out her lips, and he held himself from tightening his hold on her hand as he led her towards the green room.

'Do you like it?' she asked, looking at the painting. 'Like what?'

The confusion in her eyes turned to laughter.

'You don't care much for art, I gather. Why did you want to see it, then?'

'I never said I wanted to see it. I am more interested in the green room.'

She glanced around with a frown.

'Why? Is there something special here?'

'Two very rare commodities. Privacy and you.'

She stilled.

'I see. No one has ever called me a commodity before. I am not certain I appreciate being categorised with corn and turnips.'

'The schoolmistress should know most terms have multiple meanings. In this case as something of value or necessity.'

'It's not that I am not impressed, but don't you ever become weary of always having a suave answer ready?'

Hunter considered various less-than-polite responses to his betrothed's impertinence.

'I certainly do if my efforts aren't being appreciated. I recall a very direct request that I flirt with you.'

'And you do it beautifully, but I think I was wrong to ask it of you. It is rather like harnessing your chestnuts to a gig.'

'Good God, woman! That must be the most insulting compliment I have ever received. You might try for a touch of suavity yourself.'

Her face lit with a surprisingly shy smile and he stepped forward and stopped. He had come here to tell her he was leaving, not to settle the debate in his mind whether this was just a girl to be handled lightly or a woman to be seduced to the point of mutual combustion.

'I sent a letter to your father yesterday care of Buxted.'

The laughter drained out of her eyes and she raised her chin.

'What did you tell him?'

'That you are here and the key points you and I have already discussed. That the three of us need to resolve this issue. Reasonably.'

'I see.'

He moved back towards the picture, not looking at her.

'I think it best that you stay here and I return to London until he arrives. My being here...complicates matters. Besides, you don't need me here.'

That sentence had sounded reasonable enough when he had formulated it in his mind. There was no reason to feel just as he did when he woke from his nightmares, shaky and emptied. It was ridiculous to feel guilty about abandoning... He wasn't abandoning her. This was precisely where she wanted to be with precisely whom she wanted to be. Simply because he was aching to bed her didn't mean he should subvert her whole life and his for a bodily urge. He was neither ready to assume a burden like her nor willing to expose his weakness to her, and that was precisely what would happen if he allowed himself to think with his body rather than his mind.

'I see,' she said again, but her voice sounded distant.

There, it was done. Time for a swift exit.

'Perhaps I should stay until your father arrives. I don't want you to face the worst of his anger alone.'

She shivered or shook her head, he couldn't tell, but when she spoke her voice was clear.

'There is no need for that. He can't hurt me any more. You shouldn't stay because of that.'

The key now was to walk out and let her proceed

with her dreams, however flawed. She would probably discover soon enough that Phyllida wouldn't let go of Welbeck that easily, perhaps even less easily now that he was hankering after another, and very wealthy, woman. Phyllida would consider it piquant to deck herself in jewels purchased with another woman's money. It wasn't his business. He was probably being petty because the thought of anyone…

'Won't you stay for the jumping and the fête tomorrow?' she asked suddenly. 'It's the best day of the fair. I hate the thought that you feel you must leave because of me. It's just one more day.'

Just one more day. He shouldn't; he could do a great deal of damage in a day.

'Perhaps…one more day. But I would think you would rather remove me from the field now that you are doing so well with Welbeck, no?'

'I'm not quite that shallow. I don't know how to thank you for—'

'Whatever you do, don't start thanking me!'

She looked up, startled, but then she smiled.

'I forget sometimes how sensitive you are.'

'That's more like it. I was wondering how long before you started abusing me again.'

'I was trying to thank you!' She laughed.

'Your gratitude, like your compliments, leaves a great deal to be desired. Your abuse, on the other hand, provides a perfect excuse to punish you a little in turn.'

He moved towards her. He was surely allowed one more taste…

'That isn't punishment.' Her voice, quick, breathless, and both mischievous and touched with longing, cleaved through him and whatever shreds of suavity he still possessed incinerated in the heat that rose through him. God help him, he was blushing; he could feel the singe of fire in his face, everywhere. It was wrong. He had no business taking this any further when he had no intention to follow through. If he did one hundredth of what he wanted to do to her he would probably both terrify her and end up trapped...

He backed her against the wall and the silver-grey of her eyes darkened in an invitation as clear as the flush on her lips and cheeks and the arch of her back as her hips met his for a moment before pressing back, just enough to make him painfully aware of how hard he was. These teasing tastes were moving quickly from the realm of playful pleasure to sheer torture.

'Are you sure you haven't done this before?' he asked, tracing the line of her cheek with his knuckles, his voice husky and strange even to his own ears. 'You are far too good at this.'

'Mrs Petheridge always told me to insist on employing the best instructors if I wanted to excel.' Her own voice sank to the melodic rasp that did so much damage to his control. How on earth had she managed to make the mention of her headmistress erotic?

He gave in and sank against her, gathering her to him, moulding his hands down the dip of her back and to the soft round curve of her behind. He groaned, his hands tightening on the pliant flesh, and she rose against him, her hands twisting into the lapels of his coat, her hips arching against his again, and he held her there, trying to remind himself why it was not a good idea to toss up his virgin betrothed's skirts in the unlocked and very exposed drawing room of his hosts and discover if she was as damp as he was hard.

She pushed away so abruptly it took him a moment to notice the door opening.

'Hunter,' Phyllida Melkinson's silken voice admonished from the doorway. 'Not the hackneyed "come see the painting" ploy. So *déclassé*. You are usually much more original.'

Hunter resisted a powerful urge to toss her out, under no illusion she had just happened to enter the green room by chance.

'I think you have mistaken the room, Phyllida. We left your quarry in the main drawing room.'

She unfurled her fan with a smile, her eyes shining bright blue victory above the ivory sticks.

'Under the circumstances don't you think it wise to revert to calling me by my title, my dear Lord Hunter?'

Hunter held Nell's arm as she tried to pull away. He was definitely off form to have made such a foolish error.

'I was just taking a leaf from your book and leaving your poor husband out of it. Now if you don't mind, we are busy.'

'So I see. Appreciating the livestock. Such fine sturdy beasts, don't you think, Miss Tilney? I do believe I heard Lord Welbeck mention that you were wont to ride astride as a child? Very daring. I am almost jealous.'

'Of what, Lady Melkinson?' Nell asked and Hunter felt the tension in her arm. 'I would have thought you well versed in riding all forms of sturdy beasts.'

The fan dropped to dangle by its ribbon from Lady Melkinson's wrist and Hunter, too, slackened his hold in shock and amusement at the unexpected vulgarity of Nell's comment. But Phyllida recovered swiftly.

'Oh, most amusing. I see all those years in the stables have given you a certain finesse, my dear. Perhaps you might be a match for Hunter after all. He is quite worthwhile, even if one has to share. Oh, don't bite my head off as I see you wish to, Hunter. I shall remove my presence so you can continue your campaign to secure the heiress, but really, my dear Miss Tilney, I assure you you have no need to buy yourself a husband as your equally horse-mad mama apparently did. You do see such alliances do not always prosper...'

Her words petered out as Nell tugged out of Hunter's hold and took three long strides towards her.

'You will not mention my mother, or I will...'

Lady Melkinson shrugged, but there was a flicker of fear in her eyes and when she spoke again she had put a *chaise longue* between them.

'Or you will what? Really, there is no need for such histrionics. Everyone knows Tilney married your mother so he could expand his stables, no pun intended.'

'Or I will have a tearful word with your husband about how you are throwing yourself at my betrothed,' Nell continued with resolution, the words grinding out between her teeth, but Hunter could hear the quiver of tension in her voice and moved towards her. 'Downstairs gossip has it that Lord Melkinson has already threatened to curtail your pin money after a certain scandal in London. If I hear one more mention of my mother's name on your lips, I will happily add wood to that fire and you might have to make do with whatever baubles you can cozen from your lovers. So I suggest you watch your words carefully from now on, you little...'

'Nell?'

They all turned to the door where Charles stood staring in shock.

'What on earth is going on here?'

Lady Melkinson sank onto the *chaise longue* with a small sob and drew out a lace handkerchief from her reticule, pressing it to her eyes.

'I merely remarked that Miss Tilney shouldn't be here unattended and she... I have never been so insulted in my life.'

'Somehow I doubt that,' Nell muttered, and Hunter crossed his arms, trying not to smile.

Charles entered the room, his hands raised placatingly.

'I suggest we all return to the drawing room. It really is quite improper for you to be here alone with Lord Hunter, Nell, engaged or not.'

'Please, Mr Welbeck,' Phyllida said prettily. 'There is no need to chastise Miss Tilney. She is clearly unused to polite society.'

Nell rounded on her.

'I may be unused to polite society, but I am very used to spoilt girls like you who think they can manipulate people around them with impunity. Certainly in the lower forms of the school where I work. As for you, Charles, I will accept rebukes regarding my conduct from your mother, not from you or Lady Melkinson. I certainly won't remain silent while she insults my mother.'

'I am certain Lady Melkinson did not intend to insult—'

'Are you, Charles?' Nell interrupted. 'On what precisely do you base that certainty?'

Charles's glance flickered over to Lady Melkinson, who dabbed her handkerchief to the corner of her eye. He held his hand out towards Nell, smiling.

'If she did, then naturally it was most improper and

I will ensure she will not do so again. You were right to chastise me as well, but I really did mean it for the best. Won't you please come in to supper with me, Nell?'

Hunter wondered that Welbeck had not realised how telling his words about Phyllida were. He could see Nell noticed the familiarity immediately and her mouth bowed, her eyes darkening. She shook her head.

'You are very kind, but I have the headache. I will ask for something to be brought to my room. Good evening.'

Welbeck moved towards her, but she evaded him and left the room.

Nell refrained from taking the stairs two at a time, but only just barely. Clearly the same considerations didn't apply to Hunter because he caught up with her halfway up and she wished it wouldn't be considered childish to shove him back down. First he raged at her, and then he disappeared for a whole day only to turn up and pull the rug out from under her with that apology, then to tell her he was leaving her to her fate. And after he had unsettled her once again with his flirting and his embrace he hadn't even come to her defence when that woman, who had also probably once been one of his endless succession of mistresses, tore strips off her. He was the very last person on earth she wanted to speak to right now.

'Leave me alone!'

'Presently.'

He took her arm and she tugged it away abruptly and nearly stumbled on the last step. He took it again, steadying her.

'It is a bit late to be offering assistance when I no longer need it!' she snapped, turning to glare at him.

He frowned down at her.

'If you had needed my help, believe me, I would have come to your aid. But you didn't.'

'Yes, I did. She just sat there play-acting in the most unconvincing way and he believed her...'

'Well, that's her stock-in-trade, isn't it? It's not surprising she does it well.'

'She made a fool of me.'

'No, she didn't. You were magnificent. You won that round hands down and she knows it.'

'What on earth are you talking about? I ranted like a demented schoolteacher and she sat there like a stricken kitten. I know you are just desperate to wash your hands of this whole affair, but you could have done something other than stand there smiling!'

'You had her against the ropes—can't you see that? That was precisely why she had to resort to such a cheap trick. You most certainly didn't need my help.'

'I may not have needed it, but I wanted it. Even if you don't want to marry me, I thought you were my friend.' She felt very foolish and young as the words came out, even more so because she was so raw and confused. Everything was moving too fast. She had been racked by guilt all day at hurting Hunter. She hadn't even been able to apologise because he had disappeared to Wilton in the morning. It had been almost a relief to have Charles seek her out during the day and she had even felt the warmth in his eyes was sincere and not just a manifestation of his usual offhand cheerfulness.

When Hunter entered the drawing room in the afternoon she had just hoped for an opportunity to apologise. His own apology had shaken her and probably contributed to her willingness to sink into the disturbing but increasingly familiar warmth of flirting with him, seeking to erase the traces of tension between them. But then that woman had to ruin it by practically parading both him and Charles like possessions, confident that all it took was for her to bat her lids in their direction and they would come running. Hunter's words, that she had had the upper hand, were ludicrous.

It was always hard to read Hunter's face; sometimes it was the light-hearted humour or the teasing that served as a mask, but now, like those painful and unsettling moments in her room, it was a forbidding blankness that came between them and reminded her he was far from the easy-going rake people thought him to be. She was beginning to distinguish shapes in the dark shadows in his eyes. She could see conflicting currents of anger and compassion and even resentment. When he spoke his voice was without inflection, but the calm unravelled as he spoke.

'If I had felt you needed to be saved from someone who could do you real damage, believe me, I would have had their face in the dust before they got within hailing distance of you. Why the devil do you think I made it a condition of the engagement that you board at that school and never return to Tilney? But interceding between you and that doxy would be more of an insult to you than to her. Four years ago I saw you take down a tyrant and, however hard it may have been, don't tell me you don't look back at that moment with pride. Now tell me you don't feel good about not being the one who collapsed in fake tears on the sofa.'

Her hand closed tightly on the knob of the banister.

'What do you mean you made it a condition?'

Chagrin flickered in his tawny eyes.

'That's not the point. The point is...'

'You forced Father to let me stay in Keswick year-round?'

He hesitated.

'I thought you wanted to? Was that wrong?'

She pressed her hand to her forehead and continued down the hallway, feeling rather dazed, all her anger against him fizzling. Present and past were all shifting and rearranging and her excuse of a headache looked likely to become a reality. With each passing day it was even stranger that her memory of Hunter's presence at that pivotal moment four years ago should be so tenuous. Her future had changed during those two days in so many ways and this man had been instrumental in most of them and she hadn't even known or thought twice about him except to occasionally cringe that she had disgraced herself so thoroughly in front of the handsome, troubled young man who had been so good with Petra.

He had been right about her. Again. As embarrassed and shaky as she was, it *was* a victory of sorts to stand up to someone so beautiful and experienced, and though she might have wanted a knight in shining armour or two to leap to her defence, she had done moderately well on her own. In fact, she had done quite well against someone with skills as finely honed as Lady Melkinson.

She stopped and turned to him.

'I don't know how to thank you, for everything.'

'I didn't say that to be thanked.'

His frown deepened, making her think of a proud little boy who had just been told how adorable he was and was finding the compliment vastly distasteful.

'I know, but I'm grateful anyway. You can't even begin to understand how much that changed everything for me. I was to come back to Tilney for good the following year and it would have been hell. Staying with Mrs Petheridge was one of the best things that ever happened to me.'

'Don't exaggerate my part in it. It involved no effort on my part, so all this gratitude is very cheaply bought. Besides, I think you underestimated your ability to deal with your aunt even if you had returned to Tilney.'

'Perhaps you are right. It wasn't just that one night, I was growing out of her power anyway, but it certainly was much more enjoyable staying in Keswick than waging battle, successful or not, at Tilney. But if you wish to cling to your selfish-rake façade and reject any token of gratitude, I shan't insist.'

'Don't start deluding yourself it's just a façade, sweetheart. Just to prove it I think I will accept a token of your gratitude after all. But not in the middle of the corridor.'

Before she could respond he pulled her along and opened a door by the servants' stairwell.

'The linen closet? Really?' She laughed nervously as much with anticipation as the fear of being discovered again. Her mind might be plagued by uncertainty and upheaval, but her body had a simpler view on matters and it was already tingling and heating as his arms rose to lean against the shelves on either side of her, caging her in.

'A very useful room, love. One should always know where they are located.'

'Someone might...'

'No servants will be engaged in changing the linen in the evening. Too busy with preparations for supper.'

'Also useful information,' she murmured, wondering why she wasn't more outraged. But it had been a difficult day and right now she just wanted…something. Something wholly for herself and without thought of consequence. She should want Charles here with her, but it was hard to imagine Charles in a linen closet. It was hard to imagine anything at all with the heat of Hunter's body seeping into her even though he hadn't touched her yet. She wanted him to. To start with his amazingly beautiful lips, that carved line around the lower lip was magnificent, as beautiful as any statue. She had to admit he had a finer mouth than Charles, but maybe that was because she had already felt Hunter's on hers and she knew to her core how wonderful it felt, so it wasn't fair to compare.

Especially when it was already on hers. Oh, heaven…

It felt as beautiful as it looked, she decided as she closed her eyes. Its beauty was spreading through her like dye in water, a hue of its own, colouring her as it went, making her beautiful. Powerful.

Her palms were cool against his cheekbones as she slid her fingers slowly into his hair, gathering sensations as they went, so sensitive she could feel that little scar puckered against her palm. She slid her mouth from his, rising on tiptoe to trace with her lips the line her hands had marked, the lean plane of his cheek, the scrape of stubble along his jaw.

When she lingered on that whitish L his breath shuddered in and out. Her body echoed that shudder, moving towards his heat, moulding to his length as her mouth was moulding itself to the ridge of his jaw just beside his ear. She was back in that wonderful *sleep-wake-buzz* realm except that she wanted more.

Apparently so did Hunter because his passive acceptance of her exploration gave way. His arms left the shelf, one hand tangling in her hair and the other wrapping around her back, pulling her even more firmly against him. Pins clinked on the stone floor and she felt the weight of her hair slide and roll off her shoulders, then the tug and pull as his hands sank into it, tilting her head back. His eyes were gathering all the last glimmers of light from the high window above them and turning them to tawny flames.

'Nell... I want to see you with just your hair between us...'

His voice rubbed against her like rough velvet and her legs pressed together involuntarily as if it had scraped against her just there. The thought of her hair, sliding pale and silky against the warm tan skin she had glimpsed in the stable yard, trailing down over his waist, his hips. The same hips which were now pressing against her, hard and bulging and rigid as a real statue. It was surely unthinkable to actually want to see his hips, to see his everything, to bare him as he was baring her, slipping the dress from her shoulder.

Her skin danced as his mouth moved down her neck, tasting, licking, lashing at her nerves and dragging little moans from her she couldn't silence. She wanted closer; she wanted to tangle her body with his, merge it, lose it.

She wanted more.

'Hunter, please...' That wasn't her voice; her voice could never sound like that. But it had a clear effect on Hunter. His body surged against her, pressing her back against the piles of linen, between her spread legs, his fingers biting into her thighs as his mouth opened on hers, moving from coaxing to consuming.

He was devouring her, burning her, absorbing even her breath. She didn't need to breathe. She gave back everything until he groaned as well, pulling away a little, his hands denying his withdrawal by tightening around her, and then he gave way and was kissing her again with an abandon that she instinctively knew was out of character and she revelled in the gift of it.

He might not be a knight in shining armour, but her body felt revered as his lips seared and teased and feasted on hers until it started happening again, that rising of her body, a gathering into a powerful, throbbing unity telling her there was so much more and she needed it now. She was so hot it was becoming unbearable; she needed to do something. She dragged his body towards her and the moment the hard muscles of his thighs pressed against her the chaotic heat gathered into a fireball between her legs.

'I don't know what to do,' she moaned, squirming against him, and his arms tightened around her, pressing his mouth to the soft skin of her neck, his voice shaky with laughter or something else.

'Yes, you do. God help me, you do.'

She didn't care if he was laughing because his mouth was suckling at the skin there and now the fireball had grown and she could feel it in the tingling, aching tips of her breasts. Was it mad to want his mouth there as well, doing just that, tasting, sucking? She must be mad because that was her hand taking his and pressing it there. Oh, heaven, that felt right…

'This is madness. We can't…' he groaned even as his hand tightened on her breast, his thumb finding and brushing that ache into a cascade of fireworks along her nerves.

She was about to argue that they not only could but must, when their combined weight proved too much for the shelf behind her and with a creak it gave way and tilted. Luckily the snowy mountain of linen hit the ground before them, but Nell's backside still struck the padded ground with enough force to wake her. They remained motionless for a moment, Hunter's arm still around her, his other braced on a pile of pillowcases.

Her eyes met Hunter's and she covered her mouth to stifle a laugh. Immediately the lines at the corners of his eyes crinkled in response.

'I told you a linen closet was a bad idea,' he whispered, his head canted as they listened to see if someone had overheard the fracas.

She smiled guiltily and reluctantly pushed him away.

'We need to put the linen back.'

'We need to return you safely to your room. You look as tumbled as the sheets.'

She didn't know if it was possible to flush further, but she certainly felt her temperature rise.

'We can't leave it like this. Apparently linen closets have distinct disadvantages. Has this ever happened to you before?'

His arms tightened on her as he drew her to her feet and for a moment his mouth settled lightly on the curve of her neck before he bent to pick up a pile of sheets that had somehow remained folded.

'Since this is my first time to ever make use of a linen closet, I have to say it hasn't.'

She swiftly picked up another pile.

'I thought you said…'

'Knowing where they are doesn't mean I have made use of them before. Now I know why it is better to employ one's own rooms. There, that looks almost respectable. Come, we should return you to yours before our luck runs out. You need to rest before the fête tomorrow.'

He was clearly in control of himself now, both the passionate lover and the vulnerable boy tucked away as neatly as the piles of linen had been before they had tumbled them. So she held back all manners of answers and thoughts and allowed him to lead her to her room and push her in gently but firmly, closing the door between them.

She stared at its blank surface. She had no idea what she would have done if he had chosen to stay. She hardly recognised herself any longer. How had she allowed this man, this…rake, to so undermine her plans and in a matter of mere days? He had just told her he was leaving; he had told her what he thought about passion being short-lived, and surely he lived his life like it was a game for him, one long wild hunt, without aim or object but his own pleasure. Even now he was, to all intents and purposes, betraying another woman, even if she was his mistress and not his wife. Somewhere in London was the beautiful and experienced Lady Felton, awaiting his return. At no point had he made pretensions of any deeper feelings towards her than lust. What she had always wanted from Charles was utterly different—she wanted companionship and trust. She wanted to feel safe. With Hunter she felt about as safe as a cork bobbing in a stormy sea and he made no pretension of offering anything more.

She slumped down on the bed. It was no excuse that this was all new to her or that Hunter was so very skilled. She had to remember that learning how to flirt and discovering her enjoyment of…of physical contact was all well and good, but it was not the object of her visit to Welbeck. The only problem, she thought as she turned wearily and went to ring for Betsy, was that having started down this path, she was no longer quite certain how to stop.

Chapter Eleven

Peony's powerful body shook with the thumping of hooves as they approached the fence in the middle of the jumping course. It was high for a horse of Peony's size, but Nell had her measure and breathed in, checking the mare's headlong speed and feeling the mare's muscles gather, and then they left the ground behind. Everything fell away—Hunter, Charles, the crowd watching the jumps, even her own treacherous body and confused mind. For those few precious seconds she knew exactly who she was.

She took the jar of the landing easily, laughing in pleasure as she guided the mare towards the exit. Hunter was standing there waiting for her and she let him help her down, forgetting her embarrassment and awareness.

'I can see why this is your favourite day of the fair,' Hunter said as they went to lean on the fence to watch the other jumpers. 'You made all us mere mortals look half-asleep. Especially on that last jump.'

'Nonsense. You took the black you were riding over with inches to spare.'

He turned to her with his half-mocking smile.

'Placating me again, Nell? I remember that about you even four years ago. I felt like a four-year-old being measured for my first pony. It was a very humbling experience.'

She flushed, but couldn't help laughing.

'Oh, dear, I'm so sorry. It's true I can be very condescending about the way other people are with horses. I do try not to be. My only excuse is that it is the only thing I am good at.'

'Just a middling teacher, then?' he asked politely.

She frowned.

'I am an excellent teacher. Mrs Petheridge says she has never had girls actually asking for more Latin and history lessons before I started teaching.'

'I see. And we've already established you are a precocious pupil. Therefore your excuse for being rude is hereby revoked.'

She considered him, trying not to smile.

'That was sneakily done.'

'I'm learning from an excellent teacher. I've yet to meet anyone who makes her insults sound so reasonable and her compliments so suspect.'

'I'm only like that with you, because you don't seem to mind.'

'That comment is a case in point. If you had been a man you would undoubtedly have been a solicitor. In case you were wondering, that was a knowingly suspect compliment.'

'It was still a compliment and I shall take it as such, thank you.'

'You're the only person I know who would think being likened to a solicitor is a compliment. They're just one step above that hawker over there selling horse quackery in glass bottles.'

Nell looked over towards one of the fête stalls already set up, this one exhibiting a colourful array of horse tonics.

'I used to spend all my pin money at the stalls in under an hour. I even bought a most horrid-smelling potion because that hawker promised it was a miracle cure for spavins.'

'I take that back, then; no solicitor would be so gullible. I wouldn't pour those on the grass, let alone down one of my horses' throats,' he said.

She laughed, about to respond in kind when she spotted Charles. He was standing with his father and Lord and Lady Melkinson by the enclosure, and with a strange sense of fatality she realised she didn't want him to see her. She turned back to Hunter.

'I think I would like to go back to the house and rest before the fête. Would you mind walking me back?'

Hunter nodded and took her arm, leading her through the stalls. He hadn't missed the way she had turned away from the sight of Welbeck standing near Phyllida. Surely, however painful it was, she was finally realising the man was utterly wrong for her? She couldn't possibly cling to her belief she cared for Welbeck while responding with such abandon to another man's touch.

Her problem was that she had the body and soul of the most gifted of lovers. Or rather, it was his problem. Every time he thought he was in control of the situation she kept swinging him between desire and pique and confusion with a skill that would have done a court flirt proud. It didn't help that her dark blue riding habit fit her lean figure like a glove, making his fingers itch to bare what lay beneath so he could finally satisfy his curiosity as to how she would look covered with nothing but the shimmering silk of her hair.

He opened his mouth to say something, anything to distract him from his thoughts, when a burly man came around a stall stacked high with apples and stopped in surprise.

'My lord!'

It took Hunter a moment to place the weathered face, but the name came before he even remembered it.

'Mr Pratchett!'

The man's face creased into a smile that brought to life a multitude of wrinkles and craters.

'What are you doing here all the way from Bristol, Mr Pratchett?'

'My daughter married into these parts, my lord, and my wife and I are here to see our first grandson. Pardon the liberty, sir, but when I saw it was you I had to come and speak. About Jamie.'

Hunter tensed, waiting. It shouldn't matter. He knew not everyone could be reached. It shouldn't grab at him like this. It was already emptying him, preparing him not to feel.

'He married early summer. A fine girl who never minded about his leg. There's to be a child come spring. If it's a boy they want to name him Timothy, if it's no offence to you, sir. He said as it was those talks with you in his dark moments and looking at that picture as kept him afloat until he reached land, so to speak. I don't mean to take liberties, but my wife and I know matters might have run a very different course but for Hope House and we're right grateful.'

'It's no offence. Tim...Timothy would have been honoured. Tell Jamie that. My congratulations as well.'

'I will, sir. Good day to you, miss.'

He nodded to them and disappeared between the stalls.

'He was talking about the portrait of your brother in the memory room, wasn't he?' Nell asked.

He had almost forgotten she was standing there. He was so tense he was certain she saw the danger, but she just waited for his answer. *It's none of your business and it has nothing to do with us.* He formed the words. Carefully, so they would be unequivocal, absolutely clear.

'Who told you about the memory room?'

'Your aunts showed me. That was how I knew he had passed away just before you came to Tilney four years ago.'

'He didn't "pass away". He killed himself.'

He had expected to shock her with his bluntness, but though her brows drew together, she just nodded and he found he was still talking.

'He was barely twenty-one. He drank a whole bottle of laudanum. I don't even know where he found it. I kept all the medicines in a locked cupboard in my room because he was already taking too much. But he was always in pain and he had nightmares and he was afraid to sleep. They had taken off his left arm because the wounds wouldn't heal and there were so many broken bones in his other hand they thought of taking it off as well, to stop the pain, but he wouldn't let them. He said his left hand still hurt him as much even though it wasn't there, so there was no point. He wouldn't go outside and he wouldn't talk to anyone but me and Nurse. My mother couldn't bear seeing him in pain and he couldn't bear seeing her suffer, so she stayed away. He had attacks where he would just sit there, white and shaking, and there was nothing I could do, not even hold his hand because it hurt him too much. He couldn't even escape into sleep. He kept dreaming the man who tortured him had found him again. I wish the English hadn't shot that vicious bastard so I could have done it myself.'

He dragged himself to a halt. There was no reason to tell her any of this. There were only two people in the world who knew and that was only because he would... he *had* trusted them with his life. What would this little girl know about anything, with her sheltered life and unformed dreams? He must be a little mad to be telling her any of this. She would probably run for the hills now and would be right to do so. Charles Welbeck would certainly never subject her to such an assault.

He waited for her to turn away. The last thing he expected was for her to take his hand and lead him out of the crowd towards the wooded path to Welbeck, drawing him with her like a child or one of her schoolchildren. He wanted to hold his ground, but his feet followed his hand. She didn't speak until they had reached the place where the path split off towards the pond by the lower paddocks.

'I wondered how you knew so well how to help me that day at Tilney Hall. You were so kind without appearing to be. That's a very rare skill. I'm sorry it was so dearly bought.'

He looked out over the pond, still trying to find the resolve to shake off her hand, feeling more and more like a child being taken on an airing for their own good. Except that it did feel good. Side by side with the usual roiling guilt and pain was the calm of moving through fields and paths that were as removed from devastation and pain as anything could be.

'It didn't work with him.'

'Didn't it?'

She stopped to look at him and he met her gaze for a moment before looking back out on the dark green water with its edges feathered by surrounding willows. The image of Tim's pain-racked face stretching into a sweet smile as he came out of an attack and his words, hoarse and unsteady, thanking him for 'being there'.

'I don't think I could bear anyone else, Gabe. Some day, maybe, but not just yet. I'm sorry…'

'*Some day, maybe*' hadn't come, but Hunter was free now. Except he wasn't really free. The person he had loved most in the world, who had been his to care for since they were boys, no longer existed. He had lost a limb himself that day and, like Tim's non-existent arm, it still ached just as fiercely and brutally shattered his nights.

'You were just three years older than I.' Nell frowned.

'What?'

'I just realised. You weren't much older than I when you had to care for him.'

'So?'

'That's very young for such a burden.'

'It has nothing to do with age. It has to do with accountability.'

'I see. Is that why you founded Hope House?'

'I don't believe it. My aunts told you that?' He was truly shocked. Amelia and Sephy knew they were never to mention his and his friends' involvement to anyone. It was no one's business. How had she managed to drag that out of them in one day?

'No, *you* did just now.' Her sudden smile glinted and he didn't know whether to feel like a fool at being tricked so easily or indulge the need to bask in the admiration he read in her eyes. He pulled his hand away.

'It's guilt money. For failing him. As you know I can afford it without even noticing.'

She nodded and took his arm.

'I know. And sitting with Mr Pratchett's son means nothing, either. Come, let's go see Meecham's grey. I heard it arrived last night.'

He followed, but didn't answer, his tension lasting all the way to the stables. He should never have told her anything. This was precisely why he had always insisted on keeping his part in Hope House as quiet as possible. He didn't want people prying and feeling sorry for him. At the stable doors he stopped. He was letting this girl manage him like a blasted nurse.

'Not all the world's ills can be salved with horses, you know,' he said, detaching his hand.

'Very few, I imagine. Come, I hear Courage is well over sixteen hands and very good-natured for a stallion.'

She opened the stable door and didn't wait for him to follow but he did anyway, telling himself it would be churlish not to see the horse now he was here; it would be to give too much importance to his discomfort or admit that any discomfort existed at all.

Nell crouched by the enormous grey, wondering what she was thinking to have dragged Hunter here when it was obvious the last thing he wanted was to look at the horse. At least being here was calming her, if not him. The urge to comfort and encompass which was always part of her existence at the school was out of place here, but she didn't know what else to do. Hunter certainly wouldn't appreciate if she did what she really wanted to do, which was wrap her arms around him and hold him until he softened.

She breathed in the familiar smells of the stables and disregarded her unladylike position and the straw that caught at her skirts. For a stallion Courage was very well behaved and merely whickered and turned his head to nuzzle her hair as she examined him.

'He's sprained his fetlock in the past few months, hasn't he? What happened?'

The dismay on Meecham's chubby face was so obvious she wished she had been more diplomatic. Meecham was a serious and conscientious breeder; of course he wasn't hiding the mild injury on purpose.

'Three months ago. George, my brother, tried to jump him. I thought he had completely healed. I never...'

She smiled reassuringly. 'I don't think there is lasting damage; there is no swelling I can feel. He just reacted a bit differently when I touched him there. He is a beautiful horse, Lord Meecham.'

Meecham's shoulders visibly relaxed.

'He is, isn't he? It's rather a shame to sell him, but I have Golden Boy and Spangles for breeding already and it is such a shame to geld him. You did say you were looking for a grey, didn't you, Hunter?'

Hunter, who had stood silently throughout her inspection, nodded and moved towards the stallion with the same calm and fluid movement she remembered from all those years ago, showing none of the tension that had flared in him just moments ago.

You could tell so much from the way someone approached animals. It wasn't just that, like the stallion, Hunter was an exquisite specimen of his breed. As she followed Hunter's progress, the slide of his hands over the silky, slightly dappled coat, the way his long fingers gently eased back the horse's mane and ran down the revealed neck, the beautiful grey stallion faded into the background. It was hard to look away from Hunter's hands; they suited him so well, sleek and powerful, and it was easy to see why women would want those hands on them. It was hard not to react to their calm and purposeful exploration, to imagine it was her own skin being skimmed and tested.

She forced herself to turn away, but the image lingered—of his strong profile outlined against the horse's shoulder, his mouth uncharacteristically soft as he murmured something soothing to the horse as he tested the injured fetlock. The stable suddenly felt too hot and oppressive and she wished someone would open the doors wider and let in a breeze.

'You are a beauty, aren't you?' Hunter said lightly to the grey before moving back towards them. 'I'll take him out for a ride, but as far as I'm concerned you can name your price, Meech.'

The words released Nell and she half-sighed and moved towards a mare stabled by the door as the two men began discussing terms, steadying herself as she stroked her, drawing calm from the familiar motions and sensations.

It made no sense, the way she kept reacting to his presence. How was it possible when it was Charles whom she had loved for years? When it was Charles who had always made her feel flustered and full of hope? Not that that was how Hunter made her feel, which should have reassured her, but it didn't. It was more inexplicable, uncomfortable. There was nothing magical about it. It was too earthy and low and it worked its way up from the ground like an encroaching vine. She felt restless and turned inside out and needing to act. To do something. Take something. Touch him.

'Shall we?'

His voice was so close it sounded as though he was speaking inside her, his very voice had become part of her. It ran rough and warm through her, like brandy. She almost asked 'shall we what?' until she realised that would be a deliberate provocation.

'Shall we what?'

He didn't answer immediately. Then he placed his hands on the stall door behind her, bracketing her body. The anger was gone, but this was worse, because this look was the one that had sent her heart thudding and tightened its merciless coil around her last night. His eyes were molten honey and amber, spilling heat over her. She forgot where they were, that Meecham was a few yards away fussing over Courage, that stable hands and guests might come by at any moment.

Then abruptly he took her hand and drew her out of the stable and down the path leading into the trees. She followed, matching her stride to his long legs, stumbling as they turned off the path and into a tiny clearing hedged by stunted oaks.

There was no pause, no discussion, not even a warning before he turned her and captured her mouth with his.

It was raw, punishing. His hands untied and pushed back her bonnet and dug deep into her hair, locking her to him while his mouth took possession of hers. It wasn't a seduction; it was a demand. It should have scared her, but it just opened a new door. If he could demand, so could she. She met the thrust of his tongue against hers, wrapped her arms around the hard expanse of his back under his coat and pressed herself against him. It felt so good. Surely this meeting of her body with the hard surfaces of his was her natural state. Almost. There was too much between them, her skin chafed at her dress, at his coat and waistcoat. She wanted to be as bare, as immediate as her mouth under his, to take and be taken as she was.

'You're driving me insane, Nell,' he muttered against her mouth, his hands skimming over her body, shaping curves and dips and reflecting the urgency and impatience that was plaguing her. She wanted something. She *needed* something. The thought that he felt it too, that she had the power to do this to someone else…to Hunter…

The image that had been tantalising her, of touching his warm skin, became a need as urgent as breathing. She dragged his shirt from his buckskins and with a moan of relief spread her hands as far up his back as his clothes allowed. His skin was heated silk over muscles that bunched and shifted as she caressed him.

She needed to feel him. Soon it would be over, he would leave and she had to remember what it felt like to explore, to remember this freedom and this sense of control. She could even feel his breathing, shallow and unsteady as he started drawing back. The thought that he might stop made her slide one hand around his nape, grasping his silky dark hair in her fist and anchoring him as she pressed her mouth back to his. She wasn't done yet, not even close.

There were limits. No one could expect him to be in control when her body was all but glued to his, one hand like a burning brand on his bare back and her lips drinking him in, coaxing his soul out with sweetness and fire.

He never should have marched her out of the stables like a troglodyte dragging his woman off to a cave. But right now that was precisely what he felt like, reduced to a pulsing mass of need without brain or common sense.

Oh, how he wanted her. She was becoming a compulsion. How he was going to stop himself from stripping her, touching her, tasting her everywhere... It was beyond him.

He cradled her face in his hands and gave all his attention to that lush, delicious lower lip, mapping it, caressing it with lips and tongue, following it inward, outlining its corners where her smile bloomed. She stilled under his exploration. He could feel her arms shaking slightly but otherwise she remained motionless as he took possession of her mouth. He would make it utterly his; no one had ever known it as he did, made it tremble like this, made her shake with need like a racehorse at the gate, ready to surge when the restraints were dropped. He wanted to feel that leap against him, but he held her there, tense and needy and waiting for him, as if holding her at bay would keep him safe, keep them both safe.

She would make the most incandescent of mistresses if only she wasn't a damn innocent. It felt as though it would kill him at the moment to stop kissing her, to put away her long elegant body when all he wanted to do was drag her down onto the grass between the trees and leave her as bare as nature and pay the same attention to every inch of skin, visible and hidden, as he was to her mouth.

He had never entered an embrace wondering if he would be able to stop, knowing there was a point he was fast approaching that would challenge his control. He had told her she was testing his sanity, but it was worse than that. She kept encroaching on boundaries he had erected before he had even understood what the word meant. He had loved his family, but he had never needed them. It had been his job to be needed and that was fine with him. It was power, being the centre of the universe. He didn't *need* anyone; that was anathema to who he was. He had had more women than he felt was quite fair to remember and he had enjoyed them mightily, but he had never once mistook lust for need. He gave, he took, he didn't need.

This wasn't need either, he told himself. This was just lust, glorious and painful though it was and unfulfilled as it was likely to remain. On her part as well. She didn't need him any more than he needed her. This was sheer want, take.

His mind insisted and his body categorically ignored the lecture.

'Nell. Kiss me back, now. Please.'

Was he reduced to begging? But he got what he wanted. His words released her from her passive acceptance of his exploration. Her hand twisted back in his hair, her other hand just skimming his cheek, and her lips parted against his in an assault that rocked him backwards and made his arms tighten around her as if she could keep him from falling. She wasn't gentle. She tugged his lower lip between hers, tasting it with her tongue, catching it with her teeth and letting it go only to sink into him, her tongue searching for and finding his, her breath filling him with her whimpers of pleasure and impatience.

This was the girl who galloped as though she owned

the universe, who would ride him into heaven if she was his.

He couldn't help meeting her assault, leading and following as she grew bolder. Her hands slid under his shirt again, but this time they skimmed the line above his buckskins, and the heat became unbearable. He could feel the surface of his skin, prickling with perspiration and raw nerve ends, adding to the clamour of every part of his body that wanted to be touched by her, kissed by her, with precisely that total abandon.

'Hunter, tell me what to do to make this stop,' she moaned against his mouth, her hands biting into his waist as she pulled herself against him.

'I don't want it to stop,' he all but growled at her. Ever. Not until I'm lost in it, erased. Not until I surrender.

That thought, clear and sharp as splintering ice, finally woke him. If he had needed an answer to the question would he be willing to throw himself off a cliff to bed her, he had it. It was—pretty damn close, but not quite.

'I don't want to, but we have to stop. Now.' He managed to quiet his voice even if his body was screaming at him. She froze, too. Her fingers trembled against his back, sending darts straight into his groin, and he closed his eyes tightly, praying she not take the surge in his already painful erection as an invitation to continue. But when she pulled away he gritted his teeth even at the brush of her arm against his side.

They stood silently for a moment, both staring off into the woods, as if waiting for someone else to arrive.

'You should return to the house. Meecham will be waiting for me with Courage.' He couldn't help how curt he sounded, but when she turned to leave he reached out to tuck a wisp of hair as light and airy as a down feather behind her ear and cursed himself for his pathetic inconsistency. He took another step back, putting her out of easy reach.

'You should go rest before the fête this evening.'

She nodded and headed towards the house.

'Will you save a dance for me?' The question was out before he could censor it and she turned and he thought he could read both surprise and relief in her eyes before she nodded with something approaching her usual smile.

'From what I remember, what takes place on the village green is nothing quite as orderly as dancing. More like a cross between wrestling and a mad game of croquet.'

'We'll wrestle, then.' He firmly resisted the now-reflexive rise of his hands towards her. Finally she was gone and he returned to the stable where Hidgins was standing with Meecham and inspecting Courage. He had told her horses couldn't solve all ills, but he hoped they would help him reclaim his equilibrium because he needed to think about what he was going to do about her and right now that question only had one answer.

Chapter Twelve

The grounds of Welbeck Manor were so obviously constructed to accommodate equine matters that the modest ornamental gardens where Hunter had taken her the
first night at Welbeck were of scant interest to anyone
but Lady Welbeck during daylight hours, which was precisely why Nell made her way to them. She needed to
calm down. She needed to think. She needed to understand what on earth was happening to her. She needed…

She hugged her arms around her as she turned down
the yew-hedged path. She was unravelling, just like her
hair; every time she managed to pull herself back on
course some other part of her took flight. She might
want to blame Hunter's seductive skill, or her treacherous body, but it felt larger than that. It wasn't just her
body that was waking and rushing beyond her control.
Just a week ago she had thought she had known herself
rather well, her strengths and her many weaknesses. She
had felt quite content with the life she had built and the
only thing she had felt was missing was love and she
had actually been proud of the constancy of her adoration for Charles. She had thought it proved she pos-

sessed that precious gift the poets eulogised—true love for a perfect man.

She shivered, though she wasn't in the least chilly. No wonder Hunter had been so scornful. She had sat there lecturing him about love when she had had no idea what she was talking about. She deserved his scorn. Within mere days he had unintentionally undercut her foolish fantasies and worse—he had planted another more damaging fantasy in their stead.

She leaned against the wooden frame of the bower. A few late autumn buds were still trying to push forth and their sweet scent lingered as she rubbed their soft cream petals, just tinged pink at the edges. She wanted to go home. Back to Mrs Petheridge and safety. She didn't want to even think what had happened to her. If she did it might make it real, inescapable. No, she needed some space to think. Perhaps this upheaval was just the product of fear? Perhaps it was a reaction to the transition from the fantasy to the reality of Charles? He was a nice man and perhaps it was even a good thing he wasn't unsettling like Hunter.

Unsettling. She closed her eyes as her body was swamped by the sensations he had evoked. Unsettling wasn't quite the right word. Dangerously cataclysmic was closer to the mark. She wanted to go back and stop him from stopping; she so wanted to find out where this was taking her. She felt like Odysseus's sailors, about to cast herself onto the reefs for the price of a siren's song.

He wants you in his bed, not his life, Nell. He entered this engagement under the influence of grief and guilt and very misplaced chivalry. He doesn't really want *you*. Why would he when he has his experienced Lady

Felton? If you hadn't all but thrown yourself at him, he probably wouldn't have even touched you.

She wished Anna was there; someone to tell her to be sensible. Odysseus had tied himself to the mast so he couldn't follow his sailors to their destruction. Perhaps she should tie herself to sweet, pleasant Charles and eventually she would forget siren songs even exist. Or perhaps Charles's kisses would excite her just as much. It was possible, though it didn't feel very probable.

You are a fool, Nell Tilney.

She was so deep in her confusion and misery it took her a moment to react when a couple entered the garden. Charles didn't see her, his attention wholly on his companion, but Lady Melkinson's eyes met hers for a moment before Nell instinctively moved deeper into the bower.

The fading leaves weren't much of a barrier and she watched as the beauty raised her hand to stroke the fair-haired hero's cheek, as she drew his head down to hers, as her eyes met Nell's the moment before the kiss.

Surely she should feel something? This was Charles, the man she had been in love with for as long as she could remember. How could she feel nothing but embarrassment at witnessing their embrace? Perhaps she, like Hunter, was only capable of physical passion? Perhaps her dreams of something deeper were just mawkish fictions as Hunter had said. Perhaps there was no answer to this deep loneliness, this need to share her life with someone…

'You can come out now, little girl. I've sent him back to the house.'

The contempt in the other woman's voice on top of her confusion was like a blow to the stomach. She didn't want to face that perfect, petite beauty who had taken part in the shattering of her dreams from the day she had arrived. She wanted to be spirited away until she could recover her balance.

'I hope you learned something useful spying; if you mean to deal with men like Hunter you need to acquire some skills, my dear. Oh, I forgot. You're in love with Charles. Such a pity his interest lies elsewhere. Still, he knows he cannot marry me, so he might make do with you. All that money and adoration make you quite tempting, you know...'

Nell wanted more than anything to move away, but she wouldn't run. She had come too far, hadn't she? But holding her ground in the face of the avid enjoyment on Lady Melkinson's perfect features was costing her. She had seen that look before. For years and years and years. Like the yellow-eyed focus of a wolf, intent and predatory.

'I do admire you, my dear Miss Tilney. The undeniable charm of your oh-so-tempting inheritance wasn't enough for you, was it? You had to get them all hot and bothered, playing them off against each other. I started the week ready to applaud the masterly performance Hunter was giving of actually being attracted to a beanpole like you, but I must admit you rival him in bravura. Even Charles has started eyeing those long legs of yours. But do you think Hunter or Charles would even look at you without your acres and gold? I know what makes these men tick, believe me. I've learned the hard way. I've had to earn every privilege, every dress on my back, every ribbon, using the one gift God gave me. You're as bad as any of the men who think they can buy me for the price of a necklace. You make me sick, you pathetic little girl. You're no rival to me. You're nothing but a scrawny, spoilt…'

Somehow Nell started moving, but Lady Melkinson followed and the words kept coming, soft spoken and vicious, hardly above a whisper, making everything fade but the poison. Even her face shifted, the bloom of anger in her cheeks and the perfect teeth giving way to another face, older, uglier, leaning towards her just like that, spewing just like that. Nell's own cheeks were icy, her hands sagged limp like two flaccid sacks filling with ground glass, and though she kept moving, her legs were beginning to shake. There was still a voice shouting inside her to fight back, to do something, but she had no defence. She had already realised the truth of Lady Melkinson's accusations. Her childish dreams had no more substance to them than she had ever had in standing up to her aunt or father. She was no one and no one wanted her, not really.

Her blood pulsed thickly in her head and whatever part of her searched desperately for a way to stop this assault was fumbling in the dark for a weapon that didn't seem to exist. The words came like a litany, again and again. She was no one and no one wanted her. She was a child again, alone, abandoned without explanation, and now without even the comforting fantasy of her knight in shining armour.

'What's wrong? Nell?'

She hardly noticed when Hunter approached. He said something to Lady Melkinson, but all Nell heard was the hammer blows of blood in her ears, like waves striking again and again. She was hiding inside her treacherous body, but it was no sanctuary, just a familiar prison. She had so wanted to believe these attacks were far behind her, that she had managed to become strong enough never to fall back like this, and yet here she was, no better than a kicked, cowering dog. Lady Melkinson was right; she was pathetic.

His hands pressed into her arms and she could feel her muscles shaking against them. She didn't want him here. She didn't want anyone. She just wanted to be left utterly alone. Because that was the truth.

'Nell.'

His voice was gentle and she squeezed her eyes shut harder, like a child, as if that would prevent him from seeing just how weak she was. His arms went around her and the will went out of her, every inch of her body begging to lean into his warmth, his strength. Oh, she was spineless, useless. Pathetic.

'No.' She dragged enough strength to push away from him, but he still held her.

'Phyllida said you saw her and Charles embracing.'

Shame finally penetrated the fog.

'She *told* you that?'

Nell used a word she rarely even heard in the stables, but somehow had stowed away in a corner of her mind. She clung to the coat-tails of her rising fury as she would to a rope being tossed to her as she sank into a bog, the words exploding out of her.

'I hate and loathe her!'

'She isn't really worth hating, Nell. A woman like Phyllida is all about her beauty and for the next forty years she will have to watch her very essence fade. It's not an enviable fate. She has nothing to do with the fact that you're not really in love with Welbeck. You're not twelve and he isn't a fairy-tale prince. Grow up.'

The stain of anger that entered his voice did what his

gentleness didn't. The scrape and thud of her nerves and the flagellating anger of self-loathing gave way to anger at him. This was all his fault anyway.

'I don't need your lectures! As you said, I'm not twelve. My feelings for Charles aren't so puerile!'

'Aren't they? Do you still think you're in love with him?'

It was humiliating to admit that for ten years now she had built her future around an emotion that didn't exist. That in this, too, she was pathetic, weak.

'He was all I had! Oh, damn you!'

She squeezed her forehead with both hands.

'I needed someone to love. He meant something to me. You don't understand…'

She laughed at the childish words, a strangled sound. That was just what her schoolgirls would say. *You don't understand.*

'I needed him.'

That at least was true. He had always been there for her. His sweet teasing smile had guided her through many dark hours at Tilney.

'Well, it isn't him. You had no idea who he was and now you do. So tell me—do you still think you are in love with Charles Welbeck?' It was a challenge, not a question.

Her arms and legs were tingling now. She had no idea whether he had done this on purpose any more than she had known if he had four years ago, but he had somehow dragged her out of her little hell. Not that she felt very grateful at the moment. She was still shaky and, even more than that, ashamed, and she didn't appreciate being pushed.

He surprised her again, his hands cupping her face,

very gentle, tilting it up. His thumbs brushed lightly over her cheekbones, his palms warm against her still-clammy skin.

'You don't need Charles any more, Nell. Not the one in your mind and definitely not the real one.'

'I don't need anyone.'

His fingers stilled. There was such calm conviction in her words she was surprised by the truth in them. He had told her before that she didn't need rescuing and he had been right. If she had really cared for Charles, she would be in pain. The after-effects of her attack were still there in the faint tingle in her hands, the over-awareness of her skin, but the thought of Charles was already fading, like mist clearing, revealing a very different landscape. Not a prettier one. It was still lonely and bare like the view across the tarn far above Keswick and now without that mystical promise of a rainbow to tempt her forward.

Perhaps Hunter had been right all along. She was a naïve fool to be hankering after something beyond physical passion or companionable affection. It would be beyond foolish to transfer her fantasy of love from Charles to Hunter, wouldn't it? But standing there, feeling utterly hollowed out and exhausted, she felt that question had already been answered and to her disadvantage. She shook her head. It felt stuffed with wool and she needed to think.

'What I need is to pack.'

He drew his hands away and, because she wanted to move towards him, she stepped away. It would be so easy to take his comfort, to sink into the drugging warmth of the physical excitement he offered, but Lady Melkinson's words kept ringing in her ears. This man was clever and passionate, but he didn't love her any more than Charles and, unlike him, she needed that. She might have been utterly wrong about Charles, about herself, but she wasn't wrong about that.

'I think it is best I leave tomorrow as well. My father can find me at Bascombe.'

She looked at him as she spoke. He hadn't moved and she couldn't read his face. He looked very much as he had that night in London, cold and watchful. What was he thinking? Was he worried that she might not hold to her side of the bargain now that she was turning her back on Charles?

Why can't you love me?

The words were so loud inside her, for one panicked moment she thought she had spoken them aloud. But he still hadn't moved and so she did, hurrying towards the house, wishing she could leave her treacherous thoughts behind. This time she went straight to her room and locked the door.

Chapter Thirteen

A band of musicians was beginning to play on a small
dais by the inn, their sound just barely rising over the
happy pandemonium of the fête. It was chilly, but the air
was fuzzy with smoke and the scents of apple and clove
and roast pork mixed with charcoal and pine. The excitement of the music and the crowd that filled the village
green was infectious and she was glad she had decided
to attend the fête with the other guests rather than hide
in her room until her departure tomorrow. Not just her
departure, Hunter's as well.

Once again the thought struck her hard, starting from
her stomach and spreading out in a sick ache. Tomorrow she would be leaving—not Welbeck, but Hunter.
She turned instinctively towards where Hunter stood
next to Lord Welbeck and Lord Meecham, his mouth
held tight and his gaze on the shifting raucous crowd
of dancers. She looked down at the tips of her sandals
under the dress and shivered, rubbing the rise of goose-
bumps along her arms.

'Are you cold?'

Her head jerked up. How had he moved so quickly?

She shook her head, but changed it to a nod. It was better than the truth. Even if she had been cold, just having him standing so close was warming her from within and without.

'A little.'

He picked up the lapel of her cloak, fingering the pale fabric with absent concentration.

'I'm not surprised—this isn't very substantial. You should have worn your other cloak.'

It was such a prosaic thing to say an edge of her tension relaxed. At least he didn't appear angry with her any more. She didn't want the last exchange between them to be acrimonious. She didn't want there to be a last exchange between them. She searched desperately for something to say, but already he was turning away.

'Wait here.'

She watched as he disappeared into the crowd, resisting the urge to follow him, trying to shake off the tension that refused to release her from its grip. How was she going to do this?

'Here, this will keep you warm.'

She turned. Hunter had come behind her and was holding out a glass of cider, its coil of milky steam carrying all those smells upwards, as if he had somehow encompassed all the joys of the fête in a single receptacle. Most potently the joy that welled up in her just at seeing him. It was ridiculous to feel so happy just at another person's presence, but she did. For a moment all the agony of unrequited love and impending loss fell away under the weight of the joy of the moment. For right now Hunter was with her, a smile beginning to form in his eyes as he looked down at her. She took the glass, breathing in the scent of the cider, and sighed.

'It's just cider,' he said with a laugh, his expression losing the remainder of its uncharacteristic grimness. 'You look like I am offering you the elixir of the gods.'

She shook her head and tasted it. In all her years attending the fête with her father she had never been permitted to taste this hedonistic brew and it had achieved mythical proportions in her mind. It didn't disappoint. It slid down her throat, evoking a thoroughly sensual response like stepping into a warm spring swirling amber and amethyst and gold. She closed her eyes to let the taste spark the colours and surround her, fading away at the end, leaving just the fundaments of apple and cinnamon and a hint of clove. She opened her eyes with another sigh, letting it go.

'That was my first time.'

As the silence stretched and with the glow of the bonfires lighting the same colours in his eyes, she might have believed she had conjured Hunter from the same pagan spring in her mind. It took her a moment to even realise her words might be grossly misconstrued.

'My first cup of Wilton cider,' she explained.

'You have an interesting way with firsts, Nell,' he remarked and the spirits in the cider, which had been tumbling through her quite leisurely, chose that moment to expand in a rush of heat that spread through her like the birth of a sun.

She turned to watch the dancing, waiting for the heat to fade, and when Hunter plucked the glass from her hand and took her arm, leading her towards the green, she protested.

'I'm not finished yet.'

'You're already swaying like a willow in a stream.'

'I was moving to the music.'

'There's more room for that here.'

She glanced around the rowdy, swirling dancers. He was drawing her deeper and deeper into the mayhem, holding her close against the buffeting. She clung to his hand, raising her voice to be heard.

'I don't even know the steps.'

'Neither do I. Can you waltz?'

'Yes, but this isn't...'

Apparently there was more than one way to waltz. Nothing that would pass muster at Almack's, but much, much more enjoyable. They were on the other side of the green, far from the Welbeck crowd. There was too much chaos around them to move more than a couple of feet in either direction and Hunter's arm around her was as much a guard against the merry jostling as a guide for the rhythm.

'This most certainly isn't a waltz.' Nell laughed as he swung her out of the way of a portly couple who were clearly interpreting the music as a reel.

Her laugh collapsed into a gasp as her attempt to avoid stepping on his boot brought her sharply against him and somehow his leg slid between hers, straining her skirts against her thighs in a manner that definitely didn't happen in a waltz.

'I never said it was. No, don't pull back yet. Trust me.' His voice was as warm as the cider still tumbling through her and she didn't even manage to scoff at this outrageous demand, too stunned by the sensation of being held there in the middle of the chaos, just swaying gently against his thigh, his head bent next to hers.

She had ridden astride more times than she could count; she knew what it felt to have something firm and muscular between her thighs, the pull of fabric over that sensitive inner flesh. But not this. They continued to move, with no regard to the rhythm, his leg shifting between hers, hard and muscled, scraping and pressing in a way that should have been thoroughly uncomfortable and it was, it was, just not in any way that she wanted to stop. It made her skin heat and tingle and begin to shake, and for one mad moment, still misted in the fumes of the cider, she thought it might be the return of that horrible fear, but that thought passed immediately. It wasn't that kind of shaking. It was... She was coming apart and re-forming around a completely new heat at her centre. That burst of sun had sunk from her chest and stomach and settled between her legs, insistent and aggravating and in a dialogue with his body she could barely follow.

There were other things occurring, his arms around her, still masquerading as shields against the crowd except that his hand was moving so softly up and down the small of her back she wondered if it had somehow worked its way under her gown, she could feel his fingers so distinctly on her flesh.

He bent his head, his mouth beside her ear as if talking to her, and perhaps he was, if talking was that gentle slide of breath over the curve of her ear and every now and then his lips brushed its tip and the heat between her legs would gather in and prepare to shoot up through her to capture that caress and out into the heavens.

It never occurred to her to do anything but to hang on and survive this multiple-fronted assault as she would have clung to a bolting horse, focusing on keeping herself safe until the horse wore itself out and could be checked. But soon hanging on wasn't enough.

The kiss by the paddock had been a revelation, a ripping back of curtains on a part of the world she had only known at the level of gossip or myth. That heat and pleasure had been sensuous and unnerving and made her yearn for something more. The kisses in the linen closet and the copse had confirmed her suspicions that she was probably a thorough wanton. Now she was being dragged higher or deeper and once again all she could think was that there must be more to these amazing sensations—everything he was doing told her so, was an invitation to proceed and discover what she was capable of. She. *She* was capable of this, not just him. She knew it.

Her hands had just been clasped on his coat and she loosened them and let them slide around him, her body sinking against his as it had yesterday. As her breasts pressed against his chest she realised they had wanted this. Every part of her body, which she had always thought of as a rather necessary unit for getting about the world, was now a clashing collection of needs and demands. Right now quite a few of them were making utterly new demands of her and of Hunter and rewarding her with wonderful but also thoroughly frustrating sensations like a band of musicians engaged in a cacophony begging to be drawn into a single tune.

'Hunter.' She turned her head to breathe against his neck, and his scent, his essence, warm and spicy and inexplicably vivid, flowed through her like the cider, twisting through to every one of those elements of her body taking part in the uprising. It did something to him, too, because he wrapped around her with a sudden shiver, pulling her against him painfully, breaking the rhythm. Then they were separate again. The only point of contact was his hand on her arm as he led her out through the crowd back towards the relative calm of the stalls. She kept her eyes on her pale slippers darting in and out from under her skirts as they threaded through the chaos and did a little tripping stumble as Hunter stopped abruptly.

'May I have this dance, Nell?' Charles asked over the noise and she looked up. He had stopped directly in front of her and the light from the torches and fires that turned his hair into a blazing sunset was also in his eyes and for a moment she stood mute and breathless before the embodiment of a dream. She had actually daydreamed of this precise moment. That in the midst of the fête this man, his hand held out to her, would single her out. It had been with her for so long, clung to during her aunt's vicious scolds or during the quiet hours before sleep at school. She would sail away in his arms dancing in this very clearing, with the world fading away around them as he looked into her eyes. It wouldn't be like the chaos of sensations and heat of dancing with Hunter that left her confused and frustrated. It would be as light as gossamer and would empty her of doubts and fears because Charles wanted her.

He stood, hand outstretched, with the boyish smile she had revered, and she had an urge to slap him. She couldn't blame him for his affair with Phyllida, but she could for this shameless attempt to take advantage of an infatuated young woman. She held firmly to her smile, but it felt like a grimace.

'Of course,' she answered and held out her hand.

'You look lovely, Nell,' he said once they began dancing at the edge of the green.

'Thank you, Charles.'

'I mean it. You're so lovely I wish...'

'Please don't insult me by feigning emotions that

don't exist, Charles. I am betrothed and I know you and Lady Melkinson are lovers.'

He stumbled, but didn't let go of her hand.

'Nell! Really! Someone might hear you!'

'Is that what concerns you? What a hypocrite you are.'

He looked both shocked and rather desperate.

'Lady Melkinson and I are merely acquaintances. You are the only woman who has touched my heart.'

'Do you often kiss your mere acquaintances in the garden? Oh, don't bother explaining. I thought I cared, but I must be as shallow as you because I don't. Please don't say anything else, Charles. Let's enjoy the dance and part friends. Please.'

She could feel him struggling, but thankfully he complied with her request and they completed the dance in silence. As the music slowed she stepped back and smiled.

'Goodnight, Charles.'

She turned and searched the crowd lining the green and her eyes met Hunter's. She moved towards him without thinking and he took her arm and they walked through the stalls of roasting, sizzling and bubbling fare. She didn't particularly care where they were going, just that he was with her, his hand securing hers on his arm and the press of people forcing her often against his side. There were jugglers and a man with dogs who danced on their hind feet and a man tossing lighted torches into the air. People gasped as sparks burst upwards like comet tails. One torch fell to the ground by her feet and Hunter pulled her back, his arm about her waist.

'It's dangerous to play with fire,' his voice murmured close to her ear. She turned her head towards him without thinking and his mouth grazed her cheek. Around them the crowd kept moving from one spectacle to another, a pulsing, noisy current around their stillness. Not that she felt still. The heat that had been suspended restarted the inner drumming, feeding off every point of contact with his body. It made no sense that never during her dreams of Charles had she imagined him kissing her. Now all it took was for her to stumble into Hunter, for his hand to brush against her, for him to speak…

She wanted to cry out in anguish. Hunter had ruined everything! She had been within sight of land after years adrift and he had pushed her back into the treacherous current that would eventually leave her becalmed and alone again.

But she didn't stop him when he finally moved, guiding her out of the crowd and towards the tree-lined path towards Welbeck. Not even when he stopped and turned her to him, pulling the hood of her cloak over her hair.

'It's getting chilly,' he explained as he tucked back a tress of hair that must have fallen free during the dance, but it slid free again and he stood with it draped over his palm for a moment before raising it.

'Baked apples, with cinnamon.'

'What?'

'Your hair smells of baked apples and cinnamon.'

The very earthy statement eased her rising tension slightly. She tried to gather her hair, but only succeeded in dislodging Betsy's carefully positioned pins and a hunk of hair tumbled down her other shoulder.

'You're just making it worse. Here, let me.'

Hunter pushed back her hood, inspecting the damage, and Nell felt the return of the familiar embarrassment at her unfashionably straight-as-sticks hair.

'It's hopeless. It just won't curl.'

'Thank goodness for that; why on earth would you want to torture something so beautiful into curls is beyond me.'

'That's because you're a man.'

'You noticed. I have clearly done something right, then.'

He picked up another tress that had slipped free and ran it between his fingers, watching her.

'This one is cider and cloves.'

She presented him with another felled tress.

'The whole fair smells of cider, so that is nothing extraordinary. What about this?'

With his eyes on hers Hunter brushed it just gently with his lips and all conscious thought faded like the last gasp of a sunset.

'This is Nell.'

How did he make his voice do that, reverberate through her like a musical instrument? It made her body dance, but it was still an intrusion and a warning.

His words were like the cider, warm and drugging, and like the cider she wanted more of them. He wasn't looking hard and grim any more. The fire that was pulsing away inside her was in his eyes as well and she wanted it so much it terrified her. He wasn't hers to keep, but how could she let him go? The thought was so terrifying she withdrew, trying to find the stable ground of the laughing, sophisticated flirtation he had taught her.

'That sounds rather unappealing after all those delicious scents. Try another one. We need some more substantial fare than baked apples and cider.'

He shook his head, dismissing her weak attempt to bring them back to the mundane.

'You're wrong. This…' He ran the lock of hair between his fingers, just an inch, but enough for a shower of tingling heat to cascade from her scalp downwards. 'This is the most exquisite scent of them all. If I could describe it, all your poets would have to bow before me.'

Far behind them she could hear the roar of the crowd, but it was all just a rumble of sound around the reality of a man holding her hair and turning her body, turning her, into the rest of the universe.

Her mind and senses were raw, but enough of her remained to be scared she might never regain her footing. If she stepped into the void now, how would she return? There was no one she could really trust to guide her back to safety. No one. So it made no sense to let him secure the hood of her cloak again and take her hand and lead her up the path towards Welbeck knowing that it wasn't over. As they walked down the dim and silent corridor towards her room she was conscious of a growing elation that something was going to happen. Tomorrow she would have to go back to her old life, but right now she could take this. Him.

Outside her door she turned, straightening, preparing herself to do something she never would have imagined was within the realm of the possible just a week ago. With one hand already turning the knob, she held out her hand to Hunter. He took it and held it against his lips for the space of two breaths.

'Goodnight, Nell.'

No!

She grabbed his coat and pulled him in and either she took him by surprise or he didn't offer much resistance, only stopping once he was inside the room.

'This isn't a good idea. It's the cider and the dancing. I took advantage of your inexperience, Nell, but I have my limits.'

He spoke very slowly, enunciating each word as if she were dim-witted. She knew the moment would come when he would push her away, bring down the curtain on their little play. A more experienced woman might take this dismissal with a laugh and a teasing comment, but she couldn't. The best she could do was to try not to show him how much this hurt. She raised her chin.

'Goodnight, then. I'm going back to the fête.'

She pushed past him, opening the door, but he shut it again, hard, his hand flat against it.

'No. You're not.'

'I most certainly am!'

'Nell, listen to me.'

'No. You will say something clever and convince me whatever you want is for my own good and I don't want to hear it. Let me go.'

'Nell, it's precisely because what I want is far from your own good that I am trying to be sensible. You don't even know what you want!'

'Oh, and you do?'

'I do, which is why I am trying very hard not to accept your offer. But there is no possible way I am letting you go back down to the fête alone.'

'I wouldn't be alone. I am certain Charles would be only too happy for another dance.'

As a threat it was rather weak. He knew very well she wasn't in love with Charles and that Charles was only interested in her inheritance, but it was all she had in this uneven struggle. She didn't expect him to react so fiercely.

'You're not going,' he said, his hands tangling in her hair. 'I won't let you.'

She raised her mouth to feel the words against her lips, leaning into him as she had in the dance, and his arm came around her again, not so smoothly now, dragging her against him.

'Nell, tell me you won't go.' The certainty was gone; there was just entreaty and something else that made her want to wrap her arms around him. She slid one hand into his warm hair and it felt like a sigh between her fingers. It might be playing with fire, but this was *right*. Now her body was coming back to her, gathering, defined by every point of contact between them. This time she must have been the one to start the kiss because for a moment he still held back and then with a half-groan his hands shifted, positioned her, and she lost all control of the situation.

She was no longer playing with fire. She was fire, he was living flame and he was devouring her. She gave him everything he demanded, opening herself, helping when his hands untied her cloak, unfastened her dress, slipped down the sleeves of her gown. He paid homage to every inch of skin he uncovered with his hands and mouth, bringing it to tingling life, finding places she had never realised could make her writhe merely with a breath and flick of his tongue, like the dip below her collarbone, and further, where the skin of her breasts began to rise... She tried to tug down her chemise and stays because they were in the way. Then they weren't and the cool air gathered around her breasts and her breath shook in relief and agony.

Do something.

For a moment his hands just held her arms and his

gaze mapped her. Then he reached out and did the same with one finger, very lightly, first over the delicate swells, dipping between them to gather and release the pearl at the end of her necklace before following the curve under her breast. Then his hand cupped it and she watched, transfixed, as he bent towards her.

'Nell.' His breath was torture enough on her exposed nipple, but when he touched his lips to it, the lightest feather touch, she gave a little cry, digging her fingers into his hair, not knowing whether to stop him before something terrible happened or to press herself to him, to be consumed utterly, demolished utterly.

She moaned and gave up all thought as he took the hardened bud into his mouth and the pleasure echoed in the thudding heat between her legs. Every touch and lick on her breast was answered by a pulse of pleasure, a damp heat that was gathering.

She didn't resist as he nudged her legs apart with his knee, and when he pulled up her skirts she helped him. She didn't even have enough shame to stop him from releasing the string of her drawers and then caressing the heated, shaking skin above her garters. Quite the opposite. She wriggled her undergarments to the ground and when he raised his head to kiss her again she anchored her hand in his hair and kissed him with all the confused need bursting inside her.

She was lost. Her body was acting without her because she would never have dreamed of taking his hand and pressing it against her aching breast. And when his other hand skimmed up her thighs, between her legs, she had no idea how but she moved towards it so that it pressed his large hot palm against the fire at the juncture of her thighs. Her legs tightened instinctively, locking him there, and the hard texture of his fingers pressing against the most intimate part of her condensed the fireball into molten lead that was begging to spill free.

'Hunter…' His name was one long plea for the pleasure she knew awaited her. But just in case she wasn't being clear enough, she added, 'Please…'

It was an eternity, but finally he moved again, and though she should be shocked or ashamed, all she could do was move to the rhythm of his fingers in total wonder that this was even possible. She had thought the kisses were magical, bringing extraordinary revelation about her body, but this… Where had this been all her life? How could this completely ignored and negligible part of her have transformed into the whole universe and Hunter's hands and body and lips become the very essence of the laws that governed her new reality?

She heard his voice against her mouth, a deep growl that made her legs tighten about him again.

'I want to taste you there…kiss you and take you until you unravel.'

She was unravelling already. His fingers circled and skimmed and tugged and then the chaos became a new rhythm. She was riding his fingers, back and forth, clinging to him, saying things she couldn't even understand until everything faded into a litany of 'yes, yes…' and then that gave way as the ground fell out from under her. She was being torn apart by waves of pleasure so intense there was even a moment of fear that she might never escape this, and then with a long moan it all gave way to warmth, like sliding into a steamy, viscous bath, sliding into a new body.

Her mind came out of its cave and noticed that he was holding her tightly against him, but rigidly. Her body tingled all over, very aware of the cold air against her damp skin, of his hand still pressed against her, but not moving, just holding her. She could feel her pulse there against his fingers, hard thumping beats that slowed as she waked.

Then came embarrassment and she squirmed away from his hand and he let her, but his other hand was still tangled in her hair. Her skirts slid back down her legs and he leaned his forehead against hers and drew in a shaking breath, before stepping back and pulling up her sleeves.

She shuddered and his hands rose towards her again, but fell back, fisting.

'Are you all right?' His voice was rough and strained.

'Yes. I was afraid for a moment.' Her voice was just as rough and she cleared her throat, adjusting her bodice. His dark brows drew together.

'I'm sorry, Nell. I swear I didn't mean to frighten you.'

'No, I didn't mean that. There was a moment I didn't know if I would be able to get back. That I might lose myself.'

He didn't answer right away, but then he took her hands in his. She could feel how stiffly he was holding himself, but she didn't know what it meant or what to do.

'You are a humbling experience, Nell. I was trying to find a way to apologise for taking advantage of you, but I don't think I will. That would be to sully something amazing. You are amazing. Now I am going to thoroughly amaze myself and leave.'

When he reached the door she stepped forward impulsively.

'Hunter, may I ask you something?'

He paused at the door and took another long breath, as if preparing to plunge into a lake. Then he nodded warily.

'Why didn't you...? I don't think I would have stopped you just then, before. I mean you could have. Didn't you want to...?'

'Are you trying to kill me? I am barely clinging to the tatters of honour here which at the moment are so threadbare they are practically transparent. Now, I'm going to my room and you are staying here and I am giving you fair warning that the next time you...we... Goodnight! And lock this door!'

Nell stared at the closed door. Her laugh startled her and she looked guiltily about her room. It didn't look any different, but it was. She was.

Hunter closed the door to his room and leaned his forehead against it, debating whether to lock it just to make the point very clear that on no account was he to head back down the hallway and take advantage of his impossibly seductive betrothed.

Except that he was in absolute agony. If someone had told him a week ago that he would be standing with his hand on the doorknob of his room, desperately trying to prevent himself from going to complete the seduction of an inexperienced virgin, he would have drunk a toast to their fertile imagination.

Inexperienced. Not the most experienced of his mistresses had ever reduced him to such a state of quivering need and it certainly wasn't her innocence that was doing the trick. She had given herself over to pleasure with a hedonistic abandon and her release was the most beautiful surrender he had ever seen. Her eyes, warmed to melting, had fixed on his, giving him more than he was giving her, locking him into her joy, promising him the same if he would just let her.

The girl was a natural wanton. He should have known that was so even years ago from the way she had ridden Petra. She had been freedom and joy incarnate, just waiting to slip the leash that life and her brutal aunt and apathetic father had cinched around her. Well, she was slipping it now and he was just slipping.

'Oh, hell.' He groaned, shoving his forehead harder against the door. This was pathetic. Every single one of his stratagems was coming back to bite him. But what he couldn't do, no matter how much he needed to, was take further advantage of her state of arousal and confusion. Maybe he should. Just go bed her and have done with it. Then the choice would be taken away. Maybe it already had. He might not have taken her maidenhead, but he had done something worse. He had seen her joy and right now he felt he would kill before he let another man see her as he had. It would also finally put to rest whatever idiotic girlish fantasies she might still harbour about Welbeck, because if that man touched her just one more time, he would... He had been so entangled in the moment he had been completely unprepared when Welbeck had waylaid them as they left the green. He had just watched dumbly as she had taken the man's hand and followed him back towards the chaos of dancers as if she hadn't all but melted against him a moment earlier. She hadn't even looked back once, just smiled at Welbeck and placed her hand in his like this was the one moment she had been waiting for.

Could she still, even after what she had witnessed, be caught in her childish fantasy? He had really begun to believe she no longer cared for Welbeck, but perhaps that was just wishful thinking. He had barely held himself back from following them, pulling her hand from Welbeck's and staking his claim like the cave dweller he was deteriorating into. But if that was what Nell had been waiting for—her dance with her prince—to ruin that, to do anything at that point, would be cruelty incarnate. He couldn't do that to her, whatever it cost him to stand there and suffer the spears of hell as she looked up at Welbeck, her lips parted and a ribbon of pale gold hair loosening down her back...

He was becoming well acquainted with all forms of agony these past few days. He might have years of experience having pugilists pummel him, but these kinds of levellers were new to him and that scared him.

For the first time in his life he wanted someone to see him as he was.

Heat and clammy cold spread through him in waves, just like they did when he woke from the nightmare, as if the admission itself was a virulent disease. He had never needed anyone. People needed him, not the other way around. His mother, his brother, his aunts, his mistresses. Just as it should be. Not one of them had ever taken him by the hand and tried to soothe him and he had never wanted them to, until now. This girl had reduced him to a fool barely worthy of a lending-library novel. The worst was that some no longer hidden corner of himself was enjoying it and looking forward to more of the same.

He had to clear his mind and think.

Even if he succeeded in seducing her into marrying him, playing on her pain and disappointment with Charles, what did he think was going to happen? Nell would not be easily stowed away at Hunter Hall while he went about his business. Sooner or later he would slip up and she would discover his weakness and then what? In fact, it had been getting progressively worse this week. At least until recently the nightmare, horrific though it was, had been a kind of fixed constant. She had forced her way into his horror, making it a thousand times worse as he was helplessly forced to witness her destruction. How could he cope with watching himself fail her every night? What if one night he actually acted on that terror and hurt her? Biggs and Hidgins knew better than to approach him at night and at Hunter Hall his own wing was far from the servants, but what would happen if she became curious? How could he protect her from himself?

He gritted his teeth, trying to force a way through the physical and mental confusion. He wanted to go to her room and just tell her what she had done to him. What he needed from her. Then he would slide the remaining pins from her hair and finally do something about this raging fire that was surely damaging his higher faculties.

The only stable points in his seething mind were the need to go to her and the determination not to. He groaned and locked the door. The way he felt right now, he doubted he would manage to sleep, but right now he would even welcome the nightmares if they gave him some respite from this aching need.

Chapter Fourteen

Nell stopped in the doorway of Lady Welbeck's parlour and the mid-morning sun bounced brightly off Charles's curls as he turned towards her.

'I was told your mother was here.'

He glanced around the room, looking flustered.

'I was looking for her as well. I dare say she'll return soon. But I'm glad you are here, Nell. I want to speak with you…'

She took a step back, shaking her head. 'I really must pack. I just wanted to thank her.'

'You're leaving?'

'Yes. If my father does arrive, please inform him I will be at Bascombe. Thank you for your hospitality, Charles.'

He grasped her hand, stopping her.

'Wait, Nell. Please don't leave. We were just becoming reacquainted. I realise you saw me and…well…but it doesn't mean anything!'

'Please don't deny your relation with Lady Melkinson, Charles. I really don't care.'

His hands tightened on hers.

'I don't know what Phyllida told you, but I promise there is nothing serious between us.'

She tugged her hands away.

'Your affairs are of no interest to me. This is not only unnecessary but improper, Charles. I am engaged.'

For the first time she saw anger and frustration mar his pretty face.

'Are you? You didn't really discourage me this week, betrothed or not. So what if I had another interest? Everyone has them. I promise you that once I'm married I'll be faithful, which is more than your fiancé is likely to offer. Together we can turn the Welbeck stables into the finest in England. Think of it, Nell…'

His voice and face softened again, lighting with the smile that had been the staple of her dreams for years.

'What do you say, Nell? Tell Hunter you've found what you want right here. You'll make me the happiest man on earth…darling,' he murmured, his arms sliding down her back.

His mouth settled on hers, soft and coaxing. She had been searching for certainty in the chaos of feelings and revelations this past week and now she had it, just not the kind she had expected. She felt the scrape of her lips over her teeth as he pressed his mouth to hers and his taste was all wrong. She twisted away.

'Charles, stop. I don't want you to kiss me.'

'Yes, you do. You've been begging for this since the day you showed up. Don't play coy now, Nell. You're a passionate woman now. Let me show you, darling.'

She pulled away sharply as his head descended again and they both stumbled backwards, his foot catching the flounce of her dress with an ominous ripping sound. She tried to grab at a small table, but it just came with them and the garish figurine of a courting shepherd and shepherdess bounced and somersaulted onto the wooden floor, sending porcelain lovers and sheep in all directions as they landed on the floor, her shoulder making painful contact with his cheekbone.

'Blast! Now look what you've done!' Charles accused, rubbing his reddened cheek.

'What *I've* done? I told you not to kiss me!'

'You wanted me to!'

'I did not!' she snapped, scrambling to her knees and gathering pieces of the shattered statuette. When he didn't respond to her juvenile denial she glanced up and realised they were no longer alone. Standing just inside the doorway were Lord and Lady Welbeck, Hunter and her father.

'Nell!' her father bellowed.

'What on earth is going on here? Oh, my shepherdess!' said Lady Welbeck, hurrying towards the debris.

Nell remained where she was, vaguely wondering where her father had sprung from, but her attention was on Hunter as he strode towards her. She took his outstretched hand, shaking a beheaded sheep from her skirts. Charles also moved towards her, but stopped as Hunter turned, the look on his face as palpable as a blow. Without thinking, Nell tightened her grip on Hunter's hand and they stood suspended. Then the moment of near violence passed as Lord Welbeck went to right the table.

'What has happened in this room?' Lady Welbeck demanded.

'Yes, do tell us what precisely happened to your face, Welbeck,' Hunter added. 'And to Miss Tilney's dress as well.'

'I fell,' Nell said quickly.

'I…uh, tripped,' Charles said at precisely the same time. Hunter bared his teeth.

'I suggest you practise to be less clumsy in future, Welbeck,' he said, pulling Nell past her father's immobile and frowning figure. 'Or if you must trip, do so as far from my betrothed as possible.'

Nell didn't particularly like being all but dragged along like a child, but the truth was that she was glad to be extracted from that room. At her door Hunter merely opened it and walked in.

'You can't come in here!'

'It's a bit late for prudery, isn't it? I've been here twice already. Besides, in light of your tryst with Welbeck, protestations of delicacy are out of place right now.'

'We didn't… It wasn't a tryst.'

'I see. You merely fell. Oh, sorry, it was Welbeck who "tripped". You should co-ordinate your stories ahead of time when next you plan to "fall" or "trip".'

'I was merely looking for Lady Welbeck to tell her I was leaving, but Charles was there and…he proposed to me.'

She went and sat on the side of the bed, feeling a little ill. Her father was here and now she would have to gather the strength to follow through on her agreement with Hunter. He would receive his water rights and she would receive her freedom… She was shaking inside, not like an attack, just with loneliness and the anticipation of pain. What would Hunter do if she asked him to sit down by her and just hold her hand? Maybe even ask him if he would reconsider his offer?

Silly fool.

'So the little girl gets her prince.' Hunter spoke at last, his words harsh and mocking. 'Phyllida had the right of it after all. You played us all finely, didn't you? A bit melodramatic for my taste since it was clear from the moment we arrived Welbeck was more than willing. Flirting quite that outrageously with me was a bit of a risk, though, don't you think? Or were you having too much fun playing all fronts by then to care? You probably expect me to congratulate you, too.'

'I don't expect anything.' Her words were as muted and dull as she felt. There was no point. He had begun his acquaintance with her feeling pity and now it would end with him feeling contempt. She must have been mad to think there was something she could offer him.

She hardly even noticed the knock until Hunter spoke.

'Get rid of whoever it is,' he snarled under his breath, moving in the direction of the dressing room.

Nell walked over and cracked open the door.

'My dear, dear Nell, may I come in?'

'Lady Welbeck! What? No! I mean, is something wrong?' Nell remained lodged firmly behind the door and Lady Welbeck glimpsed worriedly up and down the empty corridor before hurrying into speech.

'My dear, how can you ask me that? I am quite distraught at my failure as a chaperon and hostess. Lord Welbeck and Charles are with your father now, trying to explain... What will Sir Henry think of us? You must believe it is only because my poor Charles is so very passionately attached to you that he has allowed his emotions to overcome his judgement. He is quite, quite broken-hearted, my dear. I know you have always loved him and surely such deeply rooted tender feelings cannot be dislodged merely by a momentary lapse in dear Charles's restraint. Men, my dear, are often swayed by urges us women know little of and it behoves us to show patience if—'

'Lady Welbeck,' Nell interrupted this flow as firmly as possible, 'there is no possibility of an alliance between Charles and I.'

'None?' asked Lady Welbeck wistfully.

'None, Lady Welbeck. Thank you for your hospitality, but I really must pack.'

Gently but firmly she closed the door.

'You refused Welbeck's offer? Why didn't you say so?'

Hunter had himself under control now, and though his eyes were still intent and darker than usual, the anger that had pressed at her was, if not gone, at least well hidden. Was he worried now she had abandoned her plans to marry Charles he might have to marry her after all?

'When during your tantrum was I supposed to do that?'

'My tantrum… Did you refuse him because of Phyllida?'

'No, not because of your precious Phyllida. Now if you have nothing useful to say, would you please leave? I must send for Betsy so I can pack.'

'She's not mine, thank heavens, and we're not done yet.'

'If you won't leave I shall start packing anyway.'

She marched over to the dresser and ceremoniously extracted a carefully folded stack of chemises, placing them on her bed. If she had expected to embarrass Hunter into leaving she had clearly miscalculated, for he just leaned back against the wall and watched. She wavered, realising she had chosen a very inappropriate threat, and though she might have come a long way from the inexperienced girl of a week ago, she still wasn't comfortable standing in front of a man with a stack of undergarments in her arms.

She was saved from backing down by another knock on the door. Hunter shifted against the wall, but otherwise didn't speak as she laid the stack on the bed and went to open the door a crack. When she saw who it was, it took all her determination not to slam the door shut again.

'Father!'

'Let me in, Nell. I want a word with you.'

His voice boomed down the corridor, but she put her foot firmly against the door.

'Whatever you have to say you can say from there, Father. I'm already undressing,' she lied.

'You insolent girl! I can see that what I have just heard from the Welbecks about your conduct this past week is only too true. You had no business coming to Wilton without my express permission and making a fool of yourself over young Welbeck. You are an engaged woman, not a fanciful child, and I wouldn't be surprised if your antics have given Lord Hunter a disgust of you. Hester was right that you would ruin matters if given half a chance. I should never have agreed to his demand that you remain in that Petheridge woman's care. We will leave for Tilney Hall in the morning and meanwhile I will speak with Lord Hunter and see if I can yet salvage this debacle.'

Nell felt her cheeks were as red as her father's. She didn't know what she had expected of this man after four years. Had she secretly been hoping he would be glad to see her? Might even say he had missed her? His whole handling of the engagement should have reminded her of her father's limitations. It was ridiculous to be so hurt, to feel the dampness of her palm against the metal knob and the skittering of nerves gathering in preparation for the rising storm. She had a sudden urge to lean her head against the door and cry. No—to slam the door in his face. Several times. Hard. Until it splintered into smithereens.

'No, Father. I will not go to Tilney Hall. Have you forgotten? I am of age and you are no longer even my trustee. I can go where I wish, with whomever I wish, and if I wished to marry Charles I would and there is nothing you could do about it. What are you worried about? That the Bascombe money might make the Welbeck stables more successful than yours? Are you so petty? Now excuse me because I really must pack.' She started closing the door in his stunned face, but stopped. 'Oh, though I might consider inviting you to Bascombe if you could ever bring yourself to apologise to me, you can tell Aunt Hester she will never, ever be welcome in my home. She is a mean, vicious, pathetic b—witch and you can tell her I said so. Goodbye, Father.'

She locked the door before he could respond and leaned her forehead on the door frame, waiting for the shaking to stop. She didn't move even when Hunter's hand settled on her shoulder or when there was a tentative knock on the door. She must have scared her father quite seriously for him to knock like that.

'I meant it! Leave me alone!' She gritted her teeth and tried to shake off Hunter's hand.

'Nell?'

'Charles?'

Hunter's hand fell away, flattening against the door

by the side of her head. She could feel the heat of his body behind her, anger emanating off him like waves.

'I must speak with you. May I come in?' Charles's voice was muffled by the wood as if he, too, was leaning against the door.

'You most certainly may not. What do you want? I am packing.'

'I wish you wouldn't. Leave, I mean. Please give me another chance. I love you.'

'No, you don't.' Nell was burningly aware of Hunter behind her.

'Yes, I do. I always liked you and I think you'll be an excellent horse-breeder's wife and—'

'Oh, for…! You don't love me, you are enamoured of my inheritance, and I wish, I really wish, Grandmama had succeeded in convincing Grandpapa not to will Bascombe to me because if ever there was a poisoned chalice this is it. Goodbye, Charles.'

'Nell…'

This time she didn't answer and eventually she heard his footsteps recede.

'Do you think Lord Welbeck might also be coming to throw his hat into the ring, or is that the lot?' Hunter asked behind her.

Nell felt a sob expand in her throat and she covered her eyes, leaning her forehead on the door.

'Nell, I'm sorry… I didn't mean…'

She hadn't cried for years. Not even when she had ridden out of Tilney for the last time, furious and scared and tentatively triumphant. The last time she remembered really crying had been a month after her mother's death and her arrival at Mrs Petheridge's. Then Mrs Petheridge had sat and hugged her on a sagging brocade sofa, her plump arms surprisingly strong.

The strong arms that drew her onto his lap as he sat on the side of the bed were certainly not plump, but Nell leaned into their embrace with the same weary abandon as the long-ago girl had leaned against her headmistress's pillowy bosom. Mrs Petheridge had patted her back, but Hunter was stroking her hair, which was unravelling again, and his hand was steadier than his voice.

'Nell, Nell, I'm so sorry. Oh, don't cry like that, sweetheart. You're tearing me apart.'

She shook her head and cried harder. Her eyes burned and stung and her shoulders and throat ached. It was splitting her from the inside. She was lost again, and alone again, but this alone was a thousand times worse than before because loving Charles had never ached. It had been wistful and hopeful and embarrassed and a host of other timid things. But loving Hunter when he didn't love her in return felt like being thrown from a horse, both the moment of shocked protest at having the world snatched out from under her and the jarring, biting pain of impact. It wasn't her bones that were shattering, but an inner structure that held up who she was, an entity she was only beginning to recognise as herself.

'Sweetheart, Nell…' His voice was husky and pleading.

He was probably desperate for this to be over so he could escape and she couldn't even walk away because her face probably looked as blotchy as if she had been ill for days. She grabbed one of the chemises from the bed and shoved her face into it and tried to stop the way her breath kept catching as the sobs finally subsided.

She resisted when he tried to pull the cloth away,

but not when he folded her back against him, his breath on her temple as his lips gently brushed her hair. Trust Hunter to use seduction to stop a sobbing fit, she thought, but she still didn't move away. Soon it would be over and right now...right now she needed this. Him.

She was drained hollow and so weary she just wanted to stay right there, held just like that. Today he would leave and she might never see him again but as a neighbour and she couldn't bear it. The agony of that thought shivered through her and his arms tightened, pulling her more securely against him, cocooning her.

'It's all right...' he murmured into her hair, and though it was a ridiculous thing to say when it was clear nothing was all right, it comforted her. She rested against him, thawing into softness, just breathing, the world evening out and slipping away. She no longer felt weary, just tired, very tired, and very safe...

She jerked awake at the sound and it took her a moment to recover her bearings.

She was lying on her bed, fully dressed, and she wasn't alone. She opened her eyes. Hunter's arm was draped over her breasts, holding her against his length, and her foot was pressed between his legs. By the small clock on the dresser it was just past midday, which meant they must have slept less than an hour, but she was marvellously rested. The events of the past days and her sleepless night must have exhausted her more than she had realised but she never would have imagined she would just fall asleep like that... It was so embarrassing! And why hadn't he just left her? He had also looked exhausted. Perhaps he also had trouble sleeping, or perhaps he had been otherwise occupied that night... She shut her eyes against the snake of jealousy uncurling inside her. It would be better just to soak in the warmth of the moment, how peaceful it felt, how right...

Hunter shifted and she opened her eyes, realising what had woken her. He was dreaming.

'No! Stop!'

His voice was muffled against her hair and his body twitched, his hand jerking against her, and she picked it up gently, pressing it between hers. He had been re-laxed a moment before, but she could feel tension gathering through his body, his fingers splaying, and she frowned. The next move when it came was so abrupt she was completely unprepared. He pulled away from her, his hands fisting on the sheets, anchoring himself to the bed, his mouth moving, but she could make no sense of the hoarse mutterings. He looked so tortured she raised herself on her elbow and reached out instinctively, but she had hardly run her hand down his cheek when he suddenly grabbed it, pulling her towards him so that she fell across him, his chin striking her forehead. She cried out more in surprise than pain, but it was enough and suddenly she was thrust away from him and he was out of the bed, staring down at her in horror.

'Nell! I hurt you! What have I done?'

She scrambled to her knees, holding out her hands.

'You didn't hurt me. I'm fine!'

But he had covered his face with his hands and she could see he was shaking. She moved towards him, but he stepped away, turning his back on her.

'I can't believe I fell asleep. I just didn't want to wake you, you were so tired, but I never should have...'

He sounded so agonised she shook her head, trying

to understand. His reaction was completely out of step with what had happened.

'Gabriel…'

'No! I never should have let this happen…'

'Hunter, calm down…'

He rounded on her, his eyes so fierce she took a step back this time.

'Calm down? Calm down? I almost… I might have… Just who do you think I am? Do you think you can just use me to play your little seduction games on that pretty boy and then when you find out he has feet of clay you can come cry on my shoulder and expect me to play the comforting protector? Is that my role now? Haven't you figured it out yet? I am no one's protector. I can't even protect you from myself!'

'I don't expect anything of you…'

'Good! At least you learned something useful from me even if it's only to lower your expectations. Now, get dressed. As for this betrothal, there is no reason we can't co-ordinate the denouement by means of the post. I think it is preferable if we don't see each other until this is all over. Goodbye.'

Nell stared at the door that snapped shut behind him, her hand still outstretched towards him and her mind still reeling.

Chapter Fifteen

If Hunter had hoped that escaping back to the familiar territory of London would relieve some of his confusion and pain, he had not taken into account being balked by his own servants. They had not taken kindly to being told, in graphic terms, that their questions about why Miss Nell was staying at Welbeck while he departed precipitately were strictly unwelcome.

Not that they said anything aloud. Their commentary was passive, but very clear. They went about their duties as usual, but the act of being shaved by Biggs had taken on such a menacing cast that Hunter had decided to forgo the experience altogether. Hidgins, for his part, had discovered his ancestors' Gaelic gloom and on the one time since his return that Hunter had forced himself to take Valiant out to try to gallop out his depression, the only words Hidgins had deigned to address to him had been a very non-subservient 'You're a fool' and, adding insult to injury, 'My lord'.

Hunter hadn't even been tempted to land him a facer. He had swung onto Valiant's back and said nothing because there was nothing to say. He had considered pointing out to the two of them that their punishment was superfluous because he was already sufficiently deep in hell. There were two versions to that hell—it hadn't taken as far as Potters Bar to realise he wanted to turn back. That the thought of leaving her, even if it was the right thing to do, was…frightening. Instead of turning back he had forced his poor horses to the edge of their ability and probably broken the Wild Hunt Club's record on the road to London.

Back in London the nightmare had shifted once again—even here she had completely taken over. For the first time neither Tim nor his mother were present, just Nell; there was no blood, no disintegrating bodies, just the inexorable rise of fear as Nell headed towards the cliff, and though he ran as fast as he could, she receded into the distance and then he had woken, not in his bed, but in a casket, the sound of earth striking above, and he realised they were burying him instead of Tim. He had finally woken in earnest, but not before scoring his wrist with bloody scratches as he tried to escape. He had lain there, frozen and panting and ashamed.

There was even relief in having Biggs and Hidgins angry at him. It was certainly more palatable than the solicitous or pitying looks that the truth would likely elicit. He also would have happily avoided his friends, but the evening after his return Biggs knocked once on the library door and announced to the ether, 'Lord Ravenscar. My lord.'

Ravenscar strode in without waiting to be invited.

'What has bit Biggs?'

'What do you want, Ravenscar?'

'That's a fine welcome from master and man.' Ravenscar went over and poured himself a brandy. When Hunter didn't answer Ravenscar poured him a glass as well.

'So, how fares your engagement?'

'It's over.'

Ravenscar raised a brow.

'I don't know whether to offer condolences or congratulations.'

'You can offer me the sight of your backside as you leave. I'm in no mood for company.'

The knocker sounded again and Hunter surged to his feet to tell Biggs not to let anyone else in. But Biggs was already taking Lord Stanton's hat and cane.

'Et tu?' Hunter said, resigned. 'Biggs, do me a favour and tell everyone else I've gone to the country or to hell or something.'

'To hell? Most assuredly. My lord.'

Stanton stared in surprise at Biggs's receding back.

'What's wrong with Biggs?'

Hunter shrugged. He was raw and restless, but the thought of being left with his own thoughts was almost worse. No, it *was* worse. He still hadn't got thoroughly drunk because he hadn't taken that path in years. Since Tim's suicide. But with each passing hour the temptation of revisiting that oblivion grew. He downed the brandy Ravenscar had poured him and walked over to the sideboard to pour a more substantial glass.

Ravenscar answered Stanton's question.

'Biggs is sulking and our friend here is in a foul mood. Makes one wonder what happened at the horse fair. Didn't know losing those water rights would have such an effect on you.'

'I didn't. She's selling me part of the riverfront.'

'Is she? That's very generous. So what's the problem?

You don't actually need the estate itself. By all accounts you should be celebrating.'

Hunter smiled down at the brandy and raised his glass.

'I am. I got what I wanted. To have my cake and eat it, too. Clever me.'

He drained his glass and Stanton moved towards the fireplace, frowning.

'Are you guilty about the girl? If you manage it carefully, you might be able to avoid too much scandal, and quite frankly with her inheritance she won't have a problem finding a husband, so...'

'I'm well aware of that!' Hunter snapped. 'She already had the offer she wanted from her childhood hero, Charles Welbeck.'

Ravenscar's brows rose, but there was a considering look in his eyes now.

'That was quick! My hat off to the girl.'

'That's enough, Raven,' Stanton said quietly and Hunter poured himself another measure of brandy. He had been right—solicitude was worse than anger. It was clear they saw through him. What was the point?

'I can't stand it.'

There was a moment's silence. Then Stanton came and poured himself a glass as well. Ravenscar went over to the fireplace and crouched down to shove twists of paper between the logs. Hunter forced himself to break the silence.

'Never mind. It's for the best.'

Ravenscar lit the fire and stood up, brushing his hands. 'As little as I want to see you hitched, man, I think you're an idiot. Why the devil did you just leave the field if you actually wanted her?'

'What the devil can I offer her? I can't promise I could even keep her safe from myself, let alone from life. She deserves better.'

'Damn, I take offence on your account. She won't find anyone better. If you care for her, go do something about it. Might be a little uncomfortable for you if she marries someone else and settles into Bascombe Hall and you have to watch her crooning over little ones that might have been yours, but you'll recover eventually.'

'Very helpful, Raven,' Stanton said curtly as he watched Hunter.

Hunter took his glass to the armchair by the fire and sat down. His mind had dubbed it 'her armchair' since every time he saw it he remembered that first night she had appeared on his doorstep. The thought of going through life at Hunter Hall, just a few miles from her, watching her married, having children, a life... He sank his head into his hands. It hurt. Physically. He never would have believed that. Even his grief over Tim had been more internal and it had been easier to turn it into rage at the world, and into that wilful self-destruction that his friends and their joint commitment to help men damaged by war had finally put an end to. But this— this locked him down, it filled his body with lead and sank him.

She's better off without you. Remember what you did to her? No wonder she had looked so appalled. If that hadn't happened he might have even succeeded in convincing himself he could keep her safe. It hadn't even been night time! He hadn't even noticed he had fallen asleep. That just showed how dangerous she was. No, how dangerous *he* was. He hadn't hurt her badly this time, but what would happen next time? If he ever really hurt her... It was unthinkable. She deserved better.

She was probably still at Welbeck and the shining prince was hard at work wearing down her defences. She had been shattered by his betrayal. He had noticed only too well she hadn't denied outright that she still loved him. Perhaps in the end she would...

He had been outsmarted, outmanoeuvred and felled by a twenty-one-year-old Saxon witch. And she...she deserved someone honest and serious and who would cherish her...love her...

Every time his mind presented this commendable resolution his heart fought back with a less articulate but much more visceral protest. *I* would cherish her. With every breath in my body. I would love her. Lust for her, love her, live for her, whatever it took. The words, childish and insistent, kept beating at him from inside. *I need her.* For the first time in his life he needed someone. He didn't even understand what she did to him, but something had just begun to happen to him. He wanted desperately to be selfish and take that risk. It wasn't right that she hold his hand and offer to let him rest, then leave him to writhe alone.

He should never have played God in her life, but this punishment was just unfair.

In his mind he conjured her into the study and sank to his knees and knelt against her, which was as pathetic as anything he could imagine, but there it was. He should have known from the beginning... He had known. There had been enough signs. Even trivial gestures like lacing his fingers through hers after finding her in the paddock with Daisy. He hadn't done anything that mawkish since he was a child being taken for a walk—no, not even then.

With her it had been so natural he hadn't even noticed the incongruity. He didn't just want her. He wanted her with him. In whatever ditch he next found himself in life, he needed her with him.

Everything was narrowing down to one need—to be with her. None of the arguments he had carefully formulated had put the slightest dent in that conviction. It was as futile as trying to explain to a three-year-old that there weren't really monsters in the dark. He needed her.

He stood abruptly and the way the room tilted and the level of amber liquid in the decanter made it clear he was well on his way to achieving his ambition to get drunk. He ignored his friends and tugged on the bell pull. When Biggs appeared he moved towards the door as steadily as he could.

'Pack a bag for me. Tell Hidgins to bring round the curricle.'

'Bring…now, my lord?'

'Now.'

Biggs lost his stiffness, his eyes darting to Ravenscar and Stanton, but they both shrugged helplessly.

'It's almost nine in the evening, sir, and you're drunk. In the morning we…'

'Biggs. Pack a bag and send for Hidgins or I'll do it myself.'

'All right, I'll find him, but he will drive. You're in no fit state…'

'Fine. You find him, I'll pack.'

'You most certainly will not…'

'Then I'll find him, you pack.'

Biggs planted himself firmly in front of Hunter, feet apart, chin up.

'My lord, you will sit down and I will bring some

bread and cheese because you haven't eaten all day and then I will speak to Hidgins and I will pack, and if once you have eaten you still wish to drive your precious horses through the night in a state of inebriation, you may do so. Otherwise I shall instruct Hidgins to lock the stables and swallow the key.'

'I can pick locks, you know.'

'I do know. I taught you. Lord Ravenscar, Lord Stanton, do make him sit down and talk some sense into him.'

Biggs disappeared and Hunter went and sat and a wave of dizziness and despair washed over him. He sank his head into his hands. Even his hair ached.

'I can't stand this,' he mumbled. 'I need to return there. Now.'

Stanton spoke, his voice gentle.

'We'll take you there if you want, but Biggs is right— you can't go like this. The only place you will end up in this state is a ditch.'

Hunter squeezed his head. They were right, he knew he was in no state to drive, but even the thought of waiting until morning was unbearable. Now that he had admitted his weakness, it was impossible to wait. He needed to see her now.

The knocker sounded and for one mad moment Hunter thought he had, by sheer force of will, conjured her up on his doorstep. He groaned.

'Whoever it is, tell them to go to hell.'

Chapter Sixteen

Nell looked up at the door. There was a light in the same room as a week ago and she prayed that meant he was at home. Alone. She remembered he had said he didn't entertain women here, but the thought of encountering Lady Felton was painful even in the realm of pure possibility. She took a deep breath and marched up the stairs. This time she not only succeeded in knocking, but it seemed a long wait for the door to open. Biggs's expression when he saw her shifted from haughty dismissal to shock.

'Miss Nell!'

'Is his lordship in, Biggs? And alone?'

'No, miss. I mean, yes, miss. I mean his lordship is in, but he isn't alone. Come in.'

She took a step back, trying not to let the burning turn to tears.

'Never mind, Biggs. Just inform Lord Hunter…'

Biggs moved down the stairs towards her.

'Lord Ravenscar and Lord Stanton are with him, miss. They are his closest friends and utterly trustworthy. But you must come in, please. You cannot be alone in the streets at this hour. I will make you some tea. And sandwiches.'

She gave a watery laugh and followed him into a room as he hurriedly lit a couple of candles from the taper he held.

'I am going to inform Lord Hunter you are here. Will you promise not to leave?'

The door closed behind him and she tugged her cloak more tightly about her. She heard another door open and before she could even move towards the unlit fireplace Hunter entered the room.

He was never very fastidious about his dress, but he looked almost as unkempt as he had after his brawl with Hidgins. He wore no coat or cravat and his shirt hung loose, and his hair looked as if she had definitely interrupted a tryst, so she wondered if Biggs had lied to her.

'I'm sorry. I didn't mean to interrupt your evening.'

'It's no bother. We were just leaving,' said a voice from the doorway and she turned to see two exceedingly handsome men, one dark and one fair, inspecting her.

'Go away,' Hunter said without turning to them. The fair one smiled at her and bowed out of the doorway, but the dark one lingered for a moment with an assessing smile on his face before the fair one tugged him away.

'Are you all right? Has something happened?' Hunter asked as the door closed and Nell shook her head.

She had meant to launch into her prepared speech, but the words that came out were an expression of all the wonder and confusion she felt.

'I was here just a week ago.'

Surely it was impossible to be so transformed in a matter of days? What would have happened if he had not come to Tilney four years ago? If eventually her infatuation and dowry had enticed Charles into offering for her? She might never have realised that she wasn't even very fond of him and that Charles hardly knew her and didn't really want to, not as she was, flawed and thirsting for life. How could she have known she needed a man who could make her laugh, and burn, and make her worry about him and want to hold him?

It had taken all her resolution to navigate these past couple of days—her father's anger and Charles's repeated attempts to make her stay at Welbeck had been difficult, but nothing like the disappointment when she had gone in search of Hunter only to find he had left immediately after their confrontation. Her tentative knock on his door had been answered by Biggs and she had stared past him at the open trunk and the pile of clothes on the bed. She didn't know what she had expected, but to hear that Hunter had already left had held her frozen. It was only the obvious compassion on Biggs's face that had set her moving again and she had retreated to lick her wounds in the privacy of her room.

It wasn't possible to force Hunter to care for her, not the way she needed, but it made no sense that she wouldn't see him again. It just wasn't possible. This was Hunter—of course she had to see him again. That single-minded thought clung to her, warping everything else around her.

In the end it was Betsy who helped tip the scales— her sniffling and red eyes as she had dressed Nell for dinner had distracted Nell from her own misery enough to realise that she was not the only sufferer from Hunter and Hidgins's disappearance. But if Betsy had no power to control her fate, Nell did—she was a wealthy woman and had to answer to no one. If she could not marry the man she loved, she could at least love him in the only way open to her. It might be outrageous and scandalous, but she would deal with the repercussions later. She didn't doubt that he wanted to bed her, and if all he could manage at this point was a mistress, she was determined to be that mistress. Later she would do her best to find her way through his defences to the generous heart she knew was there. She might fail, but she had to try.

Betsy had been only too happy to help her arrange for the hire of a post-chaise and to give her notice at Welbeck to become Nell's maid. Together they had collected Mrs Calvert from her sister's at Stoke Newington and continued to London. She had no idea what Mrs Calvert and Betsy thought of her actions when they reached London but they were quite content to trust her, probably more than she trusted herself.

She had fully expected to find that Hunter was out, or busy, and she still expected him to try to send her packing—but that at least she was determined to resist.

'You shouldn't have come here,' he said into the silence, confirming her thoughts. 'It isn't fair.'

She must have shivered because he took her hand and she followed him into the other room where the fire was still high. She sat down in her chair gratefully and he picked up a half-full glass and stood watching her. There was more light here and she saw he hadn't shaved and there was that bruising beneath his eyes that reminded her of how he had looked four years ago. He had moved deep inside himself and was watching from the battlements.

There was a knock on the door and they both started.

'Tea, sir, and something to eat for Miss Nell.'

Biggs set down the tray.

'Shall I send word to Miss Amelia?' he asked the silence.

'There is no need, thank you, Biggs,' Nell answered as she took the cup of tea he offered. 'Betsy and Mrs Calvert are waiting for me at the Red Lion. Or rather for Mrs Jones, widow.'

For a moment Hunter's eyes warmed with laughter before closing down again and that and the tea started thawing her out.

'It's nice to see you follow at least some of my advice, however dubious. But you still shouldn't be here.'

Nell sipped her tea.

'Am I keeping you from something?' she asked politely once Biggs had withdrawn.

He just shook his head, his eyes fixed on her so intently he seemed to be looking through her. She put down her tea.

'Good. I was worried Lady Felton might be here. Even though you said she doesn't come here, I still wondered if you might be with her. But I dare say you saw her yesterday, didn't you?'

He shook his head.

'Today?'

'No, and I won't be seeing her tomorrow either. Whatever relationship we once had was effectively over before I left London. I am apparently more honourable than I had once thought.'

He put down his glass. Some of the amber liquid sloshed onto the table and he stared at it and rubbed his forehead. 'You shouldn't be here.'

'You said that before. Twice.'

'It's still true. Why are you here?' His voice was less assured now.

'I have a proposition to make.'

'A proposition?'

Even though the fire had warmed her, she was shaky and cold inside. Now she would have to find the strength to tell him what she had come for and the strength not to tell him what she was really here for because that would undoubtedly drive him away, back past those battlements that kept him safe and separate. She needed some of that cider to give her courage again. She needed him to touch her instead of just watching her like that. Even if he didn't love her, even if it was just the kind of lust he obviously took so lightly as to dismiss his latest mistress without a backward glance, he could still hold her until this aching became bearable.

She fumbled at the strings of her cloak. She had come as a prospective mistress and so it was best to begin somewhere.

'What the devil?'

Nell flushed as she removed her cloak to reveal the low-cut Parisian evening gown Anna had convinced her to commission, but which she had been convinced she would never have the nerve to wear. She had made Betsy cinch her stays to the point where her breasts balanced precariously against the silvery lace and embroidery of the bodice, making it a miracle they hadn't yet decided to escape. She had come ready to compete with the Lady Feltons of the world, well aware she was in a losing position and needing whatever added inducement available to her. But his shocked response shook her confidence.

'Don't you like it?'

'Are you trying to kill me?' His knuckles stood out sharply as his hand closed on the back of the armchair opposite.

That was better.

'So you *do* like it?' she asked, lowering her voice.

'Nell…you can't do this to me. Come here. Like this. I warned you.'

His eyes rose to hers and she read hunger in there and leashed desperation. Her heart surged ahead and her lungs strained at her tight stays. Perhaps she shouldn't have had Betsy cinch her quite so well. It was time for the next stage in her battle and she needed to breathe to do that.

'I know you did. You still haven't answered my question. Do you like it?'

'Like is not the word that comes to mind. In fact, very little is coming to mind at the moment. It's all going elsewhere, which is why you need to put your cloak back on. Now.'

'I'll take the dress off if you don't like it,' she offered, shrugging the delicate lace sleeve just an inch off her shoulder.

Hunter groaned and shoved the armchair aside, pulling her to her feet and sinking his face into her hair.

'Nell, I'm in agony, I'm half-drunk and I have no willpower left. If you don't leave now, I'm going to strip off that impossible dress before it disintegrates and take everything on offer and not Beelzebub himself will be able to stop me from ravishing you. So—leave. Now!'

His stubble scraped against her cheek as she turned his face to hers, her mouth seeking his. The most beautiful mouth in the world, she thought, her whole body flooding with desire as she tasted him. She started with his lower lip first, because it was tense and needed extra attention. Slowly, lovingly, tracing it and drawing it in between hers very gently. His body vibrated against hers and his hands were fisted in her dress. It would probably be ruined, but it would be well worth it if only she could be ruined alongside it. Ruined and rebuilt. This amazing man was all about ruin and rebuilding and whether he knew it yet or not he was hers. Not just his body, but all of him. No matter how long it took or how many mistresses she had to circumvent to win him.

She gave his lower lip one last lingering caress with her tongue and leaned back against his arms. His eyes had turned pagan again. Apparently Beelzebub wasn't going to interfere with his minion after all.

'More?' she asked. 'Or shall I stop?'

The hard ridge of his arousal was pressing under her stomach, a hot, thudding presence that was in dialogue with its twin soul between her thighs, and she wanted nothing better than to shift so that they could carry on a much more intimate conversation. As the silence stretched she turned, reaching for the hooks at her waist.

'Could you help undo my laces? Betsy tied them dreadfully tight and I'm afraid I might swoon if we carry on like this. I won't be needing them again tonight, will I? I told Betsy I probably wouldn't return tonight and I am very glad you were here and there wasn't anyone with you. Anyone female, I mean. Well, are you going to help? Oh, never mind. I'll do it.'

He shoved her hands away, his own fumbling with the laces.

'You're killing me, Nell. I'm done playing fair. Do you hear me?'

The relief as the stays were released made her sigh with pleasure and she leaned against him, kissing and licking at the hot skin of his throat, tasting him with avid joy as he peeled away all the unnecessary layers, giving herself utterly into his care.

It was still a shock when his hand very gently cupped her breast, hot and hard against her though he didn't move, just held her, his hand warm and peculiarly gentle against her sensitised skin. She rested her mouth on the galloping pulse on the side of his neck, feeling its mirror under her own skin where he held her, feeling the gathering of her flesh, tightening, hardening until the bud of her nipple pressed against his palm. The moment of contact coursed through her body and his, a shared shudder that set him in motion, and her dress, her flimsy petticoat and drawers were sheared away, disintegrating as he had threatened.

He touched her everywhere, her back, her buttocks, dipping between her thighs, receding, finding her breast again, more insistent, his palm and thumb caressing the sensitive nipple, sending spears of fire through her, weaving a web of fire around and through her body, everything gathering towards the new centre of her universe.

It was everything she had wanted, but still not enough. Her stockings, his shirt and pantaloons were all in the way. She wanted *him*.

She dragged up his shirt, sighing as her hands skimmed over his back. Later she would explore this beautiful surface, inch by inch...and his waist. No blows below the waist, that was very clever. She didn't want anything to harm Hunter anywhere and especially not where that heat was pressed against her and she wanted so desperately to touch.

'I want to touch you again. There,' she said against his mouth, or tried to say because her voice would hardly form, so she made her point by pressing her hips even more insistently to his.

Once again he stopped and his arms closed around her, freezing them for a moment.

'Not a good idea right now.' He sounded underwater. 'This is your last chance to draw back.'

She tightened her arms around his neck, rising on tiptoe to say the words against his mouth.

'You will have to forcibly remove me from this house if you want me to leave. You should probably dress me first, but don't expect any help from me.'

He grunted and swung her into his arms and turned towards the door and for a shocked moment she wondered if he would carry through on his threat and put her out as she was, but then his long strides took them up the stairs and she leaned back against him, smiling in relief.

'I'm awfully heavy,' she said apologetically as they made it to the top.

His arms tightened on her.

'You're perfect.'

'You must be drunk.' She laughed and he nudged open a door and slid her down his body, his hands shaping her, curving and lingering over her buttocks, and her legs tried to separate, to make room for something.

'Not any more. Not on brandy. Wait here. I'll light a fire.'

She grabbed at him as he started to move away.

'I don't need a fire. I'm already on fire. I need you to do something about it.'

He cupped her face in his hands and rested his forehead on hers for a moment.

'Very well. There are other ways to keep you warm.'

Not warm. Ablaze. That was what it felt like when

her breasts finally were pressed against his chest. How on earth would she ever be able to move away again? He was as hard as a sculpture, but silky smooth and hot, and the hair on his chest teased her breasts, making it impossible not to move against him, rub herself over him like a cat begging for a caress. His growl did sound like some species of the larger of the feline family as his hand obliged her, gathering her against him again. With his other he released the fall of his pantaloons to strip them off, but before she could even register the long hard heat of his arousal pressed against her she found herself on her back on a bed that must have been one of the biggest she had ever seen.

She lay there, absorbing this new state of affairs, one of her legs bent on the bed, the other dangling over its side, her hair scattered everywhere. She was naked except for her stockings while a very tall, very large, very naked and very aroused man stood over her with a look that gave credence to all his talk about marauding. Then he smiled, a very marauding smile. His gaze moved over her, slowly, his expression shifting with each curve and dip travelled, heating her as he went. It was an invasion and a branding and when he reached her abdomen her legs drew together protectively, but he leaned his knee on the bed between them so that they clamped against him. He traced her cheek with his knuckles, so softly she had to turn her head into the caress to feel him.

'Don't hide from me. You're beautiful. All of you.'

She could feel her body shake and she sank her teeth into her lip to hold back the words. It was too soon, too much. She said the words loudly inside her head so that they wouldn't escape.

Mine. Hunter. My love.

* * *

Hunter watched her teeth sink into the plump rise of flesh and his own lips were singed with heat. He wanted her to sink her teeth into him, into any part of him. The need to see her lips part, open for him, just as he wanted her legs to open for him, felt like a compulsion. He was still sane enough to know he was falling off a cliff, but there was nothing to grasp to slow him down. He needed to be closer; he needed to feel her pliant, lithe body under him, over him. He needed her scent, her heat. It felt as though he needed to be inside her more than he needed to breathe.

He was still not clear how his erotic dreams of Nell had become a reality. How he had gone from black despair to this wanton display of long sleek limbs and impossibly silky hair on his bed, but it didn't matter. He would deal with the challenges somehow. Nothing mattered but that she was here, with him, his. She was his and would soon be irrevocably so. He was done being sensible.

He lay down beside her, sliding one leg over hers to anchor the warmth of her thighs in case she had any ideas about moving as he worked his hand upwards from her hip. When his fingers reached the shadowed curve below her breast her chest expanded on a panting breath and her lip finally slipped out, moist and reddened, and it was all he could do not to just haul himself on top of her, spread her legs, thrust into her, disappear into her damp heat until he erased himself completely.

His erection was as hard as a rock against the bite of her hip bone, but he stayed where he was, just cupping her beautiful cream and rose breast, his thumb brushing just below the nipple, watching it harden, gather, as it had downstairs, until her neck arched back in a cry she wouldn't release. He bent and tasted that arch, salty sweet and filled with her wildflower scent. He breathed it in, trying to capture it, like the last breath of air before sinking to the bottom of an unrelenting sea.

'You're mine. Mine...' he whispered against her skin, tasting her, kissing her, grating his lips and teeth and tongue over her skin until she began to squirm against him, her panting breath raising her body against his, her legs trying to part under the weight of his. One of her arms had anchored around his shoulder and her fingers bit into his flesh, sending sharp spears of pain and pleasure through him.

'Hunter,' she moaned. 'Stop, please, do something!'

'Do you want me to stop?' he murmured against her breast, his lips drawing in her nipple, tracing it with his tongue, rough and soft. He slid his fingers through the silky curls at the juncture of her thighs. She was so damp and hot his own hips surged against his will.

'No, oh, don't stop. Please...' She twisted and he shifted, letting her spread her legs to his fingers, her own leg sliding between his, seeking his tension, his weight. It pressed against his erection and he breathed in, concentrating only on the music of her body. He wanted... he needed to pleasure her, to watch that golden moment of joy and light once again.

'Just relax,' he whispered against her lips, coaxing and sliding. 'Trust me. Open your legs for me, sweetheart.'

A shudder ran through her and she sighed, lying supine as he stroked away the tension from her body, until she shuddered again, half-rising on her side to press against his body, her legs parting, and he slid his hand between her thighs, finding the silky skin, so hot and damp he couldn't control his own shudder of desire. But he concentrated on the slow torture of teasing her towards ecstasy with his fingers and body and mouth, using every skill he had and every ounce of self-control that remained to focus purely on her. Her body rose against his hand, finding her rhythm, now guiding him, her hands moving to touch him as he touched her, testing his control to its limits.

Almost as devastating as her hands were her little moans as she began to writhe under him, telling him she was so close. He wanted desperately to taste her, drink her in, but he held back. There would be time enough for that, for everything. She was his.

'Hunter, don't stop, please, I need to feel you.' Her voice was sapping his concentration and his resolve and when she pulled him to her he didn't offer much resistance. She moaned as his weight pressed her back onto the bed, her legs spreading for him, rising against his erection and burning through whatever part of his mind was still conscious and in control.

'I don't want to hurt you,' he managed to gasp out as her legs anchored around him, pulling him closer, sliding against his arousal and his fingers.

'I want this,' she whispered, her gaze holding his as she traced her fingertips down his chest. 'Even the pain.'

Her hands ran down his back, sliding over his buttocks as she raised her hips slightly. He groaned at the friction.

'If it hurts too much, stop me. I'll stop, I swear.'

Her hair gleamed gold as she shook her head.

'I want you.'

His last coherent thought as she began following and

matching the motion of his body was that he hoped she would still feel the same when she eventually realised what he was. Then he was only sensation, the rising build of beautiful tension he could feel in her body until her head arched back as she climaxed, calling out his name, and he abandoned scruples and control and sank into her, pushing past the resistance of her maidenhead, a confusion of contrition and joyous possession and physical exultation.

She froze for a moment, her nails digging into his shoulders, but then her body shifted, taking him in, and he heard his voice call her name again and again as he moved, the waves of pleasure crashing over him, reducing him to a single point of joy. Just her name, but inside the vastness of his body as it rose to break into a million shards of pleasure was a deeper cry.

I love you. My Nell. I need you.
Just don't let me fall asleep.

He was crushing her, he realised sleepily, forcing himself to shift his weight and pulling her on top of him as he groped for the blanket. He wasn't in the least cold himself, not with the blood flowing tangibly through his veins and her long body was stretched the length of him and her breath against his neck and her beautiful breasts...

Nell. Here, in his bed. His. If this was a dream, it more than compensated for his years of nightmares.

He opened his eyes in the dark. He didn't want to, but he couldn't afford to go to sleep.

'I'll light a fire.'

She murmured something and reached for him, then

snuggled deeper under the blanket, and he fought the urge to climb back into bed with her and just...

He took his dressing gown and went to bring a candle from the hall, stopping as Biggs climbed the last stair with a neatly folded pile of very feminine clothes in his arms.

'Here are Miss Nell's clothes, my lord. Will you be needing anything else?'

'I...' Oh, what was the harm? 'Yes. Some hot water and linen.'

'Shall I send word to Hidgins you will be needing him to drive Miss Nell to the Red Lion afterwards, sir?'

Hunter grimaced at the unspoken rebuke, but nodded. He didn't want to let her go, but considerations of propriety aside, he couldn't allow her to stay the night. He didn't yet know how he would keep her and still manage to keep her safe from him. There had to be a way, but right now his brain was too contented to think clearly. She was here. She was his. He would deal with reality later.

Back inside the room he crouched down to light the fire and then with a deep breath he went to sit down on the side of the bed, gently stroking her thigh through the sheet, enjoying the very feeling of having her here in his bed. He was glad no woman had ever been in this bed before. This was Nell's place now. When she was in London he would have to find somewhere else to sleep, perhaps fit one of the rooms on the empty floor above. Even if he wasn't sleeping in it, he wanted to know she was in his bed.

The nascent flames struck her eyes with silver and her hair with gold where it spread over his pillows. Then her eyelids fluttered down and in an instant he was submerged in scalding heat again, as if his release had merely been a prelude. He bent towards her, but drew back at the soft scratching on the door, and she disappeared under the blanket with a faint squeak. Hunter suppressed a groan and drew back. He should have sent for cold water instead.

'You can come in, Biggs.'

Biggs entered, his eyes firmly on the broad tray he carried, but his voice was suspiciously shaky.

'Hot water, linen towels and a spare dressing gown. Anything else, sir?'

Once Biggs left, Hunter rose resolutely and took the dressing gown from the pile. Nell sat up, clutching the blanket to her, and he draped the dressing gown gently over her shoulders. It swallowed her up, drooping over her arms, and he remembered how she had looked in his jacket in the Welbeck gardens just a few days ago, a whole existence ago. She looked up and he saw the memory mirrored in her eyes and he kissed her quickly and moved back.

'Later I will have Biggs prepare a bath and join you in it, but for the moment we will make do with this. Are you very sore?'

She shook her head, but her flush was so extreme he could tell she probably wouldn't tell him if she was. He really should leave her, give her some privacy to deal with this herself, but he didn't want to, not yet. The ritual wasn't complete. It would be like leaving a wedding before the vows were spoken.

'Don't worry,' he said gently as he dipped the linen into the water. 'Just relax.'

'You said that before,' she answered, her voice hitching on the end as he moved towards her.

'So I did. I'm consistent. Just open your legs… And don't tell me I said that before as well.'

Her hand shot out and grasped his arm, stopping him. Then she let go.

'You did.'

'I told you; I'm consistent.'

When he was done she looked up suddenly and smiled. He turned away, battling another wave of pain, this time in his chest. He should feel calmer now that she was unequivocally his, but he didn't. In fact, a peculiar fear was taking hold of him and he fell back on the safety of practicality.

'When you are dressed I will see you back to the Red Lion and tomorrow I will go to Doctors' Commons to procure a special licence so we can make an honest woman of you.'

She sat down on the side of the bed, holding her clothes to her chest.

'No, Hunter. I didn't come here to entrap you into marrying me.' She was pale, but her voice was very clear and he felt his nerves stretch further.

'I know that. There is no question of entrapping. We are far beyond that. We have other matters to discuss.'

'Such as?'

Her eyes narrowed into her stubborn look and he hesitated.

'How we are going to proceed. I didn't want you… anyone to know about…my difficulty sleeping. But I can't very well push that under the rug now, can I? I will just have to make sure you aren't…exposed to any risk.'

Her eyes narrowed.

'Putting aside the question of marriage for the moment, how precisely would you propose to do that?'

'Well, you will be at Hunter Hall most of the time and I will arrange for a bedroom in the East Wing which is closer to the servants and where you won't be...disturbed.'

'I see. And here in London?'

'You will probably spend less time here and when you are here I will sleep in a bedroom on the next floor. The house is big enough.'

She crossed her arms.

'No.'

'What, no?' he asked, wary of her expression. That determined look typically boded ill for him.

'I told you, I didn't come here to force you to do something you so obviously find onerous. I came here knowing that I wanted to be part of your life, even as a mistress, and I am willing to pay the price for that choice. But I am not willing to marry you because you think it is the right thing to do. If you ever do wish to marry me...I mean *really* wish to marry me because you want to be with me, I will consider it, but I will not agree to a cold-blooded arrangement based on your arbitrary conditions.'

'Damn it, they aren't arbitrary conditions. They are measures. For your safety.'

'No, they're for *your* safety!'

'Nell, don't you understand how serious this is? I cannot allow myself to fall asleep with you and if you are here...all the time... Damn it, you must see why there has to be some distance between us. I had to fight to stay awake just now! If I start relaxing my guard... I have to protect you...'

He was begging again, but she didn't look in the

least understanding. She looked adamant. She stood and picked up her clothes.

'You loved Tim and you felt responsible for him and frustrated with him and it all mixes up to feeling responsible for his life and his death, and however much I don't think you have any grounds for guilt, I can understand that in a way it is inevitable. But this is different, Hunter. I do not need to be protected from myself or from you and I won't allow you to dictate my life based on considerations of safety. I am willing to risk my heart with you. I am not willing to be put in a box because you are scared of risking yours. Now, I really should return to the Red Lion. When you are willing to talk sensibly, we can discuss this further.'

'You *are* mad! There is nothing to discuss. We have already anticipated the wedding night. Now there is only a very simple "Yes, I will"!'

She shrugged her dress over her chemise.

'No, I won't.'

He turned away and grabbed his own clothes and began dressing, trying to ignore the eager rush of heat that had burst in him at her melodramatic nonsense about risking hearts. He might have revised his own assessment about whether or not love was a fantasy, but he couldn't forget that a week ago this girl had thought herself head over heels in love with another man. Now simply because she had fallen out of love with Welbeck and into sexual excitement with him, she fancied herself in love again. Well, however much he might want it to be true, he wasn't so gullible. Besides, none of that changed the fact that the issue wasn't even in question— of course she was going to marry him.

'You don't have the prerogative of saying no, not after

last night. Has it escaped your notice that you might even now be carrying the next Lord Hunter?'

Her hand rose towards her abdomen and he was shocked by the possessive heat that swept through him at the thought of her holding his child, a little girl with her eyes. A boy. She would be an amazing mother. Oh, God, if only she wasn't trying to destroy him. Because if he hurt her, it would. He wouldn't be able to find his way back from that. Ever. That would be the end.

Her whole body had tightened at the mention of a child, gathering herself to shield that hypothetical being. He looked so tortured and guilty that Nell's resolution faltered. He was offering her so much already; so much more than she had dreamed possible just a few hours ago. She had come here because the thought of not having him in her life, in whatever guise, had been unbearable. But she could see that her actions had pushed him into a corner—he was not really a rake worthy of the name. If she refused to marry him, their association would end—he had only succumbed to temptation on the assumption that they would marry. But if she agreed, on his terms...

She flexed her hands. She didn't know how to fix this, but at the very least she owed him some honesty.

'Perhaps I never should have put you in this position, Gabriel. I should have realised you would find it hard to accept me as a mistress, but I wasn't strong enough to just let you walk away. I know you don't love me as I love you, but that is all the more reason for me to insist not to be put into a neat little drawer and kept separate like everything else in your life. If you do choose to marry me one day, it will have to be on the understanding that I will not respect those boundaries.'

Her voice began to shake and she tried to rally herself.

'If you will only let me be there with you…'

She gave up and reached for the stocking that had wrapped around the bedpost. He hadn't moved and when he spoke his voice was unlike him, cold and derisive.

'I thought I told you it was unwise to confuse sexual pleasure with love. Until a few days ago you thought yourself in love with Welbeck, or have you forgotten?'

She deserved that, but she wouldn't back down.

'You were right that I didn't understand what it meant then.'

'Oh, and now you think you do?' he mocked.

'Yes.'

His mouth closed tightly, but she waited, watching as he grabbed a cravat from the back of a chair and began winding it around his neck.

'Is that all it takes with you? A few days and some fun in bed? At that rate you'll find someone else to fantasise about in a week.'

She was surprised how little his contemptuous comment hurt. It was so unlike him that it rang utterly false and contrarily it fed the determination that had brought her to London. He was mangling his already crumpled cravat and he looked so defiant, so determined to keep her at arm's length, so…young.

'I love you, Gabriel.'

'You should be a stickler for accuracy, schoolmistress—"I lust for you" is the proper term. What the devil is so amusing?'

She couldn't prevent her smile from widening at his outrage.

'I was just remembering that I called you a dandy a week ago. Your poor cravat.'

He dropped his hands from the abused linen.

'Nell…!'

'I love you, Gabriel. If I do agree to marry you, you will have to accept that I intend to share your bed, your nights and your nightmares. I'm not scared of you. You may think keeping apart from people makes you safer, but it doesn't; it just makes you scared.'

'Nell…'

'You should be grateful that my conditions don't include a demand that you love me in return, but I will stand firm on the others.'

He covered his face with his hands.

'But that is the only demand I *can* comply with. What the devil do you think this is all about? I love you. I had no idea this was even possible until I was in the middle of it; it felt like it was killing me to leave you there. Can't you see that is precisely why I can't let you too close? If I ever hurt you…it would destroy me, Nell. I'm not strong enough to survive hurting you.'

She stood up slowly. She wanted to believe him so very badly.

'I am not so easily broken, Gabriel. I am asking you to trust me.'

'You're asking too much.'

She nodded. Perhaps she was asking too much, too soon. For now perhaps his admission was enough. She, of all people, should know how powerful fear was and that rushing her fences wasn't wise.

She went to him and gently pulled down his hands, clasping them in hers. It was amazing how expressive his face could be when he wasn't on guard. She smiled at him. He was so beautiful and he was hers. She was sure of it now. How clever of her to be brave and come to him.

'Very well. For now we will go ahead with the marriage. We can discuss terms later.'

He looked down at her, his mouth tight. His hands rose to clasp her face, tense, pressing.

'You have no intention of conceding an inch, do you?'

'How can I? I love you and you are asking me to let you suffer alone. I could never promise that.'

He dropped his hands.

'You're not really in love with me. Nothing that will survive the reality of what I am and how little I have to offer.'

'Now who is being insulting? I know you think I am weak, but I don't think I am, not when it really matters; I'm much stronger than you think. I will go to Bascombe tomorrow and…'

He pulled her against him, pressing her face into his shoulder, his own voice unsteady above her.

'I don't want you to go.'

She pushed away, reaching up to brush back his tumbled hair.

'I'm just going to Bascombe, not the Antipodes. Or you could try to convince me to stay. I would like that.'

He wavered, his eyes turning into tawny fire, but she could see the fear was there in the way his gaze flicked to the bed behind her.

'If you do fall asleep and make a nuisance of yourself I'll push you out of bed,' she offered, tracing a line from his cheekbone down the groove by his mouth to his jaw. It was going to be very tiresome, making it clear to all those women he wasn't available any longer. It was almost a pity he was so very handsome. 'Perhaps we should put a mattress on the floor so you don't hurt yourself when I shove you off.'

'This isn't amusing, Nell.' She didn't know if he sounded more annoyed or desperate.

'I will never force you to do anything you don't want to do,' she replied, tracing the line of his lower lip now. 'If you can't bear living with me, then you won't. But we both know this is more than a fear of falling asleep with me.'

He dragged her against him again, his mouth pressing into her hair.

'This is torture. I don't know what to do.'

She managed to turn her head enough to kiss the side of his neck. She loved the velvet-smooth skin under his ear, the cooler softness of his earlobe. She loved the way his breathing caught as she tasted him there.

'That's a good sign,' she murmured. 'Until now you've known precisely what to do and you've been completely wrong. If I had been foolish enough to listen to you, I wouldn't have come here. Why don't you try listening to me for a change?'

His arms didn't release their near stranglehold on her, but a reluctant laugh shook through him. 'You don't pull your punches, do you, schoolmistress? What makes you think you know better?'

She put enough distance between them to take his face in her hands again.

'I don't. But the thought of not being with you is worse than any alternative. I would rather brave a thousand terrors than lose you. Can't we try? Even if we fail? I am quite certain you don't *want* to hurt me...'

'I would rather kill myself than hurt you!'

'Well, I would rather pursue a third option instead.

I'm beginning to see that having horses with such melo-dramatic names as Valiant and Courage might not be purely coincidental.'

As she had hoped he laughed, brushing his mouth over her ear, slipping over its curves until she started to quiver under him.

'I think I've had enough insults from you for a life-time, love. How the devil do you always make them sound so reasonable?'

'I'm clever like that,' she murmured, turning her head to give him better access to the sweep of her throat.

'My clever, brave love…' He kissed the hollow be-neath her ear, drawing her skin gently into his mouth, and a shudder ran through her, arcing her body against him, her legs parting invitingly, and he slid his leg be-tween them. 'We'd better lock the door before Biggs comes demanding I deliver Mrs Jones, widow, safely back to the Red Lion for the night.'

'Does that mean I can stay?'

'It means I can't let you go, heaven help us. But one more insult and I'll…'

'You'll what?'

'Once I regain my sanity I'll think of something.'

'I look forward to it. Meanwhile, kiss me, please…'

* * * * *

LORD RAVENSCAR'S INCONVENIENT BETROTHAL

To my fearless editor Nic Caws, who swoops in and saves me from myself and my babies from creative quicksand.

Raven and Lily are particularly grateful for your superpowers.

Chapter One

Alan Rothwell, Lord Ravenscar, drew his team of black purebreds to a stop on the uneven drive of Hollywell House. It was fitting that each mile passed on the road from Bath had added a shade of grey to the clouds. It suited his mood and it certainly suited the gloom of the sooty stone and unkempt lawn of Hollywell House.

The estate had seen better days and with any luck would see them again, but first he would have to buy the place. The only problem was that he had no idea from whom. The news that Albert Curtis had dropped dead in church in the middle of his sermon after recovering from a bout of fever was doubly unwelcome—now Alan would have to renegotiate the purchase with whoever inherited the house.

'What now, Captain?' His groom tilted his head to inspect the clouds and Alan handed him the reins and jumped down, avoiding a muddy rut. Even the gravel was thin on the ground and the drive in worse shape than the country lane leading up from Keynsham. No wonder poor Albert had wanted to escape to a mission in the jungle; he had not been cut out to be a landlord.

'The door's open. Perhaps the new heir is inside, come to inspect his new domain. Walk the horses while I see what I can do about this setback, Jem.'

'Matter of time before we get soaked, Captain.'

'Isn't it time you stopped calling me Captain? It's been six years since we sold out. Don't think I don't notice you only revert to rank when you're annoyed with me, Sergeant.'

'It's coming through this stretch of Somerset, Captain. Always makes you jittery.'

'With good reason. What's *your* excuse?'

'Your foul temper the closer you come to Lady Ravenscar's territory, Captain.'

Jem grinned and tapped the whip to the leader's back, setting the curricle in motion before Alan could respond to his old sergeant's provocation.

Jem was right, of course. His temper was never one of his strong points, but it undeniably deteriorated the closer he came to Ravenscar Hall. Stanton had warned him to steer clear of Hollywell and find another property, preferably on the other side of Bristol, and Stanton had a damn annoying tendency to be right. No doubt he would tell him it served him right for trying to poke one in his grandmother's eye. The satisfaction of imagining her reaction to his plans for Hollywell House was fast losing its appeal the closer he came to his childhood home.

No, not home. It had never been a true home. He had been six when he, his parents and his sister had left Ravenscar Hall for the first time, but old enough to be grateful it was behind him. The last thing he had wanted was to be dragged back there with Cat when his parents died, but at least he had spent most of those long years away at school rather than at Ravenscar, and the moment Cat had married, he had enlisted and sworn never to return as long as his grandparents were alive.

Hollywell House was another matter altogether. He had been here only last month on his return from Bristol, but his strongest memories of Hollywell were still those of a boy. For an angry and grieving twelve-year-old, Jasper and Mary Curtis's library had been a sanctuary from the brutality of his grandfather's tyranny. It was the library that had sparked the idea to acquire Hollywell for the Hope House foundation; it was light enough and large enough to make a fine memory room like the one they had established in London. After the fire at the old structure they had been using for Hope House in Bristol, it was no longer merely a good idea, it was a necessity. Whatever pressure he had to bring to bear on Albert's heir, he would do so.

He took one step into the library and stopped abruptly.

Just last month he and Albert Curtis had shared a glass of brandy in what had been a perfectly ordinary and orderly library. The only unusual features were Harry and Falstaff, two weapon-wielding suits of armour which had taken pride of place in the centre of the room, standing guard over what was once a small ornate bookcase where old Jasper had kept his favourite books, and a pair of worn leather armchairs he had brought from France before the revolution. This unusual if pleasant arrangement had been reduced to a pile of tangled steel breastplates, helmets and books, and at the edge of the chaos stood a young woman wielding a very large flanged mace which had once been held confidently in Falstaff's metal gloves.

'Did you do this?' she demanded.

The absurdity of her question when it was apparent she was not only the author of this destruction but probably also mad roused him from his shock. He surveyed the room again. And then her, more leisurely. She must be quite strong, because though the mace was substantial, she held it aloft very steadily, rather like a cricketer waiting for him to bowl. She was also reasonably pretty, so it was a pity she was mad.

'Why would I do this?' he temporised. 'You can put that mace down, by the way. I'm not coming near you, believe me.'

The tip of the mace hit the floor with a thump that shook the room, but she didn't release the handle.

'Who are you and what are you doing here?'

'What I am doing is giving you a wide berth at the moment. Is your mania general or is it directed against anything medieval?'

She looked around the room for a moment and her mouth drooped.

'I don't understand. Why would anyone do this? It makes no sense.'

'That is the definition of madness, isn't it?'

She frowned at him.

'I'm not mad. You still haven't explained who you are and what you are doing here.'

'Nor have you.'

'I don't have to. This is my house and you are trespassing.'

'You are Curtis's heir?'

She nodded, her mouth quirking at the incredulity in his voice.

'Albert Curtis was my cousin, or rather he was my mother's cousin. Are you with Mr Prosper?'

'No, I represent the people who were about to acquire the house from Albert before he inconveniently passed away.'

'That's not very nice. I think his death is much more inconvenient for him than for you,' she said, a sudden and surprising smile flickering over her face and tilting her eyes up at the corners, transforming her looks from passable to exotic. He noticed the hair peeping out from her fashionable bonnet was auburn or reddish brown, which suited the honeyed hazel of her eyes. Warm colours. He was partial to light-haired women, but he could always widen his range. He moved into the room, just a couple steps so as not to alarm her.

'Not at all. He's dead. Nothing can inconvenience him now.'

He really shouldn't be trying to shock the woman he now had to convince to sell them her legacy, but teasing a mace-wielding young woman was a temptation hard to ignore. She might be mad, but she was definitely entertaining.

'You can't possibly be a solicitor. I've met dozens and not one of them would dare say something like that.'

'Dozens? You are perhaps a criminal, then?'

'Worse. So if you're not a solicitor, what kind of representing are you doing? And why are you pursuing it now Albert is dead?'

Worse? Perhaps she *was* mad. She didn't seem addled, but neither did she seem very affected by her cousin's recent death or even by being alone in a vandalised and empty house and in the presence of a stranger. Ravenscar knew his worth when it came to women and he wasn't used to being treated with such cavalier insouciance; Rakehell Raven usually caused a much more gratifying response. Women either ran from him or ran to him, they rarely held their ground.

He nudged one of the books at the edge of the tumbled bookcase with the toe of his boot. *On Customs of the Dje-Dje Tribes of the African Plain* by Reverend John Summerly. That must have been Albert's, poor man.

'I didn't know he had died until a few days ago.'

'That still doesn't explain why you entered, knowing full well you had no business here anymore. Why?'

He took another couple steps and bent to pick up a copy of Aurelius's *Meditations* from under Harry's gauntlet with a satisfied sigh. The spine had split, but that could be fixed. He tucked it under his arm and returned his attention to the young woman and her peculiar comments. She was still watching him with suspicion, but without a glimmer of real fear. Did she really think that mace would do an ounce of good against him if he chose to divest her of it?

'What's worse than a criminal, then? A nun?' he asked.

Her eyes widened.

'On what scale is a nun worse than a criminal? And please return that book. It's mine.'

'On the scale of flirtation material. I don't flirt with nuns. Criminals are fair game.'

Her eyes widened further, the honey even more apparent the closer he came. Her skin also had a warm cast to it. This was no milk-and-water miss, despite her clothes. There was also just the faintest musical lilt in her voice which was neither London nor West

Country. Perhaps she wasn't as proper as she looked, which would present some interesting possibilities...

'You are standing in what closely resembles the ruins of Carthage, facing a woman armed with a mace, and you are considering flirtation? You don't look addled, but I'm beginning to suspect you are. Either that or quite desperate. Please put down that book. It's mine.'

'So you pointed out, but my advice is that you might not want to argue with someone you suspect is either addled or desperate or both.'

'Thank you kindly for that advice. Now put down the book and step back.'

He moved closer, making his way around the pile of books.

'Not until you tell me what you believe is worse than a criminal. Somehow I can't quite see you as a nun.'

Her smile flickered again, but she mastered it. She raised the mace slightly and let it hit the ground again with an ominous thump. He stopped.

'I shall take that as a compliment, though I am certain most would disagree. You have three chances to guess. If you do, I will make you a present of Marcus Aurelius. If not, you leave quietly.'

He put his hands on his hips, amused by the challenge. This unusual creature was brightening up a dreary afternoon quite nicely. He would very much like the truth to be that she was a very permissive courtesan so he could see if she could wield something other than a mace in those surprisingly strong hands, but her dress certainly wasn't supporting that theory. He considered the bronze-coloured pelisse with just an edge of a muslin flounce embroidered with yellow flowers peeping out beneath. Simple but very elegant and expensively made. Her bonnet, too, though unadorned by all the frills and gewgaws young women favoured, looked very costly. Had he met her in an assembly hall or a London drawing room, aside from avoiding her like the plague as another one of those horrible breed of marriageable young women, he would have presumed she was perfectly respectable. But respectable young women did not wander through empty estates on their own, even if they had inherited them, and they didn't threaten strange men with maces. They came accompanied and in such circumstances they swooned or burst into tears.

'Let me see. You're an actress. Your last role was Dido and you are reprising. I don't think the mace is historically accurate, though.'

'No, an ox hide would be more apt, but I feel safer with a mace. Try again.'

His brow rose. He added well educated to his assessment. Not many women...not many people knew the tale of Dido's clever manipulation of calculus to capture land from the Berber king.

'A bluestocking with a penchant for the medieval.' She considered.

'I would consider that a compliment, but that isn't quite accurate and certainly not what I was referring to. One last try.'

Before he could respond, the door opened and Alan turned to face an exceedingly burly man. The mace hit the ground definitively as the young woman let it go.

'Finally. Where have you been, Jackson? Distracting him is tiring work. I thought he might be the one who did this, but probably not, so do escort him out.

Oh, and please leave the book as you exit, sir. You haven't earned it yet.'

Alan considered the glowering man. *She* might not be a criminal, but her henchman certainly looked the part. He added it to his collection of facts about her, but he still drew a blank.

'I have one last try, don't I? Just like that fairy tale with the spinning wheel, no?'

She laughed and nudged the mace with one pale yellow kid shoe. An expensive one, he noted. He should know, he had paid for enough female garments.

'That's true,' she conceded. 'I'm nothing like that silly woman, though. Who on earth would barter with their unborn child's life? I would have either thought of some better way out of that fix or something less valuable to bargain with. Well? One last try, sir.'

He moved towards her, ignoring the movement behind him. Her head lowered and she looked more wary now than when they had been alone in the room together. At first glance he had thought her pretty but unexceptional, but either closer examination or her peculiar chatter had affected his judgement. Her warm hazel-brown eyes, like honeyed wood, captivated him, and when she smiled, her mouth was practically an invitation to explore the soft coral-pink curve. She would taste sweet and sultry, honey and a hint of spice, he thought. It was a pity she was one of the most despised subcategories of the already despised species known as respectable young women. His only consolation was that they usually feared him almost as much as he wished to avoid them.

'Very well,' he replied. 'My last chance at Aurelius. You're a member of that dreaded breed of females who believe themselves deserving of all forms of homage and adoration for qualities that they have done nothing to deserve. You are, in short, an heiress.'

He had expected outrage, not amusement. She might be respectable, but she was not predictable. That at least might be a point in his favour when it came to negotiating the purchase of Hollywell House.

'How do you know I have done nothing to deserve it? I'll have you know being an heiress is hard work and not just for me as Jackson here will attest.'

'Does this bruiser keep fortune hunters at bay, then?'

'In a manner of speaking. Well, you have earned your Aurelius. Goodbye, sir.'

'In a moment. We still have the matter of the sale of the house to discuss. We will offer you the same price as we did your cousin. It is quite generous, I assure you.'

'As you pointed out, until after probate is granted, there is no point in discussing anything. Who is "we", by the way? I thought you said you merely represented the prospective buyers. The use of the pronoun "we" seems to indicate otherwise.'

For a moment he debated telling her the truth about Hope House. She was just unconventional enough that she might not see it as a disadvantage, but he and his friends had long ago learned to keep their involvement in the Hope House foundation for war veterans private. It was no one's business and certainly not the business of a pert and overly perceptive heiress he was still not convinced wasn't also a little unhinged. Intelligence and madness often went hand in hand.

'Does it matter, as long as we offer you fair price? You can't possibly live here.'

Her mouth flattened and a light entered her eyes that in a man would have conveyed a distinct physical menace. Perhaps he had misstepped.

'Do you hear that, Jackson? Here is another man who has an opinion about what I can and cannot do.'

The giant clucked his tongue.

'I heard, miss. Shame.'

Alan tried not to smile.

'I dare say now you are going to tell me the last fool who dared do so is buried under the floorboards?'

'No, but I am very tempted to be able to tell the next fool precisely that. The door is behind you, sir.'

'Do you really think you could carry out that threat? Or is it just a variation on the age-old cry of the spoilt heiress when her will is thwarted?'

'You keep a civil tongue in your head around Miss Lily,' the giant rumbled behind him.

'Jackson, no!' she cried out as a bulky hand settled on Alan's shoulder.

Alan turned in time to intercept the anvil-sized fist heading his way. It wasn't hard to dodge and the counterblow he delivered to the giant's solar plexus was more by way of a warning than an attempt to do damage. But clearly this Jackson was in no mood to heed warnings. Even less did he appear to appreciate being tripped and sent sprawling on to the pile of books.

'Careful of the books,' the girl cried out with a great deal more concern for them than for her protector. The giant grunted, stood up, dusted himself off, smiled and lunged.

Alan did not in the least mind brawling. He and his friends often indulged in sparring either in the accepted mode at Jackson's Boxing Saloon or in the much less respectable tavern yards and village greens occasionally set aside for such sport. This giant clearly also appreciated the fancy, but despite, or perhaps because of, his size, he was used to winning by *force majeure* rather than by skill and it was no great stretch of Alan's skill to avoid or deflect most of his blows. He was just beginning to enjoy himself and was even considering offering the giant a pause so they could both take off their coats and make the most of this opportunity for some sport when the door opened and an elderly woman entered the library. But her shriek, either of shock or outrage, wasn't enough to stop Alan's fist from making contact with the giant's face.

'Alan Piers Cavendish Rothwell! What on earth is the meaning of this?'

Luckily the giant fell back under the blow and conveniently tripped over the books again, because the sight of his grandmother dealt Alan the stunning blow his opponent had failed to deliver.

Though they were a mere mile from his childhood home, the last person he had expected to see in the doorway of Hollywell's library was Lady Jezebel Ravenscar, the only woman on earth he could safely say he despised and who fully reciprocated his disdain and had done so ever since he could remember. The only person whom he disliked more was her thankfully defunct husband, his grandfather and the late and most unlamented Lord Ravenscar.

Before he could absorb and adjust to this ill-fated turn of events, the girl spoke.

'You needn't have come, Lady Ravenscar. I merely wanted to see the place before returning to the Hall. Here, Jackson, put your head back and hold this to your nose.' She wadded up a handkerchief and handed it to the giant.

Alan had no idea what connection existed between his grandmother and this young woman, but he could have told her there was no possible way his grandmother would let her off so lightly. He was right. Lady Ravenscar turned her unsympathetic dark eyes to the young woman.

'When George Coachman told me you had directed your groom to stop at Hollywell on your way back from Keynsham, I instructed him to come here immediately. While you are a guest in my home, Miss Wallace, you are under my care and that means you cannot dash about the countryside unaccompanied as your departed parents clearly allowed. At the very least you should have taken your maid. You are no longer in the wilds of Brazil or Zanzibar or Timbuktu or wherever—'

'You were right the first time. Brazil,' the girl interrupted, her hands clasped in front of her in a parody of the obedient schoolgirl.

'Brazil. Yes. Well, this is England and young women do not…'

'Breathe without permission. Yes, I know. My schoolmistresses were very clear about what young women can and cannot do in English society and the latter list is leagues longer than the former. I even started writing them down in a journal. It is a marvel that any of our beleaguered species can still place one foot before the other of our own volition. My parents did me a grave disservice by raising me to be independent and an even graver disservice by dying before I was old enough for people to no longer care that I was.'

She bent to pick up the book Alan had dropped during the brawl and handed it to him.

'This is yours, I believe. I would have given it to you anyway. There was no need to break poor Jackson's nose.'

He shoved the book into his coat pocket, keeping a wary eye on his grandmother.

'It isn't broken.'

'Just drew my cork, miss,' Jackson mumbled behind the handkerchief. 'Thought you were a toff. You'll not get over my guard so easy a second time.'

The girl correctly interpreted Alan's expression.

'Don't encourage him, Jackson. This is my house now and I won't have you silly men brawling in it. There is enough disarray here as it is. If you want to beat each other senseless, kindly step outside.'

'It's not your house till after probate,' Alan couldn't resist pointing out. 'We will contact you presently about the sale.'

'Enough of this,' Lady Ravenscar announced, ramming her cane into the floor with as much force as the girl had smashed the mace into the worn floorboards. 'What is all this about a sale? And where are you going, Alan?'

'Back to Hades, Jezebel. You needn't worry I was thinking of contaminating the hallowed grounds of the Hall with my presence. That's the beauty of your husband forcing my father to break the entail. Believe me, I am as glad to be shot of the Hall as you are of me.'

'Nanny Brisbane is ill. I dare say if you are already in the vicinity, she would be grateful if you would show a modicum of respect and visit her.' Lady Ravenscar's tones were dismissive, but she didn't move from her position in the doorway. She didn't have to because he stopped in his tracks. Once again she had dealt him a very effective blow.

'Nanny Brisbane is ill?'

The girl glanced from him to his grandmother, her brow furrowed.

'Are you the rakehell?'

'Lily Wallace!' Lady Ravenscar all but bellowed and the girl shrugged.

'Sorry, the black sheep. Mrs Brisbane contracted the fever as well, but she is mending. Still, she would likely be happy for a visit, unless you mean to scowl at her like that and go around bashing things. You can't possibly be her Master Alan, you don't look in the least like the miniature of you and Catherine she keeps on her mantel, but then those are never very good likenesses.'

Alan abandoned the effort to determine if she was mad or not and moved towards the door again.

'I will see Nanny before I continue to Bristol.'

Lady Ravenscar hesitated and then moved aside to let him pass.

'Catherine and Nicola would no doubt expect you to pay your respects as well.'

He didn't stop.

'I don't need lessons from you on family loyalty, Jezebel. Though it is very typical of you to preach what you don't practise.'

As he climbed on to the curricle and took the reins from Jem, he cast a last look at the classical façade of Hollywell House with its pillared portico. He hated the burning resentment and anger his grandmother always dragged out of him, but it was his fault. It served him right for trying to exact a very petty revenge on her by trying to acquire Hollywell. In fact, he should have continued to avoid this particular corner of England like the plague just as he had for the past dozen years. Nothing good came of tempting the fates.

Chapter Two

'Lily, might I have a word with you for a moment?'

'Of course, Catherine.'

'Don't hover in the doorway, Catherine!' Lady Ravenscar snapped from the great winged armchair placed near the Rose Room's fireplace but angled so she could survey her domain. 'There is no call for secrets. If this is about your brother, you may share your information with the rest of us.'

Since Lady Ravenscar was the only other occupant of the room, her words were less a polite invitation than a command. Poor Catherine wavered and Lily stood, moving towards her.

'Is Nicky faring any better this morning, Catherine?'

Catherine met her eyes with a clear expression of gratitude.

'Her fever has diminished a little, but she is still restless. That is what I wanted to ask you. I have a basket to take to Nanny Brisbane, but I don't wish to leave Nicky with only a maid. Would you mind sitting with her until my return?'

'Of course,' Lily replied, ushering Catherine out

of the room before Lady Ravenscar could react. Poor Catherine had no stomach for opposition to her imperious grandmother and it was not merely because she and her twelve-year-old daughter were financially dependent on Lady Ravenscar. Lily wondered if Catherine had always been this way or whether marriage to an impecunious parson, widowhood and now almost a decade under her grandmother's thumb had leached her will away. Looking at her reminded Lily why she had returned to England after her father's death in the first place.

Like the intrepid traveller Lady Hester Stanhope, Lily had discovered that life as her wealthy father's hostess was vastly different now that he was gone, but she had no ambition to end her life an indebted recluse like Lady Hester. She had spent her year of mourning in the house of an aged and distant cousin, which had been even more stultifying than the weeks since her arrival in England. Even after she had come out of mourning, she had discovered there was no role to be played by a young woman of marriageable age unless she handed herself over body and soul to some respectable duenna while society tutted over her advancing years. She didn't even have the freedom to manage her own inheritance—the lawyers managing the trust, who had obeyed her every word while her father lived, now balked and held her to the rigid letter of the trust. Her father's death had been a shock on so many levels Lily was still reeling from the loss of everything she valued.

'It has been three days since Mr Marston has been to visit you. Is he travelling?' Catherine asked as they climbed the curving staircase.

'Yes, on business to Birmingham and then he is bringing his daughter back to Bristol to prepare for her debut in the spring.' The words were stiff and she tried to smile.

'Are you worried whether she will like you?'

Lily almost wished she had not been tempted to share some of her story with Catherine. It made it so much more inescapable.

'Mr Marston said she is as lovely as an angel, but that is the least of my worries. I know his offer makes good sense. I had no idea how restrictive life could be when my father passed and it is even worse now I am out of mourning. Everything the Kingston gossipmongers didn't say while he was alive, they happily whispered over his grave. The only thing that kept them from saying it to my face was the hope I will marry one of their sons. I cannot even carry on with my business concerns because Papa tied it up in a ridiculous trust when I was born and never thought to change it, because he believed he was indestructible. Right now the only thing I have any control over is Hollywell House, or at least I will after probate. I must marry or I shall go mad. Sometimes I wish Papa had left me on Isla Padrones in Brazil when my mother died instead of bringing me to Jamaica and forcing me to enter society. At least on the island I had become accustomed to being alone and having few expectations.'

'You could always stay here with us if you don't wish to marry. I know my grandmother isn't an easy person, but she is not quite as bad as she seems. When Nicola returns to school, it is just the two of us and it can be rather...lonely. I am certain she will agree.'

They stopped at the top of the stairs.

'That is very generous of you, but I already feel I have encroached too much on our very distant relation. It is only because Mr Marston's home is in Bristol…'

She touched the little gold pendant at her throat. She knew this feeling. The same one that would catch at her breath every time her father sailed away, leaving her and her mother on tiny Isla Padrones. The world closing on her, shutting her in, but also a sense of safety, of the world reduced to the familiar once more. The move to Jamaica when she had been fourteen had taken away that safety without really opening the world any wider. Her school and then Kingston society had been even more oppressive than the isolation of the island where she had run wild. She had not known how rare the freedom of being alone was until she had lost it.

'Perhaps I should remove to Hollywell House…'

Catherine's blue eyes widened.

'But, Lily, you could not live there on your own!'

'I could find someone to lend me countenance. My pin money is still generous enough to support a companion. Surely there must be an impecunious relative somewhere on the family tree who would be willing to…' She pulled herself to a halt at her selfishness. She might be scared of her future, but there were many women whose fates were indescribably worse than hers, or even than Catherine's.

She had seen that only too clearly the day she had walked into the brothel near the Kingston docks that her lawyers had tried to prevent her from visiting after her father's death. Any one of those eight women would have traded places with her at the bat of an eyelid. The worst was that the lawyers had made it clear that though she could evict the women from the structure her father had bought, under the trust she could not sign over the house to them. She had done the only thing she could think of—at least her mother's jewellery was hers outright and she had sold the most expensive necklace and given an equal share to each of the women, much to the lawyers' shock and dismay.

'You would do better to marry him, you know,' Catherine said in her quiet voice. 'He is handsome and intelligent and I can see you are fond of him and he is very fond of you and he respects you, which is just as important. Otherwise he would not be so very patient and accommodating. Believe me, waiting for a… for a perfect solution usually means waiting for ever.'

'I know. I probably shall. You should go to Nanny Brisbane before it begins raining again.

Catherine smiled. 'Grandmama was right, you know. I do want to take a basket to Nanny, but it is true I received a note from my brother. He is coming to visit Nanny and I would like to see him, but I didn't want to tell Grandmama.'

'Well, since she is the one who mentioned Mrs Brisbane's ill health to him at Hollywell House in the first place, she wouldn't be surprised.'

'Did she? Still, talking about him makes her so crotchety I really would rather not.'

'I am not surprised. The way he called her Lady Jezebel sounded like he hated her.'

'That is what Grandfather called her, never Jezebel or Lady Ravenscar. She was an earl's daughter, so Lady Jezebel was her courtesy title and my great-grandmama, the Dowager Marchioness, insisted Grandfather continue to call her that when they wed because she didn't want two Lady Ravenscars at the Hall. Then when we returned from Edinburgh, Alan refused to call her Grandmama and would call her Lady Jezebel just like Grandfather.' She sighed. 'They will never forgive each other. Nicky and I don't see him often enough, situated as we are. He did visit Nicky up at her school last month, but I wish...'

There was such weariness and pain in Catherine's voice Lily wished she could do something for her, at least say something reassuring, but she had never been good at polite lies. Then the moment passed and Catherine opened the door.

No twelve-year-old of any spirit enjoyed being confined to bed and Nicky was a very spirited twelve-year-old. The fact that she was leaning back against her pillows and allowing a maid to brush her hair was a testament to how weak she was. But when they entered, she sat up, frowning.

'Sue said Uncle Alan is staying at the Ship in Keynsham! Is it true, Mama?'

The maid blushed under Catherine's accusing eyes, curtsied and hurried away.

'Do lie down, Nicky. Lily has been kind enough to offer to sit with you while I take a basket to Nanny Brisbane.'

Lily picked up the book lying by Nicky's side and smiled.

'*The Mysteries of Udolpho.* I haven't read this in years.'

'I am halfway through, but my head hurts too much to read.' Nicky was distracted only for a moment. 'But, Mama...is Uncle Alan really in Keynsham? Will he come see me?'

'Nicky, you know your uncle doesn't come to the Hall.'

'Then I want to go to Keynsham.'

'My dear, you aren't well enough…perhaps when you are better…'

'No! By then he'll be gone and I shall return to school and I won't see him for months! It's not fair that Grandmama is so evil and has cut him off and is going to leave everything to some doddering, preachy old cousin of Grandpapa's we haven't even heard of and doesn't care a straw for the Hall! It's not fair!'

'Nicola!' Catherine scrubbed her palm over her forehead and then with a gesture of defeat she headed towards the door. 'We will discuss this later, but right now I must go. I will return very soon.'

Nicky watched the door close, her hands still fisted by her sides and her eyes red from unshed tears. Lily could feel the frustration and confused pain in her own bones. It was around this age that she had begun to actively resent her father's frequent disappearances. Her poor mother had borne the brunt of her temper as well.

She kicked off her kid slippers and curled up on the bed by the girl, picking up the discarded book.

'Where were you? Here? *"'Surely, Annette,' said Emily, starting, 'I heard a noise: listen.' After a long pause… 'No, ma'mselle,' said Annette, 'it was only the wind in the gallery; I often hear it when it shakes the old doors.'"* Lily added a rattling groan for good measure and was rewarded by a faint smile. She kept going, investing as much melodramatic nonsense into the story as she could, rising to a distressed falsetto when Emily hurried to greet the man she thought was Valancourt and promptly fainted when it was not.

'What a great deal of fainting they do engage in!' she interjected. 'I haven't fainted once in my life, have you?'

Nicky giggled again. 'No, but perhaps that's because we haven't yet been in love.'

'What do you mean, "we"? How do you know I haven't?'

'Have you?'

Lily sighed.

'No, never. It's very disheartening, though I still doubt I will faint if ever I am foolish enough to fall in love.'

'Don't you want to be in love? I do!'

Lily considered Nicky's flushed cheeks and the dark eyes glistening with hope. *She is merely a girl, Lily. She has time enough to discover the futility of dreams.*

'Well, yes, but I don't think I shall be very good at it. I am not very suited to adore anyone, certainly not someone like Valancourt. Never mind, let's discover what horrors and creaking and groanings next lie in store for our intrepid and oft-faint Emily, shall we?'

'You're funny, Lily. I wish I had a sister like you.'

Nicky leaned her head momentarily against Lily's shoulder and Lily blinked against the peculiar burning over the bridge of her nose. Not a sister. A daughter, someone like Nicky who would curl up beside her while she read… And a son leaning against her as well until he was too old for such sentimental nonsense.

She would take them to Isla Padrones and teach them to swim like the gardener Joao had taught her after her father had sent her and her mother to live on the island. Her mother had been frail and despondent after the nervous illnesses that had plagued her in the jungles of Brazil, where her father had been searching for his precious gems, and the Jesuit doctor from the nearby mission had recommended sea air. He had probably meant one of the coastal towns, but her father's romantic soul had remembered a short visit to the islands of the Amazonian delta and had sent them to one of the smallest. They were supposed to be there only until her mother recovered, but perhaps her mother's realisation that she was healthiest when she didn't have to witness her husband's infidelities had turned a convalescent retreat into a permanent home, regardless of the impact of this isolation on their only child. Ten years after leaving the islands Lily could fully appreciate what was wonderful and horrible about their seclusion there. If... *When* she had children, she hoped she could show them the pleasures of being alone, but also create a broader world than her parents had provided.

'Well, so do I,' she replied lightly, thinking of how often she had prayed for a sibling during those long years. 'A sister like you, I mean. I always wanted a sister.'

Nicky snuggled closer and closed her eyes with a sigh.

'I always wanted an older brother, too. Someone like Uncle Alan. You know, dashing and dangerous so all the girls will want to be my friend just so they can flirt with him. Well, they already do even though he's so old.'

Lily tried not to laugh.

'Don't tell him that. The old part, at least. As for the flirting, I am certain he knows that already.'

'Oh, that's right, I forgot you have met him. Sue told

me he was at Hollywell House when you and Grand-mama were there.'

'Is there nothing the servants don't know?'

'Certainly nothing worth knowing. So, what did you think of him? Isn't he handsome? The girls at school said he was the handsomest man they have ever seen!'

Nicky looked up at her, her face a study of curiosity, defiance and need. Lily tried to tread as carefully as possible over the ground of Nicky's hero worship and through the unsettling sensations that accompanied the resurgence of the memory of their encounter in the Hollywell House library.

It wasn't surprising she hadn't recognised him as Catherine's brother. She had heard a great deal about the notorious Rakehell Raven since her arrival, but she had still expected him to look more like his sister. Catherine herself was a very handsome woman, but there was a softness to her that had no echo in her brother's harsh, sculpted face, and though her hair was also near black, it was slightly warmed by mahogany lights rather than the jet sheen of her brother's that added credence to his Raven epithet.

The biggest difference was in the eyes. Catherine's were a clear sky blue, slightly chilled around the edges. Her brother's were a world away, a very dark grey she had at first thought as black as his hair. She had seen such colouring in the Venetian sailors who had manned the ship that brought her to England, but Lord Ravenscar's face was pure Celtic god—sharp-cut lines of a deity bent on the destruction of lesser mortals. Perhaps his eyes also were merely black and the impression of the complex shades of an evening sky were just an illusion that would dissipate if she had a longer look. Not that she would ever have the chance to examine the man's eyes, she reminded herself. After his visit to the old nanny, he would probably return to his gambling and womanising and whatever other dubious activities he enjoyed. She smiled at Nicky and told her what she wanted to hear.

'I think your uncle is very handsome and very aware of his charms.'

'Oh, it isn't just that he is so handsome. It is because of the Wild Hunt!'

'The what?'

'Haven't you heard of the Wild Hunt?' Nicky was practically shimmering with excitement, her ills and aches forgotten. 'It is said that when the dark huntsmen come riding through the night with their hounds, everyone should hide in their homes or be swept up in the hunt.'

'Is that what your uncle does? It sounds very tiring.'

'No, silly, those are just tales. But Uncle Alan and his friends were known as the Wild Hunt Club because they were all very wild and excellent riders and it was said that no woman's heart was safe around them and no man could win a race or a wager against them because they made a pact with the devil so they would always win. Not that I really believe that silly thing about the pact. That is just what people say when they are envious.'

Lily schooled her smile, a little envious herself—she knew all about the challenges of a girls' school.

'I am not the least bit surprised your friends at school are in love with him. I could definitely have used an older brother like him to smooth my path at the Kingston Academy for Young Ladies.'

'Were the girls horrid to you?'

Oh, God, how did one explain such things to a child? And why was she trying to? It wasn't like her to share her stories and to do so with a girl half her age…

'Not horrid, really. My mother had just died, you see, and my father sent me to a school where I knew no one. I was very used to being on my own and I was just a little…well, perhaps more than a little defensive. Like a cornered cat. I even tried to run away several times.'

Perhaps this was a little too much. Nicky's eyes were wide and compassionate, more like her mother now.

'That sounds sad.'

'It was, but it passed. Then I started making friends and it wasn't so lonely any longer.'

'I like school. I don't know any children my age here and at school I have lots of friends who like the same things I do.'

'Like novels with things that creak and groan and lots of swooning.'

Nicky grinned.

'Especially novels.'

'Shall we read some more, then?'

'Yes, please. And could you do those funny voices? The story is so much better that way. I can almost imagine I am there…'

Chapter Three

'You'll come by again tomorrow, Master Alan?' Nanny Brisbane struggled to keep her eyes open.

'Tomorrow,' Alan assented and her eyelids sank on a long childish sigh and her worn hand relaxed in his.

There was nothing for it. He could stay in Keynsham for another night, pay a visit to the Hollywell solicitor and come by in the morning before he continued to Bristol. It was the very least he could do for the woman who had all but raised him and his sister and almost lost her life doing so.

Even in sleep Nanny had the face of a devout elf, caught between mischief and adulation. She should have married and had a dozen children instead of being saddled with two sad specimens of the breed. The love that would have spread easily among her potential brood had been concentrated on them and his parents whenever they chose to come out of their little scholarly world and until their deaths from putrid fever when he and Cat were young.

Cat was waiting for him in the low-ceilinged parlour, tidying up the remains of the tea she had prepared for Nanny. He waited until they left the cottage before speaking.

'Are you certain she will be all right?'

Cat smiled and tucked her hand in his arm.

'She is over the worst of it and one of the tenants' wives, Mrs Mitchum, comes to tend to her every few hours.'

'She looks so frail…'

'She is getting old, Alan, but she is still strong. It is just this fever. Practically everyone in the region has fallen ill these past weeks, but it often passes as swiftly as it comes, sometimes as briefly as a day, and there have been very few deaths.'

'Few… Albert was one of them, though. Were you ill as well?'

'Grandmama and I were, at the same time. She was quick about it, but I was quite miserable for three days. Thank goodness Lily…Miss Wallace was here to help.'

'The heiress?' He couldn't keep the incredulity out of his voice.

'Why, yes. She may not be very easy-going, but she is utterly unshakeable, which is useful in a household descended into chaos.'

'Unshakeable. I noticed that. From my meeting with her I would have guessed you would dislike her thoroughly.'

'Well, you are not as clever as you think, Alan dear. Is it strange being back?'

'I'm not back, Cat. A visit to Nanny Brisbane is my concession to childhood debts. That is all.'

'Still, I thought you swore never to set foot on Roth-well territory as long as Grandmama is alive.'

'I was never a reliable fellow; why expect me to stand by my word now?'

'That's not true, Alan.'

'You're too soft, Cat.'

She sighed.

'I won't be so obvious as to say you are too hard. I'm still glad you came to see Nanny. She misses you. What did you think about your meeting with Miss Wallace?'

'*Meeting* isn't quite the word I would use. The only thing I nearly met was the business end of a mace. What on earth is someone like her doing at Ravenscar and how is she Albert's heir? This family is altogether too complicated. Is she another dreaded Rothwell? I thought they were all safely tucked away north of the wall.'

'Goodness, no. Her mother was a distant cousin on Grandmama's side and made what initially was a *més-alliance* with an impoverished young man, only to have him become one of the wealthiest men in South America. He died a year ago and now Miss Wallace has returned to England to marry... Oh, dear, I shouldn't say anything because it is not yet announced. You mustn't repeat that.'

'I couldn't be bothered to, Cat. It is no business of mine.'

'Well, it might not happen anyway. Mr Marston is...'

'Marston? She is to marry Philip Marston?'

'You know him?'

'Very well. We share ownership of several loom manufactories. This is a small world indeed. I had no idea he was contemplating marrying again, but I'm not surprised he has set his sights on an heiress. He is one of the savviest businessmen I know.'

'I believe he is truly fond of her.'

'Of course he is, Cat.'

She sighed.

'You would do well to take a page from his book. Perhaps if you married, Grandmama would relent and change her will in your favour.'

'We all know Jezebel won't leave me a crust of bread, married or not. She and Grandfather were clear enough about that when I left.'

'She might if you only tried to…to be conciliating and mend your ways. She has become much less rigid since Grandfather passed.'

He stopped for a moment, raising his brow, and Cat flushed.

'Sorry. I know it is none of my concern. Well, it is, but it isn't. But I think pride is a poor substitute for all this. It isn't just the money, but the Hall. This is your home, Alan.'

Alan smiled grimly at her tenacity. Cat might not have the Rothwell temper, but she employed a water-dripping-on-stone approach to attaining her ends.

'No, it ceased to be my home over a decade ago, or longer before that, when Grandfather forced our father to break the entail and disowned him for wanting to be a doctor. Let's not rehash this. I have no intention of mending my ways, as you so quaintly phrase it. I like my ways and they like me. Since I have no intention of ever spawning heirs, the Hall would be wasted on me anyway. Our Hibernian cousins are welcome to the Hall and all things Rothwell. I have to go, Cat. I have some pressing affairs to see to.'

She tilted her head as they approached the stables where his gelding waited.

'You're probably wise not to linger with everyone feeling poorly. You wouldn't want to fall ill.'

'That's not why and you know it!'

'Nicky was feverish last night and woke up with a headache. I'm worried she might also have caught the infection. She begged me to let her see you in Keynsham before you disappear again, but I cannot risk her leaving her bed while she is so poorly.'

'Blast you, Cat. Very well, I will see her quickly, but I'm not staying. I don't know why you even stay here after what that old witch put us through.'

'To be fair, it was mostly Grandfather. Yes, I know you can't stand it when I defend her and she is a horrid old harpy sometimes, but Nicky actually cares for her and I have her future to think of; I cannot afford to be cut out of the will like you, Alan. It is my responsibility to make my peace with her for Nicky's sake.'

'I can provide for you. I have enough to leave you and Nicky comfortable when someone finally puts a bullet through me.'

Cat wrinkled her nose.

'All from that mill you won gambling.'

He laughed.

'How the devil is my sister such a prude? My money is quite the same colour as Jezebel's, believe me.'

'Even so, who's to say you might not marry, and then where will Nicky be?'

'Let's just say there's more likelihood of my forgiving Jezebel than of my willingly entering a state of matrimony, Cat.'

'Oh, good.'

He sighed.

'I surrender. Come, I will sit with Nicky for a while and then I must leave. But we are entering by the back door.'

The sight that confronted them when Cat opened the door to Nicky's bedroom was not entirely that of a sickroom. Nicky was indeed in her bed, propped up against a mountain of pillows, her dark brown hair down about her shoulders and a glass with a viscous liquid on a tray by the bed, but she was laughing and she wasn't the only occupant of the bed.

'That's just silly—' Nicky stopped when Cat and Alan entered the room, crying out joyously, 'Uncle Alan, you came!'

Alan directed a wary look at Miss Wallace, who was leaning against the headboard with her feet tucked under her and a book in her lap. He walked around the other side of the bed and bent to kiss his niece on the forehead.

'Of course I came. Not that there seems to be much wrong with you, pumpkin.'

'My head feels like I'm wearing a bonnet three sizes too small and I can hardly hold up my book and I had a fever last night and Lily says fevers often worsen in the evening. Are you staying? Please say you are.'

Lily. The name was far too whimsical and delicate for the spoilt heiress who had addressed his harridan of a grandmother so impudently. He sat on the bed and took his niece's hand, wondering why the heiress was still sitting there. Anyone with the least manners would have removed herself. She didn't even make way for Cat. Clearly she was used to the world arranging itself to suit her rather than the other way around. He focused his attention on Nicky.

'I can't stay, Nicky.'

'Because of Grandmama? If I ask her, she might let you. Shall I ask her?'

'You saw me last month when I came by your school.'

'That was last month. Just for a little while? You must hear this story. It's called *The Mysteries of Udolpho* and it is even funnier than *The Romance of the Forest.*'

'I didn't realise Mrs Radcliffe wrote comedies.'

'Well, they aren't really, but Lily makes them so. Especially the swooning and the groaning.'

Alan raised his brows and turned to the heiress. Any normal, proper young woman would have been off the bed and out the room like a scalded cat the moment he entered; instead she was curled up like a kitten against the pillows, her fingers tracing the gilded lettering on the leather-bound book, and her honey-brown eyes warm with laughter. The presence of his niece in the bed as well should have made her look less like a very expensive mistress holding court in her boudoir, but his unruly imagination compensated. His mind had already pulled the pins and ribbons from her glossy hair and set it tumbling over her shoulders, cleared the room of his sister and niece, and significantly enlarged the bed. Now he was left to imagine what she might look like under the fine powder-blue sprigged muslin, if the sleek lines of her figure were spare or carried some pliant padding waiting to be warmed, softened.

Cat's assessment came back to him—unshakeable. It was a sad trait of his that he hadn't yet met a cage he didn't want to rattle and right now the thought of shaking this pert heiress out of her amused condescension was adding fuel to an undeniable physical curiosity. He caught her gaze with his.

'Groaning? Is it that kind of novel?'

If he had expected to finally shock her, the shimmer of laughter in her honey-gold eyes at his suggestive question sent that hope to grass. Here was the same gleam of mischief in her eyes he had glimpsed in Albert's library and it had the same impact on his hunting instincts. He reined them in reluctantly. This was a game without a prize.

'I don't know what novels you are wont to read, Lord Ravenscar, but in this book the groaning and creaking is confined to the castles,' she answered, and her voice, at least, was prim.

'Still, hardly suitable reading material for a girl of twelve, don't you think?'

'Oh, but everyone reads her novels at school, Uncle Alan,' Nicky interjected. 'There's even a girl who swoons when we read them at night.'

'I think it is a very healthy sign that a twelve-year-old finds such novels amusing,' the heiress added.

'Are you speaking from experience, Miss Wallace? Were you also a voracious novel reader as a schoolgirl, then? That might explain it.'

'Explain what?' Nicky asked.

'I think your uncle is referring to my flair for dramatics, Nicky.'

'I would amend that to histrionics.'

'Would you? I believe I was rather calm in the face of a ransacked library and an intruder with a punishing left hook.'

'If being calm is brandishing a mace at a stranger, then, yes, you qualify. Besides, you didn't know about my boxing prowess until your burly protector arrived.'

'That is true. I dare say you would have thought better of me had I shrieked and swooned like a heroine from a novel. Would that have gratified your male pride and preconceptions of proper female behaviour?'

'It would have certainly been less tiring. Conversing with you is like going ten rounds with Belcher.'

'Alan,' Cat admonished, but without much conviction.

'Who is Belcher?' Nicky giggled.

'Belcher is someone who would have given your uncle the black eye he deserves, Nicky.' Lily laughed and again he found himself wondering whether there was anything that could truly unsettle this peculiar young woman. Either her defences were legion or she was truly without any depth and took nothing seriously.

It shouldn't matter and he should know better than to treat her laughing dismissal of his barbs as a challenge, but he leaned towards her, his weight on his arm, his fingers just skimming the spread of her skirt where it fanned out on the bed, pressing it into the coverlet, the embroidered blue flowers silky bumps against the pads of his fingers.

'If you are so bent on blackening my eye, go ahead. I won't retaliate.'

Lily Wallace's eyes narrowed, assessing, and he wondered if she might actually try to meet his dare. Her gaze scanned his face, as if she was searching for the right spot to place the invited blow. He should have been amused, but instead he felt a peculiar rise of heat follow the path of her inspection, pinching at his skin, and with a sense of shock he realised he was blushing. It had nothing to do with embarrassment and everything with a spike of undiluted lust thrusting through his body. Until now the heat of attraction had been speculative, familiar, unthreatening. In an instant it flared beyond that, like brushfire after a drought, unexpected and cataclysmic. It took every ounce of his self-control not to draw back from the fire, to keep his breathing even. It cost him, though, both his body and his vanity suffering—he should be well past the age for such conflagrations.

'I would never be so uncouth as to strike a man while I am a guest under his roof,' she said, but her eyes did slide away from his, her first sign of disquiet. It should have gratified him, but it just added to this unexpected agony. His mind reached for the lifeline of anger at her words.

'This isn't my roof, thank God. Ravenscar Hall is no longer entailed and I am certain old Jezebel has enlightened you that she would rather see it razed to the ground than left to the profligate Rakehell Raven.'

There was no amusement in her eyes now, but the emotions in them were anything but gratifying—he needed neither contrition nor pity, certainly not from someone like her. She turned to slip off the bed and for a moment her skirt caught beneath his fingers, riding up her legs, exposing the sleek line of her calf and the shadowed indentation of her ankle before escaping him.

Just like Nicky's headache, his skin felt far too small on him. The absurdity of reacting to the glimmer of a smile and the glimpse of a woman's ankle as if he had never seen an inch of female flesh in his life when just a few nights ago he had seen in full naked glory the whole extent of another woman's anatomy was not as obvious to his body as to his mind. He tried to look away but didn't, watching as she extended her leg to put on her slipper, like a dancer. What would she be like to dance with, this strange girl? In some dark room, music entering from outside so he could be alone with her and explore those curves under the expensive fabrics, test their softness, whether he could make the unshakeable Miss Lily Wallace quiver...

'We can continue reading this later, Nicky. Enjoy your time with your uncle.' Her gaze lifted to his from the preoccupation of putting on her slippers. For a moment she stood there and then turned and left, closing the door quietly behind her.

Then it was just the old nursery room that had been Cat's until her marriage, with her books and now Nicky's dolls on the shelves. The last time he had been here had been twelve years ago, the very last day he had set foot in the Hall until today. It had hardly changed, but he had. It was important to remember that.

He gathered himself and smiled at Nicky. She and Cat and his friends and his work were all that mattered in his life. In a few moments he would leave this house and hopefully never set foot in it again at the very least until the witch was dead and buried.

Chapter Four

Alan recognised his grandmother's old landaulet coming up the drive of the Carr property in Saltford before he even saw the occupants and braced himself. Having to face the old witch twice in a week after not seeing her for over a dozen years was surely a punishment not merited by any of his sins, at least not any recent ones. What on earth would she be doing coming to see an empty property up for sale a good forty minutes from the Hall?

The open landaulet drew abreast, revealing its occupants, but his tension only took a different turn. The fact that it wasn't his grandmother, but Miss Wallace seated beside Mr Prosper and an older woman who was clearly her maid, was just as unwelcome, but for very different reasons. By the hunted expression on the solicitor's face he shared Alan's discomfort at this development.

'I do apologise for my tardiness, my lord.'

'That is quite my fault,' Miss Wallace interceded. 'Since I not only insisted on taking up Mr Prosper in the landaulet when we drove from his offices to Hollywell, but then kept him overlong on my business there,

I felt it only proper to ensure he arrive here as swiftly as possible rather than wait for his clerk to arrange for a gig to convey him here from the Ship. So I offered to see him here myself while his clerk arranges to bring the gig.'

'You are too kind, but there really was no need for you to put yourself out, Miss Wallace,' Mr Prosper replied, removing his hat to mop his brow despite the cold wind blowing. 'My clerk will be here presently with the gig, so you needn't linger. I assure you I will see to your requests for Hollywell with all promptness.'

Completely ignoring this polite attempt to send her on her way, Miss Wallace extended her hand and poor Mr Prosper had no choice but to help her descend.

Alan doubted Miss Wallace had been motivated by kindness. Curiosity was probably nearer the mark. But there was something in the smile she flashed him that put him on alert. Mischief and even anger, which surprised him. She hadn't struck him as resentful and, if anything, she might be considered the victor in their two previous encounters. His treacherous body was certainly declaring its utmost willingness to surrender if that would get him past her battlements. It was a sore pity she wasn't already married and disillusioned with wedded bliss. He would have enjoyed broadening her horizons, and his.

Other than the martial flash in her gold-flecked eyes she exemplified the perfect society miss. She was dressed in a very elegant forest-green pelisse with dark-gold military facings and a deceptively simple bonnet with matching ribbons. It enhanced her warm colouring and was far too elegant for the Somerset countryside. In fact, she looked more elegant than most fashionable women he knew in London. With her money and sense of style, she would do very well once she was introduced to London society. Though she would probably ruin it the moment she opened her mouth. London was not very forgiving towards pert young women, heiresses or not, especially if their background was anything but conventional.

On the surface she would make Philip Marston a perfect wife, but the more he saw of her the more he doubted whether Philip understood what he was taking on. In fact, if he had had to guess, he would have thought Philip would choose someone more like his own daughter—classically beautiful, well mannered, wealthy and biddable. Of those criteria Lily Wallace fulfilled only the requirement of wealth.

Not that it was any of his concern. His only concern at the moment was finding a new venue for Hope House, fast, and returning to London. However pleasant it was to watch the outline of her legs against her elegant skirts as she descended from the landaulet, there was nothing to be gained flirting with an heiress who was tangled up with his grandmother and the possible matrimonial target of one of his business partners, no matter how outré and intriguing. She might be different from the usual run of women he enjoyed, but then so would the inmates of bedlam be different. Boredom in the bedroom was no excuse for putting his head into the lion's mouth...or rather the lioness's.

She approached him and her smile widened. It wasn't a welcoming smile and he instinctively reacted to it with a contrary spurt of determination. His initial look around the grounds of this property and others in the environs had only reinforced his conviction that Saltford would not do and that Hollywell House was still the perfect choice for a new Hope House. The odds were long and getting longer, but he wasn't ready to admit defeat quite yet.

'Lord Ravenscar.' Even those two words were a challenge.

'Miss Wallace.'

'I'm surprised at you. Was it *The Mysteries of Udolpho* that gave you the idea?'

He frowned, confused. Was she incapable of a normal conversation?

'I beg your pardon?'

She cocked her head to one side, walking towards the house, and politeness required he keep pace with her.

'You do innocent very well for someone who has very little connection to that concept.'

'I must be very dense, but I have no idea what you are talking about.'

A crease appeared between her brows and she stopped at the foot of the stairs.

'The broken urn?'

'The what? Is this some form of biblical charade?' He had discarded his initial opinion that she was mildly deranged, but he might have to reconsider.

'The creaking door?' she tried, her eyes narrowing.

'Miss Wallace, either you have developed the fever or that rubbish you were reading Nicky is having a dilatory effect on your mind. What the deuce are you talking about?'

'Have you been back to Hollywell House in the past couple of days?'

'No, I have not. Why on earth would I?'

The society smile had completely disappeared and she was frowning as she watched him, as if waiting for him to slip up.

'It appears whoever vandalised the library has been back. That horrid large urn in the hallway was smashed and the effect was embellished with some atmospheric creaking of doors. The latter part might have been accidental, since the latch on one of the doors from the servants' quarters doesn't close properly, but the urn was too heavy to topple over merely because of the wind.'

Alan's fists tightened. The image of her standing in the middle of the mayhem of helmets, breastplates and books returned. With a wary look, Mr Prosper hurried past them up the stairs, a set of keys clinking in his hand. Alan took Miss Wallace's arm and pulled her slightly to one side. Mr Prosper and the house could wait.

'I admit I want Hollywell House, but I don't usually have to resort to such puerile tactics to get what I want and I assure you my taste doesn't run to the Gothic.'

He spoke casually, matching her lightness, but he felt anything but light-hearted. If she had wreaked havoc to the library the other day and was now breaking urns and hearing noises, she was indeed deranged. If not, someone was actively vandalising the property, which was just as bad.

'I am not fanciful, Lord Ravenscar,' she said coolly. 'When such incidents occur in a house that should be standing empty, I presume someone is up to mischief. I admit I thought that you, rather melodramatically, had decided to add not-so-subtle persuasion to other inducements. If it wasn't you, it was someone else, and not a ghost. But whoever it is, and for whatever reason they may be doing so, it won't work.'

'If you don't know why they are doing it, how do you know it won't work?' he asked, just to annoy her, but his mind was half-focused on other matters. On who indeed might be behind these pranks and on how cold she could look when she chose to; she looked even more the perfect London hostess like that, but then her roguish smile broke through again.

'Must you ruin it by being clever? I had quite set my mind on you being the villain; it would have been so neat. Maybe you still *are* being clever. This could still be some devious machination so you could vanquish the ghost and hope to earn my undying gratitude so I would sell you Hollywell House after all. That would be a plot worthy of Radcliffe.'

'I haven't the imagination or energy for such nonsense,' Alan replied, thoroughly exasperated. Her laughing dismissal of the situation was even more annoying than a fit of hysterics would have been. What was wrong with this woman?

'No, I suppose not. You are not in the least romantic.'

She sounded so dismissive he couldn't resist mounting a defence.

'That is not the general consensus, I assure you.'

'I didn't mean *that* kind of romantic. The *real* kind of romantic.'

'I won't ask for the distinction. I haven't a strong enough stomach.'

'See? That is precisely what I mean. Well, this is most annoying. If you aren't my ghost, then who is?'

She frowned at the ground, scuffing at the gravel with the toe of a fine kid slipper. Why couldn't she act like a normal young woman and be scared? Not that he enjoyed hysterics, but it would be a nice change if she would look at him with something other than disdain or amusement. Those were not the emotions he ordinarily evoked in women. Not that trust or confidence were emotions he tended to evoke in women either, thank the gods, but at the moment he would prefer she not be quite so…unflappable.

'Aren't you in the least bit concerned? At the very least you should avoid going there until the source of this vandalism is uncovered.'

'I have requested that Mr Prosper put it about that the new tenants of the house are moving in, which I hope will discourage any further incidents. Why don't you go a step further and try to convince me that it is after all in my best interest to sell you the property?'

Alan gritted his teeth against the urge to tell her what she was welcome to do with Hollywell.

'I admit I want Hollywell, but I am perfectly capable of separating the two issues. Are you?'

She sighed.

'I don't know what I'm capable of any more. Come, I'm curious to see this house.'

'You aren't invited. Thank you for delivering Mr Prosper, but now you had best return to Lady Jezebel before it begins to rain.'

He wasn't in the least surprised she ignored him and turned towards the stairs.

'You are, without doubt, the most aggravating woman of my acquaintance. Barring my grandmother and that only by a very narrow margin.'

She turned on the top stair, her eyes narrowing into slits of gold, but the tantrum he had almost hoped for didn't materialise. For a moment she didn't answer, just stood there, her eyes on his dreamily, as if lost in an inner conversation. He couldn't remember ever being so disconcerted by a female who was doing absolutely nothing. Young women either fled behind their mama's skirts or used all their wiles to engage his interest, sometimes from behind their mama's skirts. He didn't mind either reaction. He very much minded being scolded, threatened, laughed at or ignored, all of which appeared to be this young woman's repertoire in her dealings with him. If she was doing it on purpose, he might have appreciated her tactics, but though she was clever, she was also peculiarly transparent and it was very clear she was not playing with him, not in that manner at least. Her gaze finally focused and she continued inside.

'I hadn't realised I had such power to provoke you, Lord Ravenscar. I am honoured to receive such an epithet from someone who has undoubtedly met more women than he can properly remember. I believe I read an adage somewhere that notoriety is preferable to obscurity.'

'You misread, then. The phrase is that notoriety should not be mistaken for fame.'

She wrinkled her nose, inspecting the empty drawing room Mr Prosper indicated. They entered and Mr Prosper hovered in the doorway, clearly uncertain whether his role included chaperon services. The maid, surprisingly, merely occupied a chair in the hall and took out a small skein of wool from a bag and began knitting.

'That sounds very stuffy and English. Was it from

a morality play, perhaps? One of your grandfather's charming tomes?'

'Greek. Aesop.'

'Ah, that explains it. Wasn't he the one with the tale of the vainglorious Raven?'

'The same. And the crafty fox. How fitting. Your colouring does have a rather...vixenish hue.'

'Thank you. Most often the references are to lionesses, tigresses and other felines. It is a pleasant change to elicit associations to other animals, and a resourceful, intelligent one at that. I dare say given your colouring and name you are only too used to Raven and other fowl references.'

He laughed, crossing the room to where she stood by a window overlooking a scrappy lawn already giving way to the weeds and the weather.

'Especially foul. But I don't mind. Here's another quote for you: *"Censure acquits the Raven but pursues the dove."* So are you certain you wish to be practically alone with me in an empty house? What if I am overpowered by licentious and lustful urges?'

He didn't really expect her to be shocked, nor was she.

'I thought I was a vixen, hardly a dove, but in either case I at least am not so vain as to believe I am capable of evoking overpowering urges in anyone, let alone in someone as jaded as you, and certainly not under the watchful and censorious eyes of Mr Prosper and Greene.'

'You are quite right you are no dove. Doves are soft and padded and coo when petted. What do you do when petted, Lily Wallace?'

Finally a blush. But getting a rise out of her came

at a cost of triggering an unwelcome reaction at the thought of petting her. First of peeling away those fashionable layers to the fine cotton muslin underneath. Such expensive fabrics would be near transparent once he stripped away the stays and chemise, a gauzy cobweb of a dress, like wearing the morning mist. Her hair would be a wavy tumble of warmth, a mass of shades, darker than her eyes. She might be no dove, but her body would still be soft...

'Shall we see the other rooms, my lord?' Mr Prosper asked from the doorway.

Alan nodded.

'Yes. Let's start with the bedrooms.'

Within fifteen minutes of their arrival Alan knew the property wasn't suitable. The only reason he didn't call a halt to their exploration of the old house was Miss Wallace—her curiosity and her attempts to manoeuvre him into disclosing his agenda were too amusing to curtail. Curiosity seemed to work on her in the same way greed worked on some people. In that way she reminded him of his friend Stanton—he could never abandon a problem until he had cracked and subjugated it. But if she was like Stanton, once her curiosity was assuaged, she would be off in search of the next challenge and Alan was rather enjoying her persistence and the effect it had on her natural wariness.

She still didn't trust him an inch, but she was showing a surprising degree of faith in his honour merely by being with him for so long with only a timid solicitor as chaperon. There was an aura of dismissive superiority about her that was worthy of the most spoilt of heiresses and yet she had none of the calm ease of entitlement that women like Penny Marston had. She was no pampered house cat, but a prowling half-wild feline, used to fending for herself. Catherine must have misunderstood—there was no possible way someone like Philip Marston would contemplate marriage with a woman who would challenge his authority at every level, not even for a fortune.

Mr Prosper opened the door into what had probably been an attempt at a library and stood back to allow them to enter. 'This is the last of the rooms,' he announced from the doorway, his eyes darting from them to the darkening window, where the sun was still battling with the clouds lying heavily on the trees. 'We really should leave before it begins to rain in earnest. Shall I find your maid and have the landaulet ready for you, Miss Wallace?'

'Thank you, Mr Prosper, that is very kind.'

Alan waited until the solicitor left the room and went to stand by Lily, where she was inspecting the moulding on the fireplace, her long fingers tracing an elaborate engraving that had long since been worn down to runic incomprehensibility.

'You should have fled while you could, Miss Wallace. I'm afraid your curiosity is about to be repaid with a soaking.'

'I have survived worse.'

'So have I. Even during the last hour.'

She laughed and began pulling on the gloves she had removed while inspecting the carvings.

'What, the house or my presence? Was it so very terrible?'

'It could have been better.'

'How?'

'We could have been alone.'

Finally there was a little surprise and even more wariness. But as he expected, she gathered herself and ploughed forward rather than succumb to the momentary confusion.

'Is Keynsham proving so thin of female company, then, my lord?'

'Not in the least. We are close enough to Bristol to provide for all matter of needs. But variety is the very spice of life and my fare has been somewhat bland recently.'

'Oh, you poor, poor rakehell, are you bored? How simply awful for you.'

Her tone dripped mock-concern, her eyes wide in a wonderful parody of tragic distress, and he tried and failed to restrain his grin. He kept playing into her hands and the worst was he didn't mind it in the least. The only thing he minded was that this flirtation could not be carried to its natural conclusion. Society's mores and rules might be hypocritical, a bore and a nuisance, but up to a point he abided by them simply because it was less of a bother to do so than flout them.

It was rare that his mind parted company with his body so categorically, but as he watched her concentrate on securing the glossy pearl buttons of her glove, her lashes lowered, fanning shadows over the faint dusting of freckles on her cheeks, he felt the distinct separation of those two entities.

She was not the kind of woman he enjoyed and she was not the kind of woman who enjoyed him, but his thumb very much wanted to brush over her long dark lashes and those freckles and down the soft rise of her cheek. He could almost feel it just watching the way those dark spikes, touched with gold at the tips, dipped and rose as she secured her gloves.

The urge became a distinct ache as his gaze descended. Despite her humour, her lips were pressed together, betraying a tension he had sensed from the moment he met her. She might be an indulged heiress, but she was not some frothy confection one could sink a spoon into and taste with impunity. He had never liked syllabub anyway. He preferred spice and this girl was definitely on the spicier end of the female scale. He wondered what she would taste of…if he could coax those tightly held lips into relaxing…

'I counted ten bedrooms and four larger rooms downstairs and two smaller parlours. Smaller than Hollywell House. Does that meet your needs?'

He could almost see her mind working away at the problem, taking every piece of information he had dangled in front of her and trying to shove it into place to create some conclusive picture. It was so tempting to throw in a few red herrings and watch her grasp at them with that mix of puzzlement, suspicion and determination, like a kitten pursuing a dangled string as if it were a lifeline.

'Do you know what you remind me of?'

Her eyes narrowed.

'I'm not going to like this, am I?'

He laughed.

'Probably not. Forget I said anything. What do you think of the gardens?'

She looked out the window.

'I wouldn't precisely call that a garden. Would you need a garden?'

'A ferret.'

'You need the garden for a ferret?'

'No, you remind me of a ferret.'

He waited for the inevitable outrage to darken her eyes before he continued.

'Not physically, of course, though ferrets can be quite elegant in appearance. It was a reflection on your tenacity and curiosity. Ferrets are also very hard to catch.'

'They also bite. Hard.' Her teeth snapped shut and steam practically rose off her in waves, her fingers unfastening and refastening the last few pearl buttons on her left glove like prayer beads. He removed her hand from the maligned buttons and pressed it between his. It was warm and vibrating with the energy caged inside her, a tingling force.

'I'm surprised any of your buttons survive to the end of the day, the way you worry at them.'

She surprised him again. He had expected her at the very least to pull away and more likely to slap him or resort to the verbal attacks she had engaged in at Hollywell, but instead she smiled and for a moment he had the sensation of the sun thrusting conclusively through the clouds. It certainly had the same effect— a need to narrow his eyes to protect himself.

'They often don't,' she admitted. The tension seeped out of her hand, but she didn't remove it from his grasp. She was doing absolutely nothing, but the sensation of her gloved hand in his was spreading through him like dye in water, swirling and expanding. It hadn't occurred to him his teasing would circle back and take his flank with a full attack of lust. He waited for it to peak and settle into place as all surges of physical attraction did. These pleasant sensations came and went and meant very little in the end. He had outgrown the need to pursue and indulge them, preferring to find physical release with a few very select female friends who knew the rules of the game as well as he and who could be trusted to be discreet and clean and emotionally detached from the act. He had nothing against window shopping, but he no longer bought anything on a whim, certainly nothing as expensive and impractical as a malapert, opinionated heiress.

He dropped her hand and returned to the gargantuan and very ugly fireplace, seeking a mental rope with which to haul himself out of this particular pit, something that would categorically drive her away.

'What do you think? Is it big enough for my harem?'

Lily watched as Lord Ravenscar ran his hand along the dark marble mantel that topped the oversized fireplace, his fingers rising and falling over the moulding. She clasped her own hands together, quashing the tingling heat that lingered from his clasp and made her gloves feel too tight. She had needed just this kind of comment to centre her. It was her fault for initiating the game in the first place. It took her three breaths to find her place again in the order of things. Lily Wallace, heiress. Needs no one and no one tells her what to do. Certainly not a rakehell like Lord Ravenscar.

Almost an hour had passed since they had arrived in Saltford and so far every one of her attempts to uncover his objective had run aground. The only thing she had learned was that he enjoyed dangling decoys and watching her twist to his taunts. She turned resolutely to inspect the fireplace.

'The fireplace? If you like your women short and round, it might fit three.'

He smiled and she felt petty, like a child who was being ignored by her elders and who had just thrown something merely to draw attention to herself.

'Do you like it?'

The change in his tone shoved her further off balance. He had done that before, reach inside her with his voice, set her insides reverberating like the cavern of a bell.

'What?'

'The house, Lily. Do you like it?'

She turned away from the focused force of his eyes and the taunting intimacy in his use of her given name. She was being ridiculous. For the past hour she had trotted after him, provoking and needling, and now that she had his full attention on her, she felt a panicked need to deflect it. She could hardly imagine he was being serious about a harem. He was just poking fun at her thwarted curiosity. But those questions had rumbled, no, purred through the cold room and shot heat through her just as that short clasp of her hand had. She could feel it in her cheeks and in her chest, like brandy swallowed too fast.

Do you like it?

She went over to the window just in time to see the sun lose its battle against the clouds, casting the overgrown lawn into shadow with the suddenness of a dropped blanket. It made the world, the house, the room, smaller. Maybe these peculiar sensations were a sign she, too, was falling ill. It would almost be a relief. No one would expect anything of her if she were ill. She could hide in her room and embrace oblivion, and maybe when she came out the other end of the tunnel, this discomfort would be gone and by some miracle her fate would be decided for her.

'It's not a complicated question, Lily. Do you like the house?'

He was standing directly behind her now.

'No, I don't.'

'Why not?'

She breathed in and answered only the question.

'It feels sullen. Everything is a little too small, a little too low. I would stifle here. The only thing generous here is the fireplace.'

'You need space.'

Yes, so move away, you're crowding me. She didn't say the words aloud because that would be to pander to his vanity. She frowned up at the clouds. They were gathering in the east. That way was Bristol and ships heading out towards the West Indies and what had once been home but could never be that again.

'Don't you?' she asked.

'I am used to making do with what is at hand.'

'I see. We are back to that. I'm spoilt, I suppose.'

'Most heiresses are. It's not a matter of choice. Or rather it is a matter of too much choice. They can't help themselves from expecting more than they need.'

'How kind of you to be so understanding of my flaws.' Lily thought of the life she had led until her mother's death and wondered what he would have made of their spartan existence on the island or in the mining towns in Brazil. As far as he was concerned, she was the product of the life she had led in Kingston.

He moved to her side, looking out over the grass and weeds as they snapped back and forth in the rising wind. He was so close she felt the fabric of his coat against the sleeve of her pelisse. She wouldn't turn to look because that would give him the satisfaction of knowing how aware she was of him. How many times had she played this game in the drawing rooms and ballrooms of Kingston? She was good at it. It was just another tactical game. His move, hers, his move, hers. In the end she always won because for her it was merely tactics, she had no strategy, nothing she wanted to gain. What she wanted from life had no connection to that game any more than it had to a game of chess. Less. But now that her father was gone she knew those games were over. Now, when Philip Marston returned from Birmingham, she would likely concede and start her new life.

'Since I have so many flaws myself, it would be rather hypocritical to be intolerant of others,' he answered. 'Besides, perfection is vastly overrated. My closest friends are deeply flawed and much the better for it.'

'I will hazard a wild guess there are no spoilt heiresses among them.'

He laughed and his coat brushed against her arm, raising and lowering the fabric against her arm, and her skin bloomed with goose pimples.

'Not one. One very unspoilt heiress, but she is married to one of my closest friends.'

That was a good excuse to turn towards him and put some distance between them. She was also curious. There was something in his voice. The same tone as he employed with Nicky—intimate and affectionate; a combination that didn't match what she knew of him.

'So you admit the possibility of an unspoilt heiress?'

'There are always exceptions to the rule. In this case Nell wasn't spoilt by being society's darling for years.'

That struck home. She couldn't deny that that was precisely what she had been since her father had brought her to Jamaica after her mother's death when she was fourteen and especially since she had been introduced to Jamaican society four years after that. Not that she had ever believed it meant more than an avid appreciation of her father's fortune.

'Once you start admitting exceptions to rules, you rather undermine the whole point of having them. How do you know I'm not an exception as well?'

'Are you?'

'That is hardly a fair question. Even if we aren't special, we all want to believe we are. Otherwise how could we believe we are worthy of being loved?'

A gallant man would have entered through that wide-open door, but he merely smiled and changed direction.

'I think I've seen enough of this house. We should leave before the weather turns against us completely.'

She didn't move, piqued even though she knew that was precisely what he intended. They were unevenly matched—he was much more experienced in this game, especially since his livelihood probably depended on his performance. She flirted out of boredom and resentment against the constraints society imposed, while he did it for survival. The tales of the Wild Hunt Club that Nicky had delighted in might be grossly exaggerated, but not this man's skill at the game she merely dabbled in. She would hardly sit down with him for a game of cards and put her fortune at risk even if she had control over it, and she should adopt the same caution when it came to the game of flirtation.

It was clear he wasn't really interested in her as an heiress; he would hardly be showing his cards so generously if he was. Well, she wasn't interested in him, not in any way that mattered. She would never marry a man she didn't trust and she would never trust a rake; a fortune-hunting rake famed for his wildness was just adding insult to injury. At least she knew Philip Marston was at his core a man of honour.

But whether it was intelligent or not, the truth was she didn't want to leave yet. Just another sip of champagne before teatime.

'Was your friend who married the heiress part of the Wild Hunt Club as well?'

He leaned against the window frame and crossed his arms.

'Is that nonsense still circulating?'

'Is it nonsense? It was Nicky who told me. Quite proudly, in fact.'

At least she had managed to catch him by surprise.

'Nicky? What on earth would she know about it?'

'You would be surprised what one hears at a girls' school. It's not all Gothic novels and sighs, you know, even though her version of your exploits did sound rather Gothic. Apparently association with you is quite a cachet for her at school.'

'Good God. Does Cat know about this?'

'I don't know, but I presume she does. Your sister may be quiet, but she's no fool. You didn't answer my question.'

'You see, this is precisely what I was talking about. You seem to think you are entitled to answers simply on the strength of asking a question. Life doesn't work that way.'

'I know that. Everything has a price. I can't force you to answer. I am merely inviting you to do so.'

'Inviting. I see. Tell me what Nicky told you—I'm curious what nonsense they are allowing in that very expensive school of hers.'

'Nothing too outrageous. Merely some nonsense that you and your friends always win races because you made a pact with the devil for that privilege. Oh, and that when the three of you ride at night, virtuous women must hide indoors or be swept up in the wild hunt, never to return.'

She didn't know what the amusement in his eyes signified—a male appreciation of his potency or a reaction to the absurdity of the tale?

'Nicky told you this? What nonsense you women subscribe to. I assure you virtuous women are probably the segment of your sex most likely to be safe from the members of the so-called Wild Hunt Club. We prefer responsiveness from the subjects of our midnight raids and virtue is… What is the opposite of an aphrodisiac?'

'Marriage, apparently.'

He burst out laughing.

'Damn, you're wasted as one of that group. You would have made an excellent courtesan.'

He meant to shock her and in a way he did, but it wasn't her virtue that was shocked, but her body.

The thought of being free from all the restraints that held her, body and mind. The possibility of being free to walk up to this man and demand what she wanted…

She shook free of the foreign urge. Because his words also raised the unwelcome memory of that house in Kingston, of the shocked faces of the women who had faced her after her father's death, aware their fate was now in her hands, scared and defensive and even pained. Some of them had truly cared for her father. As far as society was concerned, those women were worse than nothing; they were succubi who destroyed the lives of good men. She hadn't seen that when she stood in that opulent room with its red velvet sofas and lewd paintings. She saw women…some of them younger than she, whose fates had never been their own, at her mercy as they had been at her father's mercy and at the mercy of men like him. As long as they were young and performed their duties, they were adored and then… That night had been the first time she had cried for her parents and especially for herself.

In a less fortunate life she might have had no choice but to become one of those women who had nothing to trade but themselves. Then she, too, would have been at the mercy of men like her father and the members of this Wild Hunt Club, who thought they were somehow redeemed because they didn't pursue virtuous women.

'I don't think so, Lord Ravenscar. No one could ever pay me enough to endure the life those poor women have to endure. Now, as you said before, we should leave before it begins to rain.'

He stopped her by moving to block her path.

'I didn't mean to insult you. Believe it or not, that was a compliment.'

'I do believe it, which is precisely why I find it so offensive that you would assign any positive value to a fate where women have to sell their bodies to survive. It might be a better fate than many women have to face in this world, but it is no compliment. As someone dependent on the frailties of others to make your living, Lord Ravenscar, you should know that better than others.'

There, she had crossed a line and she was glad—finally Rakehell Raven was beginning to show his true colours. The transition from amusement to contrition to fury was as rapid as the explosion of a tropical storm, and the complete collapse of his façade fed her own anger and pain.

'See, it isn't quite so complimentary to be labelled a whore, is it?' she all but spat at him.

'I didn't label you...'

'No, you merely thought it amusing to pay me the *compliment* that I would make a fine doxy. You might not mind the label or the role, but excuse me if I fail to find it entertaining.'

'Not that it is any of your business, but I do not frequent courtesans. I prefer women who enter into arrangements of mutual pleasure of their own accord.'

'Even if I believed you, it only means you would label me somewhere below that breed, so excuse me for not finding your excuses any better than your insults, Mr Rakehell.'

She was too angry to prepare for the move, and once he had grasped her shoulders and pressed her back against the wall, she was damned if she would show fear.

'Careful, Lily Wallace. The fact that you are a woman offers you a certain measure of protection, but no more. Don't push your luck.'

She flattened her palms against his chest and pushed.

'Don't threaten me. I am not gullible enough to be cowed by that Wild Hunt Club nonsense. You insult me, I'll insult you right back, Alan Piers Cavendish Rothwell.' She tossed back his name at him, in conscious imitation of that moment when Lady Ravenscar had walked into the library at Hollywell. He was not myth. He was just an ill-behaved boy used to people bowing and scraping before his undeniable beauty and charm. Well, she *never* bowed.

She had expected more ranting, not capitulation. She had expected to push him over the edge, but contrarily the fury receded, lightening his eyes from near black to the stormy grey reflecting the building pressure outside the window. They were still heavy with anger and heat, but there was also speculation there. Though he didn't give an inch to the pressure on his chest, the hands that grasped her shoulders softened and shifted—one to cover her own hands where they pushed against him, the other to slide softly down her cheek, leaving a scorched trail as it went before settling on her neck, his thumb just brushing her jawline.

'That was ill done of me. I'm sorry.'

The *bastard*! A sincere apology was the sneakiest, most dastardly tactic of all. It tugged back the tide and left her high and dry and defenceless. If she had held the flanged mace in her hands in that moment, she would have been so tempted to swing and let loose this explosion of fury and confusion. Either that or burst into tears. Something, anything to reflect the extremity of the pressure inside her.

'I'm curious why you flared like that,' he continued, his voice soft, musing. 'That was quite a nerve I touched, wasn't it? What is it, Lily? Is it not the first time someone has called you that?' His eyes were softening as he spoke, releasing his anger like an extended breath. 'No, it's not that, is it? Your impassioned defence indicates all your sympathy appears to be with the women you don't wish to be associated with. Strange.'

She pressed harder, but he didn't move. If anything, he leaned in against her palms, forcing her to feel the hard surface under the superfine linen, his scent closing around her, warm and musky like a tropical evening. The coolness of the wall behind her was no antidote as his heat poured through her, filling her.

'If you want to hit something, go ahead. I think I'll survive.' He didn't remove his hand from her throat, but with his other he curved the fingers of her right hand into her palm and held the fist against his chest.

She never allowed Greene to lace her stays too enthusiastically, but they felt tight now. The invitation to let the pressure inside her loose was so potent she didn't know how she would draw back. She had been so wrong about him. It might not be night-time, but she could feel the pull of this wild hunt. She didn't know what to do with everything inside her; it was all crowding at the door he was forcing open. The only thing holding her back was the conviction that even this was probably a game to him. He was back in control and she was within an inch of losing hers utterly.

'I wish to return to the Hall now.'

His thumb lingered on her chin, rose to skim the line of her lower lip and withdrew. He glanced out the window and exhaled slowly.

'That is probably a good idea. The world has decided to drizzle.'

Chapter Five

Lily wiped the drops from her cloak, but it was a losing battle. She was clearly being doubly punished for her foolishness in forcing her presence on Mr Prosper and Lord Ravenscar. The open landaulet had been a reasonable choice for a quick trip to Keynsham and Hollywell, but less suitable for a longer ride to Saltford in the swiftly shifting autumn weather. Right now the wind was driving rain straight at them and poor Greene was hunched on the seat by her side in mute misery, grumbling under her breath about English climes, English food and English roads.

The coachman glanced back at them, the rain running off the brim of his low-crowned hat.

'There's an inn just over that rise, miss. Small but respectable. Mayhap you should put up there until this blows over or I could go to the Hall and bring the closed coach.'

Greene looked up at that, her face damp and mottled in the cold, and Lily sighed. It was only half an hour further to the Hall, but it was enough for them to be thoroughly soaked.

'Thank you, yes. The coach is a lovely idea.'

The inn was a modest white-and-grey building, but smoke was billowing from the chimney and at the moment that was all Lily cared about. The coachman set up a shout for the landlord and helped them down. Inside the low, narrow entrance the landlord stared at them in some dismay.

'You're more than welcome, miss, but as you can see this is just a country inn and the only private parlour I have has just been...'

'Taken. You are proving exceedingly hard to shake, Miss Wallace.' Lord Ravenscar stood in the doorway at the back of the public room. Even with her cheeks damp from rain, Lily felt the heat rise in them and was thankful for the absence of lighting. Even after her anger and their tense parting, there was no denying the pleasure she felt just at the sight of him.

It had been a very long time since she had felt this kind of fascination and never about a person and she knew that was dangerous. Watching him drive away from Saltford while Mr Prosper had climbed into the gig with his clerk, she had told herself it was all for the best that this was probably the last time she would see this man. She had repeated that uncomforting conviction the whole drive and it just made her pleasure at seeing him again so soon all the more bitter.

'Since the drizzle has become a torrent and there aren't many other inns on this road, it is hardly surprising we sought refuge here, too, my lord. I don't see why my presence here should discommode you.'

'Don't you? Pilcher, bring a warm drink to the parlour for Miss Wallace.'

'There is no need...'

'Don't be a fool. There's a decent fire in the parlour

and none out here. Your maid can sit there and glare at me with her basilisk eye. Or if you are so concerned, I will take my ale out here.'

'I didn't mean…'

He stepped back, opened the door and waited, and with a sigh she entered the parlour. It was a cosy little room and the fire was high and welcoming. It was pointless to argue—with him or with herself.

'This is lovely, thank you,' she said, untying her bonnet and cloak. Greene took them and tutted.

'I'll take these to the kitchen and see if we can brush the rain and mud from them before it settles, Miss Lily.'

Alan watched the door close behind Greene with a twisted smile and motioned Lily to the chair closest to the fire. She sat and extended her gloved hands towards the warmth while he settled on the other chair, folding his arms and stretching his boots out towards the flames.

Seated he appeared even larger than when he had loomed over her. It was ridiculous to be nervous because he was between her and the door, but the room constricted around them to just the small sphere of warmth around the fireplace. She had an outrageous, childish urge to smile at him. Foolishness.

'The maid appears to trust me more than the mistress,' he said after a moment.

'She trusts *me*, at least.'

'I noticed that. You cannot be quite the spoilt brat you appear if you command such loyalty from your groom and maid.'

'My heavens, that was nearly a compliment. Perhaps it is merely that I pay them exorbitantly for their unquestioning fidelity.'

'I can tell the difference.'

'How?'

'Distinguishing between varying shades of loyalty is a skill one develops when one's life depends on it. Where is your bruiser of a groom by the way? Why isn't he driving you?'

'I have sent him on an errand regarding Hollywell. Why, were you hoping for a rematch? Jackson would be happy to oblige. What did you mean about lives depending on knowing true loyalty? Were you referring to the war?'

Just as before he sidestepped her question and returned with one of his own.

'Have you reconsidered selling Hollywell?'

'Will you tell me what you want it for?'

'The ferret is back in force, I see. What difference does it make?'

The door opened and the landlord entered and placed a tray on the table, and the scent of apples and cinnamon filled the air. Lily's mouth watered.

'Miss's maid is helping your groom with your coat, Lord Ravenscar.'

'Thank you, Pilcher.'

Lily picked up her glass and breathed in the scent.

'Cider. I missed this in Brazil.'

He picked up his ale and smiled at her. For once, his smile was neither taunting nor seductive, but it hit her hardest. It felt so right to be sitting there with him. So comfortable and right.

'The simplest pleasures are often the best. Cheers.'

He would know, she reminded herself, struggling to dispel the completely inappropriate fog of wellbeing. He knew all about pleasure. That was all he cared about. His *own* pleasure.

'Will you be visiting Catherine and Nicky again before you leave?'

The cynical gleam returned, both disappointing and reassuring her.

'I'm afraid not. I have some business in the area and then I will be on my way.'

'Nicky will be disappointed. Catherine will, too, though she won't say a word, of course. She never does, but that doesn't mean she doesn't feel it.'

'Are you trying to work on my conscience? It is a futile effort, believe me.'

'I don't waste my time on lost causes. I was merely suggesting you might consider taking her with you to Bristol while you are in the vicinity.

'Why should I take her to Bristol?'

He looked genuinely puzzled, which added fuel to her fire.

'You must know Lady Ravenscar isn't given to entertaining, which means your poor sister spends most of the year cooped up at the Hall with no one to talk to but Lady Ravenscar and Nicky when she is down from school. She is barely thirty years old and she should not be behaving as if she were seventy. Would it have been so hard to make some time to take her shopping or to an assembly, or are you too busy with your gaming hells and brothels?'

As the words poured out, she knew she was once more crossing a line, that her annoyance was in excess of its stated cause. It wasn't his fault she was marooned at the Hall until she made her decision, that she had no idea what that decision should be, that he kept pushing her out of her hard-earned equilibrium. None of it was his fault and yet it felt like it was. She drew breath, dragging herself back, and looked away from the smoky fury in his eyes.

'I apologise, Lord Ravenscar. It is quite clear you care for your sister and niece and I have no right to interfere in what I don't understand.'

'You're right. You don't.'

She wasn't given to blushing, but she felt the heat of mortification in her cheeks. She probably appeared both childish and shrewish, two attributes she hated. Perhaps he was right that her privileged position as heiress had spoilt her. Usually her sense of humour kept a rein on her temper, but this time she had gone too far.

She waited for the counter-attack, focusing on the buttons of her gloves, sinking into the familiar ritual of buttoning and unbuttoning them to calm her nervousness. She had never worn gloves on the island and they had been harder to accustom herself to even than corsets. They felt clumsy and unnatural, separating her from the world and hemming her in. She slipped out the buttons one by one, counting out memories for each of them, far-gone memories of the little house in Somerset before their departure to Brazil, then her favourite corners on Isla Padrones, all the people she loved, living and dead, until she was calm and collected again. With each sleek slide of pearl through its loop, her mind settled a little: this one was for her little treehouse the gardener had built for her out of a shipping crate in the mango tree; this was for tickling the manatees with her bare feet when they came to beg in the bay for crusts; this one was for Augustus, who had been her favourite from the island's many half-domesticated dogs; this one was for...

His chair scraped against the floor and she looked up. He hadn't moved, but his gaze was on her hands. For some reason she froze, her fingers still with a pearl button partly unfurled. He had the most amazing lashes, long and definite and the only feminine element in a face that was too virile and male to be truly beautiful. They rose now as she watched and he was close enough for her to see a ring of darkened blue, the colour of night that makes the eyes ache as they search it for shapes.

'If you're going to take them off, then stop playing with them and take the damn things off!'

'What?'

He moved with a suddenness that didn't even give her time to tense, grasping her wrist and swiftly unhooking the final buttons and tugging off her glove, tossing it next to his on the table. His hands were brusque, like an impatient parent, but she didn't notice that, just the slide and scrape of his fingers against her wrist as he worked.

When he took her other hand and unhooked the first button with the same businesslike movement, she turned her arm over and pressed it down on the table, blocking him. She didn't want to be treated like an aggravating child.

'I'll do it.'

But he didn't let go, just sat there clasping her wrist in his hands. She tugged at it, but he tightened his hold. This time she didn't resist when he turned her hand over, because this time it was different.

She watched his hands, dazed. Was it possible that they were even more beautiful than his face? No, they were too rough-looking to be beautiful, with a series of small white scars along the back of his right hand and one cut still unhealed along the softer skin between his thumb and forefinger. They were the hands of a man who used them for more than gambling and seduction, but they were still mesmerising. They also had to be quite large to make hers look so small by contrast. She didn't have the dainty hands and narrow wrists so admired by men. Her father would make fun of what he called her pianist hands that could span a whole octave when she played on the warped old pianoforte for the islanders. But as Lord Ravenscar's long dark fingers uncovered the pale length of her forearm and the greenish veins at her wrist, she felt fragile, breakable.

He was moving even more slowly now than she had, as if it was a physical effort to continue. Then as the edges of her glove peeled back to reveal the heel of her palm, he raised it and with one finger traced the line between wrist and palm. Her fingers twitched and her body breathed in that faint flush of skin on skin. It lit up the whole right side of her body, ending in a tingle along her cheekbone.

She wanted him to kiss her there. Press that beautiful taunting mouth right there, just as lightly. And then...

'Damn.'

His curse was soft and didn't seem connected to anything, but it rang through her like a stone dropped into a well. His face had an abstracted look as he inspected her hand. It should have sobered her, but it didn't.

She held herself completely still, waiting, but inside her was a rising blaze of a fire that demanded she *do* something. She just had no idea what. He might think her bold, but to do what she wanted to do right now, grab his hand and pull him towards her, make him kiss her, make him peel back much more than her glove, was so outrageous she could hardly believe she was even thinking it. Not thinking it, feeling it, her whole body drawing life at the moment from the contact of his fingers on her wrist. Her legs were clenched, pressing together hard, trying to hold something down.

Maybe she *was* falling ill after all. It must be that. This heat and discomfort and…and *something* made no sense otherwise. This was the fever and it was hitting her hard. She should tell him she needed to get back to the Hall. Soon. Before it became worse.

But she didn't say anything. Not even when his hands started moving again, his thumb sweeping over the skin he exposed, from the line he had traced gently over the hills and valley of her palm and up each finger, curving over its crest and resting at each tip for a moment before continuing to the next. She looked away from the damage he was wreaking, but her eyes caught on his face, intent, calm, utterly focused on what he was doing. Until he looked up.

The dark grey had melted into night and she was just melting. No one had ever looked at her like that, or if they had, she hadn't noticed. No, no one she had ever met *could* look like that. She could give credence to tales of the Wild Hunt, of seductive devils rising from the depths of hell to tempt unwitting maidens who wandered out after dark. Except that it wasn't dark and they were in the private parlour of a small English inn in Somerset in the middle of a rainstorm and she didn't believe in devils any more than she believed in ghosts.

He was just a man.

But she was just a woman.

She hardly noticed her hand stretch under his, her fingers scraping against his palm as it lay lightly on hers, but it had the desired effect. His hand closed on her wrist and he drew her towards him, over the table, his other hand closing on her nape as he stood up, drawing her to her feet, moving towards her.

She opened to the kiss as if it was the most natural thing in the world. As if she had known this man for years rather than days and this intimacy was part of her own existence, natural, reaching deep inside her to places no one else was allowed.

She didn't know what she had expected, her experience of kissing was just another part of her role as heiress pursued—she had toyed with it and discarded it as interesting but hardly worth the annoyance when kissing turned to pawing. God, had she been wrong. She had had no idea...

She hadn't expected the very contact of his mouth on hers to pour liquid heat through her, to reach even to her toes and fingertips like an ancient spell bringing a statue to life. She needed more; she wrapped her arms around his neck, raising herself on tiptoe, unable to stop her body from pressing against his hard length. A sound burst from deep inside her, a cry of yearning that she had no control over. It was a mistake. He pulled back, his eyes narrowed as if in pain.

'Lily...' It sounded like a protest, but she ignored it. She wouldn't let him stop. She could touch him; her hands realised it before her and were already moving over him, feeling the grain of his skin from the hard angle of his cheekbone to the scrape of stubble on his cheek, then into the warm silk of his hair at his nape, the taut rise of muscle and sinew as he held himself rigid. But when she pressed her mouth to his, sliding against the smooth heat of his lips, he groaned and dug his hand into her hair, angling her head and taking control. No one had ever dared kiss her like this, hard, demanding, his tongue seeking hers, torturing her sensitised lips, nipping at them before suckling them into quivering submission as he moulded her body to his. Her hesitant exploration was submerged in the force of the embrace and she just clung, waiting for disaster or salvation, little whimpers coursing through her without even realising, gathering force.

'Lily…' The single word shivered through her, a whisper of wind high above the storm. He had warned her. She understood the danger of the wild hunt now that it was too late.

She didn't hear the knock and didn't understand why he was suddenly halfway across the room until Greene walked in and laid Lily's cloak over a chair. Without a word he picked up his gloves and hat from the table and left the parlour.

Chapter Six

Alan opened his eyes and stared at the sooty beams.

Had the already cramped rooms at the Ship shrunk overnight?

The dun-coloured walls leaned in, mean and oppressive, and a draught whistled past the warped window frame. No wonder the room was so cold; it felt even icier under the blanket than out of it. He debated staying where he was. What was the point of getting up anyway? The sky outside was still depressingly grey and he would likely only get soaked a third time. Neither he nor Jem had enough clothes with them to spare another dousing like the past couple of days they had spent driving around looking for a new property, none of which had proved any more suitable than the house in Saltford. The only benefit of the massive discomfort had been to distract him, partially, from the persistent and uncomfortable memories of his idiocy at that inn.

Idiocy. The word felt woefully inadequate in the face of the physical torture that careened through his body just at the memory. His mind had never before clung so tenaciously to the sensations of a body pressed against his, to the unique, intoxicating flavour of a woman's mouth and skin. It lingered at the tips of all his nerves and at his core, an aching accusation.

How had he allowed a kiss to so completely escape his control? Her avid response had surprised him and all but knocked him off his feet, but that was no excuse. That was just it; there was no excuse for what he had done.

He turned on his side, trying to stifle his treacherous thoughts and gather the resolution to get out of bed and send for some firewood. His back ached, probably from the sagging bed. His head ached, probably from sheer frustration at being in this cursed corner of the world where everything always went wrong.

But the most abused organ at the moment was his pride and it was about to get worse. After a whole day and a half of marshalling every argument against debasing himself, he knew there was no getting around it—he would have to apologise to that vixen. She might have given his temper plenty of provocation, but he was responsible for losing it and his pride dictated he swallow it and apologise.

Damn the girl. She would have served him better if she had swung that mace at him the day he came across her at Hollywell House so he could have been knocked out and not fallen into Jezebel's trap in the first place. Then he would have taken himself off safely to Bristol and could have avoided making a thorough fool of himself.

It served him right for teasing her. What the hell had he been thinking…or rather why the hell *hadn't* he been thinking? He never should have succumbed to the informality of her behaviour and engaged in conversations with her that were as improper as he could imagine with a gently reared young woman who might one day become the wife of a business partner, no matter how unconventional. Whatever the merits of his reputation as a rakehell, not even in his wildest days had he crossed the line with marriage material, out of pure self-preservation if nothing else, because if there was one price he was unwilling to pay for his pleasure, it was matrimony. There was a little grey stone by the Hall to remind him precisely why he would never proceed down that path, no matter what Catherine or society thought. There were certain mistakes in life one didn't make twice. Catherine had been too ill to remember, but he could never forget. He had lost his will and his right to a family before it was even a thought in his young mind. There would be no home and no children and that meant he stayed away from virtuous young women. In London he was careful not even to engage them in conversation unless he was safely in the despised but controlled confines of society's playgrounds. However little society trusted him, he trusted it less—it was the hypocritical domain of the likes of his grandmother, and if he gave it a finger, it would snap off his arm, pick the bones clean and beat him over the head with it.

So how the bloody hell had he crossed that acid-etched line with the impertinent heiress? Not just crossed the line, but all but pitched a tent on the other side. He had taunted her, insulted her, kissed her and was well on the way to doing worse if her maid hadn't appeared in time.

He groaned and shoved back the blanket, shivering as he tugged on the bell and went to put on his dressing gown. His head felt heavy and he wondered if the ale he had drunk last night had been bad. It hadn't tasted off, but then the Ship wasn't the type of hostelry he was used to any more and anything was possible. It was too close to Bristol to cater to serious travellers and both the bedrooms and the fare were mediocre at best. He smiled at the thought—he had accused the heiress of being spoilt, but he himself was becoming quite spoilt. Either that or he was getting old. A few years ago he wouldn't have thought twice about staying in a much less commodious inn and a few years before that he had spent more nights than not sleeping on the rocky ground in Spain with nothing more than a scratchy, filthy blanket as cover and a knapsack as a pillow, hoping to make it through another day without being shot or skewered by a bayonet. Now he felt like a creaking, groaning octogenarian because his bed sagged and the window frames weren't true.

Maybe winning that mill at cards five years ago had done him a serious disservice. At the time he had considered it poetic justice—after all, he spent a pretty penny supplying his mistresses with the best in women's clothing, so perhaps it was fitting he should be making his fortune producing the finest muslin fabrics. Not that it had started out that way. The man who had staked the mill had actually laughed at the loss, admitting it was in such bad repair and so deep in debt he hadn't even been able to sell it.

At the time Alan had been furious and seriously considered tossing the key and deed into the Thames. Instead he had dragged himself up to Birmingham, a decision which had changed his life. In two years he had taken over two other failing mills, introducing light wrought-iron power looms with swift gearing and lighter dressing frames. That had brought him into contact with Marston and together they had invested in additional mills and more interestingly in a large manufactory of their newly patented power looms that were transforming the industry. It might not be good *ton*, but it sure as hell beat depending on his skill with horses and cards to make ends meet after selling out from the army. He had staffed both the mills and manufactories with men who had served under his command and then with more and more of the veterans floating around the country in search of employment. With Stanton and Hunter's help, he had transformed an old manufactory nearby into another Hope House, drawing veterans from all over the Midlands, and now they were doing the same in Bristol, or at least they had been until the building they had leased had caught fire. It had been sheer luck that none of the men and their families had died, but the temporary solutions they had found for them in Bristol were abysmal and made the Ship look like Prinny's Brighton Pavilion by comparison. Many of the veterans were already infirm and ailing. If they weren't going to succumb to inflammation of the lungs or worse, he needed to move them to a safer, healthier and larger home. He was through with people dying on his watch when he could do something about it.

He sat down on the side of the bed, drawing the blanket around his shoulders. He had plenty to do before he left Bristol, but before all else he had to gather the resolve to deliver the dreaded apology. If only he could gather the resolve to stand up.

He straightened at a knock on the door and Jem entered with an armful of firewood.

'Well, the landlord's ill, Captain. This place is going from bad to worse; the sooner we move on, the better.'

Alan watched Jem work at the fire.

'My thoughts exactly. We can stay at the Pelican in Bristol until we're done here.'

Jem glanced over his shoulder, frowning.

'You shipshape, sir? You're sounding rusty. Not like you to sleep in either.'

'I didn't sleep in. I barely slept at all. The damn place is like an icehouse. There's nothing wrong with me a decent room won't cure.'

'Getting soft, are we, Captain?'

'Getting old, Jem. Any chance you could find some warm water for me to shave? I feel as rusty outside as in.'

'I'll take a toddle downstairs and see if there is anyone here not laid up.' He stopped by the door. 'Why don't you get back into bed, sir? At least until the room warms.'

Alan laughed. 'Good God, Jem. Talk about getting soft. What's got into you?'

Jem's shoulders hitched back.

'Nothing, my lord. You're looking a little grey about the gills, that's all.'

Alan sighed with annoyance but pulled his legs back on to the bed. After all they had been through during the long years of war, worrying about a draught was rather absurd. As was the suggestion that he might be sickening. He couldn't help the involuntary shiver that struck through him at the thought. It didn't matter how many years had passed since his parents' deaths, just being confronted with illness could make his mind dive for cover more effectively than any of the real physical threats he had faced during the wars. Seeing Nicky, flushed and feverish, had choked him, forcing him to adopt his best performance for her and Cat's sake. Cat understood, but she herself had been too ill during those weeks in Edinburgh to remember much of what had happened. He never, never wanted to be in that position again. He hadn't been strong enough then and he had only weakened with the years.

In a few moments he would dress, say his good-byes to Cat and Nicky, grit his teeth and apologise to the vixen, and leave. Then he would do his best not to venture within a dozen miles of Ravenscar for another decade at least. This corner of England was obviously unhealthy for him in all respects.

Chapter Seven

Lily stared at herself in the silver-veined mirror. Her eyes looked huge and murky, a caricature of one of Nicky's desperate heroines. She was tempted to stick her tongue out at the despondent face before her, but Lady Ravenscar's sermons were clearly having an effect and she merely turned her back on the distorted image. Such a childish gesture would be in keeping with her rather more serious act of running away.

Or was it considered running away when one had already arranged one's return and had covered one's tracks?

She crossed the library to place the ornate wooden box with one of her father's silver-tooled duelling pistols on the desk within easy reach. She had left the other one in the bedroom which Mr Prosper's housekeeper had prepared for Lily's 'guests' due to arrive from Jamaica any day now. The housekeeper had tentatively offered to find servants to occupy the house, but she had accepted Lily's assurance that her guests were arriving with a full complement of their own.

She felt worst about lying to Jackson and Greene, sending them to see their families while she was supposed to go by post-chaise for a flying visit to an old schoolfriend near Bath. Greene particularly had been offended, but the chance to visit her sister after decades abroad won out over professional pride.

So now Lily had three days of absolute solitude in a clean and fully stocked house before the post-chaise she had hired in Bitton returned to collect her and return her to the Hall. The raging wind and threatening clouds outside only made her feel safer. There was no chance anyone would be wandering about the countryside and wondering about the lights peeping out from the curtains in what was supposed to be an empty house. For the next three days she could be alone, utterly alone, in her house.

She spread her arms wide, closing her eyes to encompass the whole of the house in her mind just as she had tried to encompass their little island as a child. Part of her might fear being condemned to loneliness, but she was familiar with it, even comfortable—it was her sanctuary when the noise of life held her back from thinking clearly. Right now she needed that clarity more than ever—she was about to make the most momentous decision of her life. That was why she needed to come to Hollywell—she had a childish conviction that if she could only be utterly alone in a space that was hers and only hers, untainted by memory or disillusion, she would know what she should do about Mr Marston's proposal.

Well, not quite untainted. Just standing in the library made it very clear it was now distinctly tainted with the image of a very large, handsome and unrepentant rake, blast the man.

She lit a wax candle from the flames of the fireplace and placed the candleholder on the big oak desk, running her fingers along its age-softened edge. Albert Curtis had probably written his sermons here and dreamed of the day he would leave it all behind and travel to the mission in Africa. What a pity he had not done so sooner. Another reminder how important it was to go after one's dreams while one could. Aside from the recent rake-related dreams, that is. Those would descend all too swiftly into nightmares.

She just didn't trust the kind of love her mother had abandoned her soul and pride for—in fact, she had developed a serious aversion to her mother's radiant joy when her father arrived on the island, as well as to her father's boyish excitement whenever he was newly on the hunt. Love between men and women, from what she had seen of it, was often either embarrassing, debilitating or downright damaging.

She wanted something better around which to construct the rest of her life. Something meaningful. She knew what her answer should be. When Philip Marston returned from Birmingham, she should say yes and start down the path to her dream of a family. She might have abandoned her young hopes of finding love, but she still yearned to have children. There was abundant love in her waiting to be shared and she wanted lots of children so they would have each other if something happened to her, or just so they would have each other to play with, to read to…

She tried to cling to the images that had accompanied her back to England, but with each passing day her fear was growing that in a marriage with Philip she would just exchange one prison for another. Even the promise of children was no longer enough to calm this fear. She knew what had shifted her from her path.

Admit it, Lily, for once, you are like all those other silly misses—fascinated by a handsome face and a sullied reputation, and piqued that a notorious fortune hunter didn't immediately start chasing you. You have become a thoroughly spoilt brat, just as he said. Well, you have come by your just deserts! He made a fool of you. No, you made a fool of yourself.

She squeezed her eyes shut against the memories that surged upwards again—of his hands holding hers, peeling back the gloves, touching her, his mouth on hers, warm and demanding, setting her alight…

It was like walking around with a bee sting embedded in her skin, knowing it needed to be removed, but afraid to pick at it for fear it would hurt as much in the removal, and all along it seeped venom into her blood, leaving her as feverish as poor Nicky.

It was just a kiss, for heaven's sake! She had been kissed before. That was one of the few benefits of being an heiress—she could flirt with relative impunity. He was an impressively handsome man and clearly well-trained, so why not enjoy a little light entertainment while she was immured here? That was all it was. She was confused only because he was so much more skilled than her past flirts. By a long stretch. She should have given credit to the tales indicating the notorious Rakehell Raven was in a different league from the men she had encountered in Kingston. Older, harder, more experienced and much, much more cynical. It was a salutary lesson not to rest on her laurels. Well, she was warned now. If she saw him again, which she doubted, she would avoid him. She had had her kiss. To invite anything else would be to invite trouble indeed. She might be arrogant as he had accused her, but she was no fool.

A thud echoed through the room and she dropped her book and jumped to her feet. It had been too close for thunder. Someone at the front door? The ghost again? No. She doubted ghosts wore boots. As footsteps approached the library, she wrested the mace from its steely grip and moved towards the desk where her father's pistol was waiting in its box.

'Not that again,' Ravenscar said drily as he opened the door and saw her.

She dropped the mace.

'Not you again,' she replied, her heartbeat thudding painfully in her ears. Fear, anger, relief and unwelcome heat were as tangled as the branches outside were by the storm. She could deny wanting to see him again until the stars stopped shining, but she couldn't lie about the excitement that lit her from within.

He shook the rain from his hat and placed it on the side table. He was dressed for riding and his caped greatcoat and boots were glistening with rain.

'I was riding through the field towards the Hall to say goodbye to Cat and Nicky and I saw the light in the library window. I thought your vandal was here. You should return to the Hall before this storm reaches its full potential. I didn't see a conveyance in the courtyard. Did your pugilistic groom take the horses to the stable? Shall I fetch him?'

His voice was stiff and measured. He was clearly unpleased to see her and against her better judgement it stung. He had also ruined her plans. There was no possible way he would not tell at least Catherine she was at Hollywell.

'Jackson has gone to visit his family. I will return to the Hall when I am through here.'

She expected incredulity or annoyance, but he merely moved into the room and sat down in the chair closest to the door. With the clouds still low, there wasn't much light in the room and it took her a moment to focus away from her discomfort and realise that he was behaving quite strangely. He might be a rake, but he was, up to a point, a gentleman. Common courtesy required that he not sit while she remained standing and the insult was pointed. She gritted her teeth.

'You may continue on your way to the Hall. I shall find my way back. Unless you are angling for another chance to convince me to sell Hollywell.'

He leaned his head back for a moment on the chair.

'No. I realise trying to convince you is a lost cause. But I still must apologise for my behaviour at the inn. It was unforgivable.'

His tone was at variance with his words. It was rough and dismissive and made a mockery of his apology.

'Please don't bother. I'm aware the first offence was mine, but there was no need for you to be so insulting.'

'Was that what I was? Some women might have considered it a compliment.'

'Some women might find you attractive,' she retorted, but she derived no satisfaction from the frown that followed her childish and mendacious dart.

'You didn't resist much at the time.'

'I'm impressed you recall one incident among so many, Lord Ravenscar. As for me, I see nothing wrong in gathering some new experiences here in England. It has been quite flat, isolated as we are at the Hall with only your relations to entertain me. So thank you for alleviating my tedium.'

There, that was a masterly exhibit of insouciance. She was quite proud of herself. Even when he shoved to his feet, a frowning menace, she held her ground and waited. But he just stood there for a moment, his hand on the back of the chair, and both her shame and pique began to fade. He looked different from two days ago. His face was pale and as her eyes ran over him she realised he was wavering slightly and the arm braced on the chair was gripping it too tightly. It reminded her of her father on the mornings after he had been out until the early hours of the morning, she realised with a spurt of outrage and resentment. No doubt he had been enjoying himself thoroughly at some tavern where men of his ilk went gambling and brawling or whatever it was men did with such abandon and which women were supposed to know nothing about. Well, when they showed up like this, how on earth were women not supposed to venture a very good guess?

'You are looking a little worse for wear, my lord. You might need some coffee.' Her voice dripped contempt and he directed her a look out of half-closed eyes that was a combination of resentment and disgust.

'I need you to see reason and agree to sell Hollywell. Trust me, you don't want to live this close to Old Jezebel. Besides, if you plan to marry Marston, you will live with him and this place will sit idle.'

She stared at him. How could he know that? Had Catherine told him? It wasn't much of a betrayal, but it hurt. She had begun to feel she had a friend in Catherine, but why should she expect her to be loyal to her above her own brother? They were family, after all, and she was nothing.

'What if I don't? What if I decide to live here on my own? What if all I need is Hollywell?'

He didn't seem to register the childishness of her protest as he rubbed at a point in the centre of his forehead and frowned at her.

'You would live here alone?'

She turned away to look out at the lawn sloping down towards the swaying trees and she followed his gaze. She could imagine sitting right here with a book and a cup of tea. Would it be so terrible to give up her dreams of a family?

'No. Probably not. I want children and I am well aware of the cost gossip could have on their future were I to choose to flout convention.'

Why on earth was she telling this man all this? It was none of his business and it was a rather pathetic attempt on her part to prove she wasn't merely a selfish and pampered heiress as he had accused her. As if someone like him had any right to pass judgement. A more self-indulgent...

If she had expected her honesty would soften him, she was wrong. His face became even stonier.

'Of course, what woman doesn't dream of her perfect little home and hearth, surrounded by rosy-cheeked bairns. So we are back to Marston. He has enough houses already. He doesn't need Hollywell. We do.'

'Is that how you make ends meet? Help people find things?'

'No, as a gambler I make ends meet by helping people lose things. I'm surprised Jezebel hasn't made you a present of all my sins yet.'

'I must have become bored and stopped paying attention halfway through the list.'

He laughed and pressed the heels of his hands to his eyes in a strangely childish gesture. He really didn't look well, she realised. He was in no state to fence with her.

'You should probably return to Keynsham and sleep it off.'

He didn't answer immediately, but when he pushed away from the chair, she watched in shock as his face turned an ashy grey under his tan.

'Damn…' he muttered and leaned back on the chair.

She moved towards him and instinctively reached out to touch his cheek before she even realised what she was doing.

'You're not drunk; you are ill!'

He recoiled from her touch as if she had slapped him.

'No, I'm not. Just tired.'

Even his voice was turning ragged. He cleared his throat and looked towards the door, his eyes half-closed, as if assessing the distance needing to be covered.

'We should go.'

For once, she didn't argue. He walked with the concentration of the very drunk, and if she hadn't known better, she would have believed he was indeed tipsy.

'Is your curricle outside?' she asked as they reached the library door and he paused, reaching out to lean his hand on the door jamb.

'No. My groom took it to Bristol. You wait here

while I ride to the Hall and have them send a carriage for you.'

She gaped at him. He didn't look like he would make it from the library to the front door.

'You can't ride all the way back, you're ill. We'll do the opposite—you wait here and I will send someone from the Hall...'

'Don't be silly.' The word faded and he half-turned, leaning his back against the wall. The remainders of colour drained from his face and he watched her with a strange fascination, as if she was transforming before his very eyes. 'I might just need...to sit down for a moment...'

He was a great deal heavier than she was prepared for, but she put her shoulder into it and managed to half-coax, half-propel him towards a backless ottoman sofa which was almost long enough for his tall frame.

'My head...it's breaking...' he groaned as he sank down and then slid on to the cushioned armrest.

'It's too hard for that,' she murmured, touching her fingers to his forehead again. If anything, he felt hotter and his dark hair was clinging to the perspiration that was forming there. She must have been very unperceptive not to have realised immediately something was wrong with him. She had become so defensive around him she was losing her perspective. 'You have the fever. I will bring a pillow and some blankets.'

His eyes opened, a flickering, intense look that stopped her.

'No, I don't!'

The words were slurred, but the denial was very clear.

'I'm afraid saying it isn't so won't make any odds

in this case, Lord Ravenscar. You most definitely have the fever. Doctor Scovell told us there have even been several fatalities in the past weeks, and if you don't want to put a premature end to your hedonistic existence, I suggest you rest here until I find some way of conveying you to the...to town.'

She corrected herself quickly. She was talking too much, she knew, a cover as much to mask her own fear as to forestall any resistance on his part. He should not be riding in this state and in this weather; he would probably fall off his horse and die of exposure if he didn't drown outright in the rain and mud-filled ditches.

'No...' He shifted, trying to lever himself up. 'I won't go...'

He was no fool; he had probably guessed her intention. She pressed her hands against his shoulders, holding him down more easily than she had expected.

'Fine, don't go. Stay here. I'll fetch blankets.'

He sank back and she could see he was beginning to shiver. This meant the fever had just begun to climb and she felt a spurt of alarm. He was so hot already, hotter than even Lady Ravenscar and Catherine had been when they had fallen ill.

'Can't go alone...' he mumbled. 'The ghosts...'

'They had best not tangle with me right now, I'm in no mood for hauntings. I will return as quickly as I am able, but you must stay right here. If you move, I will be annoyed.'

She couldn't make out his response, but it didn't sound complimentary.

It took her just moments to bring some blankets and a pillow from the rooms upstairs, and though he hadn't moved from the sofa, the change was once again alarming. He was still pale under his tan, but his sharp-cut cheekbones were stained with colour, his eyes pressed shut as if in pain and the shaking was getting worse. He said something unintelligible when she raised his head to place the pillow under it, but he just lay there as she unfastened the buttons of his greatcoat and draped the blankets over him.

When she was done, she pressed the back of her hand to his burning cheek, trying not to be distracted by the contrast between the silky skin and the scrape of dark stubble. She had never seen anyone succumb so violently and so quickly. He must have been ill a day already. Anyone less stubborn would have had the sense to keep to his bed today. What was wrong with men?

'Oh, God, my head.' The words, hoarse and half-swallowed, dragged her out of the strange fog of fear that had begun to take hold of her. He shifted, his own hand falling from the sofa, and she picked it up in hers. It was as hot, but very dry, like paper just before it burst into flame. His eyes opened, dark and glittering, and she was caught like an animal in a predator's glare.

His hand tightened on hers with surprising force.

'Don't leave!'

There was outright panic in his eyes. They were dilated, the fever darkening them to black. It was clear he was caught in some delirious thought of his own, but she answered him as if he was completely rational.

'I won't. I promise.'

'Promise…'

'I promise,' she repeated, and he closed his eyes, but his hand clung to hers, hot and dry, twitching slightly.

Even as the words left her lips, she knew they were a

mistake. The storm raging outside had come as quickly as his fever, but it did not look like it was going to lighten, which meant the fields between Hollywell and the Hall would soon be waterlogged and impassable on foot, so if she was going to bring help, she should leave soon. But the promise had a superstitious power, as if by breaking it, even for a good purpose, she would be putting him in grave risk. It would be like the night she had sat with the housekeeper's tiny new baby, Bento, while her mother had tended to poor Marta as she lay bleeding after a difficult and far too early birth. She had been so thirsty and had left for just a moment to fill the pitcher of boiled lemon water. Her mother had told her the baby had been born much too early and would have died whether she had been there or not, but her ten-year-old mind had rejected that palliative. She had been tired and thirsty and she had left her charge and death had stolen him in her absence. She knew her mother was right, that to believe otherwise was hubris, a belief in her own power and importance, but ever since then she had been very careful not to promise anything she wasn't certain she could fulfil.

So the moment she spoke the words she felt the old childish weight of fear and oppression. She could not leave him. If she did, she might come back and find him too still, too quiet, the heat of fever seeping out like water from a cracked vessel, unstoppable. All her logic, that she should fetch help, that she should not be here alone with him in the descending gloom of evening, was useless in the face of her fear of the consequences of going back on her word.

A flash of lightning turned the world to black and white for a second and his eyes opened.

'Thunder…'

'That was close. Any second now…' The crash drowned out her words, but he shook his head.

'My horse…outside…doesn't like thunder.'

He struggled to rise, but she pressed him back again.

'I'll see to him. I will be right back.'

'No, you can't ride him.'

'I won't, I promise, just lead him to the stables. Just until you are recovered.'

His eyes closed and she had no idea if he even heard her.

She hurried over to the desk and after some rummaging found what she needed. When she was done, she rushed outside, wondering where he had left his horse, but luckily it was tied by the front door and was grazing at the weeds poking along through the edge of the gravel, completely ignoring the lashing wind and rain. She stared at the animal with some dismay. It was an enormous black gelding with a long silky mane and tail which glistened in the fading light. She took a step forward and it raised its head and turned to stare at her with a look that was distinctly menacing, as if daring her to approach.

Blast the man, trust him to bring a horse as ill-tempered as he.

'There, boy,' she cooed as she approached. He sidled, watching her with his head lowered and his ears tucked back. She was not deceived; this was not a submissive gesture. Still, she moved forward with a confidence that was utterly feigned and managed to tuck a note into the belt of the saddle, where it might escape the rain. Then she untied his reins, throwing them over his neck before he could react. For a moment his liquid eyes focused on her as if debating squashing her between his enormous body and the stone column, but then he merely danced sideways, becoming aware of his freedom.

'That's right, off you go!'

The gelding bent to nip at the weeds again and with a growl of exasperation she waved her hands in the air.

'Shoo! Off you go!'

He trotted for a few steps and recklessly she moved towards him, her hands still waving like a demented houri.

'Oh, for heaven's sake. Faster!' she yelled at him and was supported by a crack of lightning and thunder, almost simultaneous. Finally the stallion sped into a canter down the drive, kicking up gravel.

She pushed her dripping hair out of her eyes and watched him disappear, wondering if he would ever be found, and if so, would anyone notice the paper tucked into the saddle or whether they would merely steal this clearly valuable horse. If so, Alan, if he recovered, would have her head. She half-smiled at the fury he would probably unleash on her anyway at putting his beautiful horse at risk, but that was his own fault. He never should have ventured outdoors if he felt unwell. Any sane person would have known their limits.

Back in the library she relaxed slightly. He was still breathing and still on the sofa, but each breath seemed to be an act of will, dredged up out of a great depth. She placed her hand on his forehead and he mumbled something, twisting away. She couldn't make out the words, but it sounded rude. She was tempted to respond by telling him what she had done with his precious brute of a horse, but that would probably drag him out of his stupor and make him do something foolish, so she merely sat down by his side and took his hand. The clouds were so thick they had turned afternoon into evening, leaching the colour from the room. This was her fault. She must have been mad to conceive of such a scheme. The day her father had caught her trying to board the ship to England he had told her running away never solved anything. He should have added it only complicated matters.

'You're a stubborn, stubborn fool,' she said aloud, as much to herself as to him, and his hand twitched, closing painfully around hers. She waited for it to ease again and rubbed it gently. Someone would find his horse and perhaps even the note. She just had to ensure he was comfortable and safe until then.

She didn't try to detach her hand again, just sat there and looked. Would it be the same no matter how many times she saw him? This sense of amazement and revelation? The way her body shifted from a medium of mundane existence to an entity with its own demands. Worst of all was the sense of rightness, of coming home.

Absurd.

Undeniable.

Even at his worst, he was so painfully handsome she wondered why she hadn't realised it the moment he strode into the Hollywell library. Yes, she had noticed he was handsome, but not that it would be hard to look away. Harder not to reach out and touch.

She curled her fingers into her palm.

Be sensible. Remember his anger at the inn. Remember your own anger and contempt for what he symbolises. No, for what he *is*. Don't put any distance between him and his actions, that way weakness lies.

That way you start forgiving and explaining away and feeling things that shouldn't be allowed, like sympathy and concern and a ridiculous conviction that you know him.

But she felt it anyway, a spreading of him into her, a knowledge of him. It might be utterly false, but it was so strong she couldn't turn it into a lie until it was proved so. Conclusively. She needed him to mend so he could become himself again, between that rakish charm and resentful anger. Maybe then she could defend herself better because now she had no defence against these feelings except fear.

She eased her hand away, resisting the temptation to touch his face, and stood up. His arm swept out and bumped into her skirts and caught at them feebly. She stood looking down at him for a moment and sat down again, untangling his hand from the muslin skirt with its embroidered flowers and tucking it between hers again. The fire was strong enough for the moment. She would tend to it in a little while.

She looked at the comfortable bed awaiting her and sighed. After two hours it was unlikely rescue would arrive before the morrow and she had best take what she needed to spend the night in the library. In between bathing his forehead with a damp cloth to calm his fevered mutterings, she had prepared herself tea on the hob over the library fireplace and brought a basket of bread and cheese from the stores Mr Prosper's housekeeper had stocked in the pantry. She rolled up another blanket and pillow, her toothbrush and tooth powder, and resigned herself to a very uncomfortable night on the floor.

Halfway down the corridor to the stairway, she stopped abruptly.

That was definitely a thud, not thunder. For a moment she remained frozen, her heart beating hard and fast, wishing she had taken one of her father's pistols with her. The second thud was followed by a faint groan and alarm raced over her skin, sharp and stinging, raising goose pimples as it went. But even as her body went into a shocked crouch, her mind moved forward. Something thudding and groaning in a house whose only other occupant was a very ill and very stubborn man most likely had nothing to do with the supernatural.

She dropped the bedclothes and ran.

He had made it halfway to the front door. Kneeling on the floor and in the gleam of her candle, he looked like a medieval supplicant before an altar. His caped greatcoat was spread around him like a cloak, his dark head bowed, his weight braced on one arm.

'You fool. What on earth are you doing?'

'Keynsham,' he muttered, clearly trying to get back on his feet, but he stopped when she placed her hand on his forehead. He was burning.

'Keynsham? Really? In a storm and on foot?' she asked, fear pouring acid into her voice. 'You want to be stubborn? Then stand up. Now.'

He finally turned to her, his eyes near black, his pupils dilated.

'You…'

His voice was slurred and she couldn't tell if there was annoyance or distaste there.

'Yes, me. You want Hollywell House from me, right?'

His eyelids flickered closed and she pinched his arm and he nodded.

'You…'

'Well, if you want it, I want you to stand up. If you don't, I will crack a candlestick on your stubborn head and drag you back to the library by your heels.'

'Vixen.'

That was clearer. She turned so that she could slide her arm around his back and brace his weight against her shoulder.

'Up with you.'

She managed to get him on his legs but would have fallen if she hadn't braced her own arm against the wall.

'Sorry…' he mumbled. 'Ill…'

Her heart was thudding so hard she thought it might break something inside her. She felt the kind of fear she had once felt when a green water boa had slithered out of the swampy bushes in Brazil less than a yard away from her, enormous, shiny, heading towards her with an intentness in its tiny glinting eyes that still came back to her in dreams almost twenty years later. It was elemental, demanding action. She had never felt this scared about the possibility of someone dying.

She managed to straighten and also push back at her fear. He was just feverish. He wasn't dying. There was no need to become all foolish and soft.

They entered the library, his long lean body hard against her side, the folds of his coat tangling in her legs and nearly tripping her. He sank down on to the sofa, breathing heavily, and she sat down with him for a moment, afraid to let him go. She could feel the tremors rise through his body, like tiny earthquakes, and she could feel him try to stop them, his muscles locking down. Even this he was fighting, she thought in frustration.

'Lie down,' she whispered, and a tremor shook him so hard she locked her arms around him again, afraid he might fall forward. But then it passed and she managed to ease him down.

He sank back into a shaky stupor, occasionally muttering something about someone named Rickie, and sometimes his eyes would flicker open with that same unfocused, haunted look. She began wondering if the clock on the mantelpiece was even working, it moved so slowly, but it was already close on ten o'clock at night, so it must have moved quite a great deal since her arrival. She was fully awake and achy in a way that had nothing to do with illness, and the superstitious fear was back—she had to remain on alert or something terrible would happen.

Was this what Catherine felt sitting by Nicky's sickbed at night, afraid to sleep?

The comparison was ridiculous; this was not her child, not a child at all, but a very large and very aggravating man. Perhaps it was that he was no one's child and someone *should* be sitting here worrying. If he had been her child, would it have been like this? No, she admitted. It would be different. She would not still be scalded all down her side where his body had pressed the length of hers. She would not have to keep her hands curled so as not to be tempted to touch. Her fingers ached with the need to trace the tense grooves by his mouth, to ease the frown forming two sharp lines between his black-winged brows and to test the silkiness of his black hair. And definitely not to press her lips to his. They looked hot, too; tense, just a little parted.

She surrendered to the urge to touch, her fingers seeking the vulnerable hollow by his temple, where the skin was soft, as velvety as the inside of a hibiscus leaf, following it to where it thinned over the ridge of bone. She loved his cheekbones, they were everything that was right and wrong with him. Sharp cut, uncompromising until they gave way to this softness which was always a little in the shadow. Then there were the lines on either side of his mouth, two gauges of his mood. Even when he wasn't smiling, there was usually still a little curve in them, a curiosity or lingering warmth. But she had seen them as straight as a hanging blade when he had been angry at her.

She smoothed her fingers over one—it wasn't like that now; it was shifting, restless. Perhaps he was dreaming. She rested her fingers lightly on his mouth. His breath was the shallow swift breath of a fever, a tangible effort that fanned over her fingertips. She sank into that simple sensation—her skin on his, his breath alternately warming and cooling the spaces between her fingers. She wasn't brave enough to do it, but she imagined this against her own mouth, that hot firm surface moving against her lips like they had in the inn. That kiss had been a curse, a snatching of her soul and will—right now she could not imagine anyone kissing her again but him. Her lips were half-burned with the need to recapture that embrace; they felt thicker, stinging a little as if she, too, was fevered and dry.

He isn't even doing anything, you foolish girl. He is ill and you are not only doing something improper, it is unfair to him. You wouldn't want someone to kiss you while you slept, no matter what the silly fairy tales said about redemptive powers.

I wouldn't mind if it was him, she replied. I would only mind if I didn't wake.

Well, he isn't you and he most likely would mind.

She removed her fingers, curling them in.

'I'm sorry,' she murmured, and he opened his eyes, a sharp silvery grey, his pupils constricted, faraway. She kept still, waiting for him to close his eyes again as he had each time these brief moments of waking had occurred so far, but he just watched her, his pupils dilating.

'What for?' His voice was hardly more than a rasp of cloth on cloth, but he sounded fully rational, even curious.

She gave a little laugh. Trust him to become rational at the worst possible moment and ask the worst possible question. At least she had resisted the urge to kiss him. That might have been difficult to explain.

'Go back to sleep.'

'Why? Where am I?'

His eyes swept the room but returned to hers, now with another level of realisation.

'Hollywell. I forgot. Hell.'

Each word was dragged upwards, but fading. Another of the tremors that had scared her shook him.

'Everything hurts… Hate this.'

She so desperately wanted to reassure him, promise him he was going to be well, but he wouldn't believe her and she was afraid the words themselves would have a runic force, twisting fate to prove her wrong. She dipped the cloth in the bowl of water and wrung it.

'Close your eyes.'

That was a mistake. He had been fading, but her words changed the rhythm of his breathing, the struggle showing as clear as storm clouds in his eyes.

'No. That's how… No. Where's Cat?' His words were slurred, but the intensity was unmistakable.

'Catherine isn't ill. She is with Nicky, who has recovered enough to start making demands of everyone and everything. It's the truth, I prom… It's the truth, Alan. Now close your eyes and we shall see if we can lower your fever so you can return to running away.'

'Vixen.' But he closed his eyes and she focused on touching his face only with the damp cloth.

'Ferret, vixen… What next? Mole? Field mouse? Slug?'

The lines on the side of his mouth curved a little, then flattened.

'Sorry.'

'Don't apologise. I told you, I like your choices of fauna. Vixens and ferrets are very resourceful; they must depend on their wits rather than brute strength. Of course, you would say I need depend on neither because I am an heiress.'

Again his smile flickered, but then he was gone and she was alone with herself again.

Chapter Eight

It was white, bright and yellow at the edges, very white at the centre. He closed his eyes again and turned away, but he was so stiff his head hardly moved. Not just his head was stuck, nothing seemed to move. Was he tied down? Yes, here it was, something pressing his head into the earth. God, they were burying him! No, it was softer, just a light touch, but very hot, or perhaps that was him because he felt hot all over and in pain. Now he could feel that all over, too.

Oh, hell, he remembered.

I'm ill. I hate this.

He turned back to find that touch and there it was, soft, light, cool, just skimming his forehead and down to his cheek. He could feel his stubble catch at the caress and wished she would continue to his mouth so he could taste her. Perhaps this was still part of the jumble of dreams hovering around the edges of his mind, billowy white clouds on the horizon.

Then the hand was gone.

'Can you hear me? You should try to drink something. Do you think you could try?'

'I'm never ill.' Was that his voice? Pathetic.

'So you already told me. Twice. Well, now you are.'

'Shouldn't be here. You'll be ill.' He sounded drunk, even to himself.

'If I am going to be ill, I will be ill and finally someone will nurse *me*. Now stop arguing about everything. This is becoming very repetitive. You are ill, you aren't going to Keynsham and you have no choice about who is going to nurse you because there is no one else here.'

He forced his eyes open at that.

'Hollywell. I saw the light in the library.'

She put down the cloth she had been bathing his face with.

'I thought you were the ghost thumping around when you came in.'

He watched the corner of her smile until his eyes grew heavy again.

'You should've run. Ghosts… Dangerous…'

She laughed at that, a warm sound that pressed back at the core of pain. Even in the murk of thudding misery, some part of him was carving out spaces of awareness. One was engaged in following the movements of the cloth and her fingers over his burning face. Another was an echo chamber for her sounds—her voice, moving between brusque and soothing, the rustle and shift of her clothes. Each space expanded and took centre stage in turn, like moving from stall to stall at a village fair. Now it was her laugh, an infectious tumble of sound, at his reply.

'Too true. Now it's time to be quiet. You must sleep…'

'No!'

Not sleep. He forced his eyes open even though the

light burned, adding to the ache that was weighing him down.

She wasn't smiling now, the auburn brows were tugged together, separated by only two deep furrows, and the honeyed eyes were worried.

'You *must* sleep. The more you fight, the weaker you make yourself. This isn't a case for brute force.' Her voice had changed, lowered, or he was fading again. He didn't want to go yet. He might not come back from the darkness this time.

'Lily… Don't go.' He hadn't meant to say that, perhaps he hadn't.

He couldn't keep his eyes open, they burned so much. Everything was burning, pounding, like the siege in Ciudad Rodrigo, where they had been sent in to help hold off the French until the English and Portuguese could complete the Torres Vedras forts. They should have been just the advance force for Craufurd and the Light Brigade, but they and the Spanish had waited in vain, week after week of French cannonballs slamming against ancient rock, each strike jarring them to their teeth, covering them with dust and raising the stench of rotting bodies from the earth.

In the end the Spanish Commander, Herrasti, had warned them he was going to surrender, giving them a night to make their escape through French lines. His men had been exhausted, drained of will. They had begged to be left to sleep and he had shouted at them, 'If you sleep, you'll wake up in a French prison or not wake up at all…'

Her hand was leagues cooler than his, closing around his aching fingers. He had no skin, no muscle left, just bones, knuckles hard and white pressed together in her hand, as smooth as satin, sliding over his.

'Not tonight.' Her voice had dipped low, into the water. 'No dying tonight. The grim reaper will have to grapple with me and I don't fancy his odds at the moment. So sleep.'

He didn't trust her, but there was nothing he could do. Her voice was sinking him lower and lower, disintegrating him. All he had left was the slide of her thumb over the back of his hand and then that was gone as well. With his last breath, he clung to the lifeline.

'Lily, stay…'

He must have slept, because this time when he woke again, he was thirsty.

He knew that feeling too well from the war. It wasn't like hunger. Hunger was easy; you felt it in your gut. Thirst often started nameless, a need that shifted around the body, searching for something to lean on, aggravating the nerves as it went. He groped after it and an image rose—as sharp as if he was there—Rickie was seated on a small rug by the kitchen hearth, the warmest place in their house in Edinburgh, with one of the neighbours' kittens a ball of fur in his small lap. That much might have been a real memory, but in this image seated on the floor by his side and leaning against the rough stone wall with a book in her lap was Lily.

He must be ill, the vision had all the power of a hallucination, subverting reality and memory. It wasn't even based on a real memory. Neither of his parents had read books to them and had certainly been too proper to sit by the kitchen hearth, and though he and

Cat had read a great deal, it had been a solitary occupation. Perhaps he had read to Rickie, but he couldn't remember. He remembered them playing with a ball he fashioned from strips of rags stuffed into a sock Cat knitted. Cards. He had learned some tricks in the market near his school and Rickie loved watching him practise, his frail little hands trying and failing to mimic his movements.

He pressed his palm against the ache in his forehead, dragging his thoughts to the surface—he wasn't in Edinburgh. He couldn't be. So where the hell was he?

His body reviewed its position and reported. This bed was even more uncomfortable than his bed at the Ship. Not a bed, a sofa? The wooden scrolling was digging into his shoulder and the side of his leg, and it was much too short. And there was something on his chest. No, someone.

That and the thirst finally brought him to the surface and he forced open his eyes.

Her hair had tumbled from its pins and lay over her shoulder, a cinnamon brown in the gloomy room. She was seated on the floor, her head leaning against his chest, and he couldn't see much of her face, just the curve of her cheek, the auburn upward brush of her eyebrow and those long gold-tipped eyelashes spearing her faint freckles. His brief spasm of concern faded and he didn't move. She was merely asleep. Whether this was real or merely a fever-induced hallucination, it was surprisingly pleasant and he didn't want to disturb it.

What the hell was he doing in Albert's library with Lily Wallace, sleeping?

Then his memory reasserted itself. The light in the window. Lily. His head. Oh, hell.

He looked carefully towards the window. The storm was still raging, but it wasn't dark, which meant he could not have been unconscious for too long. He had to leave before anyone found them like this.

If he could only find a way to make his body do what he wanted.

He struggled to pull himself into a sitting position while trying not to wake Lily. It wasn't her weight on his chest that defeated him, but his muscles which were transformed into aching stalks of damp straw. How the hell was sitting so difficult? He had been sitting since he was a baby. One didn't forget how to do it, did they?

He only succeeded in shifting Lily and she woke into an alertness worthy of his best soldiers.

'You're awake. Ow!' She rose on to her knees, then squeaked and fell back on to her behind.

Fear drove him into a half-sitting position after all.

'What is wrong? Are you hurt?'

It was humiliating. His voice was weaker than his muscles.

'My legs are all pins and needles,' she replied, rubbing at her thigh. The cheek that had rested against him was red and marked from the folds of his coat and even in his pathetic state he almost acted on the urge to press his mouth to those marks and coax her skin smooth again. He closed his eyes. Not appropriate thoughts under any circumstances; right now they were as near disastrous as possible. He had to rise, get on his horse and continue to the Hall. She must return there as soon as possible. Had he been hallucinating or did she actually say she was there alone? He must have been. She could not be that mad.

Whatever the case, he had to leave. If she really was

there alone, he would ride to the Hall and have Catherine send the carriage for her right away. There was no other choice. If only he could stay on his horse long enough to make it there. That was debatable. Right now the act of standing up felt beyond him.

Mostly he was thirsty.

'I need to reach the Hall. Have them send a carriage for you. It will be dark soon.'

She had made it to her knees, but at that she stopped.

'Not for a while. It is not yet one o'clock.'

'One...' He frowned, glancing at the windows again. It looked like they were underwater and sounded like they were surrounded by drums, but it was grey, not black. 'It can't be one o'clock at night. It is still light. The clock must be wrong.'

She stood, testing her weight on one leg and wincing.

'One in the afternoon. You slept for quite a while. When you weren't trying to escape. You still sound terrible and you must drink something. I will fetch some water for a new kettle of tea. Please don't wander off, you will only fall down again and my back is aching with dragging you back here.'

Alan didn't respond. Perhaps he still was feverish, because none of what she said made sense other than the point about tea. He let his eyes drift shut. Perhaps next time he opened them the world would be cognisable.

'Here.'

He must have slept again, because she could not have brewed tea so swiftly. The smell was unmistakable and wonderful and his mouth tried to water and failed. When he succeeded in sitting up enough to take the cup, the first sip of the hot, sweet liquid was like a benediction. It filled him, shaped him from the inside, and for a moment it drained away the pain and confusion.

They didn't speak as they drank and she kept her own gaze on her cup. Her cheek had regained its customary soft lustre with its faint dusting of freckles and he wished she still bore the signs which had been proof she had been that close. She had also collected her hair into a knot low on her nape and other than her crumpled skirts she looked cool and collected once more. Which made no sense if what she had just said was true. None of this made sense. It could not possibly be that he was alone with Lily Wallace at Hollywell almost a full day after spotting the light in the window, could it?

'More tea?' she asked politely as she placed her cup on a small table she had drawn up by the sofa.

'Not yet. First… What on earth are you doing here?'

'Running away.'

'Running… Why? From whom?'

'Just for a few days. I needed to think. I didn't expect guests.' Her mouth rose at the corners, but she still didn't meet his eyes and he realised she was nervous. As well she should be. Bloody hell, they were in trouble.

'I am trying to understand. Where does Lady Jezebel think you are?'

'In Bath. She thinks I departed for a few days with Jackson and my maid to visit a friend who lives in Bath.'

'Your maid and groom are here as well?'

'No. I left them waiting for the London coach on

their way to visit their families. Then I directed the post-chaise to take me here.'

'But…why?'

'I told you. I needed to be alone. Utterly alone. Someplace of my own so I could think. I asked Mr Prosper to stock Hollywell for guests a couple days ago so that I would have everything I needed.'

She finally looked up, her eyes dark and pleading.

'This might be the last time I will have to really be alone, before… I thought I would be able to think things through in peace here. It's so quiet.'

'You're mad. You can't just… It just isn't done, Lily!'

She shrugged. 'You sound like your grandmother. Of course it isn't done and yet I have done it. Here I am. I never expected anyone to come by, certainly not in this weather. Last I looked this morning the drive looks like a tributary of the Amazon.'

He pushed himself further upright. 'My horse. I must…'

'He ran away,' she said hurriedly, raising her hands as if to press him back, but he pushed into a sitting position and leaned his head in his hands, trying to think.

He had been alone with her at Hollywell for a full day. The fact that no one knew this yet made no difference. Her rashness and his fever had just sealed their fate.

'You have to return to the Hall. Now.'

'No, I cannot. Everyone thinks I went to Bath. What on earth would I say if I suddenly appeared the following day, as muddy and wet as a bog monster and without my luggage? As soon as the rain stops and you are well enough to leave, you can walk to Keynsham. I will stay here until the post-chaise I hired returns for me in two days' time. You see, I have thought it all through.'

He didn't raise his head. He hadn't felt so bruised since the forced march out of Portugal under Moore. She wasn't mad, yet she was if she thought it was that simple.

'You aren't well enough to walk to Keynsham yet,' she continued, infuriatingly matter of fact. 'But you cannot spend another night here on the sofa. Do you think you can manage the stairs? The bedrooms have been aired.'

The bedrooms have been aired.

Lily. You're mad.

He didn't say it. Partially because he knew that under her cheerful bravado she must be as aware as he of the consequences awaiting them and partially because he couldn't help the anticipation that was building as his mind and body absorbed this new reality.

He was about to break another vow. It was becoming a habit.

Compromised by an heiress.

Marriage.

Hunter and Stanton would split with laughter.

'Very well. Upstairs.'

It wasn't as bad as he anticipated. Halfway up the stairs his legs began to remember their function and he could have made do with leaning on the banister, but he kept his arm around her for the pure pleasure of it. This indulgence almost cost him his balance halfway down the corridor when Lily suddenly shuddered and leapt to one side.

'Lily! What's wrong?' He managed to stop from

keeling over by propping himself against the wall and he pulled her against him in one movement.

'I stepped on something. It was soft and… Oh, no, it's a mouse. I killed it.'

He found what she was staring at in the faint light of the tapers she had lit along the corridor to light their way. A tiny grey bundle in the centre of the carpet. His head was pounding and his body felt it was a hundred years old, but he couldn't help it, he started laughing, then winced as she jabbed him with her elbow.

'Oh, you heartless brute. It isn't funny!'

'I'm not… I'm not laughing at that. I don't know why I'm laughing. But you can relax that conscience, sweetheart. It wasn't a vixen that did your grey friend in, but a cat. Those are claw marks.'

He felt her shudder again as she looked and then glanced away and he pulled her more firmly against him. What a strange little thing she was. To brave being alone in a haunted house and caring for a felled rake, but then to come apart at the seams over a mangled rodent.

'I forgot all about it, but Albert had a cat, a very unfriendly ginger tabby who was always disappearing behind furniture and making a general nuisance of himself. I thought someone would have taken it, but perhaps not. It might explain your broken urn if he's been chasing mice around an empty house. Come, let's leave the little fellow for now. There's nothing you can do for him.'

'I hate leaving him there.'

'I'll toss him out the window, then.'

'No…leave him. The tabby is probably hungry. I'll try not to think about it.'

He kept a firm hold on his smile until she had deposited him on the side of the bed with all the concentration of a three-year-old carrying a full glass of water.

'You should lie down.'

So should you, right here with me.

He didn't say the words, but as they surfaced in his mind he vaguely remembered asking her not to leave when the fever had been high, clinging to her hand like a child. She must think him pathetic. Even if she did lie down with him, he was in no shape yet to do anything about it. Yet.

In the light of the single candle she looked younger, unusually awkward as she stood watching him. Was she waiting for him to fall over again? What a blow to his vanity. Here he was worried about the consequences of compromising her when she probably thought him an object of pity. But whatever either of them thought, they would likely only leave this house categorically betrothed. Did she realise that? For someone so sophisticated she could be incredibly naïve. If he said anything, she would likely run away again, storm notwithstanding.

Would it be so terrible to marry her?

It might be. He remembered most of the things she had said to him and this particular comment lingered. She had been clear about what she wanted from life— a home. Children.

It was his turn to shudder and he finally gave in and lay down, closing his eyes. The darkness was filling him again, but of a different kind. Right now he would welcome unconsciousness, anything but the great yawning pit of that winter almost two decades ago. Not even the snow had held off the stench of the bodies. He had smelled death so often during the war, rank and tangy in the Spanish sun, laced with the sting of lye. But that was nothing next to the memory of the subterranean, putrid scent of the snow-dusted bodies outside their home that winter as he tried to stave off death inside. He had failed, they had died and that was that. He wouldn't willingly go there again. He had made a promise to himself.

Except that now he might have no choice. He played by the rules, and though he had never meant to break them, they were as shattered as Albert's ugly old urn.

He would marry her.

Her scent, roses and something else, told him she was closer. Then he felt the weight of a blanket on him. He wanted to pull her to him. If his fate was sealed, he might as well enjoy it, but he kept his eyes shut. She would probably box his ears and they were already ringing. Perhaps it was best not to put fantasy to the test in his present state.

'Would you like me to read to you?'

That was neutral. He opened his eyes.

'Mysteries of Udolpho?'

'Goodness, no. There are the books in the library downstairs and I brought a few with me as well. I shall fetch some. It might help you sleep.'

She nodded briskly and left the room before he could stop her. He closed his eyes again and his body seemed to sink deeper into the bed like a hot air balloon emptying of air. He had truly forgotten how miserable it was to be ill, if he had ever known. He should try to remember this feeling so he could have a little more patience when next he came across someone in this state. He didn't know if it was better or worse having someone like her as a nurse.

Someone like her. He couldn't imagine anyone quite like her. She was like one of those strange beasts occasionally paraded at Astley's or some village freak. He never knew what she would do next.

He knew what he would like her to do next and it didn't involve books, but now that he was coherent again it was unlikely she would touch him. At least until, or if, she married him. He didn't remember much of the fever, but the physical imprint of her body on his lingered. The soft pressure of her lush breasts against him as she had helped him on to the sofa…

He turned on his side, his body thudding with heat that had nothing to do with fever. He didn't know whether to hope she returned or not, but then the door opened and she came in with a hesitant smile.

'I've brought a choice.'

'As long as there are none of my grandfather's sermons among them,' he managed, levering himself back into a sitting position, too weak to look away from the line of her thigh as she pulled over the chair by the dresser and sat. His hands prickled with the need to feel that line. All he had to do was extend his arm. First above the dress and then, slowly, below.

He watched the uptilt of her chin, the line of light and shadow down her throat and down further towards her fashionable bodice. She had changed out of her rumpled gown of the previous day and even without her maid she looked cool and elegant. At least in that respect she was like her namesake, though the colouring was far too fiery. But then, Lily could be short for Lilith. It suited her, that ambiguous female who sought life and knowledge with her arms open and was condemned for her audacity. This Lily probably would have an opinion about her, too. He could well imagine it. He would save that conversation for later.

'You choose,' he said lazily. The crease between her brows deepened as she looked down at the three books, then she gave a little laugh and opened one of them, tucking her feet under her on the chair as she had on Nicky's bed, the unconscious intimacy another slap to his restraint.

'Here—*Nightmare Abbey.*'

'That sounds worse than *Udolpho.*'

'It's by Thomas Love Peacock and it's *meant* to sound worse. He makes fun of all those novels, not to mention quite a bit of fun of Shelley and of Goethe's *Werther* and of transcendental philosophy. I thought of him because Mr Glowry's butler is named Raven and the only ghost is a somnambulist steward named Crow.'

'Too much fowl.'

'Bear with me, I will read just enough to put you to sleep. *"Nightmare Abbey, a venerable family mansion in a highly picturesque state of semi-dilapidation..."'*

Alan leaned back against the headboard and closed his eyes, more to block out the sight of her than out of any weariness. It didn't do much good because her voice was just as seductive.

'*"Mr Glowry used to say that his house was no better than a spacious kennel, for everyone in it led the life of a dog..."* I wonder if he would have found Ravenscar Hall an improvement on his Abbey? Sorry, where was I...? Ah. *"...disappointed in love and friendship..."'* she continued.

Her reading certainly missed the mark, if the mark

was to put him to sleep. The only salvation came from the fact that the tale was actually amusing—especially when she acted out the voices of the Glowrys and the other characters.

When it came to a discussion comparing women to musical dolls and lottery draws, he opened his eyes to watch her face.

"'It is only after marriage that they show their true qualities. Marriage is, therefore, a lottery, and the less choice and selection a man bestows upon his ticket the better...'" She grinned and lowered the book for a moment. 'I thought you might appreciate how closely your ideas match with Mr Glowry's.'

He covered his eyes again against her elfin smile.

'You wrong me. Keep reading. But could you skim over that fool Scythorp's impassioned proclamations? If I were there, I would probably push him out of his tower rather than listen to another anguished diatribe.'

'I told you—you aren't in the least romantic. Now, stop interrupting. This is supposed to put you to sleep.'

He almost pointed out that not even the driest legal document, if read in her husky, humorous voice, was likely to put him to sleep.

He was still far too wide awake when she closed the book.

'That is enough for now. Did you like it thus far?'

'Better than I would one of Nicky's. I never understood why those novels are so successful.'

She touched the edge of the book with its worn spine and corners.

'Because they are about loneliness, our greatest fear.'

'I thought death was our greatest fear.'

'I think loneliness is worse.'

Loneliness. At least that was a topic he understood. It wasn't a word he would associate with someone as outwardly confident as she appeared, but then he didn't know her, not really. There was a whole history in those five words and they just made what had to happen all the worse. There was no possible way he could provide her with what she needed in life.

Even knowing the disaster that was looming, it was hard to regret this twist in his fate—he had never thought he would be weak enough to allow physical passion to overcome caution, but there was no point in denying the physical pull she had on him was trumping all good sense. Even as weak as he still was, he was so tempted to touch her; he was even envious of the book warming itself in her lap. He looked away, groping for an anchor.

'Cat mentioned you lived on an island in Brazil before you lived in Jamaica. Were you lonely there?'

She shrugged.

'I was, a little. I missed my father because he remained on the mainland, at the mines. I don't think my mother was lonely. Once, she told me she and my father were far happier together since she had come to the island. Every year she went with my father to Kingston, but she was always so happy to return. I thought it was because she didn't like seeing or hearing about his mistresses, but I think she felt safe on the island and she loved the excitement of waiting for him, running down to the docks when they came to tell us his ship was entering the bay. I had this little house...well, a crate on the mango tree in our garden, and I could see down the path towards the port and I would watch her run. She was like a little girl. Towards the end I hated watching her when he came.'

'Didn't you run when his ship arrived?'

'No. I could never compete with her enthusiasm, so I never tried.'

'You are too smart for your own good, Lily Wallace.'

'So we are back to the crafty vixen.' She shifted, pressing the book between her palms, her mouth flattening into a tense line.

'I didn't mean it like that. I meant that being lonely and being intelligent is a brutal combination. Hell, don't cry, I didn't mean…'

She rubbed her eyes.

'I'm not crying, I am merely tired. You made me think of them.'

'I'm sorry.'

'Don't be, I wasn't unhappy. I did have friends even if they weren't my age and then there was Rupert.'

'Rupert?'

The tension faded as she smiled at the memory. That was a new expression, too. Wistful, the faint echo of a child's joyous smile.

'I might not have run when my father's ship arrived, but I did run down to the bay when I saw Rupert from the mango tree. We would swim together and I would imagine we were an enchanted prince and princess banished to the islands, and when the spell would be lifted, we would be swept back to our kingdom and live happily ever after. There, now you may laugh at me.'

Her eyes focused again, challenging him, but the image lingered. He could see her as a little girl, tumbled red-brown hair and more freckles than she had now. The light filling her the moment she saw her friend.

He wasn't in the least amused, but he did his best to push back at the irrational jab of jealousy. She had been a child, so what if she had run to greet some boy. It was ancient history and none of his concern.

'Well, I hate to drag you out of your fairy tale, but I'm afraid no one is going to lift this particular spell. It is time we put it on the table, isn't it?'

'Put…' The last of the light faded and the society miss was back, cool and calm.

'There is no getting around it, Lily.'

She shook her head. 'No one knows you are here…'

'I *am* here. Alone with you. I won't even start on the sheer and utter madness of what you did…coming here in the first place to an empty house, on your own, lying to everyone…' He shoved off the bed, ignoring the resistance in his muscles. 'You aren't ten years old, Lily. If you throw a tantrum, because that is all this was, then you risk the consequences. You are luckier than you deserve that it was I who came by and not whoever had vandalised the library. My God, do you realise what a risk you took? For what? Just to be alone? Is your clever little mind even capable of encompassing what might have happened to you? Hell, what *has* happened to you and not just to you. You don't live on an island any longer, Lily, and you can't buy your way out of trouble. When I walk out of here tomorrow, if I don't get struck by lightning, which at the moment is not an option to be despised, we will have spent two days alone together and whether I was at death's door for that time or indulging in an orgy makes no odds. I may be a rake, as you delight in pointing out, but I play by the rules. We are now betrothed. It is as simple as that.'

Simple.

Lily stood as well, her cheeks pinched with cold. He had lulled her for a moment with that humourous charm and, worse, that compassion which appeared so real. It might even have been real, but so was this. She had seen him angry before, but not as coldly implacable as an envoy from Hades. He would not negotiate; he would take.

She could not even hide behind the defences of her own mind. What *had* she been thinking? What madness had taken her? She had planned it, sending Greene and Jackson away and hiring the post-chaise and spreading lies, but it wasn't very different from those blind urges that had sent her running from the new house in Kingston ten years ago. A childish denial of her fate. Even then she had known it was futile. She had never been surprised her father found her or that someone delivered her home. She had expected to fail. This time was no different. She had known all along that at the end of her three days of rebellion the post-chaise would bring her back to the Hall, in time for Philip Marston's return, her engagement, marriage, life. Perhaps her fascination with Alan was no more than another rebellion against that fate.

Except that she was now betrothed to him. To Lord Ravenscar, rakehell.

She had never planned this. She should not want this. She should resist it with every fibre of her being. Because unlike Philip he was dangerous to her. It wasn't merely that he would never be faithful to her, she had no reason to believe that Philip would be, but with Philip she could accept it as long as she had what she wanted—a modicum of independence and a home that was hers. Children. A family. If she married Alan, she would want more. He had given her a taste of something she hadn't known mattered—passion, honesty. He might be a rake, but he was one of the most honest men she had met and it released something in her, like the moment Greene released the laces of her stays.

She looked at the chiselled, uncompromising face. He would face his fate just as he would have faced a firing squad in time of war. Angry, but accepting. She must face hers—she was about to become her mother. In love with an unrepentant rake.

Or she could save them both—she could marry Philip. She would have to tell him everything, of course, and let him choose. But first *she* would have to choose.

She closed her eyes briefly.

'You should rest. We will discuss this tomorrow.'

He caught her hand.

'It is best to accept the inevitable, Lily. Dreaming about some boy you loved years ago is all well and good between the pages of a novel, but this is our reality now.'

The absurdity of that idea raised her for a moment above the swell of misery that had been roiling in her.

'He's not a boy. Rupert is a manatee.'

'A…what?'

'A manatee. Sometimes they are called sea cows. They are very big and fat and grey and quite friendly. There were several manatees that lived in the mangrove bay on the island and I used to swim with them as a child.'

'A manatee.'

'They are very gentle and they like being fed. I told you, I didn't have many friends on the island, so I named them and made believe they were really enchanted princes and princesses who had been turned into manatees and one day their parents would come and find them and remove the spell, but meanwhile they were my friends. Rupert in particular.'

He let out his breath.

'I still have a hard time realising how lonely you must have been.'

Not as lonely as I feel right now and that's your fault.

'Children often create imaginary friends.'

'Would it cost you so much to admit that you were lonely?'

'Didn't you yourself say something to your grandmother about practising what you preach?'

His smile was wry as he released her hand to trace the line of her jaw with his fingers, from ear to chin, lingering there, coaxing her face towards him. It wasn't fair of him, touching her like that. So soft it made her ache for more.

'Life with you is unlikely to be boring, Lily Wallace.'

She finally managed to stand and move to the door.

'Your compliments leave a great deal to be desired, Lord Ravenscar.'

He stood up.

'I always preferred actions to words. Shall I show you precisely how flattering I can be? Or would you prefer to leave before I am tempted to show you a very effective antidote to loneliness?'

She searched desperately for some clever retort that would prove how unaffected she was, but when he took a step towards her, she hurried out and closed the door.

Chapter Nine

At least this time she wasn't asleep when the noises began.

She should have been after the events of the past day, but she remained frustratingly awake, thoughts and images darting around her mind like a school of colourful fish in the bay.

She had remained resolutely in her room after their confrontation, almost expecting him to barge in and continue their confrontation, or worse…hoping he would. But nothing interrupted her futile attempts to read and resolutely reread the same pages of her book but the flashes of lightning and barking crashes of thunder. Perhaps the tropical storms of the Caribbean had followed her to England except that she was cold despite the fire, inside and out.

The sound was so soft at first, a faint scratching and clicking. It might have been a branch tapping at her window, the wind outside was high enough, whooping and hissing, except that there were no trees near any of Hollywell's windows and the sounds hadn't come from outside.

Could it be the tabby cat, come to collect its kill? Grateful for an excuse to act, she slipped out of bed and picked up the candlestick when the sound came again. A scratching and something else, just by her door. Breathing? She had no idea, but she knew it wasn't Alan. And not a cat either. Then it was gone and she let her breath out but didn't move, every cell focused, waiting.

Don't be ridiculous, Lily Wallace. Remember what you told Alan...if there are sounds, they have a perfectly rational, earthly cause. Either go see if there is anything there or ignore it and read your book.

Oh, blast it.

She tiptoed to the door and raised the candlestick ahead of her, trying to see into the gloom of the corridor. Perhaps it was Alan after all. Could he possibly be wandering about at night again? He was no longer ill enough to justify such stupidity, was he? Perhaps it was the cat. Now that she had been looking, she had seen the wet marks of its paws in the kitchens. No doubt somewhere there was a window or door that wasn't quite secure, but she had not yet found it.

She froze—there it was again, closer. Scratching and snuffling. She wanted to draw back, close the door, lock it. Several doors down she saw a line of faint golden light under Alan's door. He *was* awake. Was he ill again? She had thought he was better, but hadn't Mr Curtis been well enough to go to church and then he had dropped dead? Perhaps Alan was even now lying on the floor of his room, dying... She hurried forward and her hand was already raised to knock on his door when she saw it. Just a flicker out of the corner of her eye and she turned, raising her candle.

'Oh, God.'

She dropped the candlestick and it hit the carpet with a thump. The world went black and her imagination wild. She closed her eyes against what she had seen and groped desperately in the dark for the knob. The door opened abruptly and she propelled herself inside and slammed against something hard.

'Lily. Good God, what is it?' Alan's arms went around her.

Alan. Oh, thank God, Alan. She turned to him, practically burrowing into his side, her hands fisting on the warm fabric of his shirt.

'There's something there in the corridor. I saw it. It's not human. Alan, no…' She tightened her hold on his shirt as he started towards the door, but he merely tucked her against his other side and stepped into the doorway and stopped. He started shaking against her and instinctively her arms went around him in case he was about to collapse. His arms tightened around her as well, drawing her back into the room and closing the door, his mouth brushing her hair.

'I warned you about those novels, didn't I?'

He was laughing! She tilted her head back, between horror and outrage.

'I'm serious, there is something out there. I am not delusional, Alan!'

'It's not out there any more; it's in here now. Hello, Grim, old boy. No one told me you were still alive. How on earth did you get into Hollywell? Looking for the tabby? This place is a menagerie.'

His voice was so uncharacteristically gentle, especially after the acrimony earlier that evening, that she instinctively relaxed, but a huffing breath against her leg made her tighten her hold on Alan. She looked down into liquid eyes, filmy with age, of a tall black-as-pitch dog leaning its rain-dampened head lovingly against Alan's thigh as Alan's free hand stroked him.

'Where did he come from?' she whispered, reaching out to touch the dog's ear.

'I don't know. Haven't you ever seen him around before?'

'No. How did he enter?'

'Probably the same way the tabby did. You need to have the windows and doors checked. Or perhaps he's a ghost,' Alan suggested. 'He likes that, don't stop.'

She pulled the ear gently between her fingers, sinking into the rhythm to calm her shaking.

'You know him? What did you call him?'

'Grim. He used to be my dog. I found him when he was a pup with his leg caught in a rabbit trap a year or so before I left Ravenscar, but I couldn't keep him at the Hall because my grandfather hated animals, so Jasper and Mary kept him for me. Albert didn't mention him when I saw him last month, so I presumed he had died years ago. Where have you been, boy?'

'Could he possibly have come looking for you?'

'It's possible. He always had a keen sense of smell; he knew when I was returning from school and would meet me halfway from the coach in Keynsham. Make your apologies to the lady, Grim. You scared this fearless Amazon as white as her nightdress.'

'He did not!' She began pulling away, but his arms tightened on her and only then did she realise he had been stroking her back as well as the dog. It had been so natural and right she hadn't noticed except now to miss it.

'Whiter,' he murmured. 'That muslin is a delicious shade of rich cream. Now we just need some peaches and strawberries to dip in it... That's better. You were looking a little ghostlike yourself for a moment. Did he wake you?'

She looked back down into the adoring eyes of the aged dog, escaping from the less adoring but far more unsettling eyes of his erstwhile master. But she made no effort to move away from the heat of his body.

'I couldn't sleep and then I heard something...'

'Lily, you can't charge after ghosts in the middle of the night. It's dangerous. You are too brave for your own good.'

'I'm not, I was absolutely terrified. My mind just froze.'

He pulled her against him and she pressed her cheek into the warmth of his shoulder. In a moment she would go.

'Fear is natural and healthy, Lily. It means you have something to lose. If you weren't scared, I'd be worried about you. Whenever any of my soldiers really turned their back on fear, I knew they were in trouble. Sometimes we have to put it aside, but never put it away. You should be a little more forgiving towards yourself.'

His voice flowed over her hair, warm and soothing and his hand was caressing again. Smooth and gentle, his fingers shaping and reshaping the curve of her waist and hip. Each motion sent a shiver of heat through her abdomen, gathering between her thighs and tingling over her chest.

She drew back, remembering his cold anger from before.

'That is rather in conflict with your comments earlier this evening. I thought I was being too forgiving towards myself.'

He considered her, but the coldness she had expected didn't return.

'Perhaps both. In any case, next time you hear a bump in the night, set the bells pealing, but stay in your room. Haven't any of those novels taught you anything?'

His voice was sinking, hoarse now, a warning in itself. She tried to pull herself back behind her usual defences.

'Just that fiction is more exciting than fact.'

'That won't do. That is practically an invitation to prove you wrong.'

The wicked amusement was back, a clear invitation to match his light-hearted flirt, but it had the opposite effect on her. The absence of his cold anger was such a relief she felt ten times a fool at how willing she was to lose herself at the first sign of warmth from him.

'I am sorry I bothered you. You should be resting. You may think you are recovered, but you aren't yet.'

'Ah, the scold is back. I was wondering how long before you tried to reassert your authority. I am much better, thanks to your nursing skills. I just need a bath and a shave and I shall be human again.'

She knew what he was doing. These were Wellington's tactics—lure the enemy forward with a view of an innocuous landscape, and when they crested the hill, they would find the British lying in wait and be stormed. She had read about it, she had seen Alan use the precise same tactic on her before and still she was walked straight up that hill. Willingly. She tried to stop short of the crest and retain some dignity.

'You still should be resting. It is fools like you who do the most damage to themselves. Remember that Mr Curtis thought he was well enough to go deliver a sermon.'

'Albert was sixty and had a weak heart. But if you want me in bed, you have only to ask. Or better yet, you could help me. I'm becoming quite fond of leaning on you.'

'Lord Ravenscar...'

'Grim, remind the lady that she has already called me by my given name, on very intimate occasions, and that we are to all intents and purposes betrothed. It is a little late for formality.'

She wanted so desperately to give in, to match the light-hearted acceptance of their fates.

Right now, right here, the choice was clear. She wanted Alan.

He wanted her, too. Even if it was a different kind of need, she could feel it in the heat radiating from his body, in the coaxing pressure of his fingers against her. Mostly she could see it in the depth of his gaze—an avid, dark possessiveness under the enticing smile. He might not want to be forced into matrimony any more than she, but she wasn't the only one in thrall to this desire.

Would it be so terrible? She wasn't her mother. She wouldn't sit on an island and wait for months at a stretch. She would demand much more.

His hand was stroking her back again, lingering on the edges of her hip before moving back up. Each time trailing a little lower until she was anticipating where he would pause and retreat, tingling with both pleasure and rising expectation which each foray. Then it stopped and she could feel her pulse thumping beneath his fingers.

'If I were halfway a gentleman, I would point out that you shouldn't be alone with me in a bedroom. Grim is not an adequate chaperon.'

Even this reminder of the impropriety of being here with him, standing against him as if they were lovers, was a subtle invitation. But it was still a reminder—she could not blame him for still hoping the disaster could yet be averted. He might not believe he had a choice but to offer marriage, but she could still release him from this predicament. Marriage with Philip Marston would extricate them both from their mistakes. Not elegantly, but conclusively.

The problem was that she didn't want to be reminded. If it was up to her to move away from him, she didn't know if she could.

'I was here with you this afternoon,' she pointed out, playing for time. Grim yawned and padded over to the fire and sank down beside it with another luxuriant yawn, watching them.

'I wasn't myself this afternoon.'

'You were surly, critical and annoyed at me. I think that was very much in character.'

His fingers moved again, even more gently this time, the slide of fabric on the swell of her hip was so soft it made no sense for it to send such fire through her veins, gathering in places she hardly ever noticed but now couldn't ignore.

'I was surly, critical and annoyed because I wanted to do this, but could barely stand. I'm feeling much better now. See?'

She did see. Apparently he recovered as swiftly as

he fell ill. Even the greyish tinge that had alarmed her yesterday was gone; his skin looked…warm. Tasty. Not peaches and cream, but something earthy, heady, with depth of texture and taste. Chocolate and spices and cognac. A hedonistic feast.

'I'm hungry,' she blurted out, and the laughter died out of his eyes. The heat that had been simmering in them, singeing the surface of her skin, became an instant blaze and then like his avian namesake he swooped.

She had expected the teasing to continue, he had appeared so collected, almost light-hearted, but he had misled her again. There was no teasing this time, no slow seduction. Instead he picked up right where they had left off at the inn, plunging her into the middle of a storm and taking the decision away from her.

She didn't care; this was what she wanted—his hands on her, one curving over her buttocks, pulling her against him, his other on her nape, his fingers splayed, hot and hard, against her tingling scalp. He kissed her as he had that first time in the inn, but this time without anger, just a hunger to match hers, a deep drawing on her soul. He suckled her lower lip into his mouth, tasting and feasting on it as his body moved against hers, holding her hard against his arousal, raising her thigh against his so he could fit himself better against her.

She hadn't even felt him untie her belt, but now both his hands were moving over her hips and thighs, not on her dressing gown but under it, just the near-transparent cotton of her nightgown shifting between his palms and her skin. She wanted it gone, she wanted his hands where they belonged, on her skin, touching her where it ached.

She shuddered, finally reaching up to touch him as he was touching her, sliding her arms around him, her hand deep in his hair, raising herself to meet his kiss, her fingers pressing hard into his nape, holding him there as she tasted the lips she had so guiltily caressed when he was ill. This was what she had wanted to do...and this...

'Lily!' It was a growl, deep and shaken, and then drowned as he took back control, his hands raising her nightgown, his fingers finally finding her flesh. 'Lily...'

She clung to him as his hands mapped the soft skin of her thighs; each rise and fall was a wave crashing over her, pummelling her from inside, grinding her into a fine dust of sensations. Now her world wasn't expanding any longer, it was imploding, reducing itself to nothing more than the object of his touch and the raging, devouring heat at her centre.

'Alan.' She wrapped her arms around his neck, raising herself to bring her mouth to his, her fingers anchoring in his hair. It was silkier even than it looked, liquid between her fingers, but the muscles of his neck were as hard as rock with tension.

When the resistance broke, it was complete. He dragged her against him, his mouth closing on hers with a feral growl, his hand on her backside pressing her hard against his thighs. She had never felt a man's arousal before, but she instinctively knew what it was, her body awakening further, pressing back, urgent with the need to rise against him, do something to answer the sensitive pulsing at her core.

This is it, she thought. This was what she had been waiting for. This desire was even more potent than her terror had been. This was a doorway to a different kind of fear of destruction. Under the fire he was setting loose, something in her was shifting, opening to a new reality. With just his hands and touch and taste, with the movement of his long lean body against hers, he was showing how constrained she had been until that moment, how much more there was to the world, to him. To herself.

'Show me, Alan...'

Every time she said his name Alan lost his footing. He had resisted every urge to go to her room, apologise for his accusations, because he had been afraid of precisely this happening. He should be thinking of every possible way to avert disaster, but instead he was clinging to a cliff face and desperate to let go, slip into her heat, into the passion that blazed beneath her surface, waiting to be set free. He wanted to be the one to set it free, to strip away her defences, her clothes, everything that kept her from him. To lay her bare to the soul and the skies.

His.

This conviction might be madness, it might pass and fade, but right now it filled the universe.

His.

'Lily.'

He said her name against the kiss-swollen softness of her lips, the authors of the smile that taunted his days and his dreams. He tasted them, slowly, drawing them between his teeth, teasing them with his tongue as her fingers tightened in his hair, her breathing ragged against his, gathering into breathy, devastating moans.

If she could melt like this from a kiss, what would

she be like when he touched her? When he slid his fingers along the damp he knew was already gathering, preparing her for him. When he licked his way down her beautiful body, worshipped the breasts that still haunted him ever since they had pressed against him at the inn, high and firm.

God, he wanted to see her, touch her, feast on her. He wanted to watch her explore his body, her own body, touch herself, teach him everything she loved so he could take her to heaven. If she let him, he would show her what she was capable of…set free; she would love like a goddess, like the elements, wild and untamed. She would consume him.

'Lily…you're killing me,' he growled, but she just moaned his name again, moving against him restlessly, sending a cascading shudder through his body, pooling in his groin with an aching agony that was so powerful he froze, frightened at the foreign intensity of his need. How could she always take him so far so fast?

He captured her face in his hands, staring down into her eyes. Her pupils were pinpricks encased in golden pools, molten and full of need. If he chose, he could take her now. They had to wed anyway. What difference did it make if he took her now or waited until the formal vows sealed their fates? At least that would put a categorical seal on this fiasco. He would press her down on the bed and seduce her until she begged him for release, and when he had given her a taste of pleasure, he would sink into her, lose himself in her…

Risk leaving her with child.

He dragged his hands away from her. Never, never in his life had he risked that. He must still be ill to even have considered…

'Enough. Lily. We must stop.'

Her hands still reached out to him, her mouth shaped the last word, her eyelids sank and rose, very slowly.

He gritted his teeth and took another step back.

'Go to your room. We will talk tomorrow.'

'Talk…'

'Tomorrow. Right now you need to leave. Now.'

He saw the vixen surface with a mix of regret and relief. Her eyes hardened from honey to agate, her mouth flattened with tension and rejection. Then even those emotions were swept away under the socialite's façade, only the burn of colour on her cheeks proving this had been deadly serious. He wanted to soothe her, ease her out of it, but he was dangling from the finest thread and the charm that served him so well with other women was beyond him.

He didn't want to charm her, he wanted to possess her.

He nearly weakened, his hands rising of their own accord, when her chin went up and she shrugged. Her lips parted, but whatever response she had been contemplating foundered and she merely shrugged again and left, not bothering to close the door.

Grim whined and came to lean against him as he sat down on the bed. The fire was fading. He should either stoke it or get into bed. He had thought he was recovered, but he preferred to believe he was still unwell rather than credit Lily with this hot, shaky sensation. He should have walked out the door the moment he had woken from his fever, as weak as a kitten or not. He should have known… He *had* known she was nothing but trouble. From that first moment in the Holly-well library. What kind of woman wields a damn mace anyway? Any but the world's greatest fool would have known.

Grim rested his muzzle on Alan's thigh, closing his eyes. Alan stroked his head instinctively. Had it really been over a dozen years since he had seen this dog? It was amazing he was still alive.

He probably wouldn't live much longer.

'My poor Grim, I abandoned you, didn't I?'

Grim yawned and padded over to curl into a crescent by the orange remains of the fire. Alan had forgotten Grim would lie down like that by the library fire while he sat with Jasper and Mary. He sank his head in his hands, his elbows on his knees, listening to the dog's huffing breath. He had forgotten how comforting it had been to listen to Grim's breathing in the same room with him when he came to Hollywell to escape the cold hostility of the Hall or when he went to sit by Rickie's grave.

Chapter Ten

Lily stared out the library window at the scrubbed blue skies of a perfect autumn morning. The only reminder of the storm was the dance of wind in the trees. At least this meant Alan wouldn't be soaked to the skin if he walked to Keynsham. She should be grateful, but she wasn't. Why couldn't the roads and fields be flooded, or better yet, an early snowstorm descend upon them and give them one more day...?

She didn't want this time with him to end. She wanted to wrap herself around him, keep him here with her. These feelings were unstoppable, unbearable, and she didn't know what to do. She knew it wasn't the same for him. Otherwise he could not have been in control so quickly after she had all but melted into a puddle at his feet. He wanted to bed her, but he had probably wanted to bed dozens of women and it had meant nothing in the end. For her this was becoming everything.

The squeal was so high-pitched her mind immediately rejected the possibility that this was a trick of the wind. She hurried into the hallway in time to see a ginger streak coming down the stairs, Grim in pursuit. The ginger tabby paid no attention to Lily, its tail high and just curved at the tip as it skidded into the library, its solid body thumping against the doorway. Grim wasn't as swift, but he was large and his lean body drank up the distance in pursuit. His size was an impediment, though, and she spread her legs and planted herself in the library door.

'That's enough, you two!'

Grim's paws scrabbled on the wooden hallway floor as he curved to avoid collision. Behind her she could see the tabby had jumped on to the bookcase in the middle of the room, flanked by the suits of armour and glaring at Lily as if she had spoilt his fun.

Grim growled at the tabby and looked up at Lily, clearly waiting for permission to continue.

Curious, Lily stood back and Grim gathered his old body and proceeded according to plan.

This time only one suit of armour suffered damage. Grim's leap for the tabby did set the bookcase rocking, but the tabby leapt, landing gracefully on the helmet until it toppled to the ground, taking one of the shoulder plates with it in a muted clang. The tabby skidded past Lily's legs again, but Grim stood there, panting and content, clearly waiting to be adulated. Lily relented and scratched his head.

'I see this is a habit. Perhaps I should be grateful you two haven't wreaked worse damage.'

'So you have identified the vandals?'

Alan stood in the doorway, surveying the beheaded knight, and Grim padded over to him, his nails clicking on the wood and his filmy eyes glistening with sheepish pride. 'I found Grim's point of infiltration. It was a door to the garden from one of the small back parlours in the north wing. The catch is faulty.'

He looked much as he had when he arrived two days ago—handsome, forbidding, tense. She didn't speak and he continued.

'Grim can stand guard until I can send someone for you from the Hall. Then later we can sit down and discuss…'

He stopped just as Grim raised his head, nudging Alan's hand. Then she heard it, too. A clatter of wheels.

'Stay here. Don't say a word.'

The door closed behind him before she could respond and she hurried over to press her ear to the wooden surface. She hoped it was the post-chaise, but they weren't due for another day. Could they have mistaken the date?

'Alan Rothwell!'

'Alan! Oh, thank goodness!'

Lady Ravenscar's and Catherine's voices were unmistakable and Lily leaned her forehead on the door. At least that meant he wouldn't have to walk to Keynsham.

'What is the meaning of this?' Lady Ravenscar was demanding, but Lily was surprised to hear her voice shake. 'They found your horse…riderless…and the note. I thought I recognised the hand…but I don't understand!'

'Grandmama!'

Lily heard the clatter, Catherine's cry and Alan's curse and she pulled open the door. It wasn't Alan who had collapsed, but Lady Ravenscar, whose cane had fallen to the ground and who was now supported between Catherine and Alan. Unfortunately Lady Ravenscar hadn't fainted and her gaze locked with Lily's and her voice at least showed she wasn't at death's door.

'I knew it! Lily Wallace!'

Grim padded over and leaned his head against Lily's side in a show of much-needed solidarity as the three Rothwells sent her looks of outrage, shock and impatient annoyance.

She placed her hand on Grim's back.

'Would you care for some tea? I have just put on the kettle.'

Chapter Eleven

'If you please, miss. Lady Ravenscar asked if you will join her when you are ready. In the Rose Room.'

Lily secured the clasp of her mother's gold pendant and shook out the pale blue muslin skirts of her dress. None of her thoughts reflected in her mirror image. She looked calm, even bored, which was nothing less than amazing.

'Is she alone, Sue?'

'No, miss. Lord Ravenscar and Lady Catherine are with her, taking tea.'

That sounded so civilised. She wondered what the servants were making of all this and if they were accepting the fiction spun between the three Rothwells to explain her precipitous return or Alan's presence.

At least the horse had been found by a farmer near Bitton who knew little of the Rothwells and hopefully cared less about the particulars of the peculiar message requesting Lady Ravenscar be alerted that her grandson was ill at Hollywell and could she send a carriage. He had done as requested—driven over through the storm to the Hall, horse in tow and the note in his breast pocket. The only hitch in Lily's plans had been that Partridge, the butler, had seen the note before Lady Ravenscar. But whether the face-saving machinations were effective or not, Lady Ravenscar's words to her at the foot of the stairs upon their return to the Hall had been meant for her ears only and left little to the imagination.

'I will not allow you to add to the damage to my grandson's reputation, Lily Wallace. However, although this is not quite how I would have hoped matters progressed, it might do very well after all. Now, go bathe and dress and come down promptly, we have a great many particulars to see to.' When Lily's foot was already on the first stair, she had added, 'Welcome home.'

Home.

She paused at the door to the Rose Room, grateful Partridge was not hovering about to hurry her along. She gathered herself, took a deep breath and opened the door.

If they had been talking, they fell silent as she entered, the motionless tableau thankfully broken by Grim, who left Alan's side and padded over to her. A thankful burn of moisture in her eyes made her look down as she petted his soft head, grateful that Alan had insisted the old dog accompany them in the carriage, despite Lady Ravenscar's expostulations. She was glad he was here.

Lady Ravenscar spoke first.

'Sit down, Miss Wallace. We have a great deal to discuss. Catherine, perhaps you'd prefer to return to Nicola now.'

After a tense moment Catherine stood and with a

glance at her brother she moved towards the door, sending a reassuring smile at Lily that did little to relax Lily's nerves. She resisted reaching out to the other woman as she passed, begging her to stay.

'Sit down, Lily,' Lady Ravenscar repeated, underlining her command with a light tap of her cane on the floor.

Lily did as she was told, readying herself for the attack and wondering what Alan was thinking as he sat down as well. By the look on his face it was best not to know. She reached out to Grim and the dog settled by her side and rested his head on her thigh, waiting to be indulged.

'Well, Lily Wallace, you have gone your length.' There was a peculiar tone to the old woman's words, certainly not the disdain Lily had expected. 'My grandson has accepted his measure of culpability in what has transpired over the past couple of days, but for a change it appears that the bulk of blame lies elsewhere. It makes no odds, of course—the end result is the same. He has also agreed it would be best to proceed as if this courtship, such as it is, took place here at the Hall and with my full approval. To this end he has agreed to remain here at the Hall until we make our announcement. This will quiet any possible whispers regarding your movements these past couple of days. Given Alan's reputation I doubt anyone would be surprised to hear he has secured your favours so swiftly.'

Lily matched the rhythm of her breathing to the stroking of her hand on Grim's head. Slow and steady. The urge to look at Alan overcame caution, but if she expected comfort, there was none. His face was colder even than his grandmother's, distant and watchful. She could almost believe it had nothing to do with him.

'Your mother was a Woodcote and, though not of the first families, your father's birth was unexceptionable and thus no barrier to marriage to a Rothwell. Given my grandson's reputation, I believe we can be grateful he has done so well. Certainly your lineage can be considered superior to the woman my son married...'

'Careful how you speak of my mother, Lady Jezebel.' Alan's voice was liquid steel and Lady Ravenscar blinked at the unveiled menace.

'I was merely stating that I am not disappointed in your choice, Alan.'

'Unlike my father's, I understand. You keep my mother out of this. She was a better woman than ever you will be.'

Grim's head slid higher on Lily's thigh, his whole body angling away from the antagonism between the two Rothwells.

'She should not have encouraged him to run away from his responsibilities for the dubious fantasy of becoming a doctor. A doctor!'

'She was trying to make him happy. Which was something neither of his parents ever bothered doing!'

'Perhaps if he had applied himself...'

Alan surged to his feet.

'Yes, do remind me on how many levels my father was a disappointment and how far he fell from the stellar example set by his own esteemed papa. It has been quite a few years since I have had to suffer through those charming lectures. Perhaps if your vicious brute of a husband hadn't beaten your son into submission, he might have proven a little less of a disappointment, Jezebel.'

There was a momentary flash of emotion in the old lady's eyes and Lily wanted to step forward and intercede before something bad happened. Though obviously many bad things had already happened.

'Believe me,' he continued, 'if I ever were to discover that I was no longer a disappointment to you, Jezebel, I would take a very hard look to see where I had gone wrong. Now I suggest that, as you yourself said for the sake of this family you appear to suddenly value so highly, you and I find a better way to deal with our mutual dislike until we resolve the issue at hand. That is as much of an olive branch as you are ever likely to get from me, so let me know how you wish to proceed from here.'

He didn't even look at Lily as he stalked out the garden door and she didn't move even after the air stopped shuddering from the slam. Clearly he was mending fast, Lily thought with a twinge of contrary regret.

'That boy! Impossible!'

Lady Ravenscar thumped her cane angrily on the floor, glaring after him.

'Shall I leave, Lady Je—Lady Ravenscar?' She tried not to sound meek, but this household was definitely having an effect on her.

Lady Ravenscar turned her black eyes on her.

'He has quite a viper's sting, doesn't he?'

Lily hesitated, searching for the best answer. She gave up. 'Yes, Lady Ravenscar.'

'That was my mistake. I merely wished… He misunderstood me, of course. About his father. Please do not begin to call me Lady Jezebel as well, like my irreverent grandson. It was my mother-in-law, the Dowager Marchioness, that insisted on continuing to call me Lady Jezebel even after my marriage and of course everyone did as she demanded. If you must indulge your penchant for the informal, I prefer Lady Belle. My mother and sister called me Belle. Jezebel was my father's idea. He named my sister Rahab.'

'Good lord!'

'Precisely. Not a pleasant man, my father. Very much like my husband. I was just barely turned sixteen to Lord Ravenscar's forty-one when we were wed. Sit down a moment. Then I dare say you should go after my fool of a grandson before his body catches up with his vanity and he falls into the lake and drowns.'

Lily sat down with a thump. Sue, the timid but gossipy chambermaid who always stuttered when Lady Ravenscar addressed her, was sixteen. A plump puppy of a child. She tried to imagine her married to the type of man who named his daughters after whores and seductresses.

'Precisely,' Lady Ravenscar said again, though Lily hadn't spoken. Apparently her expression spoke volumes.

'Well, it's a pity your father and husband couldn't have married and left you out of it. They clearly deserved one another.'

Lady Ravenscar stared at her, her pale blue eyes wide with shock. Then her gaze seemed to move inside her, her eyes losing focus, and for a moment Lily worried she might be having some sort of attack, a thought reinforced when the old lady suddenly choked. Lily reached out for her but dropped her hands when she realised the choke was actually a laugh. A very creaky and unused instrument, but a laugh none the less.

'So they did. You are quite shameless, Lily Wallace. Your parents have a great deal to answer for.'

'Most of all for leaving me far too soon. For all their faults, they set high standards—they accepted me as I am, flaws, foibles and all. I wish I could have done the same for them while they lived.'

'Yes, that explains a great deal. But husbands are not parents, girl. They needn't answer to the same standards of absolute acceptance. My grandson is not an easy man, but he is nothing like his grandfather, thankfully. I hope you will manage better than I.'

Lily took a deep breath.

'Lady Belle, I realise I made a grave mistake, but any decision to marry will be made by myself and your grandson. Alone.'

'Some decisions in life are made for us by circumstance, Lily Wallace. Now run along. I am tired. He will probably be down by the willows on the lake. And take that hound with you.'

It didn't take her long to find him. She didn't know how Lady Ravenscar was so certain he would be by the lake, but she wasn't surprised when halfway down the path she saw him through the willows overhanging the embankment, seated on the marble bench with his back to the lake, his elbows propped on his knees.

She slowed. It wasn't her role to coax him out of the sullens. She had her own problems and right now he was the most serious among them. She was not fool enough to believe she was qualified to mediate the murky waters of the Rothwell family.

She sat down on the other end of the bench, but he didn't look up, his gaze fixed on the willow branches draped picturesquely over a low stone wall. Beyond the cavern of the trees around them everything glistened as the sunlight cast a sweet glaze over the damp grass and reeds. It was a perfect, restful setting, except for the man radiating fury by her side.

'Did you know your great-aunt is named Rahab?' she asked the willows.

His scowl didn't lessen and he showed no signs of listening.

'After the harlot of Jericho,' she prompted.

Nothing.

'I dare say if your great-grandfather had had another daughter, he would have named her Athalia or Delilah or some other sinner's name. At least those are pretty names. Rahab is horrid. Even Jezebel is better. Your grandmother told me her mother called her Belle, which is quite nice. Never in her father's presence of course. Clearly she was another downtrodden woman. And Rahab was Ray. Belle and Ray. Until she was married off at sixteen to your grandfather. Do you know how old he was when they wed?'

Nothing.

'Forty-one. Now admittedly he might have been a very nice forty-one-year-old. In fact, forty-one is often preferable to twenty-one. One has experience, and perhaps even patience, but in his case I don't think age improved any of his qualities. One is tempted to wonder whether his nastiness might have some mitigating explanation like another nasty Rothwell before him, which by the sound of the Dowager Marchioness might very well have been the case, but the fact remains he was a vile man and made your grandmother's life a misery even before she blessed him with your father.'

'Is this chatter ever going to end or shall I go elsewhere?'

Lily thought lovingly of the mace at Hollywell House and folded her hands in her lap.

'I am done.'

The lake gleamed pleasantly, scarred down the middle by the wakes of three ducks making for the willows at the other edge. She liked willows. If she ever had a house of her own, she would have willows and she would put a table and chairs under them and take her books there and read near the water. Perhaps one day when...*if* she had children, while she read they could feed the ducks and sail little boats among the reeds and...

'So you expect me to feel sorry for her?'

Lily started and gave up her daydreams.

'Yes. You are supposed to feel stricken by remorse that you have been too insensitive to perceive her life was one of miserable domination by a brutish fiend and you will go down on bended knee and beg forgiveness for your callousness.'

A muscle tightened in his cheek and she watched the telltale line beside his mouth curve. The memory of touching that line while he was ill tingled in her fingertips and she turned back to the ducks and willows. She shouldn't enjoy teasing him out of his sullens and she shouldn't be allowing herself to become all warm over thoughts of touching a man's cheek.

'Knee bending isn't a strength of mine. I am afraid I've exhausted my chivalric impulses rescuing a very ungrateful damsel from her own folly.'

'I wasn't in distress. Besides, I did some rescuing of my own. You would most likely have fallen off your horse into a muddy ditch and drowned. All you did was complicate matters.'

'Well, matters are about to be simplified. Marriage has a way of cutting things down to size.'

'That need not be the case. Whatever your grandmother says, we may yet avoid a scandal. Neither of us wishes to be trapped in a marriage of form. You want your freedom and I want a family, which you admitted you have no interest in.'

'You have been spending too much time with lawyers, Lily, you are beginning to sound like one. You can throw as many clauses and subclauses at this, but the basic facts cannot be avoided. We were two days together, alone. In my experience scandals of these proportions are impossible to bury and I won't have the ruin of a young woman added to my list of sins. So I suggest you accept your fate with equanimity. You needn't worry I will make any unpleasant demands on you or your fortune. I had never intended to marry, but if it can't be helped, it can't. At least you are an intelligent woman, and I think if we establish the ground rules, there is no reason we can't make the best of this. Speaking of lawyers, I suggest you send for Mr Prosper and have him help you compose a marriage settlement you find adequate to your needs. He will probably explain to you that once you marry, your husband receives all your inheritance outright, barring any landed property for which he would receive only the income. Since I don't want a penny of your money and I have no interest in your father's mines, Prosper will have to be creative about creating a settlement that will provide you with an amount in pin money that would allow you to pursue whatever activities you wish, business or otherwise. I will sign whatever you want so you may do with it as you see fit.'

It was a generous offer. It was certainly far more generous than Philip Marston's, at least with regards to her inheritance and her personal freedom. In her discussions with Marston he had promised her a generous allowance in pin money as well as a substantial jointure, but she doubted he would let her dispose of her assets or decide how she would live her life. Philip Marston wanted a mother for his heirs and a socially adept wife to further his ambitions.

But as generous as Alan's offer was, it could not atone for what he wasn't willing to offer her. She had never expected Marston to care for her, not in any deep way. She had come to accept the fact that she was not lovable, since none of the men who had wanted to marry her had seemed swayed by any strong emotion other than avarice and she certainly had never cared for any of them. But she knew she would love her children and hopefully they would love her, and that, Philip Marston was more than willing to give her. He clearly loved his daughter, but he wanted what his own wife had been unable to give him, a large family, preferably with a few sons, and in the end this was what Lily wanted as well. It didn't matter that Alan had breached walls inside her she had not known existed and awakened needs she had not imagined could exist. In his own way he was generous and honest, but he wanted nothing to do with her dreams and she had no power to change him. To live in the expectation that she could would be to invite disaster.

'Nothing to say, Lily? You were talkative enough before. I should be gratified you aren't arguing, but I worry most when you are silent. It makes me want to check over my shoulder for the descending axe, or, in your case, a mace.'

'When I do next wield a mace at your head, I won't do it behind your back, Alan Rothwell.'

He smiled suddenly, demolishing her defences further.

'I almost hope you do. I would like the opportunity to disarm you. Disrobe you, too, but that will have to wait a few weeks, unfortunately.'

She gasped. There was no other way to describe the sharp intake of air that her body forced upon her at his words. She should have just laughed at his absurd response to her absurd suggestion. After all, she had wanted to infuse a little humour into the impossibly difficult situation they were trapped in and she should be happy she made him and Lady Ravenscar smile. But his voice had lost the rasping edge of the fever and regained the sultry sensation of rough velvet dragging over her nerves. It shoved her back against a mental wall and stripped her.

She stood abruptly. This marked the end of the unevenness in their power play his illness had introduced. He was no longer a patient but a clever, experienced rake; he was back in control of himself and she had better do the same if she was to remain in control of her fate.

'Running away again, Lily?'

'I'm standing, not running.'

'You're contemplating it.'

His voice as smooth as heated syrup and his gaze

black as burning coals and hot as Hades. She knew it was a taunt, aimed at the precise opposite result. He wanted her to take him up on his dare and she wanted to. Not because it was a dare, but because she wanted to stay right there and see what happened.

'Are you daring me?'

'You seem to thrive on dares; it's hard to resist tossing them your way.'

'You're just doing this because you're upset I saw you flat on your back and weak as a kitten. If this is an attempt to recapture your sense of manhood, it is rather puerile.'

'You're wrong. That's not why I'm doing this.'

'Then why? Because I witnessed that scene between you and your grandmother?'

He shook his head and moved towards her.

'Wrong again.'

'Then because of Hollywell House. Is that it? Because I didn't want to sell?'

'No. That's also not why and you know it.'

She swallowed and stepped back, but he continued moving towards her.

'That was three guesses, but I'm feeling generous, so you get one more. If you guess right, I'll stop.'

Oh, unfair. That was no incentive to guess right. But the words came anyway, because she needed to see if they were true.

'Because you want to?'

He stopped.

'It is usually the simplest answer that's the correct one, isn't it? So what now, Lily? Shall I stop or do you forfeit your win?'

It isn't that simple, she wanted to say. Not at all simple.

'Here?'

The black fire flashed in his eyes again and he took her hand and pulled her into the shade of the willows. Nothing so tame and cosy as the tea and books she had imagined. Nothing so profound as the children playing, at least not profound for him, but she was afraid it might be for her. There was certainly nothing tame or cosy about the harsh handsome face looking down at her, scored by the lacy shadows of the willow branches that closed about them like a cage. She had stumbled into a wild animal's lair, a panther, dark and sleek and stalking her. He raised his hand and very gently skimmed his knuckles down her cheek, coming to rest just below her mouth, his eyes following his movement with an intensity that burned the caressed skin as much as his touch. She could believe he had read her thoughts, that he knew precisely what she had wanted to do to him as she watched him on the bench and he was paying her back for her foolishness. But then his thumb gently settled on her lower lip, its pressure daring her to open her mouth, to signal that she was ready and waiting for something more.

'Lily...'

She needed to breathe. She couldn't help it, her mouth opened, sucking in his scent, deeper and warmer than the green around them.

'That's right,' he murmured and bent to meet her invitation. 'Open for me.'

His lips brushed hers, gently shaping them, sliding between them only to slide away, lightly tugging and releasing. With each sweep, the urge to cling, to force him to press deeper, harder, grew.

She knew he was playing with her, taunting her into reacting, into making a demand. There was something more, much more, and he was actively withholding it. She resisted, not wanting to give him the satisfaction of begging for what she needed, but it was wearing her down, the friction and his breath soothing and warming and promising.

When he stepped back, she just stood there, disbelieving. Was he so unaffected? Was it only she who was thrumming, singed below the skin, needing…?

'You can't have something for nothing, Lily.' His voice wasn't as confident as his actions; it was rougher than usual, bordering on an accusation.

I don't want something. I want everything. You.

He was right. She wanted to give, not just take. She might have said the words out loud if he hadn't moved towards her again, but just as his fingertips brushed her shoulders he stopped, his gaze focusing on a point behind her.

'Not here. Let's go…somewhere else.'

He grabbed her wrist, but her eyes had followed his and her haze of expectant heat was cleaved through with shock as she realised what he had been staring at while seated on the bench. How hadn't she noticed the tombstone before? Perhaps it was because it was so modest and the same colour as the wall directly behind it. She moved towards it without thinking.

'"Richard George Brisbane Rothwell. 1798–1802,"' she read slowly. Eighteen years ago.

Rickie. The echo of his fevered voice, tortured and foreign, sounded in her mind. She turned to him.

'You had a brother as well. He died when your parents did.'

'We don't speak of him.'

'I realise that. Why?'

He was under control again; even the familiar mocking smile was back. Both passion and pain might never have been there at all.

'House rules. Some people don't like being reminded of their crimes. Certainly my grandparents didn't. They hadn't even known Rickie existed until my parents died; he was born after we came to Edinburgh. At least they had the decency to bring his body back, but not enough to bury him in the Chapel with my father. I used to resent that, but not any more. This is a better place. Someplace he might have played if he had lived here. My grandparents never came down to the lake, too frivolous. That's why I like it here. I can meditate on my sins and my failure in quiet. Until you showed up.'

'Sins plural and failure singular. Why?'

'Must you pick at everything?'

'It's not a question of must. Who did you fail? Your brother?'

'What a tortuous little brain you have.' He smiled at her grimly. 'There were other failures, but he was the most monumental. At least the men who died under my command were there by choice and they knew what might happen to them. Rickie was four years old.'

'Catherine said your parents died of the fever. Didn't he die of the same cause?'

'Yes. Disease and carelessness. The disease wasn't my fault, the carelessness was.'

'You were just a child.'

'So what? Do you know in the mill I won at cards five years ago half the workers were under ten years old? They and their families saw nothing peculiar about that. When I told the families we would no longer be employing children, we nearly had a riot on our hands until we found alternatives. I might have been twelve, but I was still responsible for him. My parents were ill, the whole city was in a panic at the epidemic, people closed down their houses and stores and ran for the hills. I was too ashamed to fetch the doctor again because we had nothing to give him. I actually thought I could care for him myself. My only consolation was that they died before they realised he was dead. Foolish, isn't it? They would have died anyway. What difference would it make if they knew?'

Lily remembered that night watching over the housekeeper's tiny bloodstained baby on the island. Nothing anyone had said, could say, erased her guilt. But this had been his *brother*, in his care while his parents lay dying and his sister and nanny close to death themselves, caught in a city of chaos and without resources. She could imagine nothing more lonely, more terrifying. He was no fool, he probably knew his brother would have died anyway, but the doubt would never disappear.

She crouched down and laid her hand flat on the cool stone, just below the name. How deep did his little skeleton lie?

'It makes a difference to you,' she answered. 'One less burden for you to bear.'

'A burden I will never willingly bear again.'

She shivered and stood up. He had said as much before, but she hadn't realised this wasn't simply a preference for his chosen lifestyle, but a deep rejection of what she held dear. He would do what was proper, marry her, and then she would truly be alone.

'That makes no sense,' she protested, unwilling to accept the verdict. 'What happened with Rickie wasn't your fault. You cannot go through life blaming yourself for something you had no control over.'

'This isn't only about blame. I watched Rickie die. It took days, but I saw the precise moment. For four years he had been the most wonderful thing to enter our lives, the first thing to bring real joy to my parents' lives for as long as I could remember, and he ceased to be in a second. I couldn't even tell anyone because there was no one coherent enough to understand. I've watched quite a few men die since then, but by some mercy I've been spared watching another child die. If you think I am mad enough to risk that pain again… Just spare me your self-serving lectures, Lily, and disabuse yourself that either of us still has any choice in the matter—you are going to marry me, and if you want children, you will have to do what any other married woman in the *ton* does when she needs something from a man and her husband won't oblige. I don't know what fairy-tale idea you have of our society, but though we are unforgivingly brutal about young women's reputations before they wed, and demand discretion of them once they do, the *ton* is littered with other men's children—why should I be any different?'

Her jaw ached with the weight of his loss, but the image of her future his last words conjured made her ill. She shook her head. She would never, ever go down that path, no matter how much she loved Alan and wanted to be with him. But the very fact that he could make such a suggestion dragged out the devil in her. She wanted to hurt him as much as he was hurting her.

'So you would have no problem if I seduced another man and brought him to my bed, if I undressed for him...'

'Damn you!'

He was panther swift and just as frightening as he grabbed her, but she wasn't scared he would hurt her, not in body. Part of her refused to believe he could really contemplate such a future, for her or for himself. She heard the pleading note in her voice as she tried to reach him.

'But that is precisely what would happen if I accepted your generous offer, Alan. I would be damned to a life I would hate.'

He let go and turned away, his breathing as tense as her body.

'This is the way things are, Lily.'

'It doesn't have to be.'

'You've a softer heart than you like to accept, don't you, Lily? You absolve your parents, transform my grandmother into Lady Belle... Well, don't strain it on my account.'

She gathered herself up again at the cold warning in his voice. He was at least decent enough to point out her figurative petticoats were showing. What had she expected? That her emotion would trigger his? She wasn't so naïve. But she wouldn't stand down from her own truth either.

'I'll strain my heart over whatever I want, Lord Ravenscar.' It was a challenge, not an admission. At least she hoped not.

'You should watch that soft flank of yours, Lily. That is how battles are lost.'

She shrugged and brushed her hands on her pelisse.

'You may crow from your perch all you like, Raven. At least I know I am still warm and breathing.'

'Do you find me cold, Lily? Even in light of our little interludes? I must have been doing something wrong.'

'That's not warmth.'

'I agree. It was quite a few degrees hotter than warmth. Shall I remind you?'

She stepped back but stopped. She would not run. She didn't want to run. Oh, blast. She *was* asking for trouble. She was a fool, but at least she knew that now. At least the pain that was to come wouldn't be a surprise.

He smiled and touched her cheek.

'Standing your ground can be as much an offensive move as an outright attack, you do know that, don't you? Of course you do. This vixen is more accustomed to standing and fighting than she is to running after all.'

'Careful you don't get bitten, then.'

'Right now I'm willing to risk it.' His voice dropped and he closed the distance between them. 'More than willing.'

His hands could be so gentle. She could feel the tension in them, the leashed power, but they moved over her skin so lightly, drawing her towards him, skimming over her lower lip so that it shuddered against his fingers.

'Are you willing, Lily?' His voice was also gentle as he bent to replace his fingers with his mouth. The words moved over her, encompassing her with liquid heat. This was how it would feel if they were swimming together in the warm tropical waters of the bay in Isla Padrones. She was swimming with her own shark now. She was exposed and he was lethal. At least to her.

Yes. With his lips just poised over hers, promising, she was willing to risk anything he asked.

'Yes... Alan...'

He drew away, his hand closed around her nape, his thumb pressing up against her chin. The lazy seduction in his eyes was gone. She wasn't prepared for the blaze of fire in them now, or the surge of painful heat that echoed through her in response. He pressed her back against the trunk of the willow, sheathing them in the long green darts, a cocoon of shadow.

'There's no going back now.' His voice was rough against her, impatient and demanding like the hands that brought her against him. She didn't argue, just slid her arms around his neck and let herself go, raising her head and pressing her lips to the warmth of his neck, desperate to feel him, recapture his scent.

A groan ripped through him as she nuzzled the soft skin below his ear, his arms painful around her, but she didn't care, she pressed as close as she could, her hands teasing his hair, loving how she felt against him, how her whole body was lighting, filling, becoming alive, waiting for his touch.

'God, Lily, I want to take you here, with your hair spread like a sunset on the grass. I can't stand much more of this. Do you have any idea what you're doing to me?'

She couldn't have answered even if his mouth hadn't finally caught hers, kissing her hard and deep, demanding a response. He held her, his fingers deep in her hair, gliding against her scalp, shaping the sensitive curve of her ears, sinking lower over her shoulders and down her back, curving under her behind, sliding the soft muslins against her skin as though he could rub them off like moisture with a towel, baring her against the silvery bark and the grey-tinged leaves.

He found and lit bursts of pleasure in places she had never associated with sensation, let alone this restless-seeking joy. Somehow he knew and would linger there until she was shaking, trying not to shatter. Her hands and mouth were trying to do the same to him by their own volition, seeking and touching as he did, shivering as he groaned when her fingers stroked down the ridged muscles of his back beneath his coat. His hands tightened on her behind, pulling her hard against his arousal as he bent his head and nipped the sensitised flesh of her neck.

'We have to stop. Any more and I'll take you right here.'

'Yes…' He stifled her moaned invitation with his mouth, but his words were as damaging as his hands, filling her mind with the promise of what was to come. They flowed against the skin as he kissed her, his mouth moving down her neck, tasting the slope of her shoulder, the rise of her breast.

'No. When I show you what you are capable of, I want you where no one will interrupt us. Where I can lay you bare and kiss you inch by inch, from your ankles, the soft skin on the back of your knees, over every soft slide of your thighs. I want to spend an hour on your amazing behind…' he spread his hands over it, kneading and raising her against his erection, his hands contracting as she shuddered in response '...then I will turn you over and kiss this soft skin right here...' he arched her back to trace the slide of her abdomen, from her ribs to her navel and down '...until I come home, right here, where you're waiting for me...'

His fingers curved down, skimming but not settling there. She didn't even realise what she was about to do until she felt her hand on his, pressing him against her. Her eyes rose to his, shocked at her audacity, meeting the silvered storm in his.

'That's right, Lily. Take what you want... Don't be afraid.'

She wasn't afraid, she was terrified. The exhilarating terror of clinging to a ship's mast in a storm, watching the waves gather for the next pummelling. Any second now she would shatter into nothingness.

With a cry she pushed his hand away and instantly his hold stilled, softened. They stood for a moment longer in the cage of willows, the quacking of the ducks as they flapped their wings on the lake a reminder of where they were. Eventually Alan stood back, resting his hand on a willow branch and looking out over the lake, his eyes retaining the shimmer of light reflecting off the water.

He didn't stop her when she left, but she was weak enough to wish he would.

Chapter Twelve

'What is wrong with the boy? How on earth are people to give any credence to a courtship between you if he won't show his face?'

'He is very busy, Grandmama…' Catherine said.

'Busy doing what, precisely?'

Catherine's eyes dropped before Lady Ravenscar's and Lily couldn't determine if Catherine didn't know or didn't want to tell. Either case wasn't reassuring.

'It has been two days since your return and you have not seen him for more than five minutes if that, have you, Lily?'

The interlude by the lake had been a little more than five minutes, but after that…

What had she expected? That he would dance attendance on her and woo her? The man felt he must wed her and he clearly wanted to bed her, but he had his own life and he meant to keep it that way. This was a fine introduction to the life she would lead if she wed him. She would have all the freedom she wanted, but very little else. She should be grateful that he was making her choice so very clear, but she could no more stop the hurt and the yearning that hummed inside her than she could stop her heart from beating or blood from flowing.

'Who precisely are you accusing, Lady Belle?' Lily asked. 'Lord Ravenscar or myself? Or both?'

She was saved from Lady Ravenscar's response by Partridge's appearance.

'What is it, Partridge?'

'Mr Marston, my lady. For Miss Wallace.'

'Hmmm...bring him in, Partridge.'

Lily stood.

'No, please, Partridge. Could you show him to the library?'

After a pause, Lady Ravenscar nodded and Partridge departed.

'It is hardly proper for you to meet with Mr Marston in a tête-à-tête, Lily. Especially under the circumstances.'

'We had not reached any formal agreement, but I owe Mr Marston the courtesy of explaining matters myself and in private, Lady Belle. Please respect my wishes on this.'

'Oh, very well. Ten minutes. Thorns are best withdrawn swiftly and decisively, Lily Wallace.'

'I will ignore being compared to a thorn in the flesh, Lady Belle, but I agree in principle.'

Philip Marston turned from his contemplation of the garden and smiled as she entered. He was a good-looking man, with light brown hair and blue eyes and a bearing that spoke of a man used to command, but he looked different than when she had last seen him, less imposing, which made little sense. Lily hoped the answering smile on her face didn't look like a grimace or reflect anything of her inner turmoil.

'Miss Wallace. You look radiant. Clearly time away from me agrees with you.'

'Thank you, Mr Marston, pray sit down. I trust your daughter is well?'

His light brows twitched closer, but his smile held and he sat on the green-striped chair opposite her.

'Very well and very excited about meeting you.'

Oh, no.

'She wanted to accompany me today, but she is still a little fatigued after the trip. You look a little pale, Miss Wallace… Lily. Have you been unwell? I have heard there have been quite a few cases of this fever in the environs.'

She was tempted to fall back on this excuse; guilt was rumbling inside her like a poorly digested meal.

'Not unwell, Mr Marston. It is a little more complicated than that. There is something I must tell you and I ask that you wait until I conclude my tale before you comment. Please.'

She didn't wait for his permission. She wished she was wearing gloves so she would have something to do with her fingers. Instead she held her hands tightly together and told him as much as she dared about her escape to Hollywell and forced proximity with Alan, stopping short of admitting to any intimacies between them.

'I know we had never reached a formal agreement, Mr Marston, but that there was also an understanding between us to consider a…closer relationship and so I felt it only right to explain to you as openly as I can why that is no longer possible and to express my regrets that I should have caused you any distress or embarrassment.'

'Why is it no longer possible?'

The question was so calm it took her a moment to understand it.

'I... Because... I explained what happened.'

'So you did. It was unfortunate and perhaps you will later explain to me in greater detail precisely why you felt the need to arrange this solitary retreat to Holly-well House. However, if I understood you correctly, at the moment the only people who know you were alone with Ravenscar are his immediate family, his groom who drove the carriage over and possibly Lady Ravenscar's butler.'

'Probably. The man who brought the horse handed him the note I secured in the saddle. Apparently it was smudged, but he has seen at least some instances of my handwriting when I posted letters to my lawyers over the past weeks.'

'I see. That was two days ago?'

'Yes.'

'Have you heard of any gossip regarding your escapade as yet?'

'No, but...'

'Well, then, you might be luckier than you deserve and this shall remain the domain of a very few.'

'Mr Marston...'

'Philip. I believe we can dispense with formalities, Lily. We have known each other long enough, surely.'

'Philip, then. You do realise what I am saying—for almost two days and two nights I was alone, unchap-eroned, with a man. If this were to be known, I would be beyond the pale. No man of breeding could consider marrying me.'

'My life is peppered with "ifs", Lily. My business prospers because of them. You have been a very definite "if" from the day I met you at your father's house six years ago. I think I am capable of encompassing one more, within reason. All I am saying at the moment is that we not hurry into decisions we might regret. I admit to being surprised. I briefly saw Ravenscar earlier today on some mutual business of ours and he gave me no intimation whatsoever of any of this, but then he was always a cautious fellow.'

Alan? Cautious?

'He did mention you owned a mill together,' she prompted, hating her curiosity.

'A little more than that. My strength is in shipping, but it exposes me to all forms of merchandise. When I see extraordinary demand for particular products, naturally I become curious and sometimes I dabble in new ideas. Several years ago I became interested in the new power looms being built and sold to cotton mills and that is how I became acquainted with Lord Ravenscar. We share a strong interest in the new machinery and its effect on the costs of production. And apparently now in you, of course.' He smiled politely and for the first time she saw the steel under the calm urbanity.

'I see.'

'Do you? I have the advantage of knowing both you and Ravenscar for quite a few years, certainly longer than your brief acquaintance with each other. Perhaps I shouldn't be surprised that when someone did finally breach your carefully constructed walls it would be someone not dissimilar from your father.'

Lily opened her mouth to speak, but he raised his hand.

'Allow me to finish, Lily. Then you may correct me if I am wrong. When I came to your father's house six years ago, I admit I was fascinated with the workings of your mind. Your father and I both had the cross to bear that our wives bore us only a daughter, but I remember thinking, if Penny could grow up to be as poised and intelligent as you, I would not be disappointed. Had you been a man you could have run your father's businesses as well as he, that was clear. But despite your intelligence there was something walled-off about you. During my visits to Kingston over the years, I watched different men react differently to your defences—some stormed the battlements and were predictably repelled and some admitted defeat before firing the first shot. Since my Joanne was alive at the time, none of this was of any significance, but I admit as I came out of mourning and realised that I yet could have the chance at a male heir for my legacy, it was not long before I thought of you. There are only twelve years between us, which is hardly an insuperable divide. Unlike most young women, you have a keen understanding of my world and, despite your superior lineage, I do not believe you find my more humble origins despicable. When I discovered the unfortunate nature of your father's will, it became clear to me that here was a golden opportunity for both of us and so I approached you. Everything we discussed that day in Kingston is still applicable. You wish to have a family and some financial freedom and I would like a male heir, most preferably an intelligent one who would one day be able to assume my responsibilities. I believe given our joint cerebral gifts any child we bear is most likely to fulfil my highest expectations. It is as simple as that.'

She should probably say something, but nothing came and Philip Marston continued.

'I am not surprised that Ravenscar has the power to fascinate someone like you, Lily, so you needn't feel guilty about some natural confusion. I was very fond of your father—he was a charming, intelligent and generous man and he loved you dearly, but he had a fateful need to see himself reflected in those around him, especially women. I broach this subject because it was evident you were fully aware of his weakness. I am not implying that Ravenscar is a mirror image of your father, there are distinct differences, but there are also distinct similarities. He is a man who was rejected by his family, rebuilt himself on his own terms and is, in vulgar parlance, a rake and very used to going his own way. From the little you disclosed about your mother I could tell that aside from your love for her there was also contempt for her willingness to accept half a loaf and sometimes less. I suggest you think well and long before you allow yourself to be forced into a similar alliance without even the love your parents did share and your mother's significantly more accepting nature. You deserve better.'

Her fingers were plucking at the tiny pearls nestled in the hearts of the flowers embroidered on her skirts. She stilled them, but that was worse because they were clearly shaking. Had he stepped inside her head and found that list of fears and objections prepared by her inner lawyer? She didn't know if she deserved better, but she wanted more. From Alan. But Mr Marston… Philip…was right. At least her mother had accepted her father's limitations and learned to live inside their boundaries. She could never be her mother. She would never accept Alan's infidelities and his unwillingness to give her the family for which she yearned.

'What shall I do?' Her voice shook and his hand settled on hers, trapping her fingers against her thighs like a glass placed over bees. She wanted to fling his hand away, but she kept still. If he told her she should go ahead and marry him, she would scream.

'Wait. For the moment. Most likely the threat of exposure will clear like the skies cleared after the storm. Believe me, as a father to a young woman about to take her first steps into society I am well aware of what is at stake for you, but unless fate forces your hand, this is not a decision to be made without careful consideration of the consequences. So my advice is—wait...'

'Wait for what?'

Lord Ravenscar stood with his hand still on the knob, surveying them from the doorway. By the cold lack of surprise on his face she supposed either Partridge or Lady Belle had told him where and with whom she was ensconced. It was fitting that after disappearing for almost two days he appeared at the worst possible moment.

'Wait for what, Lily?' he asked again, his gaze moving from the light flush in Marston's cheeks to her as he approached.

'Mr Marston was suggesting, quite sensibly, that I wait before I make any firm decision regarding my future.'

His gaze locked with hers.

'I was under the impression a decision had already been made. A very firm decision.'

'As long as no formal announcement has been made, I believe Miss Wallace should be allowed to consider what is best for her future.'

'For *your* future more like, Marston. Stay out of this. You don't know the particulars.'

'On the contrary, Miss Wallace has been very honest regarding the events of the past few days.'

Lily didn't try to hide from the grey ice in Alan's eyes as she waited for the axe to fall. It would almost be a relief if Alan told Philip everything that had happened between them. It would condemn her and remove the choice from her hands—no man would accept a woman who had all but thrown herself into the arms of another, whether she remained a virgin after the encounter or not.

'Have you, Lily? Honest to a fault, are we?' Lily's eyes fell, more disappointed than relieved by his restraint. He didn't wait for her to answer. 'It changes nothing. Whatever the circumstances, I was alone with Miss Wallace for two whole days in an empty house and we are now to be married. If you had really wanted her, Marston, you would have pushed your advantage before you went off on business.'

Marston's mouth quirked in a smile, not entirely of amusement.

'Can you really hold it against me that I didn't foresee this particular development? I would have thought you would be grateful to be extricated from an alliance that must at least in part put an end to your free and easy lifestyle, Ravenscar. Unlike you, both Miss Wallace and I most avidly want children. I don't believe I could begin to recall the number of times you told me you have no intention of marrying or having children.

I believe the phrase you used was "when hell freezes over". Yet here I am, offering to relieve both of you from an embarrassing situation, and you are baulking. So while I respect your sense of honour, it must be pure stubbornness that would make you stand in the way of what is a perfect solution for all those involved.'

Tension hummed in the space sketched between them. Lily knew Philip's suggestion had merit, but more than anything she wanted Alan to smash it as conclusively as he had felled Jackson, as inescapably as he had captured her. But Alan's voice remained as cool as spring water when he answered.

'I think this is a discussion Lily and I should be having alone.'

Marston half-bowed and took Lily's hand, smiling down at her.

'Of course. I must return to Bristol anyway. I came with the hope of inviting you to a concert being held at the New Music Room on Prince's Street tomorrow afternoon. A very fine Italian soprano, I am told. I thought it would be a lovely opportunity for you to meet my Penny.'

Lily smiled, thankful for his diplomacy.

'I would be happy…'

'I will bring her,' Alan said.

'There is no need.'

'I am certain my sister and Lady Ravenscar would be delighted to attend a concert as well. We will meet you and your daughter there, Marston.'

Marston bowed, squeezed her hand and, with a wry smile at Alan, left the library.

The moment the door closed Lily felt the tug of tension pull back her shoulders. She tried to gather her defences around her anger at Alan's disappearance and her painful imaginings of his whereabouts.

'You were rude to him and you had no right. He had every reason to be angry at me and yet he was extraordinarily civil and kind.'

He walked towards the fireplace, his movements abrupt.

'A veritable paragon. He was still poaching. It isn't done.'

'Poaching? I am not a property and certainly not yours.'

'You are my betrothed. I would have thought the events of those two days sufficiently clear in your mind.'

'Well, you do know what they say, out of sight out of mind. I had begun to hope your prolonged absence meant you had disappeared in earnest.'

'Is that what this is about? Are you annoyed I wasn't dancing attendance on you? I've been extremely busy, but that doesn't change the facts by a hair's breadth. We are engaged.'

'Not yet.'

As he closed the distance between them, she realised she had forgotten how tall he was and how menacing his darkness could be. Every cell in her body was begging her to retreat, but she stood, her head tilted back to meet the storm-coloured glare.

'This isn't an island off Brazil, Lily. One word can destroy your reputation irrevocably and then any fantasy you have of a happy family is just that. You do realise Marston would drop you like a hot coal if he knew a tenth of what happened at Hollywell. You should appreciate that—he is a businessman and he has his assets to consider. He is well aware his birth is merely respectable, which is why he has chosen to ally himself with someone like you, but should you prove to be a liability he will be only too thankful to me for unburdening him.'

Lily had never slapped anyone, but she could understand the urge. Her hands tingled with the need to shatter the cold beauty of his face.

'Are you threatening me, Lord Ravenscar?'

'I am trying to make you see sense. What the devil do you think he is offering you? Your vaunted freedom? You would have no more freedom than your mother.'

'At least he would be faithful. At least he would give me a family!'

She had no idea what he might have said if Lady Ravenscar and Catherine hadn't entered at that point. But there was enough of an admission in the way he turned his back to her.

'There is a musical concert at the Assembly Hall in Bristol tomorrow afternoon,' he told his grandmother without preamble. 'I suggest we all go.'

'Perhaps it is best I stay with Nicola…' Catherine began but petered to a stop at a look from her brother.

'A concert is an excellent idea, Alan,' Lady Ravenscar said. 'Will you be staying for dinner?'

Alan bowed and headed for the door.

'Try to keep me away.'

Chapter Thirteen

Pathetic. You are without question utterly and thoroughly pathetic, Lily Wallace.

Moping like a lovesick heroine from the worst kind of novel. Why, even Radcliffe's Emily was less of a milksop over her Valancourt and at least Scythorp was entertaining. You are merely pathetic. Simply because you have never been in love before is no reason to go all to pieces. People fall in and out of love all the time. Why should you be any different?

Lily raised her chin at the image in the mirror as Sue fussed over the finishing touches in her hair, pulling and tucking strands into a Grecian knot that cascaded in waves to her nape in accordance with the fashion plate she and Nicky had chosen for the occasion. Finally Sue stood back, her chubby face flushed with concentration and worry. Lily stood and smiled encouragingly, wishing she hadn't sent Greene away. She missed her gruff efficiency and unspoken love.

She slipped the ribbon of her fan over her wrist and inspected her dress once more. She wasn't overly fond of jewellery despite or perhaps because of the source of her father's wealth and his many costly and elaborate gifts to her since her mother's death. She had never worn any on the island and she saw no reason to change simply because people expected it of the daughter of the King of Mines, Frederick Wallace.

Tonight she wore only simple teardrop pearl clips on her ears and a mother-of-pearl comb that had been her mother's. Her gloves were of a pale cream satin, with a long row of tiny pearl buttons, and she carried a fan of painted Chinese silk with the image of two black-and-gold birds engaged in either warfare or rather tempestuous lovemaking. When she had bought it in Jamaica, its scandalous nature had pleased her— now both the colouring and the tension between the birds reminded her too much of Alan, just not enough to have her choose another. Finally she picked up her shawl of painted silk.

'Thank you, Sue. I'm ready.'

She was the last to enter the Rose Room and the Rothwells turned towards her and her heart, usually a steady organ, rose and fell. Alan was clearly still angry. Not that she had expected much else after the armed neutrality of the previous evening and his absence again all day. He would honour his obligation, but no more. Before anyone could break the awkward silence, Nicky bounded over.

'Oh, how beautiful! I love orange, or is that called peach? Is that real gold? Oh, they are birds!' She touched her fingers to the delicate embroidery along the edges of the short sleeve.

'Nicola,' her mother admonished, but Lily forced a smile.

'It is gold thread embossed on machine-made net over satin with appliqué birds,' Lily answered, touching the fanned tail of one of the birds. Perhaps the dress was a little dashing for an afternoon concert, but she needed all the armour she could muster. However unsettled her feelings for Alan made her, it was not like her to concede the battle without a single shot. At the very least she would go to the tumbril with her head held high and dressed to the nines and using every ounce of her ingenuity to shape her fate.

'I want a gown like that when I am grown,' Nicky said dreamily, tracing one of the embroidered gold birds. 'Mama, you would look lovely in those colours, much nicer than purple.'

'Lilac,' Lily and Catherine said in unison and laughed.

'You are probably right, though,' Catherine said with a shade of wistfulness in her quiet voice. 'I would like to say I am past the age of such fashionable gowns, but since I never wore anything half so lovely at any age, the words are sticking in my throat.'

'So they should.' Alan finally spoke, his voice terse. 'You're almost ten years out of mourning, Cat. I've sent you enough bolts of cloth to start your own warehouse.'

'It's simply that I have enough gowns already, Alan.'

'Enough *awful* gowns.' Catherine flushed a little and turned to inspect herself in the mirror. Nicky flushed even more. 'Oh, Mama, I'm so sorry, that was horrid of me.'

Catherine caught the girl to her and kissed her rumpled hair.

'It is true, though, chick. Perhaps we should visit the seamstress before you return to school next week so you can help me choose something that isn't completely horrid. In truth, I am tired of purple. All shades of purple. It is such an unsmiling colour. Still, I am a widow.'

'Yes, but you're not *dead*,' Nicky replied, and after a stunned moment Catherine burst into laughter, hugging her daughter again.

'Oh, my dear, you are so wise. That must be from your father. Now upstairs with you.'

Nicky hugged her and then turned to hug Lily, surprising her.

'I am so glad you are to be my aunt, then I will have new cousins to play with.'

The moment of stunned silence was broken by Lady Ravenscar.

'Nicola Sayers! Listening at doors is a very bad habit!'

Nicky turned at her great-grandmother's rebuke.

'I wasn't, really I wasn't. I heard you and Mama talking as I came in, I promise. Besides, I shan't tell if it is a secret yet. I can keep secrets. But I can be happy, can't I? I hope you have a little girl so I can give her my dolls and toys. I don't have much for boys, but I could buy them balls and toy soldiers.'

Catherine was watching her brother and she made a gesture with her hand as if to stop Nicky, and it shook him from the silence that followed Nicky's words.

'You are getting ahead of yourself, Nicky. Marriage is no guarantee of children.'

Nicky turned to him, oblivious to the tensions and to the unusual pallor on his face, almost dancing in excitement at her own plans for their future.

'Oh, but of course you will have children, so you can teach them to ride like you taught me when we came to stay with your friend Lord Hunter. But you must have lots because it isn't quite as nice to be just one. I could read to them like you did to me, Lily, though they would probably like you to do it because I can't do all those funny voices, but we could all sit by the fire and you could read my fairy-tale books except that I suppose they wouldn't sit still if they were very little, especially the boys, they would be climbing on things like my friend Anna's brothers. Do you think they will have black hair or red hair? Not that your hair is really red…well, reddish brown, I suppose, but it would be lovely to have a little girl with hair that colour and I could teach her how to braid it.'

'If those braids are any example, then no, thank you,' Alan finally interrupted. 'Now, it is time for us to leave, so upstairs with you.'

'But Partridge hasn't come to say the carriage is out front yet.'

'Upstairs, Nicky,' Catherine said, and Nicky sighed and hurried off, utterly unaware of the tension she left behind.

Lily pulled her cloak more tightly about her, not because it was cold, for the weather had taken on an unseasonable warmth that was in stark contrast to Lily's mood, but because she could feel the skin of her arms rise in goose pimples under the cold hostility of Alan's gaze as he sat across from her in Lady Ravenscar's ancient carriage. She knew the images Nicky's artless chatter had evoked were as powerful in his mind as in hers, but with very different emotions. Every line of his long lean body was a study in tension and rejection and even Lady Ravenscar seemed cowed. It wasn't until the first buildings of Bristol appeared in the carriage window that the old lady spoke, the words harsh and punctuated with taps from her cane.

'If the two of you intend to continue to behave at the concert as deplorably as you did last night at dinner, I shall order George Coachman to turn about right now.'

Alan didn't look at his grandmother, but Lily saw the anger bubble and hiss, darkening his eyes.

'His name is John, Grandmother.'

'What? Whose?'

'The coachman. John Storridge. He is the second son of the previous head groom. The eldest is in the Navy.'

'I don't see what that has to say to anything.'

'Clearly not. This habit of calling all coachmen by the name of George is convenient, especially when one's faculties are failing.'

'My faculties are as sharp as ever, Alan Rothwell. As is my social acumen despite my preference not to immerse myself in the activities of the local families these past years. You may know the names of the grooms—not that that surprises me given your predilection for horrid pugilism and racing—but I know that if the two of you make your first appearance in public looking like two thunderclouds, we have no hope of passing off any alliance between you as anything other than the outcome of scandal and duress.'

Alan leaned forward and plucked Lily's hand from her lap, turning it palm up and raising it to within inches of his mouth, his thumb strumming the buttons at her wrist.

'Hear that, Lily? Grandmama thinks we can't convince these provincial plods we are enthralled with one other. Care to prove her wrong about our skills as thespians?'

His breath seeped into the buttonholes, tiny licking caresses that spread up and down, sinking under her skin, into her blood, shocking her with the speed with which her body transformed. It was as close to witch-craft as anything could be. All her resistance amounted to nothing the moment he put on an act of passion. There was not even a pretence that this was anything more than a lie, but her body didn't care and her mind was fast losing ground.

'I don't doubt your acting skills, Lord Ravenscar,' she replied. 'I only hope no one looks too closely. Most thespians have the benefit of being at a distance from their audience so their lack of sincerity is less apparent.'

Seeing the anger heat behind the mockery gave her some satisfaction, but not much.

'Perhaps I need a little encouragement to bring out the best in my performance. Think you could encour-age me, Lily?'

'Alan Piers—' Lady Ravenscar cut herself off with a thump of her cane, recognising the futility of her protest, but Alan released Lily's hand and sat back.

'Apologies, Grandmama, I was carried away by my passions. Ah, here we are.'

Catherine glanced out of the window at the mean-looking brick buildings outside.

'Where are we? This isn't the Assembly Hall.'

'Nowhere near it. I asked John to stop here for a moment. There is something I must do before we con-tinue. Wait here. I won't be gone above five minutes.'

He didn't wait for them to respond. When the car-riage door snapped shut behind him, Lady Ravenscar rapped her cane against the roof of the carriage and the coachman swung off his perch and opened the door.

'Yes, my lady?'

'What is this place, Geo...John Coachman?'

'This is Mead Road, my lady.'

'Edifying! What is this house Lord Ravenscar has entered?'

'I couldn't rightly say, my lady.'

'Couldn't or won't, John Storridge?'

Lily took pity on the coachman and gathered her cloak over her arm.

'Could you help me down, please, John?'

'Miss?'

She didn't wait for any objections, just leapt down lightly on to the pavement, narrowly avoiding a muddy puddle between the cracked paving stones, and hurried into the house where the warped door still stood ajar.

'Miss!'

She hadn't known what to expect. Perhaps a brothel like her father's, or a gaming hell or opium den like she had heard of near the Kingston docks or those frequented by the miners in Belo Horizonte. Something that would further tip the scales against this persistent pull he had on her. But all those ideas were dismissed in the first steps into the narrow, ill-smelling hallway.

A group of six or so children of all ages were seated on the stairs, laughing at a young man holding two ragged puppets, but they stopped the moment she appeared and scurried up into the dark, dragging staring toddlers in their wake.

To her right a door stood open to a room and several startled pairs of eyes took in her finery. Three of the men were seated in bath chairs, two of them had no nether limbs and the third's head lolled sideways against a cushioned headrest. Two women sat stitching by a fire and beside them several more children were seated playing spillikins on the bare floor, dressed in warm but rough clothes, their hands now frozen in mid-gesture as they stared at her.

'Miss, please!' the coachman hissed behind her, obviously shocked, but she continued down the dark hallway with its damp and mottled walls, pausing before the next door as she heard Alan's voice.

'This should be enough for rent and provisions through the rest of the week, Tippet. If I don't find something by then, it will have to be the Saltford property after all. Jem is overseeing the workers while they assess what will need to be done if we must go ahead. We will still be some ten rooms short, but it can't be helped. We can always accommodate the rest up in Birmingham or London until we find a better solution near Bristol.'

'I know you don't like sending the men and families away from what they know, Captain, but if it can't be helped, it can't. They know anything Hope House has to offer is a damn sight better than the street or the workhouse, which is where they'd go otherwise. The fire was no one's fault but those new gas pipes and we're lucky no one was badly hurt.'

'Very lucky. Have everyone ready by...'

'Are you a fairy, miss?'

Lily raised her finger to hush the little girl who appeared behind her, but it was too late. Alan came to the doorway and the girl hurried off.

'Are you constitutionally incapable of doing as you are told?'

'I sometimes do as I am *asked*,' she replied. 'These are war veterans, are they not?'

'Wait for me in the carriage. I am almost done.'

'Is this what you want Hollywell for? Why didn't you tell me?'

'Would it have made a difference?'

'Of course it would.'

'It is irrelevant in any case. We no longer need Hollywell.'

She glanced past his shoulder at the man behind him. With his grey hair and zigzag of a nose, he looked like an aged boxer.

'Is that true, sir?' she asked the man, and his eyes widened in alarm.

'If the Captain says it's true, it's gospel, miss.' He ventured a glance at Alan, but Alan was watching her, his gaze the blank look he managed so well when he wished.

'Infallible, is he?' Her question won her a sudden grin from Tippet, showing a neat hole where several teeth should be.

'When it counts, miss.'

'Thank you, Tippet,' Alan interrupted. 'Come along, Miss Wallace, we don't want to be late for the wailing Italian.'

As she turned, a scurrying in the doorways and on the stairs marked the careful retreat of whatever spectators had gathered.

Philip Marston hadn't been exaggerating, Penny was indeed an angel, or as closely resembling one as a human was likely to manage. Lily hated being petty, but she would have preferred that the pale gold beauty at least be spoilt or nasty, but in a matter of minutes Lily realised she was not only shy, but quite sweet and more than willing to think the best of Lily if her father so desired.

'This is my very first concert,' she told Lily in a hushed tumble of words as Marston turned to address some comments to Lady Ravenscar and Catherine. 'I'm afraid I don't understand Italian at all. I did try to apply myself, but I simply have no ear for languages, my schoolmistress says. Do you speak Italian, Miss Wallace? Papa says you lived in many exciting places. I do so envy you.'

'Your papa is exaggerating, though I suppose they may seem exciting to others. It is true there were people from all over the world in the mines where my father worked and I learned a little of everything, but mostly they spoke Portuguese or Spanish. Your papa said you are to have your first Season this spring. You must be excited.'

'I am... Oh, good afternoon, Lord Ravenscar.'

'Good afternoon, Miss Marston. Congratulations on having finally put school behind you. Or should I be congratulating your schoolmistress?'

Penny giggled, surprising Lily. She hadn't realised Alan might be acquainted with Penny, but if he and Philip Marston shared business concerns, it was not surprising, though she would have expected Marston to shield his innocent and wealthy beauty of a daughter from a man like Alan with the zealousness of an evangelist.

'I'm afraid I didn't apply myself quite as I ought.'

'Only bores apply themselves as they ought, so that need not concern you. Now you can apply yourself as you wish. As long as you don't apply yourself wholly to what you oughtn't.'

Penny Marston's feather-soft brows drew together in confusion.

'Are you making game of me again, Lord Ravenscar?'

'He is trying to be clever and failing miserably, Miss Marston. Come, we should find ourselves a comfortable place to sit or risk being forced to stand through the wailing Italian as Lord Ravenscar so quaintly titled a woman accustomed to singing for kings and emperors.'

'An excellent idea. Allow me.'

That had not been quite what she intended, to find Alan seated between her and Miss Marston on one of the long upholstered benches arranged before the low stage where the musicians had already gathered. Lily met Philip Marston's sardonic smile, expecting him to sit by his daughter, but as he led Lady Ravenscar and Catherine over by some deft manoeuvre, he sat himself by Lily, with Catherine on his other side, while Lady Ravenscar was seated on Penny Marston's left side under the rationale that she would thus be furthest from any draught from the windows.

Lily caught the widening of Penny's eyes and turned in protest towards Philip Marston, but he merely smiled and murmured close to her ear, 'Don't worry for Penny. It will do her good to meet a tame dragon and Lord Ravenscar will shield her if need be. He has known her for many years. Here is the programme, Lady Catherine. I'm afraid there aren't enough, so we shall have to share. Do you speak Italian?'

Lily watched in trepidation as Lady Ravenscar began catechising the beauty, but clearly Philip Marston had been accurate and Penny's good manners were finding favour with her even without the threat of intervention from Alan and Lily began to relax, as much as she could seated between the two men.

If she needed any reminder of her folly, her treacherous body was only too happy to oblige. The room was a trifle cold and most women were swathed in shawls, but the whole left side of Lily's body was shimmering with warmth. She knew precisely how many inches separated her thigh from Alan's, three, and her elbow from his, two. If she just shifted a little to rearrange her shawl, she could finally bridge that chasm and...

'Do you happen to know what *strazio* means, Miss Wallace? The first song is in German, which is beyond us, but Lady Catherine and I have been attempting to decipher the Italian lyrics for the second song.'

Lily took the programme Philip Marston was extending to her and stared at the word he was pointing to, her mind untangling itself from shawls and chasms and heat.

'It means...' She cleared her throat. 'Torment. I think.'

'Is it a sad song, then?' Penny enquired.

'It is a song about a woman who is pledged to one man but keeps thinking about another,' Alan answered without inflection. 'Does that qualify as sad or merely a case of faulty judgement on her part?'

'Hush!' Lady Ravenscar said loudly as the singer, an unremarkable-looking woman with dark hair and eyes and a rather pinched mouth, finally climbed to the stage. The buzz and chatter around them thinned and stopped and then the heavens opened. The singer's voice rose above that of the violins, pure and true, the most beautiful thing Lily had heard in years. On Isla Padrones they had believed dead babies' souls were collected by angels who soothed their new charges' ascent to heaven with divine song. The villagers had sung as they took the housekeeper's baby to the little churchyard on the far side of the island, their voices radiating the same joy and hope of redemption. She hadn't cried then, she had been too guilty and too frightened and had not wanted to draw any more attention to herself as she shadowed the procession, but now it took all her effort not to sink her face in her hands and cry out her confusion, like the tired child she had been then.

The room held its breath until the last note shivered and faded and then the applause burst forth. Lily sat with her hands pressed together in a simulacrum of clapping or prayer, holding hard against the need to cry.

'Beautiful.' She hadn't meant to speak, it was hardly more than a breath, but Alan turned to her.

'Lily?'

He bent close to her, his breath smoothing over her cheek and pressing against her ear like a fluttering kiss. She shook her head and felt the careful ringlets Lady Ravenscar's maid had toiled over brush against him and then his finger touched the skin between her sleeve and the edge of her glove above her elbow, sliding down, as soft as a feather, the shawl concealing the contact. His voice was as soft, hardly a whisper.

'Don't. I'm sorry.'

Luckily the singing began again and the pain eased, but not the thudding of her pulse or the need to lean against him. She abandoned all attempt to remain in the room, letting everything fall away but his proximity, facing the truth. She had slept with her cheek against his chest, her hand in his. She knew the rhythm of his pulse. He probably didn't even remember that, but it was part of her and now her body was drawn to his as to a lodestone. Her tiny universe had expanded during those days at Hollywell and it now included one very unrepentant rake. She still had a choice, but it would require a more brutal act on her part than she had wanted to believe.

Chapter Fourteen

He had sunk low indeed. Bringing tepid lemonade to his grandmother at the Bristol Assembly Hall was not something he would have considered a possibility just a week ago. Once fate sank its talons into you, it did so with a vengeance.

'Where has Lily gone?' Lady Ravenscar hissed between clenched teeth as Alan handed her the glass. His own jaw tightened as he turned to view the room.

'Nowhere, Grandmother. She is with Cat and the Marstons.'

'Not any more, I saw her by the back door and that is not the direction of the withdrawing rooms. Why the devil is that man still fawning over her? I thought she sent him packing.'

'Lily is hedging her bets, Lady Jezebel.'

'And you are going to stand for that?'

He didn't bother replying. Anything he said at the moment would probably not end well. He had been stoking his anger at Lily for the past two days. It was a useful countermeasure to the persistent desire that pulsed through him like a remnant of the fever. It kept him focused on duty and action and away from the unsettling reactions to this impossible girl. Like that moment at the end of the first song when she had been leaning forward, her lips parted as if she had been the one singing. The candles had raised her warmth to fire, her hair shimmering with copper and gold and amber and her skin reflecting the blush peach of her dress. He didn't know what the taut, almost tragic expression on her face had meant, but she had been close to tears for a moment. It had been impossible not to reach out and touch her, however briefly, and even that tiny gesture had cost him, reminding him how much more he wanted than a chaste caress of her arm. Giving a sip of water to a man with a raging thirst was more torture than relief.

In a saner world he would have been able to take her hand, lead her out of this stifling room and...

He frowned and scanned the clusters of people talking and fanning themselves at the back of the room. On impulse he stepped into the hallway that separated the assembly hall from the smaller meeting rooms of the guildhall and glanced up the carpeted stairs guarded by a rather sad-looking Roman bust on a pedestal.

'Female troubles, too, Agrippa?' He patted the balding head as he moved towards the open door of the guild meeting hall across the hallway and paused in the doorway. A still figure stood looking up at the large painting commemorating the Battle of Trafalgar, all taut sails and thrashing waves and bursts of cannons. The room was cold and only the light from two high windows touched the lighter colours with some life.

'What are you hiding from now?'

She whirled around, her skirts billowing like a fluted flower.

'I am not hiding, I needed to think. Then I saw this painting and was curious.'

He was tempted to ask her what she had been thinking about, but he doubted it would redound to his credit. After Nicky's devastating discourse about children he didn't want to talk about anything profound. He looked at the painting instead.

'Decent, but inaccurate. The storm came after the battle was won, and the *HMS Sandwich* didn't even take part in the battle.'

'Let me guess, Nelson was a hero of yours and you know all the names of all the ships and whom they took as prizes.'

'Of course. I was fifteen. My friends and I were masters of naval strategy even though none of us had set foot on more than a barge. I would have joined the Navy when I left Ravenscar, but luckily by then I wanted Napoleon's head, so I enlisted with the Rifles instead.'

'Why luckily?'

'I get seasick.'

'Really?' Amusement warmed the gold in her eyes and some of his tension eased.

'Not really, but I definitely don't enjoy the thought of spending months at a stretch in a small space with a group of rank-smelling men eating weevil-riddled hard tack.'

'I can't imagine anyone does. Jackson, my groom, was pressed into service as a boy until my father took him to work with him. He had some horrific tales to tell. But the war must have been just as horrible. I saw those men today.'

'Peace has been just as hard on many of them. We had a purpose during the war and a family of sorts. All that went by the wayside when they returned to England, some less than whole in body or mind, and found they had no livelihood. A great deal more than vanity rides on a man's pride. Come, we need to return.' He hesitated. 'What were you thinking about?'

'Precisely that. Those men. Why didn't you just tell me you wanted Hollywell as a home for war veterans? I cannot understand why that is a secret.'

'Ah, the ferret is back. It isn't a secret, but it is private and no one's concern but ours. This is not a topic for a musical evening.'

'Why not?'

'Because. Besides, I told you we are no longer interested in Hollywell.'

'Yes, you are. You were telling Mr Tippet that Saltford is too small. If I am willing to put Hollywell at your disposal, why not take it?'

'What do you mean put it at our disposal?'

'Precisely that. I won't sell it because I understand from Mr Prosper that landed property is the only kind of property a married woman retains any form of control over, however truncated, but I will provide you with an indefinite lease at a symbolic cost and that way you could use the purchase price for any adjustments you need to make to the structure and for whatever other needs arise. I would have one stipulation, but it is a small one and we needn't discuss it now. I can speak with Mr Prosper tomorrow and you can begin bringing people there immediately.'

The words poured out of her, establishing facts and setting up barriers, and all the tension and anger he was trying to push aside returned, as hot and immediate as the desire she evoked in him so effortlessly.

'If this is some form of sacrificial apology because you think you can weasel your way out of this engagement, let me tell you…'

'It is an offer, pure and simple. Do you know that if you had a modicum of trust in people, we might have resolved this issue at Saltford and none of this would have happened? Let that be a lesson to you to be less secretive and distrustful in future. You forgo golden opportunities.'

'Is that what happened? Most people would argue that what happened is quite the opposite.'

'Oh, yes, I'm aware what a golden opportunity my inheritance is…'

He grasped her shoulders as she started moving past him.

'I actually wasn't referring to your three per cents, but to other assets altogether. But this is hardly the right place for me to clarify my meaning. Or perhaps it is, at least if we are interrupted, you won't be able to hide from your actions. This isn't a game and Marston and I are not two dolls on a shelf for you to choose from, so it is time to abandon the delusion that you have a choice here. You gambled with your fate and you lost— that is life. I suggest you stop all this soulful flirting with Marston and start honouring the hand you dealt yourself. In a week we will announce our engagement to friends and you can begin planning your bridals.'

'How could any woman resist such a sweetly phrased offer?'

She tried to pull away, but he held firm, moving in.

'Is that what you want? Once I have you somewhere we are less likely to be interrupted, I will show you precisely how hard it will be to resist a sweetly phrased offer. Stop acting like Andromeda being offered as sacrifice to some damn sea monster. And Marston is no Perseus.'

He was too angry to be conciliating, but instead of matching his thrust she withdrew in one of her disconcerting surrenders that always left him far more vulnerable than victor.

'I know that. If anyone is the sacrifice here, it is you because this is all my fault. You must think me terribly ungrateful and spoilt. But that is precisely the point, you see. I don't want anyone to suffer because of my mistakes. I've not only ruined your life, but also brought this strife between you and Philip when neither of you are to blame. It is so unfair.'

He should tell her that right now it didn't feel at all like a sacrifice. Not with her looking up at him with that mix of contrition and compassion, her lips soft and parted, just waiting for him to taste them again. Right now the only thing that felt like a sacrifice was the weeks that would have to pass before he could finally do something about this aggravating, aching need. He felt perilously close to that sea monster, focused on mindless devouring.

He needed to take her back into the main hall, he needed to keep his footing in the shifting sands around her, he needed…

He pressed her back, bringing her up against the door.

'I'm not concerned with fairness at the moment.

Just stay away from Marston. Understand?' He didn't give her a chance to answer. His body moulded itself against hers, his mouth finally lowering to find the moist warmth he was thirsting for, filling with her scent and taste. It was hopeless. He *needed* this. This wasn't the passion and pleasure he knew so well; it was like drinking the finest cognac after years of warm ale. He wouldn't be able to go back even if he wanted to and he didn't.

He felt her shiver between him and the door and he gentled the kiss and pulled away, cupping her face in his hands. Her eyes opened slowly and he waited out the inevitable burn of heat that struck him at the half-lost softness there. His once-clear vision of the future was lying in a shamble at her feet and he had no idea where he was heading. He had made wealth, he had found purpose and, until he had walked into the library at Hollywell, he hadn't wanted or needed anything else.

But everything precious came at a price. He had never thought he would have to pay this one.

He breathed in, twice.

'Come. We must return to the others.'

'There you are, Miss Wallace. Ravenscar,' Marston said as he and Catherine intercepted them as they entered the assembly hall. 'Lady Ravenscar asked Lady Catherine and myself to find you. She said she had already sent you, Ravenscar, but perhaps you were feeling unwell, Miss Wallace?'

Lily raised her chin at the censure in his voice.

'Everything is quite all right, Mr Marston. Lord Ravenscar and I were merely discussing my offer to lease Hollywell House to his war veteran foundation.'

Alan couldn't help smiling at Lily's diversionary tactics. By the look on Marston's face it was a surprise attack worthy of Wellington.

'I… What?'

'The Hope House foundation, Mr Marston,' Catherine's calm voice poured soothing oil on the rising waves as she explained the nature of the foundation and Alan's original plans for Hollywell before Albert's death. 'I think that is very generous of you, Lily,' she concluded. 'So is it settled then?'

Alan ignored his sister's double entendre.

'Not quite. I explained to Miss Wallace that though Hollywell House is the right size, we would need to make structural adjustments to it that she might not be willing to countenance.'

'And I explained to Lord Ravenscar that I will not object to adjustments as long as they respect the spirit of the original structure.'

'Could you not find a structure in Bristol?' Marston asked.

'Not of that size and with grounds where we could construct a manufactory to employ the men. We have found they mend better when they have gainful employment. Believe me, I have looked high and low this past week. We are about to lease a property near Saltford—'

'Which is inadequate by your own admission,' Lily interrupted. 'I suggest you swallow your pride and send your men to inspect Hollywell tomorrow, Lord Ravenscar. Now, we should take our places for the second act. Lady Ravenscar is beckoning.'

Finally it was over. Lily kept her smile firmly on her face and tried to listen to Lady Ravenscar, Catherine and Marston dissect the singer's skills as they moved along with the crowd towards the entrance, but her whole concentration was on the man behind her. As she was edged aside by a portly couple, her shawl caught on the arm of a chair placed against the wall and she paused to untangle it.

'Allow me.' Alan brushed aside her hands and took the shawl.

'I can do it myself, thank you.'

'Yes, I know, but it's done. Here, turn around.'

She met the challenge in his eyes as he held the swathe of silk, aware of the flow of people. To quarrel would only attract attention and more censure. She turned.

'Relax. You're as stiff as a sail in the high wind,' he murmured as he draped the shawl over her shoulders. His breath whispered along her exposed nape, stirring the soft hairs there, preparing her flesh for the kiss she knew could not follow. Then his fingers fell away, just skimming the length of her arm as if arranging the silken folds. 'Birds of paradise. Very fitting… You looked like one in this flock of pigeons and hens. Fire and light and completely out of place. And very hard to capture.'

His voice sank to a whisper and she shivered, a clammy cold skittering under the heat his words and touch were sparking. She wasn't hard to capture; she was snared, utterly. Her legs were shaking and she felt ill with the need to turn to him and either slap him for what he was doing to her or beg him to take her out of there, with him. He had hardly touched her, but just that soft brush of his flesh on hers and she was on fire again, it was staining her cheeks, as corrosive as acid.

She could hear her own pulse, sharp convulsive gasps of her heart as his fingers curved over her elbow, taking her arm to guide her towards the door and another step towards her fate.

Chapter Fifteen

Alan watched the bemused group of men trail along behind Lily as she pointed towards the shuttered windows of the north wing of Hollywell. They stopped and Tippet scribbled on his pad while the two masons stood elbows akimbo, heads cocked to one side like two curious sparrows trailing an exotic bird.

He should have known it was a mistake to concede even as much as this examination of Hollywell, because the masons and carpenters had already decided it would be easier to modify to their purposes than Saltford and had said so in Lily's presence, leading to disastrous results. She had commandeered Tippet and the masons, left Catherine and Nicky to inspect the contents of the linen closets and marched off, leaving Alan with the carpenters and workmen to inspect the roofs. Tippet hadn't even asked for Alan's approval to disappear with her, the traitor, Alan mused as he watched the mutiny disappear around the corner of the north wing.

He didn't know if he had it in him to turn down her offer. He should. If he knew one thing about Lily by now, it was that she needed the safety of an island of her own, which was precisely why she had run here when she had wanted to think. This made her willingness to sacrifice it all the more touching, but for her sake he should keep Hollywell inviolate for her. He should have thought of that before and warned the masons and Tippet to offer all forms of reasonable explanations why Hollywell was inappropriate, but he hadn't been prepared for her insistence on overseeing them like a little general.

He sighed. It would lead to another battle royal, but it was unavoidable.

'Is this what you asked for?'

Alan turned to face the tall man striding across the stable courtyard, the sun striking gold in hair the colour of late wheat and a flash of silver in the deep-set eyes. He was always happy to see Stanton, but the extreme degree of relief he felt at seeing his friend was a sign of how low he had sunk since his arrival in Somerset.

He took the extended document and clapped his friend on the shoulder.

'Stanton! Damn, it's good to see you, man. I didn't expect you to bring it yourself.'

'I'm afraid my curiosity isn't equal to the challenge of sending a deputy when one of my two best friends requests I procure a special licence from the Archbishop of Canterbury. Especially when that friend is you. What on earth has happened and who is Lily Wallace?'

Alan tucked the licence into his coat pocket.

'Straight to the crux of the matter as usual. Come, we need some brandy to make this comprehensible. At least I do.'

'That bad? When I warned you that if you ever fell you would fall hard, I didn't expect it to be on your face, Raven.'

'I was actually happy to see you for a moment there, Stanton. Would you mind saving your compliments until I have a glass in my hand?'

'Not at all. So you managed to secure Hollywell from the new heirs after all? Your last communication wasn't so promising. What did you do, threaten to set your grandmother on them?'

'No, compromise them. Lily Wallace is the heir.'

Alan had rarely seen Stanton, the master of diplomatic finesse, bereft of words. He closed the library door and went over to the cupboard where Albert had kept his brandy. He was just handing Stanton his glass when the door opened and Lily and Tippet entered.

'Lord Ravenscar, Mr Tippet and I were wondering… Oh. I'm sorry, I didn't mean to interrupt, but I'm afraid the masons need to know whether we plan to open the wall in the north wing.'

Alan subdued his various warring reactions to her appearance and tried to make sense of her question.

'Why on earth would we need to do that?'

'For the bath chairs. I thought that if we convert the north wing to bedrooms for those who cannot climb the stairs, we should still ensure those men can enter and exit the house without encountering stairs. Like a gangway. A paved one. The north wing is lower lying than the south wing and the mason said we could transform the blind wall at the end of the corridor into another door leading directly to the back courtyard.'

Her voice slowed as they remained silent, as if explaining something to the very dim. Stanton recovered first and moved towards her, hand extended.

'What an excellent idea. Good morning, Mr Tippet. I will save my graceless friend the bother of making introductions because you must clearly be Miss Wallace. I am Lord Alexander Stanton. What a pleasure to meet you.'

Alan waited for the inevitable reaction almost all women had when confronted with Stanton. When he bothered to charm them, which was rarely, they fell like ninepins. When he employed that smile, the effect was often catastrophic.

Lily took the extended hand and smiled and Alan relaxed. He knew the shades of her smiles and this one was friendly, curious, but definitely not bowled over.

'Ah, the least wild of the Wild Hunt Club. You are in the Foreign Office, correct?'

Stanton's smile widened.

'Correct on both counts. The gangway is an interesting idea; I wonder why we never thought of it.'

'I will treat that as a rhetorical question, Lord Stanton, since any answer I give is likely to offend. Are you here to help?'

'I admit I did come here to help, but I see my offices are absolutely unnecessary.'

Lily's eyes narrowed and she pulled her hand away from Stanton's lingering clasp and looked past him to Alan.

'Shall I tell them to make the measurements, then, Lord Ravenscar?'

He nodded, unequal to arguing with her at the moment, and she smiled at both of them and left, Tippet at her heels.

They both stood watching the closed door for a moment.

'I'm losing my touch,' Stanton said. 'And you've either lost your heart or found your senses. That was not what I was expecting.'

'Lily is not what anyone would expect.'

'No details until I have a glass in my hand. I'm parched after driving all the way on my mission to save my best friend from being forced to the altar against his wishes.'

'Can you?'

'Even if I could, I am not certain I would. I like her. A paved gangway. Since when is she part of the Hope House effort?'

'Since this morning. Or rather since yesterday when she offered us Hollywell. I hadn't realised my tentative agreement to consider Hollywell included allowing her to shadow Tippet and the masons and to set my sister and niece to cataloguing the linen, but to be fair it is her property.'

'A young lady accustomed to command. Interesting. Tell me about her.'

Alan handed him a glass and told him.

'If you laugh, I'll do some damage to that perfect face of yours, Stanton,' he concluded as his friend's smile hovered on the edge of a grin.

'I won't, I promise. I'm as worried as hell. I never would have placed odds that you and Hunter would both become tenants for life within two months of each other after a lifetime of evading that fate with such religious zeal. My faith in my abilities to predict the future actions of men or nations is sadly shaken. But did she have to be an heiress? You know this will

just give credence to all those tales about the dispos-
sessed rake. Does the fact that you have been allowed
back into the Hall mean you are now restored into your
grandmother's good graces as well?'

'Since she isn't restored into mine, I neither know
nor care. We are in a state of armed neutrality and I am
staying at the Hall merely to ensure our courtship, such
as it is, has credibility. I don't need Jezebel's money
and you know it.'

'Still, if you are going to marry and have a brood
of children, you will need a home.'

'Marry, yes, children, no. And I have a home. Two
of them.'

'A house by a manufactory in Birmingham and a
bachelor's residence on St James's Street most certainly
do not qualify as homes. But you cannot still be serious about not breeding. Even if that young woman be-
lieves this is merely a marriage of form, she cannot be
so naïve not to know you are likely to bed her. I saw the
way you were watching us. You were ready to drive a
carriage between us if need be.'

He shrugged. He wasn't ready yet to put into words
his chaotic thoughts and feelings.

'Wanting to bed a woman and willingly making a
pact with the devil are two different things. You know
I swore never to have any children.'

'You swore never to marry and never to cross your
grandmother's threshold, too, so forgive me for not
being impressed with your record.'

'This is different.'

'I agree, it bloody well is. You cannot possibly mean
to marry that delectable girl and keep that resolve.'

'I am perfectly capable of bedding a woman without leading to conception, I have been doing so quite successfully for almost half my life.'

'Yes, but this would be your wife, Raven. Surely she wants children?'

Alan went to refill his glass and Stanton continued.

'How long are you going to punish yourself? This makes no sense.'

'I am not punishing myself. Quite the opposite. Having a child would be the ultimate punishment.'

'So you would condemn her to a life without offspring merely because you are a coward.'

Alan winced, though it was the truth. The rushing river of fear, pain and need that had coursed through him at Nicky's excited babblings about children had still not quieted. The images clung—Lily reading aloud, with a little red-haired girl leaning on her and on her other side, more shadowy, a little boy, dark haired, small hands curved around a ball.

He made a last effort to cling to the vision of his fate he had presented to Lily by the lake.

'I won't stop her if she wishes to...go her own way. As long as she is discreet, she is welcome to conceive as many children as she can bear, literally and figuratively. The *ton* is littered with other men's offspring anyway. I don't see why I should be any different.'

Stanton shook his head.

'My God, you're even more cold-blooded than I thought. No wonder she is considering Marston's offer. Are you purposely trying to drive her away?'

'No. I am merely trying to ensure she isn't disappointed.'

Stanton stood up. 'If you set the bar any lower, she won't have any choice but to step over it, Alan. Now, as much as I would love to continue observing the details of your downfall, I've left my poor horses out there and it's been a long drive. I'll rack up at the Pelican in Bristol, so come pay your respects before I drive back tomorrow.'

'Busy?'

'Very. I'm off to Vienna to discuss how far south the Austrians can go in Italy. I told Hunter I'd come and save you if need be, but if I couldn't, it is up to him and Nell to hold your hand during the ceremony.'

'They might not have to follow your directives after all if Marston gets his way. As for you, try not to get kidnapped by pirates or shot by princes this time. I might be too busy in the near future to come to your rescue again.'

'To be fair I had already escaped when you and Hunter came to rescue me from Derna and it was the veiled bride who was my saviour of sorts on Illiakos, so I think I shall survive even if you are too busy lying to yourself about how much you are the captain of your fate, Raven. I wish I could delay sailing just for the pleasure of watching your expression as you sign the register under the parson's beaming smile, but I promise to try to be there for the christening.'

Alan watched the curricle disappear down the drive and turned to inspect the façade of the house. A little sunshine, however weak, made any house seem more welcoming and Hollywell was no exception. They had done nothing yet and already it looked more like the home he remembered from Jasper and Mary's days. It only reinforced his conviction that Lily should not relinquish her sanctuary. He might not need a home in the sense that Stanton just mentioned, but Lily did and he knew what this place symbolised for her. If she gave them Hollywell, she would have nothing that was truly hers. All her money amounted to nothing more than a banker's draft waiting to be withdrawn by whoever married her. Hollywell had come to mean something different for her, and if he took that, too… In a fair world this should be her home, someplace she could be safe and build her own world. Have the family she wanted. Not as his mistake or as Marston's property.

Could he do it? Let go that last vow and risk the pain. For her.

She would be a good mother. Both stronger and more vulnerable than his. He could see how his mother had never known how to navigate the barriers set by his grandparents. Lily would probably have put his rigid grandfather to flight and tamed his grandmother just as she had these past weeks. All that pain and need inside her only made her strong. What was she asking for in the end? A child. So what if it felt like she was the guardian of hell asking for his soul? Perhaps this was his punishment, to risk that pain again.

This was the real choice—release her to marry Marston or tell her he would marry her on her terms.

No, the real choice was whether he was willing to allow her into his life. Or whether he was capable of letting her go. If so, he had better do so sooner rather than later because with each passing hour that thought was becoming more unacceptable.

The rumble of wheels alerted him and he turned at the top of the steps to see a carriage approaching. He cursed under his breath and waited for the carriage to draw up and the footman to lower the steps.

'Hello, Marston, Miss Marston. Welcome to Holly-well. To what do we owe this pleasure?' He stood back to wave them up the stairs into the house, wishing them at the devil.

'Penny and I decided to take advantage of the fine weather to pay a visit. Lady Ravenscar's butler informed us you were all at Hollywell. Since our visit is partly motivated by some news I have heard which might be pertinent for your effort here, we decided to join you.'

He paused as three figures appeared at the top of the stairs and smiled.

'Good afternoon, Lady Catherine, Miss Wallace. And this must be your beautiful daughter, Lady Catherine. We apologise for the intrusion.'

'You are always welcome, but I'm afraid Hollywell isn't ready to receive guests, Mr Marston,' Lily said as she descended. When she was in her social mode, Alan found it hard to gauge her thoughts, but the very fact that she had withdrawn into her cool shell was telling. She was nervous and alert. He had no idea if that boded ill for him or for Marston. 'But the library is almost habitable, so we should proceed there. Unless Tabby and Grim have laid it to waste again.'

'Who?' Penny asked curiously, and Nicky launched into an animated recounting of the haunting which Lily had shared with her and Catherine. Mr Marston watched his daughter with Nicky for a moment and smiled.

'Together they look like that child's tale my daughter used to love, *Snow-White and Rose-Red*. She would imagine she had a sister like Rose-Red, dark haired and lively.'

Catherine smiled. 'That certainly describes Nicola.'

'You mentioned a proposition, Marston?' Alan interrupted.

'Ah, yes. I was in a meeting with the mayor regarding the planned installation of lock gates on the river and overheard a discussion regarding the Grantham Road Workhouse I believe you might find interesting. Apparently the Parish is in financial difficulties and will have no choice but to sell the property which has been standing empty since they acquired it a year ago. This is not yet public knowledge and I asked the mayor if we might have the right of first refusal. From what I could see outside it is a little larger than this structure and has the benefit of being on the edge of town with some fields behind it that I believe are also open for purchase at the right price. It is also no more than half a mile from the manufactory you and I were considering.'

'But they no longer need a property,' Lily interrupted. 'They have Hollywell.'

'I believe the Grantham Road building is more suitable for the purpose, Miss Wallace,' Marston replied. 'Do you know the place, Lord Ravenscar?'

'I do, but I hadn't realised they were looking to sell. Are you certain of this?'

Marston raised his brows.

'Of course. The mayor is merely waiting for our response. If you wish, we can proceed there now.'

'Oh, Papa, must we leave right away? We have just arrived here and Nicola said we could go and meet a ghost dog.'

'Perhaps Miss Marston could stay here with us while you and my brother attend to your business?' Catherine suggested, her eyes questioning Alan, and he nodded, very aware Lily had not said a word. 'Good. We shall take good care of her, Mr Marston. When we are done here, we will have tea at the Hall and meet you there on your return.'

'Oh, excellent!' Nicky clapped her hands and took Miss Marston's hand, tugging her towards the door. 'Come, I last saw Grim sniffing around the old conservatory searching for Tabby, not that it is really a conservatory, just an old parlour. His name is Grim because Uncle Alan named him after the fable of Church Grims, which are black dogs that guard graveyards, and that was where he found him when he was a puppy...'

Catherine laughed as their voices faded.

'Poor Nicola, she has been pining for someone nearer her own age after being isolated with her mama and grandmama. I should probably keep an eye on them or Nicola will not let your daughter get a word in edgeways. Are you coming, Lily?'

Lily nodded, slowly, her gaze moving between Marston and Alan. When the honey brown of her eyes settled on Alan, he felt no warmth there. She was miles away. He had a visceral urge to reassure her, but he knew there was nothing he could say with Marston and Catherine standing there. For the moment it couldn't matter if she saw this as a personal rejection. Lily might not know it, but she needed Hollywell.

'Coming, Ravenscar?'

'Yes. Let me just tell my steward and groom to meet us there.

'Well? More suitable than Hollywell House, don't you agree?'

Alan descended the stairs into the courtyard, where Marston stood waiting.

'Yes. There is no need for you to wait, Marston. We are likely to be a while. I've asked my groom to fetch the rest of the men.'

'Good.'

'I am still going to marry her, though.'

Marston's smile flattened. 'You are entitled to your opinion.'

'Is it pride keeping you in the game or are you finally beginning to realise she is wrong for you, Marston?'

'I could ask the same question of you, Ravenscar.'

'I know Lily a little better than you.'

'By George, you're an arrogant devil. You've known her for all of a couple of weeks and I've known her since she was seventeen.'

'Which just goes to show how wrong you are for her, because in all those years you still haven't got her measure, Marston. She might have managed her father's house like a social goddess, but she is no more a hostess than I am. She has discipline, that is all. There's no passion for the vocation behind it.'

'I'm not marrying her to be my hostess.'

'You're not marrying her at all. But that *was* one reason, wasn't it—you want a cool, socially adept wife to add a cachet to your business dealings. The other and more important reason is to produce the perfect heir for your business. I'll concede that any child of Lily's is likely to be intelligent, not to mention wilful, but you are doubly delusional if you believe you will have the schooling of that child. She'll trump you on every hand. If ever I've seen a woman who will command the love and loyalty of her children without even trying, that is Lily. She won't actively overrule you, but the result will be the same. Her values will win over yours every time.'

Marston faced him, feet apart and arms crossed, but Alan wasn't fooled by his cool, mocking smile. Every line of his rival's body spoke of arrows hitting home. But each arrow struck home with him as well. One piercing him with the image of Lily with a baby in her arms, laughing. Another with her as he had seen her in his fevered hallucination with Rickie, seated by a little boy, reading to him. Of a little girl with her flame-touched hair, running towards him. He clenched his hands against the assault and continued.

'Then there is the price she will make you pay for taking away her freedom because you aren't really about to allow her to manage her inheritance beyond whatever generous pin money you allow her in the settlement, correct?'

'She will have a family to keep her occupied. That is what she wants and that is precisely why she won't have you, Ravenscar, so you are wasting your time.'

'Perhaps. I'm done with my lecture. Just think about whether you want to continue pressing your suit or whether you should be looking for someone more suitable for your plans. You're a good man and a damn good business partner, Marston, and I don't want to break up a very comfortable partnership, but I will fight you over this with every weapon in my arsenal until you drive me decisively into the sea.'

'I suppose I should thank you for showing your cards so openly.'

'I'm hoping you will one day thank me for my advice and for helping you avoid a serious mistake.'

Marston unfolded his arms, shaking his head. 'Are

you certain you don't want to consider my Penny instead? If I don't have children, at least I would be sure of being able to leave my legacy in the hands of someone as single-mindedly ruthless as you.'

'No offence to your beautiful daughter, but no, thank you, Marston. My taste runs more towards fire than the ethereal.'

'So be it. It is time I joined my daughter and her charming hostesses. You might have drawn a high card with that unfortunate incident at Hollywell, but I don't know if your luck will continue to hold out, Ravenscar.'

'Any decent gambler knows never to rely on luck alone, Marston. I will meet you back at the Hall.'

Chapter Sixteen

Grim straightened, eyebrows twitching, nose raised. It gave her just enough of a warning before the door opened and Alan entered the Rose Room accompanied by Lord Stanton. Their light and dark beauty was a devastating combination, Gabriel and Lucifer. If Lord Stanton hadn't been dressed in a dark blue coat and breeches, he could have been a model for Apollo—tall and powerful and handsome as a god, the candlelight striking gold and silver in his light brown hair and his eyes the colour of ice floes. She watched as Penny Marston and Nicky stared in shy awe at the new entrant and sighed. Next to him Alan looked even more dangerous and she could see why they practically begged an epithet. It would always be like this with Alan. No wonder he was so sure of himself.

He paused on the threshold, surveying the group by the pianoforte and nodding to his grandmother, who sat on a sofa where she could watch the keys, her hands folded on the knob of her cane like a strict music master. Then he touched his forehead in a strange salute to Philip Marston, who stood between his daughter and

Nicky as they sang to Catherine's playing. After the introductions Stanton chose to sit by Lady Ravenscar, with just the hint of the devil in his smile, while Alan approached Lily in the window seat. She straightened but kept her eyes on the pianoforte, resisting the instinctive pull that struck her every time the blasted man walked into a room. However furious she might be at him, inside she felt just as ecstatic at seeing him as Grim looked. She became a puppet on a string around him, reactive, helpless. She hated it.

'What a charming scene,' he said as he sat down beside her, his knee briefly skimming her thigh as he turned to her. Another seemingly casual trespass on her space. Except that it wasn't casual, not for her. She was already aware of him in every inch of her body, but now her skin felt like brushfire. He snapped his fingers at Grim, who trotted towards him, mouth open and panting with joy. 'I'm impressed Lady Jezebel invited them to stay for dinner and the entertainment. She and my grandfather were not the most sociable of people, but Catherine appears to be right that she has mellowed with age. Marston is fitting in nicely, isn't he?'

'He has a very fine voice.'

'And delightful manners. I presume they included telling you I am making an offer on the Grantham Road property, which means we will not be needing Hollywell after all.'

'He told me.'

'It is better this way.'

'His words exactly.'

'Marston and I might not want you to lease Hollywell to Hope House, but our reasons are very different.'

She folded her hands together, wishing she had chosen a chair rather than the window seat. The velvet curtains kept the cool night air out, but now they mirrored the heat rising in her. Every time he came near her she expanded, all the emotions that should be mild and controlled filling and turning wild and too large for her skin. She had been waiting for him to come and now she wished him gone. Or to be alone with him.

'Aren't you going to ask what they are?' he prodded.

'I am certain you have perfectly good reasons, Lord Ravenscar. If you don't wish to share them, that is your prerogative.'

He leaned back against the curtain, crossing his arms.

'You bear a striking resemblance to Lily Wallace, but you can't possibly be her; she would have skewered me to the wall by now. Or has all this domestic charm finally broken your spirit?'

No, you have.

He shifted, the depth of the window seat providing cover for his hand as he traced his fingers down her spine as softly as the fall of her hair. They lingered on the small of her back, gathering the shiver that ran through her, and she saw his chest rise and fall before he drew his hand away. He might have power over her heart and mind, but she had her own power over him and that was a step in the right direction.

'I'm offering you something I have never offered any woman, or ever thought I would.'

For a moment her mind glided away on the soft warmth of his words, allowing herself the fantasy of what might have been said. If their intimate pressure was an invitation to bring their lives together, to build on those two days of mutual caring, on her instinctive knowledge that he could be so much more than he believed of himself.

The risk was so great, but so was the reward.

'I know you are.'

His hand returned to her hip, almost as if he would draw her towards him, an impossibility in the civilised drawing room.

'Tell him to stay away, then.'

'Is this a privilege you reserve for yourself or am I allowed to tell you who you may associate with as well?'

She turned to him and he folded his arms again.

'Don't be clever, Lily. You aren't going to marry him, so for both your sakes you should send him on his way. You risk hurting him.'

'So this is pure magnanimity on your part? Or are you concerned this might harm your mutual business concerns?'

'Blast it, Lily…'

They had both been speaking quietly, but his words fell into the silence that followed the final chords of the music and they shivered in the air alongside the remnants of the song.

'Do you play, Miss Wallace?' Stanton asked, moving towards them, but his arched brow was directed at Alan.

'I have had the pleasure of hearing Miss Wallace often when she played for her father's guests,' Marston said as he helped Catherine rise from the pianoforte. 'Please come play something for us, Miss Wallace.'

Lily didn't want to play, but she allowed Stanton to lead her to the pianoforte. She spread her fingers on the keys and noticed they were shaking. She had intended to play Mozart, but the moment her fingers touched the cool slide of the keys they shifted, spread, choosing for her. The Scarlatti sonata had been one of her mother's favourites, sent by her father the last summer before she died, and Lily had played it often to the sound of frogs and crickets and the lapping of waves coming in from the veranda. He had sent it with a beautiful emerald necklace as an apology for missing his visit and that had been one of the times she had seen her mother cry. All the confused emotions of a thirteen-year-old had entered the music and ten years later she felt they were still there, a tangle of need and sadness and fury held deep underwater, but under them all such a welling of love it choked her. It was more a love song than any of the ballads Marston and Catherine had just sung.

The music faded to the last chord and she took her hands from the keys. She shouldn't have looked. With Grim by his side and the window-seat curtains casting a shadow over him, he looked like a statue cast in black marble of a guardian of a portal to Hades, unyielding and unreachable. Which made her the poor soul, coins clutched in her hand, delivering herself into his world, and surely a life of watching his infidelities from her golden prison would be a version of hell, at least for her. But so would a life without him. So she would have to fight their demons and hope that in the end she won. For both of them.

She didn't hear the applause or even notice when Marston came to lead her to the sofa, his voice low and warm with appreciation. Penny and Nicky began a game of charades and even Lady Ravenscar entered the fray, but Alan just came and leaned against the side of the pianoforte and watched them, arms crossed.

* * *

When Partridge brought in tea for the ladies and something more potent for the men, Lily was surprised to find Stanton choosing the seat next to hers. She caught the tension in the look Alan directed him and the same edge of mischief in the look Lord Stanton directed him as he had sat by Lady Ravenscar. Perhaps she had been wrong that this was the tamest member of the Wild Hunt Club.

'You play exquisitely, Miss Wallace. It must have taken many years of instruction to achieve such a pitch of beauty.'

'Is this flattery in aid of something, Lord Stanton?'

He paused and the amusement shimmered to the surface.

'Actually, it is. Can you blame me for being curious about the woman who will become my best friend's wife?'

'Not at all, I would be curious myself. However, I am certain Lord Ravenscar has told you no such announcement has yet been made. I would appreciate if you respected that.'

'Of course, I can be extremely circumspect. If need be.'

She smiled at the qualification.

'You are quite used to having the world bend to your will, aren't you, Lord Stanton?'

'I do my humble best to ensure it does.'

'Why am I not surprised? Your association with Lord Ravenscar should have warned me and on top of that you are also a politician. A lethal combination.'

'A diplomat, not quite a politician, and apparently

not much of a diplomat if you see through my façade so easily.'

'Not at all. I am merely naturally wary. So, have you come to scout the enemy's landscape?'

'No, I came to deliver something of importance to Raven, but you are no enemy, Miss Wallace, quite the opposite.'

'That is politic. However, I know Lord Ravenscar has probably told you all the particulars of our predicament. Surely as his friend you are concerned about his being manoeuvred into an association against his will.'

'Alan rarely does anything that is completely against his will. He is even more used than I to having the world bend to his demands, possibly because he has had to work harder at it. That doesn't mean he is an untrustworthy fellow. I would trust him with my life. Well, I already have, in fact.'

She would also trust him with her life, just not with her heart. Now she would have to trust him with that, too.

'How long have you known him?'

He accepted the change in direction with a slight bow.

'Eighteen years. Raven arrived at Eton halfway through the year and into the middle of a rather bitter war being waged between a group of bullies against a friend of mine and myself and a few others. Raven was already very tall and very surly and they took one look at him and invited him into the winning camp.'

'So you began as enemies?'

'Not quite. He took one look at them and walked across the lines so to speak. When they tried to… reason with him, he broke Crawley's nose. He might have been sent down right away except no one would speak against him. That was that. Well, it took a few months to get him to more than snarl, but by the next year he and Hunter and I became close friends and that was that. Raven always had my back.'

'You are very lucky, you three. To have each other.'

His brows rose, as if surprised. Then he smiled and she smiled back. He had a very nice smile when he dropped his charming façade.

'We take care of each other in a way. Which is why I am naturally curious about you.'

'Of course. Now that you have seen the scheming hussy who has entrapped your friend, are you going to forbid the banns?'

He laughed.

'I believe with a special licence that practice doesn't apply.'

'A special licence?'

'Yes, didn't Raven tell you?' Stanton's attempt at innocence was distinctly unconvincing. 'That is the real reason why I came. He asked me to apply for one with the Archbishop. He is clearly taking his new role very seriously.'

'Does he know how much you are enjoying his downfall, Lord Stanton?'

'Most assuredly he does. He made enough game of Hunter when he fell in love with Nell, it is only fair he suffer a little of his own medicine.'

She shook her head. Men were sometimes beyond her understanding. They certainly had peculiar ways of showing their affection for each other. She cast a careful glance at where Alan was standing by Catherine and Nicky, his dark head bent to something his niece was saying as her hands danced expressively. She turned back to Stanton.

'Did he ever tell you about Rickie?'

His smile held, but the warmth behind it doused utterly. This more than anything told her precisely how strong the ties between these men were.

'Yes. Not until he was much older. He doesn't confide easily. It clarified quite a few things for us.'

'So you know he doesn't want children.'

'Yes. I know.'

Perhaps she had been hoping for a dismissal or a denial or even another politic qualification.

'Both my best friends lost brothers in tragic circumstances and both have to suffer the pain and, what is worse, the guilt,' he continued. 'We each have our own crosses to bear and I don't presume to be able to understand their brand of pain any more than I expect them to understand mine. I do expect them to accommodate me, though, which is enough of a presumption.'

She plucked at her gloves and he continued.

'It doesn't mean you have to let him win, though. He isn't as smart as he thinks. In fact, if anyone is a damn fool… Ah, hello, Raven. We were just talking about you.'

'Were you? Should I be flattered or should I be searching for the knife in my back?'

'Unworthy, my friend. I was just telling Miss Wallace how pleased I am at your betrothal.'

'No such announcement has been made, Lord Stanton,' Lily repeated and Lord Stanton stood up and bowed.

'Of course, Miss Wallace. I stand corrected. How pleased I am to make your acquaintance, then.'

Alan took the vacated seat as Stanton moved towards the others. He turned to her, every line of his body signalling a threat.

'You two appeared to be quite friendly.'

'Did we? I like him. He is very charming.'

'I know he's charming. Women keep falling over themselves to capture his attention and half the time he doesn't even realise it. Try not to join their ranks.'

She laughed at the absurdity.

'Surely you aren't jealous? That is rather facetious after you yourself advised me I would have to seek what I wanted with other men.'

He shifted abruptly, the mocking distance disappearing from his face.

'You wouldn't. Not Stanton.'

For a moment she saw the twelve-year-old boy who had been sent to Eton within months of losing everything he loved, faced with impossible guilt and impossible choices and still choosing to stand with what he thought was right. She reached out and caught herself, clasping her hands in her lap.

'I would never do that to you. That isn't who I am.'

She watched the tension in the etched line of his jaw and the razor-slashed grooves in his cheeks.

'*If* I married you, Alan, I would be faithful. *That* is who I am. You should put aside considerations of honour and decide if that is what you want.'

Both of them were saved from his answer by Lord Stanton's announcement that he had to return to Bristol as he was going back to London early in the morning. In her own inimitable fashion Lady Ravenscar managed to extend her farewells to the Marstons as well and within twenty minutes the room had been cleared of all guests and Catherine was chiding a yawning Nicky towards the door.

'To bed with you, Nicky.'

'That was nice. I like them, Mama. I hope they come again. Isn't Lord Stanton so very handsome? Just like a prince…'

'Yes, my dear. Upstairs with you.'

The door closed behind them and Lady Ravenscar levered herself to her feet.

'It has been a long evening. I will retire as well. Goodnight, Lily. Alan.'

Lily straightened, the numbness falling away as she realised what Lady Ravenscar was doing. No, she wasn't ready to be alone with him, but the door had already clicked shut and the tapping of Lady Belle's cane faded.

'My grandmother has significantly mellowed if she is willing to lower herself to such manoeuvres to further her ends,' Alan said as he sat down beside her on the sofa. 'This is not something my grandfather would have permitted, no matter how sublime the cause.'

'Goodnight, Lord Ravenscar.' She began to rise, but he caught her arm, pulling her back down beside him.

'We aren't done yet.'

'I am tired, Lord Ravenscar. I wish to retire.'

The dark night shades of his eyes had softened a little, revealing the silver that would flash when his compassion or amusement surfaced. It tugged an answering response from her, but she resisted it. She didn't want to soften right now. She had heard of foxes that chewed through a trapped limb to escape a poacher's snare. She just needed to gather her resolve.

'Yes, I can see that. You are escaping back to your

island, aren't you? First we are going to discuss Hollywell. Why don't you just admit you are secretly glad you can keep Hollywell for yourself?' he continued, but the underlying truth in his question opened the floodgates.

'Because I'm not. If I did agree to marry you, I would have a lifetime to be alone because in the end that is all you are able to offer me. I wanted to fill that house with people and children, even if they weren't my own. I wanted to turn the drawing room upstairs in the south wing into a schoolroom and there would be a reading room for them so I could read to those who hadn't learned yet, or who just wanted to listen. I know what you think you are doing, Alan, but you are wrong. This just proves it.'

She gasped as his hands shot out and grabbed her shoulders, forcing her to face him.

'I won't let you marry Marston.'

His obtuseness drove her pain into rage. She could feel the ebb of her tide, the rise of the destructive anger, but she had been holding back too much that day to stop it from crashing through her.

'Let go of me! I didn't say I would marry him, but I didn't say I would marry you, either. I don't like the terms, Ravenscar. If it means I am ruined, then so be it, I no longer care. This foolish dream I had about coming home to England and living the life I might have had is not worth the price. I shall sell my mother's jewels and go away, somewhere. America, perhaps, where they won't mind a little dust on my reputation in exchange for my wealth. I might even find someone who truly cares about me as I do about him. That strange mythical beast might yet exist out there. I'm not escaping to my island this time, Alan.'

She desperately wanted to shake him, to drag him off his own island, but she watched helplessly as he shut down. It was peculiar that this harsh, cynical look reminded her again how handsome he was, almost unfairly so, giving credence to that Wild Hunt nonsense of a man damned and seductively dangerous. She was beginning to forget his physical beauty, merely seeing Alan, but when he turned coldly furious, it became evident again.

'This is all very edifying, but the fact remains that you will marry me.'

'You cannot force me to wed, Alan.'

'Is that another challenge, Lily? Shall I show it will not take any force at all?'

Yes, please. There was nothing she could do to stem the swarm of blood filling her with anticipation.

'I didn't force you to rush into my arms that night at Hollywell,' he continued.

'I was scared.'

'That wasn't why you stayed there, that wasn't why you opened to me, why you moaned in my arms when I touched you, there…'

His fingers lightly traced a stripe of lace embroidered into her skirt, following the line between her thighs. Her legs shivered against each other and the memory of every moment of the night Grim had scared her rushed through her mind and body, as hot and inescapable as the most virulent fever. In a second her cheeks were throbbing with blood, her mouth dry, her lungs struggling to regulate her breath, and at the juncture of her thighs, an immediate awareness, damp and yearning. If she could have resorted to violence to wipe away her weakness, she would have. But she just waited for the worst to pass before she spoke.

'It isn't proper for us to be here alone, Lord Ravenscar.'

'We are engaged and allowed a little lenience,' he replied, his gaze moving over her face, settling on her mouth. He wasn't touching her, but she felt him, the memory of his taste filling her, and she had to fight the urge to lick her lips, capture that shimmering sensation and prepare herself for more.

She was stronger than this.

'We aren't engaged yet. How many times must I say this? Please leave the room or I shall.'

'Then leave.'

She hadn't expected that. She stood, half-expecting him to still protest, but he said nothing, his attention on a stray thread unravelling the petals of an embroidered rose on the back of the sofa.

'Goodnight, Lord Ravenscar,'

The last of the petals succumbed to a sharp tug of his fingers.

'Sweet dreams, Lily.'

She walked out before she broke utterly. She would concede this battle, but not the war.

Chapter Seventeen

It took an exertion of will over every sinew in Alan's body not to stop her. He twined the pink thread between his fingers, trying to bring to bear all the internal lectures about proceeding calmly and carefully and keep a tight rein on this need to touch her, take her…

Right now all this good counsel felt as effective as sheltering under a blade of grass in a storm. It would take more than a few pithy homilies to calm this burn of frustration. A few more evenings like this and he would do something drastic, like march upstairs and show her why all this fine talk about choices and propriety and anything but the elemental bond that existed between them was as empty as…as his life would be if she married Marston.

Damn her. He was done playing fair.

He shook the thread from his fingers and went upstairs. He would wait until her maid left and then he would make clear her fate was as sealed as his.

'Sue? Did you forget something?'

She didn't turn as he opened her door, but her arm

stopped in mid-brush. Her hair hung long and wavy and lush down her back and over her shoulder and his hands were already mapping their way down its length as he closed the door behind him, turning the key in the lock.

She turned, her eyes widening, taking in his coatless, bootless state.

'You can't come in here,' she whispered.

'I think you'll find I can.'

'Alan…'

'Let me.' He took the brush and stroked his hand down the waves of her hair as they fell over her dressing gown, covering her breasts in a mantle of warmth.

'It's even silkier than it looks,' he murmured. 'Do you know, I fantasise about what it would feel like on my bare skin and spread out on the bed when I am inside you.'

He smiled at the burn of colour that swept the coolness from her skin and wrapped his hand deeper in the auburn waves. He was done waiting and he was done playing by the rules. They never worked for him anyway. Tonight he would break another vow and categorically ruin a virgin and risk his soul into the bargain. It was a fair trade.

'I'll scream,' she hissed, recovering from the shock, but her voice shook and she didn't try to pull away.

'With pleasure. I hope so.'

'You are impossible! You know what I mean.'

He tightened his hand in her hair, bearing her head back as he bent to speak the words against her mouth. 'Go ahead. Scream…'

He smiled at the agonised little moan that met his words. She was his. Right now. For ever.

'Your lips are a little dry, let me help you.'

He caressed her lower lip with his tongue, drawing it into his mouth and letting it slide out, half-catching it with his teeth before releasing it so he could see the moist glimmer on the lush curve. He was going to taste every inch of her, find every flavour.

'One day I will discover what magical spice you use, Lily. I've never tasted anything so delectable.'

'Alan, you can't do this; this is cheating…' she whispered, but he felt her hand flutter against his chest, her attempt to push him away turning into an unconscious caress and adding to the urgent pulsing of blood rushing through him like a swarm of angry wasps. He paid no heed either to her or his body, just to his plan.

'I'm just helping you prepare for bed.' He ran the brush from the crown of her head to the tips of her hair, long, slow, definite strokes. Mirroring them with the slide of his mouth against hers, not penetrating her there, just warming and soothing and teasing until he could almost feel the confused pulsing between her legs in the way her hands were curled into each other, her thighs hard together. Her scent enveloped him, beckoning him with the fantasy of slipping into the warm Caribbean Sea with her, as bare as the elements.

'One day you'll take me swimming with you in your bay, Lily. There will be nothing between us but warm water and no one to hear your intoxicating moans but the gulls.'

He kneeled beside her, ignoring the pressure of his pantaloons on his erection as he trailed his hand down to find the ribbon that secured her dressing gown between her breasts and gently eased it free. Her eyes were on his, but dilated, lost in shock and need. If he were a gentleman, he would give her time, woo her fears away, but he was taking no chances any more with his prize. He would woo her after he secured her. There would be no more talk about America and running away.

'Do you know,' he said as he traced the embroidered pattern along the bodice of her nightgown, sinking into the valley between her breasts, curving under them and raising their weight very gently into his palms, 'this cloth might actually have come from one of my mills? I will take you there so you can see what it takes to make something so exquisite, so sheer I can see every shade of colour, every change in texture.' He marked his observations with his fingertips and her flesh gathered and shook beneath them, her breath mirroring the tremors that he could feel down to where he was leaning against her thigh.

He was shaking as well, with hunger and the need to keep it reined in, with the knowledge that he was finally going to take her, make her unequivocally his, that with each tremor that brought him closer to her his life was changing, opening.

There would be no going back for either of them, no running away. She was his.

Lily watched his hands, dark and hard against the white lawn of her nightgown, showing her the vulnerability of the flesh beneath. She knew what he was doing. She had thrown down the gauntlet and he was merely picking it up. He would win, too, because she wanted to lose. When he looked at her like that, nothing else mattered but that he not stop. She was no better than her mother and at the moment she didn't care.

All she cared about was right here, his features hard cut with tension, about to take what she had no wish to withhold.

Her eyelids sank as his fingers pressed gently against her breasts, encompassing them, but when his thumbs brushed up, catching the hard peaks, the whip of pleasure was so immediate and foreign she shut her eyes tight against it, sagging against him with a cry. In a second he was dragging her out of her chair to her feet and hard against his body, his voice hard and urgent against her hair.

'You want this… Tell me you want this, Lily.'

'Yes.' She almost choked on the word, her throat was so tight, her mouth pressed against his neck, breathing him in, filling with him. She was back in his room at Hollywell, but this time he didn't stop. This time she was tasting the silky hot skin, touching her tongue to the rough scrape of stubble along the line of his jaw, seeking his mouth. She was drunk on the need to taste him again.

'I want you…'

His body contracted around her, like the tremors of fever, and that excited her almost more than anything, the knowledge that he wanted her, that he was clinging to his control. She said the words again, like a prayer.

'I want you…Alan…'

His name was caught against his mouth as he dug his hands into her hair and raised her mouth to his. This kiss grew wild fast, capturing, tasting every corner of her mouth before claiming its depth until she lost her boundaries, as much him as herself.

It didn't stop with her mouth and now she would have fought him if he had tried to stop. Her nightgown sighed to the floor and she was as bare as he had threatened and his hands closed on her breasts again and the rough and soft drag of his skin felt as though he had reached inside her, curved over her heart and soul, and was shaping them as he saw fit. He was turning her into flame, setting free some mythical creature like the tales of the people of Padrones.

She wanted to feel him. His image of swimming with him in the bay filled her mind, of sliding her body against his, feeling his hands, his mouth sliding against the softness of the water, finding her... Her hands clenched the warm fabric of his shirt, pulling at it. She had lost all shame, all reason.

'I want to feel you on me.'

He didn't need a second invitation. He dragged his shirt off, pressing her against him, and she couldn't resist rubbing herself against the silky dark hair on his chest. It fed the restless hunger inside her, the pulsing heat gathering at her centre.

'Lily, you were made for me. You're mine.'

She didn't answer, intent on his body, his hands as they pressed her back until she felt the bed against her thighs. She looked up, meeting the naked passion in his gaze. There would be no going back, no escape, he was hers.

She wrapped her arms around his neck as he lowered her on to the bed, bringing him with her, bringing his mouth to hers, raising her hips as his hand traced down from her breasts, his fingers skimmed up and over the soft curls between her legs, gliding between her thighs and sending a tingling cascade outwards from that point like ripples on a pond. Her mouth stilled under his, too shocked to react to the intensity of the sensations. His kiss softened, a gentle brush of his lips over hers mirroring the gentle brush of his fingers on her thighs, up between her legs, finally touching her where she never even touched herself. Before she could even react and pull away, a bolt of lightning struck though her. She sank back, breathless with the shock.

'Hush, don't worry, I know what I'm doing...' His voice was hardly more than a rumble of sound, coursing through her like her own blood, but instead of soothing her it stung, sobering her. Of course he knew what he was doing. He had done this countless times before, would do it again, whether he married her or not. At no point had he promised anything else.

But sanity was a weak weapon against what his hand was doing.

'Let me show you what you are capable of,' he whispered against her mouth before his lips moved lower, trailing fire over the rise of her breast so that her nipple hardened, pushed against the muslin, seeking his touch. His fingers kept sliding against the damp heat between her legs, each stroke tightening the spring coiled about her. It would break, she knew it had to break, and her with it.

He pressed his mouth to her breast, his breath spreading over her skin, its edges reaching the hardened arc of her nipple, making her muscles clench in anticipation about his fingers as his lips approached, her whole body a collection of warring elements vying for the attention of that beautiful mouth, those skilled hands...

The next words were just a lick of heat against the apex of her breast and struck a bolt of agony through her body and her mind.

'Trust me…'

Trust me.

Finally the caged tiger struck, slashing her with the memory. Of her mother running down the path towards the docking boat, like a little girl, excited, ecstatic at her husband's return, uncaring of the fact he had probably come from another woman's bed.

'No!'

The cry of denial that burst from her was so sharp his caressing hands stopped immediately. His hand touched her cheek, his eyes narrowed and questioning. He looked beautiful and dangerous and she wanted him more than she had wanted anything in her life and he scared her more than the hosts of hell. She scared herself even more.

'What's wrong, sweetheart? Did I hurt you?'

The endearment sounded so real it stung like a slap. The worst was that she now had to choose. She knew he would stop if she asked. A choice. What did she choose?

'Alan,' she whispered, wishing she could have kept that burst of pain inside her. She didn't want him to stop, no matter where it took her. She wanted more of this. She wanted him.

So she clung to him as his mouth captured hers again, shivering as it skimmed over her cheek and down to the excruciatingly sensitive skin of her neck, lingering on the silky consistency of her earlobes, demolishing her. She didn't resist when he took her hand from where it clung to his shoulder and pressed it against the unbearable heat between her legs. She moaned as her fingers slid against the slick dampness, guided by his.

'I want you to see what you are capable of, what you can do for yourself. Someone like you shouldn't hide from her own fire. You shouldn't be afraid to touch yourself. Let me show you… I won't hurt you, I promise.'

Of course, he would hurt her in the end, in soul if not in body, but she no longer cared, as long as he was touching her. She wanted him to show her.

The pleasure was different, more muted but deeper in pitch, subterranean.

His hand moved on hers, pressing, teasing, torturing her. She was shaking with it. He was gathering her like the threads of a tapestry, weaving her into this new body, the finest of textures, from rough to soft, silky and frayed. She was everything under his hands, his mouth, being filled with his beauty. She wanted to be filled by him.

Without conscious thought her other hand reached out and met the hard pressure of his arousal through the fabric of his pantaloons and a sound between a groan and growl ran through him and into her, his hand stilling on hers and she could feel him shaking as well.

Now she could concentrate on every point of contact between them, exploring the geography of their shared passion. They were at the edge of a whole new landscape and he had given her only a glimpse of this new world. There was such a force in her to take what she could right here, right now because it was the only thing she had ever really wanted. She hadn't known what wanting was until she had met Alan. She hadn't known who she was until she had met him. Now she knew.

'God, Lily. You're destroying me. I want to be inside

you, disappear inside you… I want to go in so deep I never come out.'

She could *feel* his words, a flame rising where he was touching her, shooting up hot and hard inside her. She wanted him to make them real, to follow that heat and replace their fingers with the rigid muscle pressed against her hand. So deep he would never come out. He was already inside her soul, she wanted him inside her body. She was drowning, the only breaths she was taking were coming from the heat of his mouth on hers.

Then his fingers brushed hers away and set about demolishing her. Each sweep sent shards of lightning up through her body, tightening it unbearably. It was devouring her, but she wanted more, she wanted him with her. She wanted him as torn apart by need, but he was holding back. She could feel the acute tension in his breathing, in the frantic pulse in his blood and his tension where their bodies touched and she knew he was as desperate for the release as she, waiting for some sign from her or from himself to take the step from which there was no return.

'I want to feel you, all of you, take your pantaloons off.' Even to her it sounded like a command. He gave a choked laugh, his hand stilling, then his thumb flicked the nub of pleasure and her body arched up against him in sweet agony.

'Your wish is my command.'

She almost wished she hadn't said anything because she didn't want him to move away from her, not even to pull off his clothes. Like the unveiling of a statue she watched the linen pull away from the sculpted ridges of his chest and shoulders, the silky straight dark hair that tapered down from his chest, the angle of his hip bones as he moved to take off his pantaloons. She pressed her legs together at the sight of his erection, not in rejection but because her body contracted as if he was already inside her. Then he was leaning over her, his hand closing on her cheek and jaw almost painfully, his eyes dark and intent over hers.

'You're mine, Lily. There is no going back.'

She shook her head. She knew that. She had made her choice.

'Touch me. I want to feel you.'

'You will. Believe me, you will. I just hope you don't hate me by the end of this, Lily.'

That sobered her a little. She pressed her own hands to his face, meeting the intensity in his eyes. His words should have frightened her, but they just strengthened her resolve. Somehow she would reach him. Whatever it took.

'I'm not scared of you, Alan.'

He groaned, sinking his forehead against hers, and then he captured her mouth with a kiss that drove every thought and fear from her mind. His hands began demolishing her again, then slid deep between her thighs, parting them, stroking the soft inner flesh until she rose against him, and then his weight was between them, his erection thudding hot and hard where he had been touching her. She heard her voice, soft shuddering moans he muffled with his mouth as he poised himself at her entrance, teasing her to a pitch of need.

'Lily. You're mine.'

The words were all the warning she had before he penetrated her, the pain shooting sharp and hard through her. Her nails sank into his back and they both froze, breathing hard.

'It's over. I'm so sorry. It's over.'

She could hardly hear the words, her ears were ringing, her body torn between pain and the unsatisfied need and the pleasure he had promised. Then the shock centred and she was still there, waiting.

'What now?' she breathed.

His head sank so that his cheek pressed against hers and she realised he was shaking.

'Are you laughing?' she demanded.

'Only a madman would laugh at a moment like this, sweetheart,' he whispered, his breath warm against her ear and cheek, heating her again. 'I'm not laughing, I'm dying. Please, please don't move or you will kill me.'

She could feel the wriggling tension again, the delicate imbalance inside her, waiting for the fall.

'But if I don't move, I might die. What do we do?'

'I'll have to sacrifice myself, then.' He groaned, his body sinking against hers, shifting her legs further apart, sliding against her, not leaving her, just sliding his hand between them, finding the point of contact between them, and her shudder became an ache. The pressure of his fingers against her unleashed pleasure so powerful it spread through him and back into her, up to her breasts that were begging to rub themselves against the hair on his chest and the hard muscles underneath. As he moved inside her, over her, against her, she forgot pain, fear, the future. There was only now and the twisting, unrelenting joy that was just within reach if he would only...

He closed his teeth over her earlobe, whispering the words against her.

'You are magic. You'll come with me, love. Give yourself to me.'

The coiled spring snapped and joy spread through her, warm honeyed pleasure moving through her body, lighting her from within like a paper lantern, and then she burst and sank back, gasping for breath as his body continued to shudder and thrust against her until slowly he sank down on her, his arms gathering her to him, his mouth against her hair, repeating her name.

Alan eased off the bed. Whether he wanted to or not, it was time to leave her. Tomorrow he would leave as early as possible to sign the papers for the Grantham Road building and then come back and make the arrangements to put the special licence to use. Now that the possibility of a child was no longer hypothetical it was crucial there be no chance of scandal surrounding Lily or their children. He owed her that.

He curled his fingers into his palms against the need to run his hand over the curve of her hip under the cover, down the line of her leg, to wake her and see in her eyes that she knew what had just occurred between them. Not a seduction, but an admission and a pact.

It had not been as he expected. He had no knowledge of deflowering virgins, but he had prepared himself for the worst, to go as slowly as a mule cart and to have to comfort a tearstained and shocked young woman after the act. He should have known nothing that involved Lily would proceed as expected. He also should have known that slow was not an option. It had been impossible to go slowly. She had been so responsive, so alive and unbridled…beautiful in her joy. Tearing through whatever remained of his defences like a cannonball through gauze.

He always did his utmost to give pleasure. It was a

mark of pride. But there had been no such consideration here—he had *needed* to see her climax, to watch her melt, soften, tense into that final ecstasy. He hadn't just wanted to give her pleasure but show her she had that capacity herself. It had never occurred to him it would be as satisfying as his own physical release and much more addictive. When she had climaxed a second time, he had been completely caught in the wonder of it, in her beauty, as awe-inspiring as the shifting ocean.

But mostly he wanted to lock her to him, body and soul, as deep as he could go. He wanted to wake her and make her climax a third time while he was inside her up to the hilt so he could feel that beauty surround him, feed on her whimpers of pleasure from within. Become part of her joy.

He had come to both signal his surrender and try to tie her to him and he had only proven to himself how futile and unworthy his resistance was. He should have known that day at Saltford that she was his fate, that she had stolen his capacity for pleasure, for feeling alive.

He bent and tucked a strand of hair behind her ear and touched his mouth gently to the ridge of her cheek, breathing her in. She stirred and moaned faintly and his body clenched around the memory and promise of joy. He would give her a dozen children if it made her happy. Whatever it took to keep her, to see light warm her eyes.

'You're mine, Lily,' he repeated, but she didn't stir and eventually he left.

Chapter Eighteen

Lily pulled at the long willow leaf, stripping it from the thread-thin stalk. The pale late-autumn roses she placed on Rickie's grave were shivering in the breeze, their cream petals stained pink at the tips.

After last night she didn't know what to think at the news that Alan had left for Bristol with his groom close to first light. Nothing, probably. She knew how desperate he was to close on the new property. He had solved one problem, or so he probably thought, and now he was off to solve another. Then he would return and set about sealing their fate.

She pressed her hand to her stomach and closed her eyes in a silent prayer. How did one know if he had practised any of those means to avoid conception? Her discussions with those women in her father's forbidden house had taught her a little about what men like him did to avoid breeding bastards, but she thought she would have remembered if he had used one of the French gloves they had mentioned or if he had…well, stopped in the middle. But she didn't have the experience to judge. Could he have forgotten to be careful? It wasn't like the Alan she had come to know, but perhaps. And if he had forgotten, it meant she might even now…

What would he do if she was?

Those women had also been very clear about the means they employed if precautions failed. They were sometimes dangerous, but as they said, it was that or lose their livelihood. Such slips could mean starvation for them and the child to be born.

No, whatever happened she knew Alan would never make such a demand of her and she would certainly never accede to it. He would abide by his responsibility here, too, and it would either destroy whatever fragile bond existed between them or finally break through to him and the love she knew he possessed.

'But I would still like it to be his choice, Grim. Not something else fate forces upon him. Is that foolish of me?'

Grim yawned and lay down, snuffling at the grass, and she knelt by him, wincing at the stinging between her legs.

'You agree I should marry him and risk everything, don't you? I can see that you do. But on my terms, at least until he sees reason. You see, I can be as constant as you and much more devious.'

She pushed to her feet, brushing at the grass.

'Are you coming? No. Very well, stay here and watch over Rickie.'

'Miss Wallace. Mr Marston is here to see you. In the Rose Room. Lady Ravenscar and Lady Catherine are not yet awake, miss. It being so early still.'

'Thank you, Partridge,' she said, ignoring the

pointed note in the elderly butler's voice. Time to clear the decks.

Marston was standing, hands clasping his gloves, his expression wary as she strode towards him.

'Good morning, Philip. I am glad you came so early, there really is no point to beat about the bush any longer. I think you know what my answer is. You aren't in love with me and I am in love with another man, it is as simple as that.'

Marston drew his gloves between his hands with a resigned smile.

'You are right that I knew what I was coming to hear today. The tension between the two of you is as palpable as a pea-soup fog. But a word of advice, if I may. Don't let him have his way too easily. You are in a strong negotiating position, so negotiate.'

Lily thought of her total capitulation the previous night. It was imprinted in every inch of her body, in the throbbing sting between her legs and the rawness where his stubble and teeth had grazed the sensitive skin of her breasts; in the yearning of her skin and the occasional echo of pleasure where he had touched her and shown her how to touch herself.

She laughed at the futility of his offer.

'I don't know if I would make it to the negotiating table, let alone stand firm on my demands. I don't expect him to love me, men never fall in love with me, but I do want more than he is willing to offer.'

'My dear girl, I've watched quite a few men fall in love with you. You just never realised it.'

She shook her head.

'That is kind but inaccurate, Philip. Certainly none of them ever said anything to me.'

'Men do need some encouragement if they are to risk themselves, Lily. We are fragile vessels.'

'So are women.'

'True. Well. What will you do now?'

'I don't know... Marry him and see if I can win him over in the end, I suppose. I honestly don't know what I should do.'

She must have looked as lost as she felt because he hesitated and sighed.

'Out of pride I really shouldn't be helping him, you know...'

'You are helping me, not him. Besides, since he might be your brother-in-law one day, I don't think you should antagonise him more than necessary.'

His jaw dropped, but the flush that spread over his cheeks confirmed her suspicion that he and Catherine were rather more attracted to each other than either realised and she laughed, relieved. What a mistake she had almost made. Both of them.

'I assure you...'

'Oh, please don't. I shouldn't have said anything that might send you running.'

'Yes, well, to our business. I find when I make a mistake in negotiations it sometimes helps to make a tactical withdrawal. If you accept his terms outright, don't be surprised if they don't answer your needs. Make him come to you, on your terms.'

'How?'

'Penny is leaving this morning to go to her aunt in Bath for a few weeks to acquire some polish before I take her to London in the spring. I would be glad if you accompanied her there. She would be happy for the company on the drive and my sister is a very pleasant and easy-going woman and would be happy for another guest, especially one as charming as you.'

'This morning?'

'Yes. I gather Ravenscar is in Bristol to sign the papers with the mayor, so his absence is fortuitous. Could you be ready in an hour or so?'

She pressed her hand again to her stomach. She knew running away was no solution, but she needed to think and she couldn't think around Alan. Well, not very rationally. He would just do precisely what he had done the night of the concert—seduce her and push the decision further and further away from her. And she—she would fold like the frailest of fans because for the first time in her life she felt utterly at home with someone.

But wasn't this precisely what had eventually driven her mother into illness and melancholy and on to her refuge on the island? Why should she trust this conviction that she was as right for him as he was for her and if he only gave her a chance...if she only tried hard enough, he would learn to love her and be content with what they could build together? Was she doomed to relive her mother's fate or was there merit to this feeling deep insider her, this blind belief that Alan was not like her father and much more than he himself believed he was? Because if he wasn't, she would have to be strong enough to walk away, whatever the price.

He would follow her, of course he would, he was nothing if not stubborn, but he could hardly manoeuvre her as easily in a stranger's home in Bath as he had at the Hall. She would recover some measure of distance even if she could never recover her heart.

She raised her chin and answered, 'I could, but...

If he hears you were here before my departure, he will come asking questions. I don't want to cause you trouble.'

'I will ignore the slight to my manhood. He might come asking questions, but I am not obliged to answer, am I? I must be quite mad. You are a bad influence on me, Lily.'

'I know. Aren't you glad you discovered that now rather than after we wed? Thank you, Philip. I really do wish you happy.'

Chapter Nineteen

Alan stopped at the sight of his grandmother all but bursting from the door of the Rose Room.

'Alan. Oh, thank goodness you are back.'

He frowned, following her into the room, where she sank into her armchair. She pressed one veined hand to her cheek while her other clutched a piece of paper in her lap.

'What is wrong, Grandmother?'

'Lily. She's gone.'

'What do you mean, she is gone?'

'Gone as in gone. Partridge said a carriage pulled up out front and she hurried out to it with a portmanteau before he could say a word or summon me. She left this.'

Alan took the letter from his grandmother and turned away to read it.

It wasn't long, or informative.

A few weeks…

'It doesn't say where she went. It doesn't say if she will return. What did you do to frighten her away, Alan?'

Given her a promise he had never imagined he would give. Taken away her choice. At least he thought he had, but obviously not. Did she think she would escape him? He would find her if it was the last thing he did and then he would…

He pressed the letter down on the table, smoothing out the edges until the snarl of fury and fear and pain worked its way through him. What more did she want from him? He had risked his heart and soul to give her what she wanted last night only to have her run.

'Could she have gone to Hollywell once more? Or to that Marston fellow? Partridge said he was here this morning to see her.'

Alan turned. 'Was he?'

Her eyes widened further. 'Don't do anything foolish, Alan. A duel with Marston would be ruinous.'

'A duel? With Mr Marston? What are you talking about?' Catherine asked from the doorway.

'Lily has left. We don't know where.'

'But…she couldn't have gone with Mr Marston!'

'And why not? He was here this morning and now she is gone with nothing more than this faradiddle about going away for a few weeks with some friends and she wrote that we are not to worry. Not to worry!'

'I don't believe she would have left with Mr Marston. She doesn't even want him.'

'She doesn't have to want him. She wants what he can give her,' Alan snarled.

'No. I don't believe it. I always knew she wouldn't do it in the end and she wouldn't.'

'Well, she's done something, gone somewhere, and I'm going to find out where. Since you are so convinced she didn't go to Marston, perhaps you have some ideas where she did go.'

Catherine shook her head, her blue eyes damp with tears.

'No, none. I mean…she couldn't have returned to Jamaica or to her island, could she?'

'Literally or figuratively? It doesn't matter. I'm going to find her.'

'Where will you go?'

'I don't know. Hollywell, Bristol, Brazil, wherever I need to.'

'What can we do to help, Alan?' Lady Ravenscar's question was so practical, there was no reason why it should have brought down his defences. He paused in the doorway and looked back at his grandmother. Belle and Ray.

'There is something you can do. The Hall. I want you to change your will and leave me the Hall. I don't want or need your money, but I must have something to offer her beyond money… I need to offer her a home.'

'I have no intention of altering my will, any of it.'

She met his gaze with defiance and he tightened his hand on the doorknob.

'So be it.'

'Catherine and your cousins will receive bequests, of course, but you are and have always been my prime beneficiary, Alan. I know we parted in anger after Catherine's wedding, but if you imagine I would follow your grandfather's example and write you out of my will, then you never knew me. Your grandfather was a…a horrid man and I hated him with every fibre of my being, though I could never fully admit that to myself until well after his death. I was glad you turned your back on us and I envied you the day you left. Thank goodness you did, because if you had stayed, it would have meant he had already broken you as well. It is true I hoped one day you might return, might even ask me for the only thing of value I had to offer you, but I was proud that you never did. The Hall is and has always been yours, as well as every acre of land and the income from it. I hope you and that impossible young woman will finally make it a home worthy of the name. It is about time a Rothwell made up for all the misery of those before him. I think I shall remove to Bath. I am tired of seeing to the Hall and now that my sister is widowed as well we should rub along quite well. Oh, do stop staring at me as if I have grown a second head and kindly refrain from making any comment, either mocking or mawkish. Reserve your energies for dealing with your concerns. Now go.'

'I was expecting you earlier.' Marston rose from his desk as his butler showed Alan into the study. Alan strode forward until only the bulk of the dark mahogany desk stood between them.

'I apologise for keeping you waiting. Where is she?'

'Not here.'

'You're a lucky man, then, Marston. Where is she?'

'Perfectly safe.'

'That isn't what I asked you. If I ask you again, it will be with my hands around your throat.'

'I don't want to brawl with you, Ravenscar. Believe it or not, my objective is not to punish either of you. Lily and I understand each other tolerably well now and have decided we will not suit. She and Penny have probably reached Bath by now. They will be staying with my sister in Laura Place. She is perfectly safe and will be well chaperoned. I have the direction here.' He pointed to a sheet of paper on his desk.

Alan shook his head, trying to rearrange his thoughts, but they kept stumbling over the emotions exploding in his head like a bombardment of French cannon.

'Why Bath?' he finally managed.

'Because Penny was going there and the opportunity presented itself. I believe Lily needed some time to decide whether to accept your offer without you constantly tipping the scales. She isn't as ruthless as you, Ravenscar.'

'I think this is pretty damn ruthless. I don't need you defending Lily, Marston; that is my role. From now on find someone else to fulfil your procreative ambitions and stay out of our business.'

Marston laughed softly. 'It's a pity you never met her father. I asked him once why he was allowing her to remain unmarried for so long—she was already twenty-one then and had just sent another fellow to the roundabout. He said it was his fault she had built a tower to keep herself safe, so he owed her some leeway and that he hoped one day one of them would actually have the bollocks to storm her castle.'

Alan strode towards the door.

'What are you going to do?' Marston called after him.

'Storm a castle,' he answered before slamming the door.

Chapter Twenty

Lily looked down at the grave. Four years old. He would have been full of energy, already a boy with opinions and a sense of himself. A person. So much of what he might have become would have been there already. She wondered if he had been shy or talkative. A cautious boy or someone who threw his heart ahead of him. She wondered what Alan had been like as a boy before life had forced him to erect walls about himself. She wished she could reach into the past and shift fate to relieve him of that horrible burden, but she couldn't. All she could do was stand by him now.

'I saw you from the drive.'

She turned as Alan let the willow branches fall back into place, so filled with love she couldn't speak.

'At least this saves me a drive to Bath. Did the carriage break down?'

He spoke lightly, but she knew him well enough by now to hear the grinding mix of emotions beneath the carefully suave question. She pressed her hands together and laid her cards on the table, all of them.

'No. I decided not to go. I didn't want to leave and I

don't really wish to negotiate. I want to be with you. I can't force you to love me or to want to have a family, but I do want you to try to make more of this than just a marriage of convenience. I love you, Alan. I don't think I will be able to be with you and keep that inside me. It will be like trying not to breathe. Can you understand that?'

He looked up at the arch of the willows above them, the tendons in his neck sharp with tension, like the painting of a fallen angel supplicating the heavens. Then he moved towards her.

'Don't ever run away from me again.'

'I won't. I…'

He closed the distance between them, pinioning her face in his hand, his fingers hard against her bones. There was anger there, and more; she knew that roiling storm of feelings.

'Don't you *ever* dare run away from me again. You want something? You stay and fight for it and tell me I'm being a bloody fool. But you don't run. Do you understand?'

She nodded as best she could in his steel grip, the first buds of joy forcing their way through her fear as she began to absorb the truth revealed in his eyes, in the agony etched on his lean face. She stroked her fingers lightly down his cheek and something else appeared through the anger, and when he spoke again, his voice was muted, defeated.

'How could you do that to me? Do you know what I thought? I thought you had gone to him. I couldn't bear it…'

'I didn't. I wouldn't. I just wanted to get away to think. This morning I realised you might have forgotten to…well, to be careful and that I might even now be with child. I knew I would have to fight you for the kind of life I thought was right. For us, not just for me. I wanted to show you I would not let you dictate all the terms, but then as we were just coming into Keynsham I realised I didn't want it to be like that. So I told them to put me down and I went to Mr Prosper and asked him to bring me home in his gig. I don't want to run away from this, from you.'

He stared at her, his eyes narrowed and unrevealing.

'Forgotten? What kind of fool do you think I am? What the devil do you think I was doing when I came to your room last night? Do you think I *forgot* to use precautions like some green fool? That after a dozen years of being cautious it just slipped my mind? For someone so intelligent you are as foolish as a newborn lamb sometimes, Lily. I knew precisely what I was doing, and if you had used half the brain God gave you, you would know what that meant. I couldn't have signalled my surrender more clearly than if I walked in there with a white flag.'

She stared at him. She had been so caught in her own drama she had lost all sight of his. Marston had told her once Alan was cautious. The wildest of the wild hunters was as cautious as a mother hen when it came to things that mattered. He had seduced her knowing full well he might walk out of that night a prospective father and had known precisely what that meant and she had been as blind as a bat and fluttered away just as blindly in her confusion and fear.

He reached out and tucked her against him as if sheltering her from a storm. She clung to him, trying not to cry with the joy that was careening around in her like foolish old Grim had careened around Hollywell.

'You're more than I can bear sometimes, Lily, but I can't live without you. If you leave me again, you will discover just how terrifying the Wild Hunt can be. I'll build a damn tower if need be and lock you in and hide the bloody key.'

She laughed with joy, pressing herself against him. 'You don't scare me, Alan Piers Cavendish Rothwell. Besides, ferrets are good at finding things. Will you marry me, Alan?'

'Damn you, Lily.'

'I think I am by now, damned that is. I probably was the day you walked into Hollywell and teased me into giving you Marcus Aurelius. See the lengths I will go to get my property back?'

'Oh, God, anything I can give you, I will.'

'There's only one thing. Will you marry me and let me love you?'

Her shoulders and ribs protested at the fierceness of his embrace, but she revelled in it, and when it gentled, she raised her head to touch her lips to the tense muscles of his neck.

'That's two things,' he murmured against her hair, his hand sliding down her back, softening, bringing her against him. His other hand slid the pins and comb from her hair, and when it tumbled free, he breathed in, raising a fistful to his mouth before moving his attention to her mouth, his lips stroking hers, gentle and rhythmic, like a warm breeze.

'Will you?' she prompted.

'Yes. God, yes…'

This was the wild hunt she had been waiting for. She

could well give credence to dark powers when she found herself stripped of her garments and spread out on the shaded grass in nothing more than her stockings, a dark devil poised above her, his eyes narrowed shards of ice as they scraped over her body before her own shivered shut when he bent to kiss her, drawing her soul into his, his mouth torturing her with a trail of kisses that lingered on her breasts, before descending, making her squirm against him as they skimmed and delved the sensitive skin of her abdomen, coming closer to her aching centre. Too close. She half-raised herself on her elbow to see his night-black hair glistening against the pale moon luminescence of her skin. She was already shaking, half in anticipation, half in fear. Her hands caught in his hair and he drew back and she wished she hadn't stopped him, but she didn't know what to do with all these feelings.

'Alan. Touch me.'

'Oh, I will. Believe me. Down to your soul. Just like you've touched me, my lovely Lily. You're mine.'

His fingers playing gently with the soft skin of her thighs above her garters, sliding his fingers under them, transforming their unravelling into exquisite torture, following their descent with his mouth, whispering his love and precisely how he was going to touch her, love her, make her his. His voice was a subterranean river of lava, hot, destructive, consuming her as it coursed over her. She answered him but had no idea what she said, maybe just his name over and over, a plea and a command, but he understood, his fingers finally returning to her centre again, filling her with a luminescence that radiated through every nerve in her body, his mouth capturing her breasts again as his fingers massaged and coaxed and tortured her arousal, and when his tongue laved her nipple into an unbearable peak, she stopped thinking, obeying his command to forget everything but him and what he was doing to her, what his body was doing to her.

When he shifted her legs apart, she took him in with a gasp of need, her body arching to envelop him. There was no confusion, and if there was pain, she felt none of it in the throes of her storm. She went wild, her fingers biting deep into his shoulders, her mouth capturing his groans of pleasure as she wrapped her body around his erection, laying claim.

She moved with him, utterly open, taking him deeper and deeper with each thrust, uncaring of the hard ground beneath her, of the cold air on her bare flesh. All she felt was his body against hers, hard and soft, inside her, his muscles shaking under her hands, his mouth on hers, his hand caressing her breast, telling her how much he needed her. Loved her.

She hadn't thought the pleasure could come so swiftly. It caught her like a beast from the dark, sudden and inescapable. She shuddered around him, her fingers pressing into his buttocks, and the shudder spread to him.

This time they sank into the warm waters of the tropics. He was pulling her along with him, deep underwater, and it was warm and she didn't even need to breathe, she became the sea, warm, vast. Joyful. She felt the sweet agony of his climax, the violent shudders as his body closed on hers, but for her this time was a warm welling of pleasure that rose and rose and wouldn't stop, carrying her with it into his arms. Home.

* * *

'I should have waited. Of all places to do this… I must be mad. It is November and anyone coming down to the lake could see us.'

He dragged his discarded greatcoat over them and she snuggled against him, her leg sinking between his thighs as he shifted, anchoring her on top of him. Under the weight of his caped coat, his hand sloped down her back, warm and gentle, like sun on the surface of water. She arched into it, absorbing his heat as their bodies cooled.

'We would be truly ruined, then, wouldn't we?'

'It would certainly finally put an end to all your indecision.'

'I knew what I wanted before you did,' she protested, tracing the line of his arm from his shoulder to where it rested on her hip, a landscape of powerful muscle, fine silky dark hair, down to the definite bones of his wrist. When she reached it, his hand turned, lacing their fingers together.

'Damn, I love you. Will you marry me, Lily?'

She stilled for a moment, waiting for the mingling of pain and joy to flow through her and calm again.

'I asked you first.'

'I beg pardon, I asked you first.'

'No, you didn't. You *told* me. I asked you. There is a vast difference. And, yes, I will. Your turn now.'

He laughed, pulling her more fully on top of him.

'When you come off your island, you do it with a vengeance, my lovely vixen. I thought I was good at meeting dares, but you outdo me. You've outdone me utterly. Yes, I will marry you. This very instant, but Lady Belle would never forgive us if we don't appease the ghosts with some show of pomp and circumstance. Hunter also won't forgive me if I don't at least invite him to come gloat at my downfall so he can pay me back for gloating at his.'

She pulled her hand away and planted it on the grass, raising herself to look down at her fallen angel. Flat on his back. It suited him. She would have to do this often.

'You are certain about this, Alan? You must believe me, I don't want to force you if you don't wish to be married.'

'I'm not as generous, love. I'll not allow you a loophole to wiggle out of. You do realise that I didn't use any precautions just now either? You are now honour bound to make an honest man of me. Now come, up with you before we freeze to the ground and are found here encased in ice like fossil remains. Lady Belle will skin me alive if I allow you to fall ill. She is counting on us to relieve her of the Hall so she can lead a wild life of dissipation in Bath.'

'She... What? Does that mean she has reinstated you?'

He secured his buckskins and shrugged into his shirt as she slid the chemise over her head, then he picked up her dress from the grass, his eyes glinting at her as he gathered it into folds and slid it over her head, turning her to secure the hooks.

'Disappointed? She told me she had never respected my grandfather's wish of keeping me from inheriting. Not that I need it, but just so you know, I would marry you without a penny to my name and bear the shame of living up to your fortune-hunting slurs if I had to.

There is no possible way I would give you up over a blasted prejudice.'

She turned back to him, gathering his hands in hers.

'I would also marry you if you hadn't a penny to your name, Alan, and consider myself lucky.'

He pulled her against him, grasping her chin, his expression hardening again, a beautiful forbidding statue. He wasn't smiling, but she could see beyond the harsh tension to the fear and beyond that to the giving love she was so lucky to have reached. She touched his cheek as she had when he was ill, softly, full of love, her eyes burning with tears.

He pulled away, stroking the hair from her face.

'What's wrong, love?'

'That day we returned to the Hall, after you were ill, when we sat here, I dreamed of children playing here, but I never believed it might be true. But I need to tell you I don't need anything else other than you. If you will only let me love you.'

'So will you be disappointed if I tell you I was rather warming to the idea of children? I'm terrified of it, but I don't think I can go back to being the way I was any longer. I was thinking we would start with a daughter, just to ease me in. With your hair. And then a son. Or two.'

She laughed, wiping away her tears and wrapping her arms around him again, rising on her toes to press her mouth to his. A son and a daughter. Everything she could give him, she would. She smiled against his mouth, parting her lips to taste him, loving how the hunger was beginning to rise again, how her body was mapping every point of contact between them and laying out demands for more. What a revelation this man was. Hers.

'Alan. My raven with his broken wing. I do love you. I am so glad you shoved me off my island.'

She could feel the rigid tension recede, revealing his warm, generous core again. His fingers combed through her hair, untangling it and unravelling her all over again.

'Not shoved, coaxed. Now I shall have to coax you back. You owe me a fantasy. You and I are going swimming.'

She laughed, glancing at the lake.

'You're mad. It is November!'

'Hell, no, I refuse to spend my honeymoon in the English winter. You have been swimming around in my feverish brain since we met and it's time I introduced myself into that fantasy and ousted your fairy-tale prince Rupert. It is very demeaning to realise I was jealous of a manatee.'

She leaned her cheek against him, listening to the beat of his heart.

'You needn't have worried. Vixens and sea mammals don't mix.'

He smiled and he tightened his hands in her hair, raising her face towards his as he brushed his lips over hers.

'Ravens also tend to have a penchant for their own kind—feral field animals. Vixens, ferrets, hedgehogs...'

'Hedgehogs?'

He held her firmly as she tried to pull away, speaking the words against her mouth, his breath tangling with hers. She knew what he was doing—he was baiting her, teasing her out of her lair like the wild hunter he was.

'Small, prickly and with a soft underbelly,' he added for good measure, and she sank against him, opening for him, her outrage giving away to laughter.

'You'll pay for that, Raven.'

'With pleasure…'

Epilogue

Summer 1825

The puppy streaked down the bank and cleared the shallows with a leap.

'Good Gwimlet!' Alexander cheered as the black head strained above the surface towards the bobbing wooden boat. The dark green water shattered into ripples around him, spreading all the way to the grassy island in the middle of the lake connected to the bank by a wrought-iron-and-wood bridge.

Their first summer together Alan had brought workers to construct the island for her as well as the classical temple-like structure at its centre, where they went when they wanted to be utterly alone. Everyone knew no one was allowed on the island when the gate on the bridge was closed.

She looked across and sighed, remembering the perfect summer morning they had spent there a week ago before he had left for Birmingham.

'Very good Grimlet,' Lily agreed, detaching her daughter's chubby hands from her hair and shifting her to her other hip to allow her daughter to rearrange her hair on the other side.

'Greene is despairing of me, Emma. She thinks you are colluding with your father to keep me in a state of permanent disarrangement. And to think I was once considered fashionable.'

Emma detached her hands and raised them in the air. 'Papa.'

'Yes, Papa. I miss him, too, pumpkin, but he should be back tomorrow.'

'I will show him Gwimlet's new trick,' Alexander announced as he took the wooden ship from the puppy's grinning jaw and stood back to avoid most of the shower as Grimlet succumbed to the need to shake off the lake on his new masters before padding over to stretch himself out in the patch of sun between Rickie's and Grim's graves, his pink tongue with its black spot licking absently at the grey stone.

'Papa!' Emma insisted, squirming, and the back of Lily's neck tingled and she turned in time to see Alan push aside the curtain of willow branches.

'Papa!' Alexander got there first, but Emma made good time on her shorter and chubbier legs.

Alan hauled his children into his arms and Lily met the love in his eyes with a rush of emotion and gratitude that never seemed to dim. When Alexander's stream of news and Emma's tugging at his hair and buttons finally subsided, he noticed the mobile ball of dark fluff frolicking at his feet.

'What on earth is that?'

'*That* is Grimlet. Mr Prosper's housekeeper mentioned her son's dog had bred and invited us to see the puppies. The rest, as they say, is history.'

'Grimlet.'

'Alexander wanted to call him Little Grim, but then he thought Grimlet was better.'

'Do you like him, Papa? May we keep him?' Alexander asked with the sudden seriousness that characterised their son.

'If you can keep him from chewing my boots, he can stay.'

Alexander considered the puppy, now rolling on his back at their feet, snapping at a fly that was hovering above him.

'But he likes chewing things. Besides, you have more boots. There is only one Grimlet.'

'Impeccable reason. Yes, you imp. You can keep him.'

'Gimmit,' Emma added.

'On condition you take him with Nanny up to the house now. Mama and I have matters to discuss.'

'Must we?'

Alan beckoned to Nanny Brisbane, who proceeded to pluck Emma from his arms.

'Yes, Master Alexander. It is time for the puppy to have his nuncheon if he is to grow to be as big and strong as Grim.'

'And I shall grow to be as big and strong as you, Papa,' Alexander announced, picking up Grimlet and marching off in the lead.

Lily walked into Alan's open arms and watched the reluctant cavalcade wend its way up to the Hall.

'Are Catherine and Philip well?'

'Very well. They send their regards and said they will visit as soon as Timothy is old enough to be left with his nurse. I told them they might as well bring him as the Hall is one big nursery anyway.'

Lily laughed, leaning against him. It was ridiculous to be so grateful for his return after a mere week's separation, but there it was.

'Lady Belle wrote from Paris full of complaints about French food and manners, but reading between the lines she and your great-aunt Ray are having as marvellous a time there terrorising the French as they had the inhabitants of Bath. I'm glad you returned early. I thought you were only due back tomorrow.'

'That was the plan, but I was having trouble sleeping, so I told Marston he can deal with the rest.'

She frowned, cupping his face in her hands, warming herself against him.

'Was anything wrong?'

'Yes. The bed was too big. I kept waking up wondering where you were and thinking of you in our bed, all warm and waiting. Not conducive to a restful night.'

'I wasn't in our bed, though.'

His arms tightened around her and he raised her face, his eyes taking possession of her again, bringing her to life.

'No? Did you run away again behind my back? I warned you what I would do next time.'

'Yes, I know, locked towers and the like. I was in the nursery. I couldn't sleep either, so I went to listen to Alex and Emma breathing. We are doing very ill at being apart. We shall have to practise.'

'Right now there are much more pressing concerns that require practice.'

'Now? Here?'

'Jem is under strict orders to allow no one to approach the lake path. This is what we constructed our island for, isn't it? Not that we made it there last time.

I've been fantasising about how you looked there last time, dappled in sunlight and your hair like fire on the grass. How clever of you to have your hair down and ready for me. Are you sure you didn't know I was coming?'

'Emma helped.'

'She is shaping up to be as intelligent as her mother. I only wish she had your hair. Maybe our next daughter will.'

'Yes, well…about that…'

The heat in his eyes dimmed a little in shock.

'Are you serious?'

'I'm afraid I am—is that terrible?'

He pulled her against him, laughing.

'I leave you alone for a week and I come back and find you with child and a new puppy.'

'I beg pardon, you were very instrumental in at least one of those developments!'

'So I was, how clever of me. This time it will be a daughter with your amazing hair and tortuous mind. Come, all the more reason to gather our rosebuds while we may before I have to share these delectable beauties again.' His hands curved under her breasts, raising them to brush his mouth over the sensitive swells, and her legs sagged against him as her need gathered, fed by the joy and love he woke in her so easily.

She took his hand and led him to their sanctuary.

'I'm so glad you came home, Alan, my love.'

* * * * *